Also by
Danielle Steel

Blue

On the anniversary of a car accident, Ginny Carter meets thirteen-year-old Blue, who has been living on the streets, utterly alone. Ginny reaches out to him, and slowly, the two form a bond, becoming the family they each lost. But just as he is beginning to trust her, she learns a shocking secret. Can she can help Blue to feel whole again, and at the same time heal herself?

Precious Gifts

Veronique Parker's world is turned upside down when her former husband dies suddenly, leaving her and their daughters astonishing inheritances: a painting, a French château, the freedom to pursue their dreams, and a revelation from the past. These gifts will lead them on a journey certain to change Veronique and her daughters' destinies in the most surprising of ways . . .

Prodigal Son

In a matter of days, Peter McDowell loses everything – including his marriage. Returning to the home he left twenty years ago, he comes face to face with his brother Michael. But to his surprise their reunion is tender. Only later, as Peter mulls over his late mother's journals, does he begin to question what lies beneath Michael's perfect surface . . .

Undercover

After a job gone wrong shatters undercover agent Marshall's world, he flees to Paris. Meanwhile, Ariana knows that as the daughter of an American Ambassador, her safety is always at risk. Even when she is relocated to Paris, trouble is never far behind. Paired together, Marshall and Ariana must trust each other if they are to find freedom from their past . . .

A Perfect Life

An icon of television news, Blaise McCarthy has it all: beauty, intelligence and courage. But privately there is a story she has protected for years – her daughter Salima is blind, and lives at a year-round boarding school. But when Salima's school closes and she returns home, suddenly Blaise's life is no longer perfect, but real. Can mother and daughter together learn how to face a world they can't control?

Pegasus

On the cusp of the Second World War, a family is forced to flee Europe, taking with them one amazing gift from life-long friends. But when tragedy strikes on both sides of the ocean, what will become of each family when their happiness rests in the hands of fate?

Power Play

Fiona Carson is a successful woman in a man's world. Devoted single mother and tough negotiator, Fiona has to keep a delicate balance every day. Meanwhile, Marshall Weston enjoys the fruits of his achievements – but he harbours secrets that could destroy his life. The lives they both lead come at a high price. But just how high a price are they willing to pay?

Danielle Steel

'Danielle Steel always transports you
into a world you want to be in'

'I'm totally addicted'

'She never disappoints'

'Unique, emotional, magical'

'Fantastic, uplifting'

**'You really can't beat a good
Danielle Steel story'**

'A wonderful story'

'A truly amazing author'

'I couldn't put it down . . . finished reading
at 4.30am'

'Always gripping'

'One of my all-time favourite authors'

'The ideal holiday book'

'Another brilliant story'

'Another fabulous book from Danielle Steel. I
can't wait for her next'

'Enthralling'

Danielle Steel is one of the world's most popular and highly acclaimed authors, with over ninety international bestselling novels in print and more than 600 million copies of her novels sold. She is also the author of *His Bright Light*, the story of her son Nick Traina's life and death; *A Gift of Hope*, a memoir of her work with the homeless; and *Pure Joy*, about the dogs she and her family have loved.

To discover more about Danielle Steel and her books visit her website at www.daniellesteel.com

And join her on Facebook at www.facebook.com/DanielleSteelOfficial

By Danielle Steel

Danielle Steel

Country

CORGI BOOKS

TRANSWORLD PUBLISHERS
61–63 Uxbridge Road, London W5 5SA
www.transworldbooks.co.uk

Transworld is part of the Penguin Random House group of companies
whose addresses can be found at global.penguinrandomhouse.com

First published in Great Britain in 2015 by Bantam Press
an imprint of Transworld Publishers
Corgi edition published 2016

ISBN
9780552166195 (B format)
9780552166201 (A format)

Typeset in 12/15.5pt Adobe Garamond by Falcon Oast Graphic Art Ltd.
Printed and bound in Great Britain by Clays Ltd, St Ives plc

Penguin Random House is committed to a sustainable
future for our business, our readers and our planet. This book is made from
Forest Stewardship Council® certified paper.

To my so greatly loved children,
Beatie, Trevor, Todd, Nick, Sam,
Victoria, Vanessa, Maxx, and Zara,
May you seize the day,
and may life treat you kindly.
May your opportunities be abundant,
your joys immense and limitless,
and may all your dreams come true!

I love you so very much!
Mom/DS

Country

Chapter 1

The day dawned brilliantly sunny, reflecting the bright light on the crisp snow that had fallen the day before in Squaw Valley. The ski conditions were perfect, better than they ever had been for Bill, Stephanie, and their two favorite couples, the Freemans and Dawsons, with whom they spent Presidents' Weekend every year. It was a tradition they had observed for ten years, a sacred pact that none of them would break.

Alyson Freeman had come, even days before she had given birth to their last baby, their third child, two years before, refusing to miss the great weekend they always shared. And since Brad was a doctor, she said she felt safe being there. It was only a four-hour drive from home, and although Brad was an orthopedic surgeon and not an obstetrician, she knew he would see to it that she got the best care, if she gave birth in Tahoe over the long weekend. Their Presidents' Weekend was a date they never broke, and this year was no different. It was meant to be an adult weekend, free of children and responsibilities.

It was no longer an issue for Stephanie and Bill, whose children were dispersed and working in Atlanta and New York, for their first steps on their fledgling careers, and in Rome, where their younger daughter was spending her junior year abroad. Fred and Jean Dawson's daughters were both married and lived in Chicago, having married brothers. But even Brad and Alyson, whose children were much younger than the others', agreed not to bring their kids, and left them with an au pair at home.

Fred and Jean had been married the longest and were slightly older than the others. To those outside the close circle of friends, they appeared to have the perfect marriage. Fred had invented software that had made him a fortune, and had gotten in on the dot-com boom right at the beginning. Their palatial home in Hillsborough was testimony to his success, along with his plane, his Ferrari and Aston Martin, and Jean's stable full of Thoroughbred horses, which were her passion. They had money to burn, and Fred's humble origins were a dimly remembered dream now.

Jean had been a waitress in Modesto when he met her, from a dirt-poor family that had just lost their farm when her father died in an accident, leaving five starving kids and a widow who looked twenty years older than she was. Jean rarely saw her siblings anymore and had nothing in common with them. She had married Fred thirty years before, and was fifty-one years old. She'd had her eyes done, an excellent face-lift by a plastic surgeon in New York, she stayed in shape, took terrific care of herself, and got Botox shots three times a year. She was a beautiful woman, although her face showed almost no expression, which was fine with her. Above all, she never wanted to be poor again, and as long as she and Fred stayed married, she knew she never would be.

She knew that he had cheated on her for most of their marriage, and she no longer cared. She hadn't been in love with him in years. She could have sued him for a fortune in a divorce, but she liked the lifestyle he provided, the perks, and the status of being Mrs. Fred Dawson. She said jokingly to her friends that she had made a pact with the devil, and the devil in her life was Fred. She had no illusions about him, and no desire to change anything about the way she lived. She had her horses and her friends and went to visit her daughters in Chicago if she wanted to see them, and she and Fred had an unspoken arrangement that worked for both of them. There was an undeniable edge to her, born of the way things had worked out, and she didn't have a high opinion of her husband, or men like him. She believed now that all men cheated, given half a chance to do so, and her husband certainly did, and had for years. He slept with secretaries, assistants, and women he met at cocktail parties, on business, or in elevators, and women he sat next to on planes. The only women he didn't sleep with, she was certain, were her closest friends. At least he had the good taste not to do that. And most of them were too old for him. But he wouldn't have done that to her anyway. He wasn't a bad guy, just a cheater, with a weakness for twenty-five-year-olds.

They had a civil relationship, based on a mutual arrangement that worked for both of them, even if it was devoid of warmth. She had forgotten what it was like to feel loved by a man, and no longer thought about it. She had everything else she wanted, materially, which by now was more important to her. She wouldn't have given that up for anything in the world. They had recently bought a Picasso for their dining room, for which Fred had paid just under ten million dollars. They had one of the most important art collections in the West.

Jean's one soft spot was how much she cared about her friends, Alyson and Stephanie. She loved the weekends they spent together, and talking to them every day. She had opportunities and luxuries they didn't, but neither of them was jealous of her, and she knew it. They didn't envy the state of her marriage either, or the emptiness of her relationship with Fred, but despite the choices she had made, there was a human side to Jean, and an honesty about herself that they all found endearing. There was no pretense to Jean, she loved being rich and Mrs. Fred

Dawson, and it was worth anything to her to stay that way. It was almost like a career choice she had made. Corporate wife of multimillionaire, who was rapidly on his way to becoming a billionaire in the high-tech world. Fred Dawson had a Midas touch, which men admired and envied, and the power he exuded was like an aphrodisiac to women. And Jean bought more Thoroughbreds, fabulous Impressionist paintings, and owned more Hermès and Louis Vuitton and Graff jewelry than almost any woman in the world. And yet she was perfectly capable of enjoying a weekend in Squaw Valley with their four best friends.

They had driven up from Hillsborough in Fred's new Ferrari. And she always referred to the three couples as the Big Six. Fred had already been successful when they met, though not on the scale he was now. Even Jean admitted that the amount of money he had made in recent years was ridiculous, but it suited her just fine. She felt like a queen, and in her world she was. But her bright mind, quick wit, and honesty about herself and others kept her from being obnoxious. She could be harsh at times, born of disappointment about her marriage. But her friends loved her as she was, even if her husband didn't. He was only attracted to young women, and no matter how great she looked, Jean had been too old to appeal to him for years. At fifty-five, Fred preferred women under thirty, and considered them a status symbol to feed his ego, which Jean knew well. No matter how much plastic surgery she had or how many Botox shots, or how diligently she worked out with her trainer, Fred hadn't been attracted to her in years. And Jean had no illusions about it. It took a strong ego for her to no longer be affected by it, and she availed herself of his credit cards at every opportunity to keep her morale high. It worked for her.

Brad and Alyson Freeman were the opposite of Jean and Fred. After twelve years of marriage, they were still madly in love, and Alyson thought her husband walked on water. She had been a rep for a pharmaceutical company, and at thirty-five she had begun to think she would be single forever, until her Cinderella story happened. Brad had noticed her when she was dropping drug samples off at his office. Still a bachelor at forty-one, and enjoying every minute of it, he was the object of all his nurses' fantasies, and Alyson's as well. He was the successful orthopedic surgeon they all dreamed of, and he fell for Alyson like the proverbial ton of bricks. Eight months after they started dating, they were married, and Alyson's life changed forever. She worked for a few more months until she got pregnant, and had been busy with their three children ever since. Twelve years later, she still talked about her husband like a modern-day saint, grateful for everything he did for her, thrilled with the life they shared. He was a devoted, loving husband and a great father to their kids, and whenever Jean made one of her acerbic comments that all men were cheaters given the chance, Alyson defended Brad hotly and told her he had never so much as looked at another woman since they were married, which caused Jean to give her one of her wry smiles.

'I know Brad is perfect, and the most faithful man on the planet, but he's still a guy,' she commented. And Alyson's body still looked great, although she rarely had time to dress up anymore. She was too busy with their kids. But she worked out at the gym several times a week, and played tennis, and she loved their ski weekends with their friends. And even Stephanie teased her occasionally about how she idolized Brad and how in love with him she was. But it was sweet to see. They were obviously happy, Brad had done well, their kids were adorable and were eleven, six, and two, and they had a beautiful home in Ross, one of the most luxurious and affluent suburbs in Marin. And they really seemed to have an idyllic life. Brad was constantly loving and solicitous and was as in love with Alyson as she was with him. And he really was the perfect dad. He was their older son's Cub Scout leader, took their daughter to her soccer games and ballet on the weekend, and had a 'date' with Alyson at the best restaurants in San Francisco every Saturday night. And he was one of the most respected surgeons in his field. And at fifty-three, he was still a very handsome man, and looked years younger than he was.

Each of the two couples represented an extreme on the scale of marital bliss. Alyson and Brad were madly in love, and Fred and Jean had settled for an arrangement that worked for both of them but, even to those who knew them well, appeared to be devoid of love.

Stephanie and Bill were somewhere in the middle, having had their ups and downs and a few hard knocks in their twenty-six years of marriage. The first eight or nine years had been wonderful and everything Stephanie had hoped they would be, having babies, buying their first home in the city, Bill becoming a partner in the law firm he worked for, and doing well. They had met in college at Berkeley, while she was an undergraduate and Bill was finishing law school, and had married shortly after she graduated. She had gotten a terrific job at a very successful ad agency, which used her writing and marketing skills, and which she was excited about, until she had problems in her first pregnancy and was put on bed rest for five months. Michael, their first child, was born prematurely, and after that, with Bill's encouragement, she never went back to work. She was a stay-at-home mom and enjoyed her life, until things started to get hectic as the kids got older, and there were times when she regretted not having kept her hand in the workforce, to have a sense of accomplishment of her own. She talked to Bill about it once their younger daughter Charlotte started school, but Bill was insistent that he preferred her being at home for their kids, so for several years now she had given up the dream of ever working again.

Both of them kept busy. She had been president of the PTA for several years. She was a hands-on full-time mother, involved in all their activities. And Bill was too busy at the law firm to participate in their children's lives as much as he should. Over the years, they had both discovered that being a hands-on parent was not his strong suit. He was much better at making a living that provided a nice home for them in the city, and at keeping their kids in private schools. He was an excellent provider, and a good person, but he had no desire to spend his weekends ferrying the children from one soccer match to another, or even showing up at the girls' ballet recitals or school plays once a year. Stephanie had become artful at making excuses for him to make up for all the things he didn't do. He loved his children but never seemed to have time to spend with them. He rarely had time to come home for dinner, and often came home at night when they were asleep. And somehow Stephanie always managed to cover for him, and make him look good to their kids. Even when he played golf with clients on the weekend, she always had a rational explanation for why he really had to be somewhere else. And by the time they were in their teens, the kids were so busy that they never seemed to notice or comment on his absence, even when they didn't see him for several days. As far as they were concerned, according to what their mom said, that was what dads did. Stephanie always picked up the slack for him. She never missed a sporting event, a school conference, or a doctor's appointment. She carpooled when they were younger, listened to their problems, made their Halloween costumes, and kissed away all their hurts. Bill's frequent no-shows put additional pressure on her. She never complained about it, but she noticed, and so did Michael before he left for college.

Michael had played lacrosse for four years by that time, and one night at the dinner table he pointed out that his father had never come to a single game. Stephanie found that hard to believe, but when she thought about it later, she realized it was true. Michael left for UCLA a few months later, preparing for a program in sports management he wanted to take in graduate school after college, and moved to Atlanta to work for the Braves when he got his B.A. He had been there now for three years, and still planned to go to graduate school eventually, but not just yet. She missed him, but he loved his job, it was a great team, and she was happy for him.

The girls had never commented about Bill's performance as a father, even if Michael had. She tried to be both mother and father to all of them and never said anything to Bill about it. She knew how hard he worked, and how well he provided for them.

They lacked for nothing, and he had established a solid

base for her and the children. All three of their children had gone to excellent colleges, and good schools before that. They went on wonderful vacations in the summer, and Stephanie had never had to work. For all intents and purposes, he was the perfect husband and father, even if he didn't remember their birthdays or hers, or show up for school plays.

The subject of her going back to work came up again when Charlotte started high school, Louise was a senior, and Michael was in college, but by then Stephanie couldn't imagine who would employ her, and at what. It had been twenty years since she had worked. And before she could figure out what to do about it, a bomb she had never expected had hit their life. She discovered by accident that Bill was having an affair. Until then, she had thought that they had a good marriage, in spite of occasional bumps. By a series of unlucky coincidences, she found out that Bill was having an affair with a junior lawyer at the firm. They had been working on a case together, and once Bill confessed, he swore nothing like it had ever happened before. It came at a time when Stephanie had been particularly busy getting Charlotte into high school, and helping Louise apply to college, and she and Bill had been spending almost no time together. And the antitrust case he was working on kept him at the office until midnight every night. He and the young lawyer had spent a week in L.A. taking depositions, and he admitted later that it had started then. She was also married, and the discovery – Stephanie had seen them at a restaurant together when he claimed to be in meetings at the office – rocked her world. He had been deeply apologetic and admitted that he was in love with the young lawyer, but also said he didn't want to lose their marriage. With enormous sadness, Stephanie asked him to move out, until he made some clear-cut decisions. It was a painful time for Stephanie and they had separated for two months. He had wanted to marry Marella, who then decided to stay with her husband. He was honest with Stephanie, and said he wanted to resume their marriage and try to forget his affair. It would be better for their kids, but he didn't pretend to be in love with her anymore. Stephanie didn't want him back by default, but she had also had time to realize that she didn't want a divorce.

Alyson had been heartbroken for her when Stephanie told her about it, and Jean had said she wasn't surprised, it was no worse than the dozens of indiscretions Fred had committed over the years. All it did was confirm Jean's belief that all men were cheaters given the opportunity, and Bill was no better than anyone else. 'You can make him pay for it if you stay,' she teased Stephanie, but she was sad for Stephanie that it had happened. It had shattered Stephanie's illusions about Bill and their marriage, and made it hard if not impossible to feel the same about him again. They had gone to marriage counseling, Stephanie finally agreed to continue their marriage, and the children were aware that something terrible had happened between their parents, but Stephanie had never told them what it was. She didn't want them hating their father because he had cheated on her. She didn't think that would be fair to him. Jean was outraged when Stephanie told her and thought that they should know, but Stephanie had spent twenty years creating the illusion for them that their father was devoted, concerned, honorable, and above reproach. She didn't want to expose him to their children as the cheater he was, nor damage their relationship with him, although her relationship with him seemed to be destroyed beyond repair when he moved home again.

After the two-month separation, things had never been the same again. They were more like roommates under one roof. She believed that they loved each other, out of a sense of history, if nothing else, and they had children together, but there were no longer any obvious demonstrations of affection, and she no longer complained about how little they saw of him. Before, he had been busy, but now there was a chasm between them that neither of them had been able to bridge. And she never fully trusted him after he returned. They still had sex, but it was infrequent and lackluster. She felt it was an obligation since they had decided to stay married, and he made love to her because he knew he should. Their relationship had never been passionate, but it had been friendly and warm in the early years, and adequate after that, but all desire had gone out of it for both of them by the time they got back together.

Stephanie knew the young lawyer had left the law firm six months after the affair, but she no longer cared. Bill was still her husband, but he would never again be her best friend, or someone she was even close to. They had nothing to say to each other anymore, except about the kids. She kept him informed of their progress in school and college, and when Michael and Louise got their first jobs. Louise had recently moved to New York to work for Sotheby's in the art department. They talked about practical matters, but never about their feelings for each other, or his affair, which stood like a wall between them. She had been sad about it for a long time, but now she simply accepted it as the way marriages were after this many years. And his infidelity with the young lawyer had left irreparable scars. But Stephanie had never wavered from her decision to stay with him, for the kids, and Bill had been adamant about wanting to stay married to her. He didn't want a divorce. They were a family, and he wanted to stay that way, however impaired their marriage was.

It had been particularly lonely for Stephanie when Charlotte left for college at NYU, and even more so now that she was doing her junior year abroad, in Rome. Stephanie and Bill had gone over to see her in January, and she was having a ball. She was going to be there until June, come home for the summer, then go back to NYU. Stephanie could hardly wait till she got home. She was toying with the idea again of finding a job herself. With all three kids gone, she desperately needed something to do. She had worked on several benefit committees, but she had been bored planning charity events and raising money, and wanted more to do. But her brief fledgling career after college was a dim memory now. She had opted for family instead of career, and now the kids were all away. It made for some painfully quiet nights when Bill was working late, and awkward ones when he was home. They had so little to say, other than the news she shared about the kids. He never called them himself, but they all called her to check in. And the only evenings Bill and Stephanie really enjoyed together now were the ones they spent with their friends, the Dawsons and the Freemans, and the trips they had taken together for years. Then she could chat with the women, and Bill could hang out with the 'boys.'

All six of them were good skiers, although the three women took it easy, and the men were always competitive with each other, particularly Brad and Fred. Bill was less so and a more relaxed skier. They took the black diamond trails, while the girls took the gentler runs, and they met for lunch at the base, and went to good restaurants at night.

Stephanie was looking forward to a day of skiing with Alyson and Jean as she zipped up her parka, and walked into the living room of their suite to find Bill. He looked trim in a black parka and ski pants, with hiking boots. He had left his ski boots in his locker at the lift, with his skis and poles, where she had left hers as well. Stephanie was wearing a white ski parka, with her long blond hair in a braid, and a pale blue knit cap. She was carrying her goggles and gloves as she glanced at Bill.

'Ready?' He nodded and followed her out of the room. At breakfast, they talked about the weather and he read the newspaper. They walked out into the winter sunshine and covered the short distance to the shuttle to take them to the lift. The other two couples were staying at a hotel at the base, which was new. Bill had wanted to stay at the same hotel where they always did, and didn't mind the shuttle to get to the lift. The others were already waiting for them with their skis on, and Bill and Stephanie hurried to put on theirs. They put them on side by side, and Stephanie started to say something to him as he began to move toward the men. He turned and glanced at her with a serious look. They rarely smiled at each other anymore. It didn't occur to either of them, they weren't even aware of it.

'Have a nice run,' she said softly. She had meant to talk to him about renewing Charlotte's traveler's insurance, which was about to expire, but had forgotten to mention it over breakfast. She could always talk to him about it that night. All of their conversations were about practical matters, like roof repairs, a problem with a tree in their garden, or something for one of the kids. She never shared her private thoughts with him anymore, and hadn't since the affair. What was the point? They were no longer close.

'Thanks,' he said, smiling this time, 'you too.' There was no touch of the hand, no kiss, no hug, no tender words. They weren't part of each other's emotional landscape now. She had learned to live without it, and she always wondered if he was having another affair, or when he would. Their relationship had been inadequate and sterile now for seven years. And with that, Stephanie shoved off on her skis to join her two women friends.

'Cute hat,' Jean said, admiring Stephanie's pale blue knit cap, which was exactly the same color as her eyes. Jean was wearing a big fox hat, and a trim beige ski suit she had bought in Courchevel. She was always beautifully dressed. She had the time and could afford to be, and she went shopping constantly. She was the best dressed of the three friends, and her nails were exquisitely manicured with bright red polish when she took off her gloves. Alyson never wore any and had given up manicures, since her children were small, and Stephanie had gotten out of the habit years before. She dressed simply and practically and didn't try to look sexy or cute to Bill. Those days were over, and had been for seven years. Stephanie was wearing the pale blue ski pants she had worn for ages, only the white parka was new, and she had actually borrowed it from Louise, who had left it when she went to New York. Alyson was all in red with a red knit cap and her dark hair tucked into it.

The three women rode the chair lift together, and they could see their three men already far ahead. They hadn't lost time getting on the lift, anxious to hit the trails. The girls had taken time to adjust their goggles and hats, pull on their gloves, and get on the lift holding their poles and dangling their skis. The women could have followed the same tough trails as their men, but didn't want to. They preferred a more leisurely run. The boys were already gone when they got off the lift, chatting about their kids. Stephanie was telling Alyson all about their trip to Rome, and the weekend they'd spent in London on the way back. Bill had clients there, and Stephanie had had time to shop. Jean commented that they were going to Europe in a month.

All three women skied down the mountain gracefully, and stopped here and there to admire the view and talk, and then skied on again.

'God, the weather is gorgeous,' Stephanie said, admiring the scenery on one of their stops. Squaw was busy that weekend, but there seemed to be enough space for everyone. There was at least a foot of fresh powder since the day before. It was harder to ski in, but they had fun on the way down, and enough time for another run. It was almost noon when they reached the base for the second time, and decided to wait for the boys for lunch. They always stopped at noon, and went to the better restaurant, before skiing all afternoon.

'For an old broad, that wasn't bad,' Jean congratulated herself after their last run. She was a fabulous skier, and in terrific shape. And Stephanie was in good shape too. Only Alyson was slightly out of breath and complained that she was getting to the gym less often because of the kids, and she had gained a few pounds over Christmas.

They stood chatting for half an hour, waiting for their husbands, and Jean looked annoyed as she glanced at her watch. It was a rose gold Rolex Daytona that Fred had given her the year before. 'What the hell are they doing?' And then she rolled her eyes with a familiar expression she often used when talking about Fred. 'Probably picking up girls on the trail.'

Alyson looked upset the moment she said it, as she always did. 'Brad doesn't do that,' she defended him.

'And they ski too hard to pick up women,' Stephanie said with a grin. 'They're more interested in showing each other up than chasing women,' she said practically, and all three laughed. But they'd been waiting for more than half an hour when Jean suggested they go to the restaurant without them, and wait for them there. She wanted a

31

Bloody Mary and was tired of waiting. She almost had the other two women convinced when out of the corner of her eye, Stephanie saw Brad and Fred following a ski patrol sled, with three members of the ski patrol around them. Both of their men looked serious, and the only one missing was Bill. She saw a form under the blanket on the sled, and without stopping to say anything to her two friends, she skied toward them. Jean and Alyson exchanged a glance and followed her. And as soon as Stephanie reached them, the ski patrol stopped and Stephanie bent quickly to say something to Bill on the sled. His face was hidden by the blanket, and before she could remove it, Brad grabbed her arm and stopped her. The look on his face spoke volumes, and there were tears in his eyes.

'Steph, don't . . .' She looked from him to the others, and she could see that something terrible had happened before they said a word.

'What happened? Is he okay?' she said with a look of panic, reaching toward her husband again, but Bill hadn't moved.

'He collapsed while we were skiing,' Brad explained in a tense voice, looking stricken. 'I think he had a heart attack. I gave him CPR until the ski patrol came. I couldn't revive him,' he said with tears in his eyes as he looked at her.

'OhmyGod.' She popped her skis off and knelt on the snow then, wondering why they weren't doing anything to help him, and when she pulled the blanket back to see him, he looked like he was sleeping. Brad shook his head at the two other women then, and they instantly understood. Alyson's eyes filled with tears as she looked at her husband, and Jean was shocked as she glanced at Fred, and he shook his head too. Stephanie was still kneeling on the snow, holding Bill in her arms, but it was obvious that he was dead. Brad put an arm around her then and helped her stand up, and told her he hadn't suffered. He said Bill had died instantly, as Stephanie stared at him in disbelief.

'That can't be . . . he's fine . . . he doesn't have a heart problem. He had a checkup last week.' As though saying that would cancel what had just occurred, but it didn't.

'That happens sometimes,' Brad said gently. The ski patrol slowly led the sled away toward the first aid station, as Brad held Stephanie and she began to cry. This couldn't be happening, she kept thinking to herself. It wasn't true. Bill was fifty-two years old, he couldn't be dead. She tried to think of what he had said to her that morning when he went off with the others. Not 'I love you,' or any tender words, just 'Thanks' when she wished him a nice run. He hadn't kissed her goodbye, she hadn't tried to kiss him. It hadn't even dawned on her that something could go wrong and she'd never see him alive again. All he said was 'Thanks,' and now he was dead. She felt like a robot as she walked into the ski patrol station with the others. They had taken Bill inside on a stretcher by then, and put him in a small private room. One of the men from the ski patrol led her in, and she stood next to Bill, looking at him, unable to believe what had just happened. The man she had once loved and been married to for twenty-six years was dead. They hadn't been really happy in seven years, but they had stayed together. They loved each other in a quiet unspoken way. They expected to be together forever. He was the father of her children . . . and now he was dead. Stephanie just stood there looking at him, and gently touched his face as tears rolled down her cheeks.

Chapter 2

Alyson went to their hotel to pack for them, and check them out of the hotel, while Stephanie stayed with Bill, and Jean, Brad, and Fred were with her at the ski patrol station. Fred and Brad filled out the necessary papers, and signed the accident report. And Brad spoke to the head of the ski patrol quietly about making arrangements to have Bill taken to the city by ambulance to the funeral home there. Stephanie heard it all from a great distance, and everything around her was a blur. She stared at Jean as though she didn't understand.

'How could that happen?' she said for the tenth time in an hour. She looked as though she were in shock, and when the ambulance came, Stephanie couldn't stop crying. Their marriage hadn't been perfect, and they hadn't really been happy in a long time, but she had loved him, and she never expected him to die. They had wasted so much time being disconnected from each other after the affair. It was as though he had burned the bridge that linked them, and she had never been able to connect with him again. And now he was gone.

The two couples stood making their driving arrangements to get back to the city. Jean said she would drive Stephanie down in their SUV, while Fred went alone in his new Ferrari, and Brad and Alyson went home in Brad's Porsche. They had left the Mercedes station wagon for the kids and the au pair. For the Freemans and particularly the Dawsons, their cars defined who they were. Stephanie didn't care and drove a four-year-old SUV.

'Are you okay?' Jean asked gently as she helped Stephanie into the car. Stephanie was deathly pale. She got in seeming confused, like someone who had been ill for a long time. She kept thinking about Bill that morning, and a thousand mornings before this, and all the things they hadn't said to each other. And how was she going to tell her kids? She'd have to tell them on the phone, since all of them were in other cities, and now they had to come home. 'Do you want me to call the kids?' Jean offered as Stephanie shook her head, staring out the window and seeing nothing, and then she turned to look at Jean.

'We never really got back together, after . . . after what he did. We just pretended, but it was never the same.' Jean had known that without Stephanie admitting it to her. It had been obvious to anyone who knew them.

'It doesn't matter,' Jean said quietly as they drove away

toward the city. 'You loved each other. Those things are hard to recover from.'

'I went back to him for the kids . . . but I loved him too. I just didn't trust him anymore. And Bill was never good at talking about things, so we never did after a while. He didn't want to, and I didn't either. We just kept putting one foot in front of the other and doing all the things we had to do.' But the joy had gone out of their marriage seven years before, or maybe long before that. She couldn't remember now. Whatever it had been, or had once been, or never was, it was over now.

Jean couldn't help wondering what she would feel if Fred died now. Sad, probably. Their marriage had been a sham for so many years, but she was used to him. She liked to say to her friends, somewhat tongue in cheek, that their marriage was a genuine fraud. But in some ways they cared about each other, no matter how disappointing it had been.

'I'm sure he always loved you,' Jean tried to reassure her, whatever she believed, which was colored by her own view of men. 'Men just do stupid things. Fred has been an idiot for most of our marriage. He started cheating on me even before our kids were born, and I was young then. He figured I wouldn't know.'

'Why did you stay with him?' Stephanie asked, turning to her with a dazed look. She was still in shock, but talking to Jean was helping her try to stay focused on some kind of reality. Jean was the life preserver she was clinging to.

'I still loved him in those days. It took me a few years to get over it, but I did,' she said with a wintry smile, and Stephanie laughed. Jean was so awful about Fred, but most of the time the way she said it sounded funny. But it couldn't have been easy to live with, any more than Stephanie's situation with Bill was, after the affair. At least he had never cheated again, that she knew of. All those thoughts kept racing through her head as they drove down from Tahoe. She was grateful that Jean was driving. She couldn't have made the trip on her own, she was too distracted, and stunned. It all felt unreal.

They got to the city in just under four hours, Jean parked the car in front of Stephanie's garage on Clay Street, and followed her inside. They left the suitcases, skis, and poles in the car. And Bill's boots were back there too. The ski patrol had taken them off before they sent him to the city in the ambulance, and had gotten his hiking boots from the locker. Stephanie had put them on him herself with shaking hands before they took him away.

She stood in the front hall, after they walked in, and looked at Jean as though she were lost, and didn't know what to do. But she knew. She had to call her kids. She went out to the kitchen, and sat down on a high stool next to the phone. She normally knew their numbers by heart, but suddenly couldn't remember them.

She called Charlotte in Rome first. It was two in the morning for her, and she didn't want to call her any later, but Charlotte needed to know so she could come home the next day. There was shocked silence at the other end of the phone when Stephanie told her, a long pause, and then a long sharp scream. Jean could hear it from across the room. Stephanie sobbed as she talked to her and tried to comfort her, hating the fact that she had to tell her such terrible news over the phone without having her arms around her. She told her daughter to get the first plane home, and use her credit card for the ticket. Stephanie had given her a high enough limit on the card that she could always buy a ticket home if she needed to. She had just never expected it to be for something like this.

'Let me know what flight you're on,' she told Charlotte, who was her youngest, at twenty. She was much too young to lose her father. Stephanie had been in her forties when she lost her parents, which had seemed too young too. But at twenty, it was brutal. And Bill was only fifty-two. Who could have expected this to happen? And he had been in such good health, or so it seemed. As she had told Brad, his annual physical the week before had turned up nothing.

Charlotte was still crying piteously when they hung up, and Stephanie tried to catch her breath as she continued crying too. Jean handed her a glass of water.

'How is she?' Jean asked, looking worried.

Danielle Steel

'Awful,' Stephanie answered simply, and pressed Michael's number. He answered on the first ring. It was Saturday night, and he was home, cooking dinner for some friends, with his girlfriend. It was already eight-thirty at night in Atlanta, he said they were barbecuing, and his mother could hear music in the background. She told him the news as gently and directly as she could, and his voice was shaking when he asked her, 'How are you, Mom? Are you okay?'

She couldn't speak for a minute, then said, 'How soon can you come home?' She could hear that he was crying when she asked him, and then he said something muffled to someone standing next to him.

'I'll catch the red-eye tonight,' he said, trying to sound strong and manly for her. 'Have you told the girls yet?'

'I just called Charlotte. I wanted to tell her before it got any later, so she can catch a flight in the morning.'

'Poor kid,' but poor him too. Poor all of them, Stephanie was thinking. Bill hadn't been an ideal father, but he was the only one they had. And they were too young to lose him. And whatever his failings, he was someone they could rely on. Now all they had was her. The thought of it made her shudder. Everything rested on her now. It was awesome and terrifying being the only parent, no matter how competent she was. This was much worse than during their separation.

'I'll call Louise in a minute,' she said wanly. 'You don't

40

have to come home tonight, Mike. You can come home tomorrow, I'll be okay.'

'No, I want to,' he said, still sounding tearful. He was twenty-five years old, and suddenly the only man in the family. 'I'll see you in the morning, Mom,' he said. He had to get off the phone if he was going to make the flight.

And then she called her middle child, and older daughter, Louise, in New York. She sounded confused when her mother told her.

'What?' She was sure that she had heard wrong. What her mother had just said sounded insane to her. Stephanie told her again, and this time she began crying and couldn't stop. It was a long time before she could say anything to her mother. 'How? That's not possible. He's so young, Mom.'

'I know. I don't understand it either.' But the doctor at the ski patrol confirmed that it had been a heart attack.

They talked for a few minutes, and Louise said she would take the first flight out of New York in the morning. And then Stephanie turned to look at Jean. The first of the horrible tasks was done. Now all her children knew. Stephanie felt as if she'd been hit by a bus, as Jean handed her a cup of tea.

'Why don't you lie down for a little while? There's nothing you need to do right now. The kids have been told. You can deal with the rest tomorrow. I'll come over first thing and help you.' And then she asked, 'Do you want me to stay here tonight?' Stephanie thought about it and then shook her head.

'I'll be okay,' she said sadly. She didn't really want anyone staying there. She wanted time to think. So much had happened. She hadn't been able to absorb it yet. Nothing made any sense. She was sure that Bill would walk in any minute, and tell her it was all a joke. But the look on her friend's face told her it was all too true.

They went up to her bedroom and talked for a while. And then Fred rang the bell. Jean let him in, and he brought Bill and Stephanie's suitcases and skis inside and left them in the hall. He didn't know what else to do.

And finally, around eight o'clock, Fred and Jean left and went back to Hillsborough. Jean promised to come back in the morning. And Alyson called several times that night, and offered to come over. But Stephanie knew the au pair had gone home, and she had no one for her kids. She promised to come in the morning too.

It was the longest night of Stephanie's life. She couldn't sleep. All she could think about was Bill, and what had gone wrong between them for all those years. Suddenly she felt guilty for not working harder to forgive him and repair the damage, but he hadn't either. They had been two lost people, treading water for seven years, after the ship went down.

Jean was back at eight-thirty the next morning, and

Alyson showed up shortly after. Stephanie was working on the obituary, and she called the funeral home. She had to go in to pick the casket and make arrangements, plan the funeral, pick programs and meet with the minister at the church, and call the florist. There were so many things to do. Between the three of them, they got most of it organized by ten that morning. And as soon as they did, Michael arrived, he hadn't been able to get on a red-eye the night before, and both women went downstairs, while Stephanie and her son cried in each other's arms.

Louise arrived an hour later, from New York. And Charlotte was due to land at one. Jean stayed to do whatever she could to help, and Alyson went home to her kids, but promised to come back later.

And when Louise walked in, she sobbed in her mother's arms about what an amazing father Bill had been. Jean said nothing but couldn't help noticing that in death Bill had become a saint, to his children at least. She couldn't imagine that Stephanie was thinking the same thing.

Michael went to the airport to pick up his younger sister when she arrived from Rome, and by three o'clock all of Stephanie's children were home, all looking shell-shocked and mourning their father. Jean went to the funeral home with her to pick the casket, and then they went to the church to meet with the minister. It was Sunday, and they set the funeral for Tuesday, at three p.m. The obituary Stephanie had written was to run the next day.

'There's so much to do,' Stephanie said to Jean as they drove back to the house, 'my head is spinning.'

'Let me call the florist for you,' Jean offered, and Stephanie nodded, looking dazed.

'Do we need to call people and tell them?' Stephanie asked her, not sure what to do.

'Just call his office tomorrow. Everyone will read it in the paper.' Stephanie nodded. Her children were waiting when they got home, and Jean went back to Hillsborough, promising to return the next day.

The four of them had dinner in the kitchen that night, and sat for hours afterward talking about their father, as Stephanie listened to them tell stories of what a hero he had been, and what a great father to them. There was a disconnect somewhere, she knew, but she couldn't locate it just yet and didn't want to. They sat there late into the night, alternately crying and singing his praises, and then finally everyone went to bed. Stephanie had never been so exhausted in her life. Half the time she was in searing emotional pain and the other half she was numb.

The next day was more of the same, with more details to take care of. Everyone at Bill's office was shocked, and all of his partners called Stephanie. Jean went shopping and arrived with dresses for them to wear to the funeral, and miraculously everything fit. None of them had had properly serious black dresses to wear for a funeral, as the bereaved family of the deceased.

The day of the funeral dawned gray and rainy. Jean had called a caterer to be there when people came to the house after the service. And three hundred people trouped through their house, as Stephanie stood pale and brave and her children cried all day.

She was finally alone with Jean for a few minutes after everyone left, and she stared at her friend in shocked disbelief.

'Everybody loved him so much. They all have stories about what a great guy he was. I never knew he had that many friends.' Stephanie looked confused as she lay on her bed, and Jean sat down in a chair across the room.

'People always become saints after they're gone. No one remembers the bad things they did. And to his friends, Bill was a good guy, even if he wasn't great to you. No one's going to remember that now, or say it to you. Least of all your kids.' She had heard them talking all afternoon about what a wonderful father he'd been, and Michael had given a eulogy in glowing praise of his father.

'He never did anything for the kids,' Stephanie said softly, as though she were afraid someone would hear her. 'I had to push him into everything he did.'

'I know. You always made him look like a hero. That's all they want to remember now.' Stephanie fell silent as she thought about it, wondering if she was confused too. Maybe he had been a better husband than she thought. What was true – what people were saying about him now, or the distance and disconnect they had lived with for years after he cheated on her? 'Don't try to figure it out. It doesn't matter right now. Just get through this. How long are the kids staying?'

'Louise has to be back at work by the end of the week, and Michael has a big meeting in Atlanta on Friday. Charlotte has exams this week, she's leaving tomorrow night.' Jean realized from what she said that Stephanie would be alone by the weekend, in the deafening silence of her empty house. She hated to think of her alone.

'It would be nice if they could stay at least till Sunday,' Jean said, looking pensive. But sooner or later, Stephanie would have to face the fact that she was alone now. Bill had died just at the point in life where kids are gone, and you want to count on your husband being there while you got old. Instead, Stephanie was a widow at forty-eight, with kids who were grown and gone and lived in other cities. And Jean knew that however lacking Bill had been, or inadequate their relationship in recent years, it was going to be very, very tough on her.

She left a little while later, and Stephanie spent the evening with her children. They all agreed that the funeral had been beautiful, although to Stephanie it seemed like a blur. She couldn't even remember who was there.

After spending the day together, Charlotte left for Rome the following afternoon, Louise the next day, and Michael on the red-eye to Atlanta that night. It was over.

Country

Bill was dead, they had buried him, and their children had gone back to their own lives and worlds, and after she drove Michael to the airport on Thursday night, Stephanie came back to her empty house, sat down on a chair in the entrance hall, and sobbed. She had never felt so alone in her life.

Chapter 3

For the next several weeks, Stephanie wandered around her house like a ghost. She lay on her bed for hours, thinking about Bill, wondering what had gone wrong between them, and why. She called her children every day, and it was strange talking to them. They were mourning a father they had never really had. The perfect father, who had always been there for them. Louise even attributed things to him that Stephanie had always done, and Bill never had. It was confusing and upsetting listening to them, and she said as much to Jean when they had lunch three weeks after he died. She looked as though she had lost about ten pounds, and Jean wondered if she had been eating.

'I don't know who we're talking about when I talk to them, or what to say. All those times I covered for him, all the things I did to make him look like a good guy to them, when he was too busy to care what any of us were doing, or even show up. And now suddenly, according to them, he was there at every game, went to every recital and play. Charlotte even told me he used to pick them up at school all the time, and I never did. What am I supposed to say? Do I tell the truth, or leave them their fantasies? I know this sounds crazy, but it even sounds like they're mad at me for being alive, and sorry I'm not the one who died.'

'They're just angry, Steph. And it's safe to take it out on you.'

'Well, I'm not enjoying it a lot. The truth is that he loved them even if he didn't show up. But the reality is he didn't. He didn't show up for me either.' But he had done other things that mattered. He had left her and their children well provided for, with sound investments, a house that had increased in value, a trust for each of the children, and large insurance policies that not only covered the estate taxes but left all three children and her a sizable amount. He had been a responsible person, although he had failed her abysmally as a husband, and had been an absentee father, which no one chose to remember. Jean wasn't surprised.

'That's just the way it works. At least you're all secure. At his age, he might not have done that.' But now Stephanie had to figure out what to do with the rest of her life. She didn't have a clue. And unless she visited her children in their respective cities, she wouldn't see them until Thanksgiving, which was more than eight months away. At least when he was alive, she knew Bill would eventually come home every night and fall into bed beside her, even if they didn't talk to each other. Now she didn't even have that. She had nothing and no one. No one to take care of, or do errands for, or have dinner with on the weekends. And what if she got sick? If something happened to her? Who would be there for her now, or go to the emergency room with her if she got hurt? She felt totally alone. And just trying to say it to Jean made her cry. She hadn't stopped crying in three weeks. She wasn't even sure if she was crying for him, or herself. And she was scared. She suddenly felt so vulnerable.

'The truth is you're the one who always held up the world around here. He didn't. He was always working,' Jean reminded her, to give her back some perspective. Stephanie thought about it for a long moment and then nodded as she blew her nose.

'I guess you're right. That was always my job. But at least I knew he was around. Now he's not.'

'You'll be okay,' Jean reassured her gently. 'It's just a big change to get used to. Why don't we all have dinner next week?' she suggested, and Stephanie hesitated, wondering if it would make her feel worse. She didn't feel ready to go out yet. 'It would do you good. You can't sit here forever in ratty jeans, waiting for him to come home. He's not going to, Steph. You have to get on with your life.' But it felt too soon to do that. And she was lying awake at night now, thinking about the affair he had had, and how angry she had been at him. And suddenly for no reason, she was angry at him all over again, which made no sense. The affair had been seven years before, and now he was dead. And getting angry at him served no purpose. But she was angry anyway. It was eating at her night and day.

In desperation, after not sleeping for weeks, she finally went back to Dr. Zeller, the therapist she'd seen seven years before, when they first split up after she discovered the affair. The therapist was glad to see her. She had heard about Bill, and read the obituary, and she told Stephanie how sorry she was.

'Thank you,' Stephanie said, looking subdued, as she sat in the familiar chair across from the older woman's desk. She was tired of hearing people tell her how sorry they were about her 'loss.' It was such an easy buyout of any real emotion or compassion, and such an infuriatingly trite word. She had said that to Jean too.

'How are you feeling now?' Dr. Zeller asked. It had only been a month since Bill had died at Squaw Valley. It was still hard to believe. Some days she felt as though he'd only been gone for minutes, and at other times as though he'd been gone for years. The kids were still a mess, and singing his praises every chance they got, whenever she called them. And Louise and Charlotte had an edge in their voices whenever they spoke to her. She tried to explain how bad it made her feel.

'Suddenly, he has become perfect, and I'm some sort of bad guy because I'm still alive.'

'It's easier to be angry at you for surviving than at him for dying,' Dr. Zeller said simply. 'They'll get their perspective back eventually, but it will take a while. And it's less painful to believe he was perfect than to admit the truth, particularly since that truth can't be changed now. They can't make him a better father, or more interested in them. Now that will never change. They lost the hope of a better relationship with him when he died. They don't want to remember the truth right now.'

'So they need to beat me up,' Stephanie said ruefully, smiling at her.

'Yes, they do.' The therapist smiled back. 'What about you? How do *you* feel about him now? How have things been since the affair?'

'It was never the same again. I guess I never forgave him. I thought I had, but now I realize that maybe I didn't. And all of a sudden I'm obsessed with it again. I think about it all the time, and I'm furious with him. It's like it happened yesterday.'

'Your chance to fix that is gone now too,' she reminded her. 'Why did you stay with him, Stephanie, if you felt that way?'

'For the kids,' she answered quickly. 'Neither of us

wanted to break up our family. The girlfriend decided to stay with her husband, so he came back to me, and we both thought it was better for the kids.' She looked mournful as she said it, and felt angry again. It showed in her eyes.

'So you don't think he came back because he wanted to stay married to you and loved you?'

'Not really. If she had left her husband, he would have married her. He wanted to. She was the one who backed out.'

'Did Bill say that to you?' she asked with interest.

'More or less. He didn't have to. He said he wanted to marry her, and the facts spoke for themselves. She stayed with her husband, so he came back to me, and the kids. But he was never really there. We were both kind of dead after that. We went through the motions of being married, but it was never fun again. We never really talked. It never felt real. And once the kids were gone, we talked even less. There was nothing left to say except that the roof was leaking, or someone needed to clean out the garage. We spent almost no time together. He worked all the time, and I kept busy on my own.'

'That doesn't sound like much of a marriage. Why stay after the kids were gone?' Stephanie thought about it for a long moment, and then shook her head.

'I don't know. I guess neither of us wanted the pain of a divorce.'

'But the life you're describing sounds painful to me.'

'I loved him,' Stephanie said, with tears in her eyes. 'I just didn't trust him anymore. I never trusted him again. For a long time I thought it would get better, but it never did.'

'Did you ever think about leaving him then?'

'No.'

'What are you going to do now?' It was a good question, one that Stephanie had asked herself a thousand times in the last month. She had found no answers yet.

'I don't know. I'd like to get a job, but I have no idea what to do. Bill left everything organized and all of us very well set. I don't have to work, but I'd like to find something to do. I can't sit alone in the house for the rest of my life.'

'I hope not.' Dr. Zeller glanced at her watch as she said it. Their session had come to an end, and they made an appointment for the following week, although Stephanie didn't think it had really helped. All they had done was discuss the problems she was facing, they had found no solutions, to her anger or her children's, or to how she was going to fill her days and nights now that Bill was gone. She felt even more depressed when she left the therapist's office, and wondered if it was worth bothering to go at all. What difference would it make now? He was dead, no matter how she felt about it.

She let Jean and Alyson talk her into going to dinner

with both couples that weekend. She really didn't feel like it, but her friends insisted that she needed to get out. They had discussed it with each other, and they were worried about her. She looked like a zombie and was obviously depressed. She hardly ever left the house. It bothered Jean that Stephanie's kids were so tough on her whenever they spoke, almost as if they blamed her for their father's death.

In the end, Stephanie agreed to have dinner with her friends at a restaurant they all liked. Neither Brad nor Fred had seen her since the funeral and were concerned about her too, from everything their wives had said, although they weren't surprised.

Jean and Fred offered to pick her up in a Bentley Fred had just bought and wanted to show off, but Stephanie said she would meet them at the restaurant, she didn't want to feel like a burden on them. She told Jean she was perfectly capable of driving herself, although she had hardly been out of the house in the past month.

She was surprised at how nervous she was when she dressed for dinner, and told herself she was ridiculous. These were her best friends, and it would be just like old times, which she found made her anxious too. It would feel weird to have dinner with them without Bill. She wore a simple black dress, which hung on her now, and high heels. It was the first time she had worn decent clothes since the funeral, and it felt strange. She washed her hair and blew it dry, and put on makeup, and she was shaking when she got in the car, and scolded herself again.

She was startled, when she got to the restaurant, to realize how noisy it was. She had never noticed it before, and instead of festive, as it usually seemed, it felt oppressive and overwhelming, and she looked pale and strained when she got to the table where the others were waiting for her. The two men were on their feet instantly, and gave her a warm hug. For a fraction of an instant, she thought Brad held her for too long, and Fred looked at her with such obvious pity that it almost made her cry. She kissed Jean and Alyson while fighting back tears, and then sat down. She was about to order a drink, when she realized she had to drive, so she decided not to. The conversation felt strained at first, and finally she relaxed. But for the entire evening, she felt as though she were sitting on the other side of a pane of glass. They were just as they had always been, but they were still couples, and she no longer was. She was a woman alone, even with them. She felt different and separate and inadequate, as though she hadn't brought enough to the table to deserve being there with them. She was only a half, they were whole. She felt like a ghost, and as dead as Bill.

The conversation touched on all the usual subjects, vacations they were planning, worries about their kids, a huge construction project Brad and Alyson were contemplating to add on to their house. Brad said they were exploding at the seams, and it would only get worse as the kids got bigger. And Alyson was distraught because her au pair had quit. Suddenly Stephanie felt like she had nothing in common with the problems they were dealing with, which all seemed superfluous to her. She was just trying to survive from one day to the next, and hanging on by a thread. It was exhausting listening to them, and she felt like she had nothing to add. She had nothing to contribute to the conversation, and Jean could see how uncomfortable she was, and was worried about her.

'Are you okay?' she asked her on the way out, and Stephanie nodded and smiled. 'It will be better next time,' she reassured her. 'It's bound to feel a little weird at first. We all miss him too.' The Big Six had suddenly become the Big Five, and it felt more like four and a half to Stephanie. She didn't feel like a whole person in their midst. She was just a single woman with nothing to say.

They all agreed to have dinner again soon, and they kissed each other goodbye. Stephanie was relieved when she finally got home, took off her dress, threw it onto a chair, kicked off her heels, and lay down on her bed in her underwear and pantyhose. She had hated every moment of the evening, and felt ill at ease with her old friends. She had felt anxious all night, and wondered if she would feel that way forever now.

Jean called her as soon as they got home. 'Look, okay,

it's not the same. But this is still new for all of us. Pretty soon you'll feel like you always did with us.' Fred had commented on the way back to Hillsborough that Stephanie hadn't said a word all night, which was almost true.

'No, I won't,' Stephanie said miserably, feeling sorry for herself. 'I'm not a couple anymore.' She had lost not only a man but the status and protection that went with it, and a way of relating to people as part of a larger whole. She was different than they were now, and no longer one of them.

'That doesn't change anything. We don't care. You don't have to be a couple to be part of the group. We love you. And you're not going to be alone forever. Sooner or later, there will be someone in your life. At your age, you're not going to be on your own for long. Not the way you look.' Stephanie smiled at the compliment, but she didn't want someone else in her life. Her options now were to be alone forever, or eventually start dating, which sounded horrifying to her. She hadn't dated in twenty-seven years, and she had no desire to start now. 'Just take it one day at a time.'

She talked to Dr. Zeller about it the following week, who acknowledged that it was going to feel very strange and unfamiliar being single now, and not part of a pair.

'All our friends are married,' Stephanie said with a look of despair. 'I feel like I'm a misfit with them now. A fifth wheel. I don't belong anywhere. I can't even hide behind my kids anymore, they're not here.'

'No question, Stephanie, this is very new for you. It's also an opportunity. You get to choose what you want to do now, and who you want to be. You can change things in your life that you didn't like before, or add new people to your life, eliminate people Bill liked and you didn't. You get to choose everything in your life, and everything you do. That's a rare opportunity, even if it comes at a high price. But there are real benefits to it too. It's something for you to think about. The only person you have to please now is you.' It sounded frightening to hear her say it, like too many doors and windows open. She no longer felt secure, about anything.

She was still thinking about it on the way home. And when she called her children that night, none of them answered. They were either busy or out.

What the therapist had said made her think of something Jean had said too, about how lucky she was to be on her own. She didn't feel lucky though, she felt scared, even terrified at times. Bill had been her buffer to the world. Now he was gone, and all the protection he offered, even theoretically, had gone with him. Jean said that if it happened to her, she wouldn't want another man. But it was easy for her to say, after thirty years of marriage to Fred, however imperfect he was – she had no idea what it was like to really be alone. It gave Stephanie a feeling of panic just thinking about it. It made her realize again that she needed something to occupy her time, either a charitable activity of some kind, or a job. She needed something to do. And she had no idea where or how to start. Suddenly all the things she had put off dealing with, after twenty-six years of marriage, even if it was sadly lacking in some ways, had to change. She couldn't coast along, blaming things on Bill anymore, or wondering why she had stayed married to him or why she didn't have a job. It was all up to her. And thinking about it made her angry at him all over again. Furious in fact. Just like the affair he had had, everything that was happening to her now was his fault. He had left and taken everything with him, her sense of security, her image of herself, and her status as a married woman, along with his protection. And this time she knew he was never coming back. She wasn't sure she would ever forgive him.

Chapter 4

The second time she had dinner with the two couples went better than the first. They had dinner in Marin, at a steakhouse they all liked, and she felt more relaxed. It wasn't as noisy, and she hadn't gotten all dressed up. She had started looking into charities where she could do volunteer work, and talked about it at dinner. Brad suggested she volunteer at a hospital, and Fred thought she should take finance classes to better understand how to handle the investments Bill had left her. But she wanted to do something with young people, which was what she knew best. She had narrowed it down to two foundations, and was planning to visit both in the coming weeks. One provided housing, education, and family reunification to homeless adolescents, and the other was a shelter for teenage girls with babies, and both sounded interesting to her. And in addition, at some point, she still wanted to find a job. But at least this was a start.

This time, when she said goodnight to her friends after dinner, she felt less depressed, although she still felt different from them now. None of them had any idea what it was like to face every day alone, with no one to talk to, spend time with, or even ask her how she was. The same things had bothered her in her marriage, but at least then they had the option to talk to each other if they wanted to. Now she didn't. Her friends took for granted the fact that they had each other to rely on. They had someone to keep them warm at night. And the silence in the house was deafening when she went home.

It was a long lonely haul from February to May, but in April the two couples and she had discussed the trip they took to Santa Barbara for Memorial Day every year. They stayed at the Biltmore, and she and Bill had always enjoyed it. Both Alyson and Jean were encouraging her to come, and she wasn't sure what it would be like going away with them now alone.

They finally convinced her to go. She had recently started working at the shelter for homeless adolescents, and found it challenging and interesting, and it gave her a sense that there was some purpose to her life. She had something to contribute to the kids at the shelter after twenty-five years as a mother. Some of them didn't know who their mothers were, and had been in foster care for years before they ran away and preferred to become homeless on the streets rather than face the agonies and terrors in bad foster homes, or even on their own. The life experience of the young people she was dealing with was a whole new world to her. She enjoyed working with them, and she was able to go away before the shelter tried to set up a regular schedule for her. For now, they were having her come in on a haphazard basis, so she was free to come in when it worked for her.

Right before Memorial Day weekend, Jean tried to convince her to fly to Santa Barbara with them on their plane, and Alyson offered to have her drive down with them. But Stephanie didn't want to go with either one, and decided that she'd rather drive herself. She thought the time to think in the car would do her good. And she had often done most of the driving when she went with Bill, if he was tired or wanted to read some work. Jean said she didn't like the idea of her driving alone, but Stephanie was definite about it, even though she knew it would take her six or seven hours. She played music on the way down, and stopped for lunch at a truck stop. She left early in the morning, and arrived in Santa Barbara by early afternoon. She felt a pang of loneliness as she checked into the hotel, but then felt happy when she saw her room, and was glad she had come. It was hard to believe that Bill had been gone for almost four months by then. It felt like a thousand years since she had been fending for herself.

She met up with Fred and Jean at the beach club across the street, and Brad and Alyson joined them there when they arrived. They sat by the pool and lay in the sun, and Stephanie swam before she went back to her room. Bill would have been anxious to get ready for dinner by then, and it felt like a luxury to swim for as long as she liked.

She met the others in the lobby for a drink before dinner. Jean was wearing a slinky white dress that showed off her figure. She had had liposuction recently on her hips, stomach, and thighs, and she looked fabulous. Alyson was wearing a silk blouse and matching skirt, and said it felt great to be out of sweats for a change. It was all she wore running around with kids all day. Stephanie was wearing white jeans and a hot pink shirt and high-heeled silver sandals. Her figure looked better than it ever had after nearly four months of grief and near starvation. If anything, she was still a little too thin, but she looked less strained than she had earlier.

They had a good time at dinner, and went for a walk afterward. Fred had had too much to drink and went to bed, and Brad escorted the three women and lingered talking to Stephanie, and reminded her that he was always there to help her, if there was anything he could do for her. She knew it was well meant, but it felt a little strange. He had been extremely nice to her ever since Bill's death, and he asked her about the shelter where she was working, and told her how much he admired her for doing it.

The girls went to the bar for a drink afterward, and

Brad went to their room to read. It was nice being just the three women for a little while, and Jean reminded Stephanie of how lucky she was not to have to go upstairs to a drunken husband who would snore so loud he would keep her awake all night. Alyson laughed and said that Brad snored too. But listening to them, Stephanie didn't feel as lucky as they said. There were good things that went with it too that she no longer had. She didn't miss their sex life, which had been uninspired and tedious for years, but she did miss just knowing that there was another human in the bed with her, and someone to wake up to in the morning, no matter how uninterested he was. Old habits were hard to break, and after twenty-six years of marriage, she missed Bill every day. She missed knowing he'd be coming home to her at night, no matter how disconnected they were. A dozen times a day, she thought of things she had to tell him, about insurance, the kids, or something he needed to take care of or do, only to realize again that everything rested on her now. There was no one else to take care of anything except her, and it weighed heavily on her.

'Maybe a snoring drunk in your bed isn't as bad as you think,' she said to Jean. 'At least he's there. What would you do without him?' Stephanie said wistfully, and Jean could see how lonely she still was and how much she missed Bill.

'I'd probably have a very pleasant life,' Jean said

confidently, convinced that Stephanie now had the better deal. It was easy to think when you had never experienced it. And Stephanie knew only too well how hard it was. The other two women had no idea. Jean envied her the freedom to do whatever she wanted, but it had been more difficult than they realized. She was still working her way through anger and grief, but she was feeling better.

They sat together for an hour, talking easily, and then went upstairs. Alyson knew Brad would be waiting up for her, and they'd make love that night and again the next morning before they got up. She thoroughly enjoyed their weekends away. And as much as she loved her children, it was nice having some romantic time together. Jean admitted readily that she and Fred hadn't had sex in almost five years, and said she didn't care. Listening to them, Stephanie felt a pang of loneliness again. It would have been nice to have the option to have sex with Bill. She wondered if she'd ever make love again, and recognized the possibility that she might not. Falling in love again didn't seem likely to her at forty-eight. It wasn't a sure thing at any rate. And it made her sad to think that she might never be kissed again.

She left the others outside her room, took off her clothes, put on her nightgown, washed her face and brushed her teeth, and ordered a movie she'd been wanting to see. She watched the movie until two a.m., ate chocolates from the mini-bar, and slept late the next day. It only occurred to her when she ordered room service for breakfast, that she could never have done any of those things with Bill. And he would have hated the movie she had seen. They were small compensations for her loneliness, but maybe they counted for something.

And when she saw him, Fred looked fiercely hungover and was in a bad mood when she met up with the others at the Coral Casino Beach Club, across from the hotel, at noon.

'He always thinks he has a brain tumor when he's hungover,' Jean said under her breath, as he dove into the pool. He had seen two pretty young women in bikinis swimming, and Jean knew exactly why he had decided to swim, and didn't care. She saw him chatting with one of them a few minutes later. He never changed, and never hesitated to pursue other women right in front of her. He had been doing it for years. It made Stephanie sad for Jean. She was a good woman and deserved better than that. And spending his money lavishly as revenge was small compensation for what she didn't have.

Alyson and Brad were in good spirits, and kissed lovingly as he put sunscreen on her back. Watching them made Stephanie nostalgic, thinking of the tenderness she and Bill had lost long ago. She saw Jean turn away from watching them too.

They had lunch sitting by the pool, and spent the afternoon relaxing and swimming, and they were all in good spirits when they went back to their rooms at the end of the day to change. They had dinner at a fancy restaurant that night, and Fred had too much to drink again, and flirted with a woman at the next table whose breasts were nearly falling out of her dress. He sent her a bottle of champagne, and no one commented, although it was embarrassing for them. He was fun to be with when he wasn't chasing women, or falling asleep at the table once he was drunk. It was easy to see why Jean got annoyed at him, and thought Stephanie was better off without a man. He went to bed before the others, and Alyson and Brad went to their room early that night, while Jean and Stephanie went to the bar and sat talking for hours. Neither of them wanted to go upstairs. And when they finally did, Stephanie ordered another movie, and this time popcorn to go with it, which she spilled in her bed, and then wound up laughing all by herself. Bill would have killed her for that. She gathered it up and ate it while she watched the movie, which was even better than the one the night before. She almost invited Jean to come and watch it with her, but she was afraid to wake Fred, if she called her, so she didn't.

On the whole, it was an easy, relaxing weekend, and she had a good time with them, even alone. She was in good spirits after talking to her children, when she headed back to San Francisco on Monday afternoon. She swam for a last time, said goodbye to the others, and drove onto the freeway, thinking about the weekend, only to realize half an hour later that she had taken the wrong on-ramp and was heading south, to L.A. and Palm Springs, instead of north to San Francisco. She took another turnoff, still distracted, and found herself facing a sign indicating the road to Las Vegas, and almost laughed out loud. Now that would be a very different experience than going home. She was trying to get back on the road heading north, and didn't make the turn in time. She had no sense of direction, hated maps, got confused by road signs, and didn't know how to work her GPS. And the next thing she knew, she was on the road to Las Vegas, trying to figure out how to get back in the right direction.

And as she tried, she realized how much she didn't want to go home. There was nothing waiting for her there, except loneliness and silence and an empty house. A crazy question popped into her head: What if she went to Las Vegas instead? Who would even know? She wasn't a gambler, but doing something that different might be fun. It was a little bit unnerving thinking that no one would have any idea where she was. But what could happen to her? Would it be so terrible to do something outrageous for a change?

She felt guilty even thinking about it, and then with a sudden surge of rebellion and independence, she intentionally ignored the turnoff heading north, which finally appeared. And instead of turning on to it, she kept going straight ahead with a big smile on her face. Even if she only stayed for a night, what harm could it do? Who would ever know? She pressed her foot down on the gas, feeling wild and liberated and free. The coin had finally flipped, and she was discovering the other side of being so alone. She really could do whatever she wanted now. There was no one to stop her, or even know. She lowered her side window, and let the wind fly through her hair. She was on her way to Vegas. She was alone, and lonely, but she was also free. It was a feeling she had never had before.

Chapter 5

The drive to Las Vegas took Stephanie just under five hours. She turned on the radio and was singing to herself. She had a strange sense of exhilaration and freedom just knowing that no one knew what she had done or where she was. A simple wrong turn on the freeway had turned into an adventure. In her life until now, she would have corrected her mistake, turned around, and gone home. But this time she had done something different. She had no idea what she was going to do in Las Vegas, maybe nothing, just walk around and watch the people, or play a few slot machines. Or maybe she'd go to a show. The possibilities were endless.

She'd only been there once, for a bachelorette weekend, years before. Bill hadn't been a gambler, and neither was she. But suddenly going to Las Vegas sounded like fun to her. She felt invulnerable and very brave, driving there on her own. She wondered what her two friends would say if she told them, but she didn't want to tell anyone right now. That was part of what made it special and unusual, just disappearing for a day or a few hours, doing something totally unexpected. She would drive back to San Francisco the next day, but for now, she was on her way to Las Vegas, on a crazy adventure that was completely atypical of her, which made it even more exciting.

She had stayed at the Bellagio the last time she went, and had read about the Wynn having been built since then, and being the best hotel there now. She was mildly tempted to stay at something more exotic, like the one that looked like an Egyptian pyramid, or the one that pretended to be in Paris, or another one in Venice, but she decided she'd feel more comfortable at a more traditional hotel. As she reached the outskirts of Las Vegas, it suddenly dawned on her that in her entire adult life she had never taken a trip alone. She'd been married to Bill since college, and ever since she'd gone everywhere with him, and more often than not with their kids. Bill had never been a very adventuresome or spontaneous person, he was a creature of habit, as she was to a great extent. He hadn't taken her away on romantic weekends, and preferred family vacations they planned far in advance, usually to places they liked and had been before, or their weekends with their friends, like their Presidents' Day annual ski trip, or the Memorial Day weekend in Santa Barbara she'd just been on. She smiled to herself thinking that if Bill had known what she was doing, going to Las Vegas by herself on a whim, just because she'd taken the wrong exit getting on the freeway, he would have been amazed. And so was she.

Driving into Las Vegas, she was dazzled by the lights and neon signs. It was after six o'clock by then, and there were swarms of people on the street, going in and out of casinos, as the hotels towered over them. Even on a Monday evening, there was an instant party atmosphere that reminded her of New Year's Eve. The drive through the desert to get there had been peaceful, but now everything had come alive, with thousands of people visible everywhere. And they weren't just gamblers, they were families with kids as well. Traffic on Las Vegas Boulevard was heavy, as she glanced around her with a broad grin. This was clearly the strangest thing she had ever done, but she was in a festive mood as she drove up to the Wynn, with its gold-domed awnings. It was a surprisingly beautiful curved complex of two hotels with two towers in bronze glass, with gardens, waterfalls, pools, and an eighteen-hole golf course behind, and an artificial mountain at the entrance to the hotel. It had separate entrances for the hotel and the casino, which was unusual in Las Vegas. And it towered forty-five stories above her, as she told the doorman she was checking in. He gave her a ticket stub for her car, and she said she'd come back for her luggage if she got a room. She began to wonder if they'd have one, when she saw the lobby, filled with light and flowers, with parasols suspended from the ceiling dancing to music. There was a multitude of shops, with everything from Rolex and Cartier to Vuitton and Dior. There were a thousand distractions to entice her as she walked up to the front desk, stood on line for a few minutes, and then asked if they had an available room. It was the end of the holiday weekend, and she hoped that people had checked out. The clerk looked at his computer for a minute, and returned to her with a welcoming smile. She had asked for a standard room.

'Have you stayed with us before?'

'No, I haven't.' She almost wanted to tell him that this kind of aberration was a first for her.

'Then we'd like to give you one of our Wynn Tower suites, at a reduced rate, of course.' They did everything to make people feel special and want to come again – and possibly stay for even longer than planned if they had a good time and were lucky in the casinos. 'How long will you be staying with us?'

'Just one night.' She couldn't think of an excuse or a reason to stay for more than a night, and she was sure that would be long enough. The exciting thing was that she had been bold enough to do it at all. The victory was there.

The desk clerk inquired about her luggage as he handed her the key card to the private gated entrance to the tower and her room, and she said her bag was still in her car. He told her that the key card would serve as her casino card too, and they would send her luggage up to her immediately, after a bellman showed her to her room.

She was escorted to the private gateway of the tower suites, and to a suite on the fortieth floor. As Stephanie stepped inside the suite, she looked around in amazement. It was elegant and luxurious, with an enormous living room in soft beiges, with couches, a desk, a dining area, and a huge flat-screen TV, a large bedroom that she could see from the living room, and a spectacular view from floor-to-ceiling windows that looked down at the city, and out toward the desert and mountains beyond it. It was breathtaking as she looked around. Her room at the Biltmore in Santa Barbara had been lovely, but nothing like this. Another bellman brought her bag up a moment later, as Stephanie walked around and checked out the suite. The marble bathroom was bigger than her bedroom at home, with a glass shower and enormous bathtub, and every imaginable cream, perfume, and amenity on the marble sink. She wanted to clap her hands and grin, this was going to be fun, and just for a fraction of an instant, she wished she had someone to share it with, even her kids, who would have been stunned that she was there.

She decided not to change her clothes. She didn't want to waste time. No one she had seen on the street, or even in the lobby of the elegant hotel, was dressed in anything fancy, other than the few women already dressed for the evening in one of the better restaurants or on their way to a show or the casino. The others wore halter tops and shorts, or T-shirts and jeans. She was fine the way she was, in sandals, a white T-shirt, and jeans, which she had worn for the drive home. She picked up her bag and headed for the lobby and took another look around, and then headed for the Esplanade of Shoppes. There were jewelry shops like Graff's for the high rollers, and gamblers who had done well. There was a Chanel that Jean would have loved, and Brioni, Oscar de la Renta, all of them with fairly flashy clothes in their windows, and expensive wares to tempt people wandering by with money to burn.

She used her key card to wander into the casino, after seeing the high-limit gaming area just off the tower lobby, and then found herself among the slot machines all around her, in the main part of the casino, with blackjack, poker, and craps being played. There were eighteen hundred slot machines. People were gathered around the gaming tables, and she decided to wait until later to try her luck. She walked out of the casino, and on the doorman's recommendation, she took a cab to Fremont Street to see what was happening there, and was instantly startled to see all the neon signs suddenly go dark as a huge canopy lit up overhead with a giant film display on a screen that was one thousand five hundred feet long and ninety feet high. Everything she saw was dazzling and impressive, and it was exciting being on the street among all the people. Everyone appeared to be in high spirits, and she looked into shops and wandered through two malls before she went back to her hotel at eight o'clock. There were several fancy restaurants, and she was hungry, but she didn't want to eat alone at a proper restaurant, so she went to a more informal restaurant in the lobby, and ordered a sandwich, as she looked around.

There were families in the restaurant too, and successful-looking older men wearing heavy gold watches, accompanied by flashy young women, some of whom seemed as if they'd been hired for the night, and were no older than her girls. There were groups of women who appeared to be having a great time, and men who were laughing and talking and eyeing the women who walked by. She saw one table of them check her out, and one of them smiled at her. For the first time in decades, she felt suddenly unprotected, and she realized she could no longer hide behind the shield of her married status or her husband there with her. She was a single woman now, and it felt strange. But no one was out of line, or tried to accost her. It was a city built for fun, with the lure of sex and easy money to entice anyone who came there. It was a playground for adults, with celebrity shows and famous musical acts to entertain those who didn't want to gamble, or just needed a break. There was something for everyone, even kids, with small playgrounds with fun rides, and babysitting services for parents who wanted to park them for a while so they could go to the casinos and try their luck at the slot machines or tables.

Stephanie went back to the casino when she finished her sandwich, and stood watching the blackjack table for a while. People looked intent, as they placed their chips on the table, and a serious older woman had stacks of chips next to her and was doing well. Stephanie could hear Spanish, Italian, and French. There were two German men standing right behind her, and a cluster of Arab men were speaking Arabic. She went from blackjack to roulette, which seemed less interesting to her. The dealers bantered with the clients, and people came and went from the table, as some left to try their luck somewhere else. She watched the craps table for a while, which was harder to under-stand as people rolled the dice, and there were poker tables. She bought fifty dollars worth of chips and sat down at a slot machine just for fun. On the second turn, she won four hundred dollars as lights and bells went off, and she gave a little scream, as three older women grinned at her.

'I've been working that machine all night,' one of the women said in a heavy southern drawl. 'That's my money you just won.' But she was good-natured about it. She said they came here every Monday. They were playing two machines each with a practiced hand. They looked like someone's grandmothers. Stephanie stuck with the machine for a while, and then moved on to another one and lost half of what she'd won, but she was still ahead on her initial investment, and then she went back to watch one of the blackjack tables again. It seemed like the most interesting game to her, although she didn't have the guts to play. She stopped here and there to watch the people and the games, fascinated by the intent expressions of the gamblers.

She didn't have an uncomfortable moment all night, and people chatted amiably as they stood and watched, and several of the players laughed and talked too, particularly if they were winning, and the dealers made occasional jokes. Stephanie noticed that the dealers changed frequently. There were no windows to the outside, which made it easy to lose track of time, with no way of knowing if it was day or night. The gambling and party atmosphere went on around the clock. And she was startled to realize that it was midnight when she glanced at her watch. She had ordered several Cokes, and there were frequent offers of free drinks. She noticed too that the winners at the tables gave the dealers hefty tips when they won. And there was an English player who was making thousand-dollar bets, with stacks of chips in every color in front of him. The dealers seemed to know him well. She'd been told that there were additional private rooms for the heavy gamblers, and she saw the roped-off area, where only the heavy-hitting gamblers went. Someone told her that they sent private planes to pick them up from wherever they were, and they were comped by the hotel. This was serious business to some, and although in many ways it appeared to be Sodom and Gomorrah, it had a playful atmosphere that appealed to her. Her detour on the road home had turned out well.

She had thought about going to one of the shows, but was having too good a time in the casino to leave. She played a few hands of blackjack after midnight, lost a hundred dollars very quickly, and decided to call it a night and go upstairs. She'd had a fabulous time, and she had already decided to go home the next day. She had done what she came here to do, prove to herself that she could do something different, check out the unexpected, and seize an opportunity. But she had no reason to stay. She was going to do a little shopping before she left, because the stores were so good, and then she would drive home. She was in no rush to go back.

She got in the elevator, using her room key for the fortieth floor, when five men walked in. They had had a lot to drink, and were all handsome, about her age, and they looked her over unashamedly. She wasn't dressed to entice anyone, and realized she probably looked like their wives at home, with no makeup, in a T-shirt and jeans. She had noticed some sexy young women in the casino, with tight short dresses, lots of cleavage, heavy makeup, and stiletto heels. Just watching them made her smile. She couldn't even imagine dressing like that. Stephanie had natural, wholesome good looks, and she appeared and felt like a wife and mom, not a babe, even though she didn't look her age. The lack of makeup and elaborate clothes made her seem younger too, as did her youthful appearance. One of the men was smiling at her as they all got out on the fortieth floor.

'How about a drink?' he offered, and for a moment she was surprised, and almost wanted to turn around to see if he was talking to someone else. No one had offered her a drink in years. She had never been in a circumstance where that could happen, and she had always been with Bill.

'Uh . . . I . . . uh . . . no, thanks. My husband is waiting for me,' she said pleasantly, trying to sound calm, and hoping she didn't blush. It was startling to realize that he was hitting on her.

'Lucky guy,' the man quipped back with a smile. 'Why not let him wait? Just one drink. You can tell him you were playing the slot machines. If he's dumb enough to let you walk around alone, that's what he gets.' He looked as though he meant it, and for an instant Stephanie felt a ripple of fear run down her spine. She suddenly felt unprotected. This was what Bill had left her to when he died, strange men in elevators who were accosting her, and wanted to see how far they'd get in exchange for a drink. It brought the message home to her loud and clear that she was on her own and had no one to protect her now. No one cared whether she was a married woman, or had a husband in her room. She was fair game.

'I don't think he'd like that,' she said with a polite smile, and headed toward her room with a quick step. The man didn't follow her, but he called down the hall.

'Come on, beautiful . . . just one drink . . . there's no harm in that.' She glanced over her shoulder again with a smile and shook her head, opened the door to her suite, and disappeared inside, as her heart pounded in her chest. She had done it. She had done something brave and unusual for her, but she didn't belong here, and it was time to go home. She was relieved to be in her room alone. She sat down on the couch and looked at the view of Las Vegas, with its flashing neon signs and garish lights far below. It looked as lively and busy at one in the morning as it had at six o'clock. And she thought of the man who had just offered her a drink. There was a world of men like that out there, that she had no interest in and nothing in common with, even if they were nice guys. She didn't want a nice guy, she wanted Bill, even if their marriage hadn't been perfect. He was familiar, and she always felt safe with him at her side. Now she felt vulnerable and scared. For the first time since he died, she wasn't angry at him, just sad.

She sat there for a long time, and then undressed to go

to bed. She noticed on her cell phone that Louise had called. She hadn't heard the phone ring while she was in the casino, and it was too late to call her now. It was four in the morning in New York. Jean had called too, probably to make sure she had gotten home okay. She would call her back in the morning, and wondered what to say to her, that she had spent the night in Las Vegas? Jean would think she had lost her mind, and maybe she had, but in a good way. And even the final incident of the offered drink was harmless enough. Stephanie had proven she could take care of herself, even in an unfamiliar place. She was tired as she got into bed, but it had been a good day, and had been an adventure she hadn't expected. She tried not to think of Bill as she turned off the lights after she brushed her teeth and washed her face. And that night she dreamed of the man in the elevator who had offered her the drink, and wondered what would have happened if she had said yes.

The sun was streaming into the suite when she woke up at nine o'clock, looked around the unfamiliar bedroom, and remembered where she was. She smiled to herself as she thought about what she'd done. Coming to Las Vegas had been a crazy thing to do, but she was glad she had. She hopped out of bed and looked at the incredible view again. Beyond the strip and the bright lights that were lit and flashing even in the daytime, she could see the desert. Las

Vegas looked like a mirage, which made her think of something she had wanted to do for years, and never had. She and Bill had always talked about going to the Grand Canyon one day, with the kids, but never got around to it, and she knew it wasn't far away. She wondered if that was part of the odyssey for her now, doing all the things they had promised they would do and never had.

She showered and dressed, and went downstairs to have breakfast at Tableau, the private breakfast restaurant in the tower. She was still thinking about going to the Grand Canyon, which she thought was a few hours away. She was packed and ready to leave at ten, and checked out of the hotel. The desk clerk asked her if she'd been satisfied with her stay, and the suite, and she said she'd been thrilled, which was true. She put her bag in the car, and drove to one of the shopping malls, and by eleven she had done everything she wanted to do. She had bought a pair of shoes at Gucci, sexy black sandals with stiletto heels, a sweater, and a pair of ridiculously expensive but great-looking jeans. She put her trophies of her freedom trip in the car, and thought about heading home. She had no reason to stay, and nothing to do here, but she didn't want to go back to San Francisco either. She had even less to do there, except her volunteer work at the facility for home-less kids, but they didn't need her that week, so she was in no rush to leave. Her life was a long empty road stretching ahead of her, and aside from occasional phone calls with her kids, no one needed or wanted her. She couldn't bear the thought of going home to the empty house, and thought about the Grand Canyon again.

She stopped at a gas station on the way out of town and inquired how far it was, and the woman at the cashier desk told her it was about four hours away and added that it was worth the trip.

'My husband and I go every year,' she volunteered. 'It's the most beautiful place on earth. One of God's wonders.' She pointed to a map on the counter as Stephanie looked at it wistfully, sad again suddenly at what the woman had said.

'My husband and I always wanted to go too.' And then she added, 'He's not here.'

'Go anyway,' the woman said. 'You can always come back again with him,' she added cheerfully as Stephanie shook her head.

'No, I can't. He died in February.' She hated herself for saying it, but she always seemed to need to tell people now, as though they should know she was a widow, and feel sorry for her. The woman looked at her pointedly then and handed her the map.

'Then you need to go. It's a magical place, and it will be good for your soul. It's on me,' she said, indicating the map. 'You'll be glad you did. I'm sure he'd want you to go.' Stephanie nodded with a lump in her throat the size of a fist, embarrassed by what she'd said. She was tired of telling strangers her story. Too much information, but she was still so raw, even after a night like the one in Vegas. In the clear light of day, Bill was still dead, and she would be a widow forever. She wasn't used to it yet and didn't want to be. She looked at the woman for a long moment, holding the map in her hand.

'Thank you,' she said softly, and walked into the sunlight, and back to her car. She opened the map on the front seat, wondering if she should go. Maybe the woman was right and Bill would want her to. If he had, they would have gone together. But he wasn't here anymore. Her life was her own. And she had come as far as Las Vegas, on a whim, so why not go to the Grand Canyon too? She didn't know why, but she knew she had to go. She followed the first sign to the turnoff that would lead her there. She had no idea what she was doing or why, but just as she had gone to Vegas after taking the wrong turn, now she was heading to Arizona to see one of the wonders of the world. It was another adventure, another day, and she felt like a different person suddenly. She had no idea who she was, but this new person she was becoming surprised her every day.

'Okay,' she said to herself out loud, feeling as though she were being led by forces she had no control over, but was willing to give in to, to see where they led her. She turned on the radio in her car, and started singing, wondering if she was going a little nuts, or if she was sane.

But what was sane anymore? It made no sense that Bill had died, especially at his age. And it made no sense that she was suddenly alone and that no one knew or cared where she was, and that she had spent a night in Vegas and was heading to the Grand Canyon now. She could only assume that she was a little off-kilter at the moment, but maybe it wasn't so bad. And by the next day she'd be home, and no one would ever know what she had done, or why. She didn't know herself why she was going there, as she drove through the desert singing out loud to a Norah Jones song. And as she thought about the past two days, all she could do was laugh. 'Stephanie Adams, you are certifiably insane,' she said to herself in a clear strong voice. But the funny thing was she didn't feel insane at all. It was the most normal and rational she had ever felt. And it didn't matter what Bill thought of it, or if he liked it or not. He was gone. And she was here. She felt excited by what she was doing, and alive!

Chapter 6

Stephanie left Las Vegas on Highway 93 and drove south to Interstate 40, and finally she took the last turn just before three o'clock, after crossing the state line into Arizona. She pulled up in front of the visitors' center at the south rim, where throngs of people were coming and going in hiking boots, with backpacks on, laughing and talking and excited to be there. It was one of the most important natural wonder destinations in the country and the world, and Stephanie felt exhilarated as she arrived. She parked her car in the lot and walked back to the center, to inquire about hikes she could take that late in the day. She wasn't up to an all-day hike in the hot sun, down to the canyon floor and back up again anyway. She just wanted to be there and soak up the magical atmosphere of a place she had wanted to see for most of her life. She had an innate sense that something she was about to see and feel there would make an important difference to her, and help her find peace, which she had needed desperately, and she was ready for it now. She changed into a pair of running shoes she had brought with her, and she was wearing a T-shirt and shorts, which she had changed into before she left Las Vegas, figuring she'd be too hot in jeans. And she took a water bottle with her, feeling as though she were on an important mission of some kind. She knew to the very depths of her soul that she was meant to be there. And she lined up at an information desk to ask about the shorter hikes. She could come back the next day for an all-day hike, but she wasn't sure she wanted to do that, and she was thinking about driving back to San Francisco that night. She liked driving at night. She could stop at a motel on the way if she got too tired.

The ranger at the information desk handed her some pamphlets in answer to her question, and her inquiry didn't seem unusual to him. Many people with younger children, or older members of the group weren't up to the rigorous hikes to the canyon floor, and only wanted to walk for a few hours. He suggested Bright Angel Trail to her, which he said would work, allow her to appreciate the canyon's beauty from several stopping points, and have her back up at the top in slightly less than three hours, which sounded perfect to her. He said the paths were clearly marked, and reminded her to take several bottles of water, and to wear sunscreen and a hat. He said it was a walk for which you didn't need a guide, and he told her that while it was a healthy hike, it wasn't overly arduous, and looking at her, he could tell that it would be easy for her. She thanked him, and taking the pamphlets with her, with more general information about the canyon, she walked back outside, and got in her car to drive three miles to the head of the trail, and parked. When she got to it, the trail was narrow, and wider in spots, with benches to rest. At one of the railings, she stood gazing at the breathtaking beauty of the canyon she had wanted to see all her life. She was in no hurry and began at a leisurely pace, and as he had said she would, she found it an easy hike.

She passed several small groups of people along the way, one of older people, another with children who were about ten or twelve years old. There was a group of young women who were talking and laughing and smiled at her as she went by, but for long stretches, she found herself alone on the path, enjoying the silence and the sounds of birds and insects, and the peace of nature all around her, always with the majesty of the Grand Canyon just within sight. It was the most beautiful spectacle she had ever seen. She stopped to sit on a bench once, to drink some water, and just enjoy the view. Then she continued walking, and the path got steeper as she went farther down. The ranger had told her at what point to turn back if she wanted to keep the hike to three hours. And when she reached the farthest point of the hike she was on, she wasn't winded and sat down on another bench to just revel in the view.

She was tempted to keep going, but she knew it would get even steeper after that, and would get her back to the top too late. Hikers who were returning to the top, and not booked for campsites at the bottom, were encouraged to be back before dark. If not, they were likely to run into problems and encounter risks that the rangers strongly urged them to avoid. And Stephanie planned to follow his advice. She was just sitting there, enjoying the view, with tears in her eyes, wishing she would never have to leave, and so grateful she had come. She was thinking about Bill, and wishing they had come here together, knowing he would have loved it too, although he was never as moved by nature as she was, but this was impossible to resist. The beauty of the Grand Canyon had touched her deeply. She was mesmerized by it, as she sensed some movement near her, and turned to see a man walking toward the bench, on his way up from the trail below. He was wearing jeans and a tank top, had long hair to his shoulders, and tattoos on both arms and his chest. There was nothing menacing about him, and he looked about her age, despite the long hair and tattoos. He smiled when he saw her, and she nodded, a little disappointed that another hiker had turned up to distract her and interrupt her reverie and silent communion with Bill. She felt so close to him here, as though he too were now free, and somewhere nearby in the beauty of nature and this amazing place. She was planning to leave in a few minutes, but wasn't ready to do so yet.

The hiker sat down on a rock near the bench she was sitting on, and turned to her.

'Gorgeous place, isn't it?' he said in a heavy southern drawl, trying to be pleasant. She didn't really want to talk, but she didn't want to be rude. There was something about nature that made one feel obliged to be congenial to everyone, but this time she wanted to be alone. She saw that he had powerful shoulders and looked athletic, and he was wearing hiking boots. She wondered if he had been hiking all day, although he was carrying no backpack with supplies. All he had was an old military surplus canteen slung over one tattooed arm. She noticed that he had an old pinup-style girl tattooed on one shoulder, with a name under it, and an eagle on the other side. 'I come here every year, to get my head back on straight,' he told her, and she smiled. It was why she was there too. She wondered if most people did, or just as tourists to see one of the wonders of the world. In fact, she had come for both. 'There's nothing like this place to feed the soul.'

'I know,' she finally answered him, her hair pulled back in a haphazard ponytail with an elastic she had found in her pocket when she started to get too warm. She looked very young with her blond hair and blue eyes. 'I've always wanted to see it. It's even more beautiful than I thought it would be. It takes your breath away,' she said in an awed voice. He hadn't moved any closer, and was sitting on a rock nearby, sipping from his canteen. His face was flushed. He had walked at a good pace.

'It still does that to me, after all these years. I came here for the first time when I was a kid, and it just gets to me more every year.' She nodded, easily able to imagine that could be true. One would never tire of this, no matter how many times you saw it. And even seeing it for the first time, she knew she wanted to return. 'Did you travel from far away?' he inquired casually, just being friendly to another hiker, not with any special interest in her. She felt nothing frightening or overly personal from him, he just seemed like a nice person.

'San Francisco. I was in Las Vegas last night, so I thought I'd stop here today on the way back.' As she said it, for a flash of an instant she remembered the stories one heard of female hikers being molested and murdered in other places, but he seemed so gentle that she felt guilty for her thoughts.

'That's when I get here too. I work in Vegas a couple of times a year.' He looked like he might be a transient worker of some kind. He wore no jewelry or watch, and the torn jeans and shirt he was wearing he could have gotten from Goodwill. And his hiking boots were ancient and battered and might have been secondhand too. She didn't ask him what kind of work he did in Vegas, just as he didn't ask her why she'd been there. The rules of the road on nature trails were to be friendly but not intrusive, and he respected the same boundaries she did. They were just fellow travelers on a common path. And she could easily imagine that the hiking trails here were well patrolled. This was not a wilderness trail, but a national monument and park.

They sat quietly for a few more minutes then, and she looked at her watch. It was the one Bill had given her on her last birthday, a small gold watch from Cartier that she loved and never took off. And it told her now that if she wanted to be at the top around six, it was time to leave and head back. She stood up, took another drink of water, nodded at the man sitting on the rock, and started up the path. As the ranger had predicted, she found it a little more challenging than she had on the way down, and five minutes later, the man who had been talking to her was on the path just behind her, moving at a faster pace than hers, with longer legs. He slowed as he came up next to her at a wider part of the trail.

'It's a little tougher on the way up. I've hiked to the bottom several times,' he informed her. 'It's like climbing Everest coming back up.' She laughed at what he said, and was feeling the steepness of the path now. He showed no signs of going past her, and walked alongside her at what was a leisurely pace for him. But in some ways it was nice to have company, even from a stranger on the path. He pointed out several things to her that she wouldn't have noticed otherwise, and they watched a condor soar overhead. And they saw no other hikers for a while. They walked side by side silently most of the time, and she felt strangely as though he were walking beside her to protect her, or to help her if she needed a hand, which she didn't. He was a comforting presence, and not an intrusive one. There was something very peaceful about him. And after a while of mutual silence, he asked her a question. 'What made you want to see the canyon now?' She could have answered anything, and she didn't want to seem pathetic as she had felt with the woman at the gas station in Las Vegas, but she decided to be honest, in the way one can be sometimes with strangers you know you'll never see again.

'My husband died four months ago. I just felt like I had to be here . . . to find peace.' She hadn't even realized that was why she had done it, but she knew it was true when she said it. He nodded as he listened.

'That's a good reason. I'm sorry about your husband.' And unlike most people, he sounded as though he meant it. 'Was he sick for a long time?'

She shook her head as the path got steeper. 'No. He had a heart attack on the ski slopes. It was very sudden. I'm still trying to deal with it and decide what to do next.' She felt strangely honest with him, like confession.

'This is a good place to think about things. I always do that here too. I work in a crazy business, and sometimes I feel like there's noise in my head all the time. I come here to get quiet.' And after he said it, they both noticed the silence around them, and the sounds of nature that they both loved.

'Where are you from?' she asked, finally curious about him too, although she didn't ask about the business. It could have been anything. She wondered what he did but didn't want to pry.

He laughed at her question. 'Originally Arkansas, from a town of about seventy-five people. I live in Tennessee now. Nashville. It's a great place, but gets pretty nuts at times. I left Arkansas at fourteen and never looked back. Nashville is home now. I've lived there most of my life.' She listened to his drawl and smiled. He sounded like the country boy he was. It was a far cry from her mundane, dull life in San Francisco. 'What did you do in Vegas last night?' he asked with interest, curious about her. He didn't meet women like Stephanie very often, and had noticed the expensive watch, although everything else she had on was very plain. She looked wholesome and serious, and he guessed that she had probably been married for a long time. She was still wearing her simple gold wedding band, although he knew now that she was a widow. And he assumed she had kids but didn't ask.

'I walked around,' Stephanie said with a smile. 'I went

to the casino and won four hundred dollars on the slot machines. I played a couple of hands of blackjack, but I'm not a gambler. I really enjoyed being there, and I went shopping today.' And then she decided to tell him the rest. 'I actually took the wrong turn on the freeway, and headed toward Vegas by mistake. I'm glad I did.' She said it with eyes full of mischief, and he laughed.

'That's a hell of a wrong turn to take. Where did you start out?'

'Santa Barbara for the weekend with friends.' He laughed again. She was far off her normal path. She didn't tell him that no one knew she was there, which would have made her feel too unprotected, but to a limited degree, as best one could with a stranger, she felt safe walking next to him, and telling him the truth. 'I'm going back to San Francisco tonight.'

'Did you go to any of the shows last night? Some of them are pretty good. I love the magic acts myself. I can never figure out how they do it. David Copperfield is the best. The guy is a genius. He lifts people right off the stage, and damn if I can ever guess how he does it.'

'I saw him once in L.A. He was amazing,' she agreed. 'My son kept trying to lift his sister up for about six months afterward. He never did it.' She grinned as she said it, and so did he.

'What kind of music do you like?' he asked conversationally. They were almost back at the top by then.

'A little of everything. Ballads. Norah Jones. Alicia Keys, stuff I can sing along to.' She smiled.

'Country?'

'Sometimes. Rap when I have to, but my kids have grown past that.'

'You like to sing?' He had picked up on what she said, and she smiled and looked embarrassed.

'I used to sing with a choir, but I got too busy and gave it up. I guess I could go back to it now, but it's been a long time.'

'Singing is good for everything, the heart, the soul, the mind, like coming here. As long as you don't take it too seriously. Some people turn it into a nightmare. It's better if you just enjoy it. Music should always make you feel good, and come from the heart. If it comes from the head, or the wallet, you wreck it,' he said with a grin, and she laughed. He was full of country wisdom, but some of what he said made sense. He seemed like a smart guy. And she noticed that he had paid attention to what she said, even about singing.

They walked along silently again for a while then, and a few minutes later, they were back at the top, where the view was spectacular. The climb back had gone more quickly talking to him, and they walked toward the parking lot together. There was a big black bus with shiny sides parked nearby, and he glanced toward it, and then back at her.

'Wait here a second,' he said, and ran toward the bus in long, loping strides, and she was startled to see the door of the bus open. She watched him disappear inside. She had no idea what he was doing there, and he looked out of place next to the mysterious but obviously fancy bus. It was the kind rock stars rode in, and she wondered if he worked for them. He was back in a few minutes, and handed her something. 'I'm playing in Vegas tonight, for the next few days actually. These are comp tickets for my show, if you want to go back. You might enjoy it.' And then with a shy glance, he introduced himself. 'My name is Chase. Let me know if you come to the show.' He had handed her two tickets, and she looked surprised. 'I'd like it if you'd come. We put on a pretty decent show,' he said modestly. She wondered if he was in one of the opening acts for a more important band. But the bus that was standing by was pretty impressive. She didn't look at the tickets, but thanked him for them.

'I don't think I'll go back tonight, but thank you.' She was as shy as he was.

'You got something important to do in San Francisco?' he inquired, and she shook her head. She had nothing to do at all. 'Then maybe another night won't hurt. You came this far on your detour. Things happen for a reason, like your coming here. That wrong turn you took in Santa Barbara was no mistake. Wrong turns never are. What's your name, by the way?'

'Stephanie,' she said with a smile. It had been an odd meeting, and she was glad she'd met him, although it seemed pointless to go back to Vegas for another night. But no more so than going home to an empty house.

'We go on at eleven. At the Wynn, if you change your mind. Don't lose the tickets. It's sold out.'

'Okay.' They exchanged a last friendly smile. 'Thanks for walking back up with me.'

'Anytime,' he said, waved, and then headed back to the bus, and she watched the door open again. He waved one last time, and disappeared when the door closed and they pulled away. She stood watching for a minute and then walked back to the parking lot with the tickets in her hand. She didn't look at them, and tossed them on the passenger seat next to her, as she started the car, and then glanced over at them again and her eyes grew wide. She felt like an idiot when she read the name. She hadn't recognized him, even when he said his name was Chase. The tickets said Chase Taylor, he was one of the biggest stars in country music, she had heard his songs a thousand times, and everyone in the world knew his name. She hadn't recognized his face, particularly meeting him out of context. No wonder his show was sold out. She laughed out loud as she drove out of the parking lot, and headed back to the main road. She had a long drive ahead, back to San Francisco, or she could drive three and a half or four hours back to Las Vegas and see his show. She drove through the crossroads. It was a little crazy to drive back to Las Vegas to see a country music star she had met on a hiking trail, but maybe he was right and it was all part of the detour. She really didn't want to go home, and maybe it would be fun. Feeling like a drifter, she took the turnoff to Las Vegas. The last two days had been the craziest thing she had ever done. But why stop now?

Chapter 7

Stephanie got back to Las Vegas just after ten o'clock, and checked back into the Wynn. They didn't offer her an upgrade to a suite this time, but they gave her a very handsome room, with the same panoramic view. She felt different after her trip to the Grand Canyon that day, it was almost like a religious experience. It really was a magical place, and meeting Chase had been a bonus. She felt a little strange coming back to Vegas to see his show, like an overage groupie, but she was aware that she was willing to do almost anything to avoid going home to her empty house. And it made no difference to anyone now if she was there or not. Another day on her wandering path wouldn't change anything, as long as she had come this far. She'd had several texts from Jean, and answered them, but still didn't say where she was. They were having lunch on Friday when Jean came into the city for her Botox shots, and she had no way of knowing that Stephanie hadn't come home. It would never have occurred to her. She called when Stephanie was getting dressed. She had taken a silk top out of her bag, and was planning on wearing it with jeans. She answered her cell phone when it rang and saw that it was Jean.

'Hi, Steph, did you get home okay? I'm sorry I haven't called. We're tearing out the barbecue on the patio and putting in a bigger one and everything's a mess, and one of my horses got sick, and I spent all of yesterday in the stables with the vet. So how are you?'

'I'm fine.' She felt guilty about where she was as she said it. How could she possibly explain to Jean that she was in Las Vegas to see a country music show, and had been at the Grand Canyon? It sounded incredible even to her.

'I talked to Alyson. Two of the kids came down with chicken pox, which means the baby will get them next. So she's been crazed too. So what have you been up to?' Stephanie tried to think of a creative lie to tell her, or just say she was fine, but it suddenly seemed like too much work.

'I'm in Las Vegas,' she said simply.

'You're what?' Jean said, sounding distracted. It was obvious to her that she'd heard wrong.

'I'm in Las Vegas. I took the wrong turn off the freeway. I just didn't want to go home, so I came here.' It sounded lame even to her, and impossible to explain. None of them knew what her life was like now, and how hard it was to have no direction in her life, nowhere to be, and nothing to do. No kids, no husband, no job. Even her volunteer work didn't need her right now. No one did. Her friends' lives were so well ordered, and she had suddenly lost all the structure in hers.

'You're gambling?' Jean was shocked.

'Not really, except for the slot machines for a few minutes and two blackjack hands. I went shopping, and I went to the Grand Canyon today. I've always wanted to see it. It was gorgeous.' Jean felt suddenly sorry for her as she listened, and realized again what her life was like now without Bill.

'Did you plan that? Why didn't you tell us?'

'No. It was a spur-of-the-moment decision.' It was one of the few perks of her new life as a widow with grown children. Spontaneity was a new feature she could never indulge before.

Jean realized that Bill hadn't been great to her, but he was rock solid and an anchor, and he grounded her. Now she was like a rudderless ship, drifting loose from her moorings. The last place Jean would have expected her to go was Las Vegas, although the Grand Canyon made some kind of sense since she knew that Stephanie loved nature. But she sounded lost, and it made Jean sad for her, and she wanted to help.

'Poor baby. Are you okay? Do you want me to send the

plane for you? We can get someone to drive your car home. I can send one of my stable hands down with the plane.'

'No, I'm having a good time. I'm going to a country music show tonight.' She sounded more cheerful as she said it.

'Jesus. Now I am worried about you. Why in God's name would you do that?'

'I met Chase Taylor on a hiking trail at the Grand Canyon today. He gave me two tickets to his show.' There was a long pause while Jean thought about it, and then she laughed.

'If I remember correctly, he is a gorgeous hunk. Better than the Grand Canyon. Stephanie, now wait a minute. Are you having an affair with him?' Stephanie laughed in answer.

'Hell, no. We walked up the same hiking trail. I had no idea who he was. He's a nice guy, he gave me tickets to the show, and to be honest, I have nothing to go home to. I'll drive back tomorrow. This was just kind of a detour for a couple of days. I've never done anything like it before, and it's good for me to try new opportunities open to me now and be more spontaneous. I definitely think this qualifies.'

'Only if you sleep with Chase Taylor, and if you do, you have my blessing. The guy is amazing.'

'He's okay. He didn't ask me to, and he probably has a

Danielle Steel

dozen girlfriends. I think all those big-time stars do. I didn't recognize him while we were hiking, until he walked into his rock-star bus waiting for him at the top, and gave me the tickets to his show.'

'You're hopeless. Even I know who he is. Shit, he's one cute guy, and you're a free woman. Go for it. Why should the guys have all the fun?' She was thinking of Fred as she said it. She had had one affair with a golf pro ten years before, but other than that, she had never cheated on Fred. She didn't want the headaches that went with it. She preferred to dedicate herself to spending his money.

'I'm not going to sleep with him. The subject never came up.' She laughed. 'I'm sure he wouldn't want to, and neither would I. But it might be fun to see his show. I probably won't even see him tonight, except on stage. I'll use the tickets, come back to my room, and come home tomorrow.'

'Well, you certainly are leading an interesting life,' Jean said with a tone of approval that surprised Stephanie. She had thought that Jean would be horrified, but clearly she wasn't, far from it.

'Don't worry. I'll be back home tomorrow night, cleaning out closets and doing laundry, in my very exotic life.'

'Don't rush back,' Jean encouraged her.

'Don't say anything to Alyson. She'll think I'm nuts.'

'Probably. She's too busy dabbing chicken pox with

calamine lotion to talk to you anyway.' They both knew that this was much too far out for Alyson, who wouldn't understand. Jean was more open-minded, and had been encouraging Stephanie to go out with men now. Alyson would have been content to see Stephanie mourn Bill for years, which was what she said she would do if Brad died. Jean was older, wiser, and more realistic. And she thought an affair with a country music star was just what Stephanie needed. 'Well, call me tomorrow and tell me what happened tonight,' Jean said with a lascivious tone, and Stephanie rolled her eyes.

'Nothing is going to happen. I'm just going to a concert.'

'Then try harder,' Jean scolded her. 'I'm planning to live vicariously through you. Don't be so boring. If I want to be bored, I have my own life for that. Go have fun!'

'I'll call you tomorrow,' Stephanie promised, relieved that Jean wasn't appalled by what she was doing. It was nice to have her support. She finished dressing, put some makeup on, and slipped into the high heels she had brought with her. She was at the concert hall right on time, as an usher led her to a seat in the front row, and whispered to her that her ticket included backstage passes for after the show. She didn't think she'd take advantage of them, but Chase had given her the best seats in the house, and she felt guilty that she hadn't used the second ticket, and the seat next to her was empty.

Danielle Steel

She hadn't come to see the opening band, since he had told her to come at eleven, and a few minutes later the theater darkened, and his band started playing, and a moment later the man she had met on the hiking trail exploded onto the stage with one of his most famous songs. The audience loved him. He played everyone's favorite country music and after a while, sat down on a high stool and played some ballads, as Stephanie watched him, mesmerized. They cheered and screamed at the end of the show, and he played two more songs, and looked straight down at her with a broad smile before he left the stage. She hadn't been sure until then, but he had seen her. And as soon as the curtain came down, an usher came to her and told her that Mr. Taylor was expecting her backstage. She felt shy about going to see him, now that she knew who he was, but she felt that she ought to thank him for the tickets.

Feeling nervous about it, she followed the usher to a door at the side of the stage. He used a code to open it, and a moment later she was in a long dark hallway and walking up a flight of stairs, until she found herself standing at the back of the stage, with all the instruments and sound equipment and the roadies and technicians packing up for the night. The usher led her past them, into another hallway where all the dressing rooms were. He knocked on a door, and suddenly she was in his dressing room, surrounded by people. Chase was damp with sweat in the red plaid shirt he'd worn on stage, and was happy to see her.

'I'm so glad you came,' he said with a broad grin. 'I hope you liked it.' He seemed shy again as he said it.

'I loved it!' Stephanie said honestly, beaming at him. 'You were fantastic. I felt like a total idiot when I saw your name on the tickets after you drove away. I'm sorry I didn't recognize you today. I just wasn't expecting to meet a major music star on the hiking trail.'

'I like that better,' he said modestly, and then turned to introduce her to a beautiful, very young blond girl standing right behind him. Stephanie saw that she was one of his backup singers. She instantly assumed she was his girl-friend. She had a lush figure but a childlike appearance, and appeared about eighteen years old. 'This is my protégée, Sandy.' She smiled at Stephanie and looked even younger when she did. 'One day she's going to be a big star. We're grooming her for that.' He was proud as he said it, and Stephanie could guess that 'protégée' was another word for girlfriend, like 'niece.' He was about thirty years older than she was, but Stephanie wasn't surprised. It was the nature of his business and of men who were as successful as he was. At least he had an excuse for it, more than men like Fred, who just liked young girls because they were sexy. The girl gazed adoringly at Chase when he said it, and then she walked away.

There were at least a dozen other people in his dressing

room while he talked to Stephanie, and she recognized most of them as his band. There were the six musicians who accompanied him and two female backup singers, Sandy and another woman, Delilah, who was at least ten years older than she was, and both had great voices. The show really had been fabulous, and Stephanie was vastly impressed, particularly by Chase. And she liked his simple, natural style, which went straight to the heart. His lyrics were good, the music he composed was excellent, and his voice could rip your heart out. He had an enormous talent, and it was impressive seeing him live on stage. It had been very exciting and she was glad she'd stayed to see it, no matter how unusual for her.

'Will you come out to dinner with us?' he asked her a few minutes later. 'I warn you, this crowd can't stomach decent food. They all grew up on grits and corn pone. They won't eat anywhere but a diner, but there's a halfway decent one not far off the Strip. Come with us,' he said warmly, and she hesitated. She didn't want to impose on him, but the invitation was very appealing. They seemed like a good group and were all joking with one another and teasing Chase. They all thought the show had gone well and were pleased, and were friendly to Stephanie when Chase introduced her.

He turned to her with a quizzical expression. 'Do you have a nickname?'

'No.' She shook her head.

'Would Stevie work for you?' She laughed at the suggestion, and had to admit that in this group Stevie sounded more apt than Stephanie.

'I'll take it.' She smiled at him.

'Good. I'll take a quick shower and then we'll head for dinner.' And then he turned to Sandy, who was talking to one of the musicians. 'You coming, Squirt?' She nodded with a lopsided grin. 'What about Bobby Joe?'

'He's coming too. He's in the casino. I'll go and get him.' Chase rolled his eyes as she said it.

'The least he could do is watch our show. Just because he's in the opening act doesn't mean he can spend the night in the casino.' He gave Stephanie an exasperated look, and disappeared into his bathroom to shower. He emerged ten minutes later with wet hair, in a tank top like the one he'd been wearing earlier that day, with a blue plaid shirt over his shoulder, ripped jeans, and the battered black lizard cowboy boots he'd worn on stage. He looked every bit the rock star he was, now that she'd seen him on stage.

All the musicians came with them when they left, and hotel security was thick around them all the way to the bus, as everyone got on board. And Stephanie was surprised by the luxury she saw inside. It was in good taste, and was decorated almost like a yacht, with dark wood-paneled walls, and lush brown leather upholstery, thick carpeting, some nice paintings, and sleek modern furniture, some of it covered in alligator, that he had had made for the bus. There was a full kitchen, a bathroom, and a bedroom with a king-size bed where he could rest. He preferred the bus to any other mode of travel, for privacy and comfort. He could do whatever he wanted on it. There was even a piano.

Chase glanced around when they got on the bus, and asked where Sandy was. Delilah told him she had gone to the casino to find Bobby Joe. Delilah was the other singer, she was in her thirties, and she didn't spend much time with Sandy away from work. She was married and had kids.

'Christ, I feel like a kindergarten teacher half the time with those two,' Chase complained good-naturedly, and everyone laughed as he said it. Sandy and a lanky young boy covered in tattoos with bright red hair came running up to the bus minutes later.

'Sorry, he was winning,' Sandy said apologetically to Chase, as Bobby Joe let himself down on the couch next to Stephanie and stretched out his long legs. He had a cocky look about him, and one could sense that he both admired Chase and was jealous of him. He wanted to be him one day, and until then had to content himself with being an opening act. He was about twenty years old, and his accent was even heavier than Chase's and Sandy's. He told Stephanie he was from Mississippi, and had been opening for Chase for about a year, but had played with another band before that. They all talked about the show that night and some things they wanted to change in rehearsal the next day, and by the time they got to the diner, everyone was calling her Stevie, and acting as though they knew her. They were an easy, congenial group, and it was obvious that they all adored Chase, except for the somewhat arrogant Bobby Joe, whom Sandy circled like a shepherd dog. He was arrogant with her too, and then kissed her long and hard in front of Chase, which shocked Stephanie, thinking she was Chase's girlfriend.

'Okay, Bobby, enough, don't wear yourself out before dinner,' Chase said as they filed past him, on the way off the bus to eat, and the two young people brought up the rear. Stephanie was intrigued by Chase's casual reaction. He was a hell of a good sport, or very self-confident if she was his girlfriend. She couldn't help asking him about it, as they walked into the diner and Charlie the drummer asked for three booths. The people at the restaurant all knew Chase and were happy to see him back. They gave him three booths in the rear, where he was less likely to be bothered, although his fans always found him.

'That doesn't bother you?' Stephanie asked him as she slid into the booth next to him, after he patted the seat beside him to invite her to sit next to him since she was his guest.

'What?' He looked blank.

'Bobby Joe and Sandy.'

'Not unless he knocks her up and she can't work for the next year, and gets saddled with a baby. If he does that, I'll kill him. He's twenty-five years old and hopefully he knows better. She's just a baby, and she's crazy about him. But she's eighteen, and there's nothing I can do. And she's got to have some fun,' he said reasonably. 'Her daddy died three years ago, and left her to me when she was fifteen. I'm her guardian. Her mama died when she was two, so I'm all she's got. Thank God she can sing, or I wouldn't know what to do with her. But I can tell you, it's a hell of a responsibility raising someone else's kid. I figure that if I get her to twenty-one, she's on her own after that. Until then, she answers to me.' He looked serious as he said it, and Stephanie grinned broadly. 'I'm serious. It's not easy. Especially raising girls.'

'I know. I have two of my own. And a son,' Stephanie said just as seriously, and then smiled again. 'I thought she was your girlfriend, so I thought Bobby Joe was being pretty gutsy kissing her right in front of you.' Chase burst out laughing when she said it.

'Are you kidding? You think I'm a child molester? She may be eighteen on her driver's license, but she's fourteen in her head, or twelve sometimes, or two. I don't go out with women young enough to be my daughter, or grand-daughter in this case, by Tennessee standards. I'm forty-eight years old, and the last thing I need is an eighteen-year-old in my bed. That would kill me for sure.' He was still chuckling, and Stephanie looked amused too. 'She's a pretty girl, but that's just a bigger headache, especially at her age. I lived with a woman for fourteen years, and we broke up two years ago. As she put it, our careers weren't compatible. It's hard to keep two people together in this business.' Stephanie vaguely remembered that he had been involved with some equally famous country music singer, and they had recorded several albums together. She didn't remember the breakup. 'I married my high school sweetheart at seventeen, and we had a baby a year later. My son is thirty years old and smart enough not to go into this business. He runs a construction company in Memphis. His mama and I divorced when he was two years old. She got married again and had a bunch of kids. I never did. I got busy with my career and stayed that way. It suits me better than marriage, and I've kind of taken a break for the past two years since Tamra and I broke up. That got a little heavy. She actually sued me over some of our music together. I don't need the headache.'

'So how do you manage to stay so normal?' Stephanie asked him honestly after they ordered burgers and fries. The two musicians sharing the booth with them were arguing about a change in the arrangement of the second song of the show, and they were paying no attention to Stephanie and Chase.

'I don't know. I don't like it when people get all full of themselves. Besides, you might be a star one minute, and nothing the next. I figure keeping things simple is better. Tamra was always the big star – I just tagged along.' But the truth was, he was the bigger star, and always had been, and her career had tanked after she left him. Stephanie was impressed with his modesty and genuine, unassuming ways. After that they joined in the conversation with the two musicians, and Chase settled the argument about the arrangement. He liked it the way it was. 'Don't fix what ain't broke,' he reminded them, which was a saying she had often used too. The enemy of good is better.

The whole group spent an hour at the diner and then went back to the bus, and when they arrived at the hotel, Chase walked her across the lobby to the elevator. She didn't invite him to come up, and he didn't suggest a drink at the bar. She could see that he was tired. They had worked hard during their show.

'So what are you doing tomorrow?' he asked with a gentle smile. 'Driving back to San Francisco?' She nodded. She had had a great time that night, and she liked him. He seemed like a good man. She liked his values and his reactions, and his philosophies about life. Play fair, be honest, don't screw over the other guy, work hard. It all made sense.

'I should get back,' she said, although she wasn't sure why she said it.

'To what?' he asked her honestly. After talking to her, he knew that she had no kids at home, no job, no real reason to go home. 'Why don't you stay another day? We're only playing here for three days, and then we're going back to Nashville. Why don't we drive out in the desert tomorrow? It's beautiful. I'll show you the sights. I don't have to be at rehearsal until six.' He made the band work hard, which he said kept them all good, and him too. 'What about it?' His eyes pleaded with her, and she hesitated and then nodded. Why not? She was enjoying herself. She didn't feel like he was pursuing her as a woman, just as a friend, which was nice. There was no pressure on her.

'Okay. What the hell? I've come this far, I might as well stay another day.' She said it as much to herself as him.

'That's my girl, Stevie. You know what they say. Carpe diem. Seize the day. We only get one day at a time – we have to make the best of it. You never know what's going to happen tomorrow. Today is all we've got.' She had learned that lesson with what happened to Bill. And she knew the expression. It was Latin. Carpe diem. She just never thought it applied to her. It never had before. 'I'll call you around ten. We'll figure out something to do. I've got a car here – we don't have to take the bus.' It sounded good to her. And like fun. She was going to spend the day with Chase Taylor, just hanging out, just as she had done tonight. Who would have thought that the long-haired, tattooed guy she had met on the hiking trail at the Grand Canyon would turn out to be a country music star, and they'd make friends? He was right in what he said. Carpe diem. Seize the day.

Chapter 8

When Chase picked her up at ten-thirty the next morning, he had a plan. He waited for her in a Mercedes at a side door of the hotel where no one would see him, and he told her about the Moapa River Reservation of Paiute Indians he wanted to take her to, thirty miles away. 'It was a land grant of two million acres originally. Now it's down to a thousand,' he explained to her. 'There's not much there. They run a casino and a few stores, but there's a medicine man I met there, at the casino. He's a very spiritual person. I thought you might like to meet him,' Chase said as they drove north on Interstate 15. It was in the desert, and he said he had been there before. When they got there, they walked around. It was a bleak place, with imposing sand-stone cliffs. Chase knew where to find the medicine man at his small, dilapidated house just outside town. Chase introduced him to Stephanie, and the medicine man told her that she had far to go on a new path.

'Did you tell him that?' Stephanie asked Chase suspiciously, and he swore he hadn't. The medicine man told her then to open her eyes so she would see the path and to let go of her old ways and life. And he told Chase that he had to open his heart, that it had been closed for a long time, maybe since he was a boy. They talked for a while. Chase thanked him and slipped bills into his hand as they left.

'That's pretty scary,' Stephanie commented as they drove away. There was something very profound and spiritual about the man, and Chase said he had been impressed by him before. Chase liked to meet unusual people off the beaten path.

'Medicine men are very special people,' he confirmed.

'Was what he said about you true? That your heart has been closed.'

'Pretty much,' Chase confessed easily as he drove with his eyes on the road. 'Except to music. I don't think I've really loved anybody since the girl I married at seventeen. I loved Tamra, but it was complicated, and it was always more about our careers than the relationship. The relationship just came out of that. She's a hard woman, and she's all about herself. This business is like that, everyone is out for themselves, and they don't care who they screw over to get where they want. It destroys people's souls.' But she had a strong sense that his was intact.

'So why are you different?' she asked as they drove back toward Las Vegas.

'Maybe I don't care as much about where I'm going. I've been lucky. I love what I do, but not enough to kill someone over it or give up who I am. I'm not willing to make the sacrifices some people are. I'm willing to work my ass off, not sell my soul.' He had made the right choices and had remained whole. 'What about you? What are you going to do now?'

'I don't know. I've never had choices before. I was on a path I thought I was going to be on forever. I forgot the kids would grow up. I thought I was married forever. It never dawned on me that he might die, at least not until we were very old.'

'Were you happy with him?' Chase was curious about her.

'I used to be. At first. And then I think we kind of lost each other in the shuffle. I was busy with the kids, he was focused on his career. He worked too much. We were always tired by the time we got together. I think the excitement kind of went out of it for both of us. We were just used to each other and knew what we had to do.' She took a breath then. 'And then he had an affair. It kind of blew what was left to bits, and maybe there wasn't much left even before the affair.' She had never said that out loud before, not even to Bill. 'I never wanted to face that when he was alive, but maybe it was true. We split up for a couple of months when I found out about it. She was married too. She went back to her husband, he came back to me, and that was it, but it was never the same again. That was seven years ago. I never realized how empty our marriage was till then. The excitement and passion in our lives died a long time ago. Maybe that's why he had the affair – maybe he was just trying to feel alive again. Maybe we should have gotten divorced then, but I didn't want that for our kids. So we stayed together. I don't think we were ever happy with each other after that. There were okay days, but never great ones. There was no magic. Our relationship was like a job. I never realized that till he was gone.' She had been thinking about all of it since Bill's death.

'That's why I never got married again,' Chase said softly. 'I never wanted to settle for "good enough". I wanted "great" or nothing. I never fell in love again. I guess that's what the medicine man meant. But it's hard to find someone to fall in love with when you're in this business. So many big egos, and people who want to use you to get where they want. There's not a lot of heart, except in the music. Sometimes the people in it just suck.' She laughed at what he said and suspected it was true. And it was hard for someone like him, he was such a big star, and everyone wanted something from him, or to use him. She said it, and he agreed. 'You get used to it after a while. I don't take it personally. But I don't fall for them either. I know better now. I used to be naïve. I've gotten smarter with age. You have to in this business, and in life. Or you get screwed over every time.' It was an interesting perspective. 'But what's happening to you is like being born again. You can wipe the slate clean. You have a million opportunities to start a new life.' She nodded, thinking about it, and knew it was true.

'I don't know,' she said sadly. 'And what do I do? I want a job, but I don't know what I can do. I haven't worked in years, and I don't have a talent like you.'

'What are you good at? What do you like to do?'

'I don't know . . . being a wife and mother. Entertaining clients. Folding laundry. Making Halloween costumes. I like to sing, but I'm not talented. I used to like to write poetry and short stories, but what would I do with that? I'm doing volunteer work at a homeless shelter for kids right now. The people who run it are a little disorganized, so I never know when they'll need me, which makes it hard to plan. But I like it. The kids really need help. Unlike my own, who really don't need me anymore.'

'They probably need you more than you think. And if they don't, it means you did a good job.' He was practical and down to earth above all else.

'I need them more than they need me. And they're being difficult right now. Their father hardly paid any attention to them, but as soon as he died, they decided he was a saint.'

'They'll get over that. It's probably part of the grieving process for them.'

'Well, it's damn hard to listen to, I can tell you. I don't mind them thinking he was a nice guy, I always fostered that and made him look like a hero to them. But now everything I did, they attribute to him, and my girls act as though they're pissed that he's dead and I'm alive.' She was totally comfortable talking to him and admitting things she might not have to someone else.

'You're the safe one, and they're probably angry that he died.'

'I was kind of mad at him myself until now,' she admitted. 'I stuck it out. I paid my dues. I lived through the affair, I stayed with him, and then he goes and dies, and now I wind up alone for the rest of my life. Who's going to be there when I get old or if I get sick, or be there to walk our daughters down the aisle? He just bailed on all of it, and now I'm stuck there in an empty house. He wasn't there much, but I knew he'd come home at night. Now no one comes home. I'm there alone.' She didn't want to sound pathetic, but it was true.

'It seems like he wasn't really there even when he did come home,' Chase said sensibly. 'And you're not going to be alone for the rest of your life. Not with your looks.' He smiled at her. 'You're still a young woman. Hell, you're my age.' They both laughed. 'You're just alone for now. And there are a lot of things you can do – get a job, move to a different city, meet new people. The whole world is open to you. It's what the medicine man said, you have to open your eyes to new paths. It appears that you had exhausted the old ones anyway. With all due respect, it sounds like your life with your husband was over. Neither of you wanted to acknowledge it, but it was. You just need some time to figure it out.' She knew that what he said was right, although it scared her.

'Maybe I'll get a job as a dealer in Las Vegas,' she said with a rueful smile.

'Or a singer in a country band. How good's your voice?' He was teasing her and she laughed.

'Not good enough.' They changed the subject to Sandy then, and Stephanie commented on how great her voice was. She had a huge talent, like him. And he was a hard taskmaster, teaching her the ropes. He sounded a little guilty as he said it.

'The poor kid needs a mother more than she needs a voice coach. She's been dragging around backstage since she was in diapers. Once her mother died, her father took her everywhere with him – on tour, to rehearsal – and now I do the same. She grew up with a guitar and a microphone in her hands. But it's paying off. I think she'll make it big one day. It's kind of exciting to see. And she's a sweet girl. I try to toughen her up a little. She's always falling for some kid like Bobby Joe. He doesn't give a damn about her, she's just convenient for him on the road, and he sees her as a way of being connected to me. But if he's bad to her, I'll kick him out so fast, his head will spin. He's just a punk, and not as talented as he thinks. He won't last long in this business. She will. She's the real thing. He's just a flash in the pan, selling sex appeal and a second-rate voice. She's pure gold. She's a platinum record waiting to happen, and it will if I have anything to do with it.' He took his role in her life seriously, as her protector, teacher, and mentor, and Stephanie was impressed. It was how she felt about her kids. And Sandy wasn't even his. She had just been his ward since she was fifteen.

They stopped for a late lunch at a restaurant he knew in the desert, instead of somewhere in the city where he would be hounded. People came up to ask him for autographs even in the diner, and he was nice about it. But he wanted private time with her. He enjoyed their conversation, and everything she had to say. And she liked talking to him too. Their ideas were similar on many subjects, even though they had come to the same conclusions in different ways. And he had far more worldly experience than she did. Compared to him, she had lived a sheltered life. He had been in the often cutthroat front lines of the music world for many years, but he was neither bitter nor spoiled by it. He had remained true to himself. Meeting him and talking to him was a remarkable experience. And she admired how humble he was.

It was five o'clock by the time he took her back to the

hotel. And he had rehearsal in an hour. He said he was going to swim and work out before that. And she wanted to shop some more. She had spotted some other stores she wanted to explore. The temptations in Vegas were limitless, for both shoppers and gamblers, and she hadn't bought new clothes in a long time. Jean filled the void in her life by shopping constantly, Stephanie was wearing five-year-old clothes and never bought new ones. The stores in Las Vegas had caught her eye.

'Thank you for a fantastic day,' she said with a warm smile.

'I guess yesterday was my lucky day,' he said, smiling at her. 'I went to the Canyon to clear my head, and look who I met.'

'I think you have that reversed,' she said, touched by what he said.

'Do you want to come by rehearsal? We'll just go through some stuff for a couple of hours. If you'd like, you're welcome to hang around.' She said she might, and he left her in the lobby of the hotel. She went back to her room for a few minutes to wash her face and relax and then went back out again to look around. And an hour into their rehearsal, she dropped by to see them. She had given up her plan of leaving that night, and was driving back to San Francisco the next day. She had already called the shelter to let them know that she wouldn't be in, and they told her they didn't need her for another two weeks.

Their rehearsal was in full swing when she slipped in. Chase was doing one of his ballads, and she loved listening to him. Sandy came off the stage and sat down next to her and squeezed her hand, as Stephanie remembered all he'd said about her, and how much she needed a woman in her life. She looked like a little kid, in jeans and a T-shirt with a ponytail and no makeup.

'What did you do today?' Sandy whispered with wide eyes, as they sat together in the darkened room, listening to Chase.

'I just went shopping,' Stephanie said, looking guilty, and showed her a pair of flats she'd bought at Marc Jacobs, with mouse faces on them. Sandy giggled silently and said how cute they were. 'What size do you wear? I can get you a pair tomorrow.' Sandy looked surprised and said she wore an eight, the same as both of Stephanie's girls.

Sandy had to go on stage after that, and Stephanie stayed for a while. Chase came down during a break while they were adjusting the sound and gave her a hug. After two days, and their lengthy conversations, he felt like a friend. And then she left, and went to Marc Jacobs to get the shoes for Sandy and went back to her room. Chase called her when they were through.

'Are you coming tonight?' He sounded worried that she might not.

'Of course.' It was why she had stayed.

'Do you want to be backstage or have a seat?'

'Backstage might be more fun.' It was something new. Her life was new these days, or had been since she came to Vegas and met him.

'You can wait in my dressing room if you get bored,' he offered.

'There is nothing boring about your show, Chase. I'll be there the whole time.' She smiled as she said it. She was becoming an avid fan.

'Why don't you come half an hour early? You can sit in my dressing room with me before I go on. Come to think of it, come at ten. We can have dinner after, if you don't mind waiting that long.' It was the life he led, of endless nights and midnight dinners, rehearsals, and waiting around all day in hotel rooms. It was better than it used to be when he was young, and they went on ten-week road tours with him and the entire band in a van, driving from town to town, day after day, performing all night, to filthy, disgusting venues, and dressing rooms that hadn't been cleaned in years. Now he was a star, but he had earned it the hard way and paid his dues.

Jean called her that night again when she was getting dressed and wanted to know what was going on and when she was coming home, and had she slept with Chase Taylor yet.

'Stop that. We're just friends. He's a really decent guy. I'm just having fun, hanging out with the band.' She felt like a teenager as she said it, and Jean laughed. 'I'm driving back tomorrow. I'll see you on Friday for lunch.'

'I can't wait.' Jean felt like her partner in crime.

Stephanie still hadn't heard from her kids in several days, which was typical, and no one knew where she was except Jean. She wouldn't have told them anyway. They would have thought she'd lost her mind.

Stephanie showed up at Chase's dressing room that night at ten, carrying a shopping bag. He was stretched out on the couch with his long legs, reading the paper, and he stood up as soon as she walked in. He kissed her on the cheek and offered her a drink, but she was happy to just sit there and relax with him. It felt good to be a part of it, and she was surprisingly comfortable with him, like an old friend. Several members of the band came in to ask him about various technical details, and Sandy walked in and was happy to see her there.

'Hi, Stevie. What are you doing here?' She looked surprised and pleased.

'Hanging out,' she said, laughing at her words. As she said it, Stephanie handed her the bag. Sandy reached into it with a puzzled look, and found the mouse shoes in her size. She gave a squeal of delight and threw her arms around her benefactor's neck. She tried them on and they fit perfectly, as Chase watched the scene looking touched. After she left, Chase turned to Stephanie.

'That was sweet of you to do. I never do things like that for her, and I should. I just give her money and tell her to go shop. That's what I meant. She's starving for a woman in her life. Delilah takes her out shopping sometimes for clothes to wear on stage. Thanks, Stevie. I really appreciate it.'

'I enjoyed it, and it's a small thing to do.' She made little gestures like that every day for her kids when they were around, and sent them small gifts when she found something she knew they'd love. She was good at it, the motherly duties she enjoyed for so long, and missed so much now.

He chatted easily with her before the show, and then took her backstage with him before he went on. He found a chair for her, in the wings, and Sandy blew her a kiss as she flew by on her way to take her place on stage. The show was even better than it had been the night before. She couldn't see Chase except on a monitor, but she could hear him. She was starting to know some of his songs.

She told him how good it had been when he walked back to her after the show, and he smiled and put an arm around her shoulders.

'Come on, let's get out of here. I'm starving, let's go eat.' He let the band go to dinner on their own and took her to a small restaurant on the edge of town with Cajun food and chicken wings and ribs. They ate with their fingers, and it was delicious. He had a hearty appetite, and was always hungry after a show. They sat there eating and talking until almost three a.m., and then he drove her back to the hotel.

'Can I talk you into staying for our last night? We're leaving on Friday. You could go back to San Francisco then.'

'Now I really am a groupie,' she said, laughing, but she was easy to convince this time. She was enjoying herself too much to leave, and he was pleased. He walked across the lobby with her, with his long easy stride. People noticed him immediately and wondered who the woman was with him. He kissed her quickly on the cheek at the elevator and disappeared, before anyone could start asking for autographs. They were all drunks at that hour, and he wasn't in the mood. He called her as soon as she got to her room. And she was tired too. It had been a long, busy day.

'Sorry I ditched you, Stevie. I didn't want to deal with fans.' She understood, and she lay down on the bed with the phone.

'It's fine. I had a great time tonight. San Francisco is going to be even more miserable now. What am I going to do at night?'

'Come to Nashville, then. I can show you around. We're recording next week, and you can sit in the studio with us. And we're playing a concert that weekend. Nashville is an amazing place. You can be our good luck charm.' He felt as though she already was, and everybody liked her.

'I'm not sure that's a proper job. It might be a little hard to explain.'

'Then don't explain it. Just come.'

'I've already been here for two days, and I'm staying tomorrow. I have to go home sometime.' But she could no longer think why. She was having too much fun here with them.

'We'll talk about it tomorrow,' he said firmly, and she laughed. They both knew she had to go home. But in the meantime, she was having the best time she'd had in years. 'See you tomorrow, Stevie. Sleep tight,' he said in a tired voice. He had given the show his all tonight. He always did. And Sandy had been terrific too, and put her mouse shoes on the minute she came off stage. 'You can become Sandy's mentor, or mine,' he said warmly. He liked spending time with her.

'There's nothing I could teach you that you don't already know,' she said kindly. He was a wise man, and she agreed with the wisdom he had shared about life.

'I don't think that's true, Stevie. You're a very special woman. You just don't know it yet. Come to Nashville and find out.' She didn't know what he meant by that and didn't want to ask. She liked the friendship that they shared, and she wasn't ready for it to be more, with him or anyone. And he had sensed that from the moment they met. He was satisfied with what they had. He just liked being with her. He hadn't enjoyed anyone this much in years. 'Get some sleep. We'll figure out something to do tomorrow, or just lie by the pool and relax. I'll call you in the morning,' he promised.

'I'd like that,' she answered, and they both hung up. It had been another perfect day. And she was thoroughly enjoying her new friend. And so was he.

Chapter 9

They spent the morning at the pool the next day, until people started hounding him for autographs. And they went back to his suite, and ordered lunch there. It was still impressive to Stephanie to see how fans chased after him and intruded on him every place he went. He was always gracious about it, but it was wearing after a while.

They were halfway through lunch when Chase brought up the subject of Nashville again.

'I know this isn't the kind of thing you do,' he began, 'but it's a hell of an opportunity to see the city with someone like me. It's a two-day drive from here. I can drive your car for you, or one of the boys in the band. You can stay a few days and then drive back to San Francisco. And you can visit your son in Atlanta while you're there. Come on, Stevie. We're having such a good time. Don't leave now.' His eyes pleaded with her when he said it, and she was touched. And he was right, it was an opportunity, but it made no sense in her real life. What was she doing following a country music band around the country from Las Vegas to Nashville, and then driving back west alone? It was really a stretch for her. But the alternative was depressing. Sooner or later she had to go home. Why not have some fun before she did? He did all he could to convince her, and by the end of lunch she still wasn't sure. The chance to visit Michael in Atlanta appealed to her and almost seemed like a good excuse, but not quite.

'I don't know, Chase. And you have work to do when you get home.' He had told her about the new album they were doing.

'Yes, but I'd love to show you around. Just come for a few days, and you can see your boy.' He was touching every chord he could.

'If my boy wants to see me. He has a girlfriend I don't like, and she's not crazy about me either.'

'A local girl?' She nodded. 'Ah, a Georgia peach. They're the worst kind. Saccharine sweet while they knife you in the back.' He had described her perfectly, and Stevie laughed.

'You're a very convincing man,' Stephanie said with a serious look. But she knew it was something she might never do again, and what better way to see Nashville than with him?

'So have I convinced you?' He looked hopeful, and she shook her head.

'Almost. I just don't know how to explain this to anyone. It's so not part of my normal life.' But her normal life now was loneliness and grief. She dreaded going home, which was how she had wound up in Las Vegas in the first place. But Nashville felt like she'd really be pushing it, and leading someone else's life, not her own.

'Then don't explain it. Who do you need to explain it to?'

'My son, if I show up.'

'Can't you say you were visiting an old friend? You have nothing else to do right now. That might sound okay to them.'

'Yeah, it might,' she said, looking pensive, and then she sank her chin into her hands with a sigh. 'Maybe I should just stop worrying about it and do it. I can figure out some explanation later. I don't know why I feel like I need to explain things to anyone, or make excuses, or have their permission. I'm just not used to doing whatever I want. Maybe they don't give a damn anyway. My kids are grown up, so am I.' She looked troubled as she glanced at him. 'Okay, I'll come to Nashville. I can tell my grandchildren about it one day, about when I made friends with a famous country music star and followed his band to Nashville.' He smiled at what she said and her expression, and he was happy she agreed. He was enjoying her company too much to want to see her go. It was one of those rare encounters in life that seemed important to both of them, although neither of them knew why. And he knew that sooner or later she had to go back to San Francisco, where she lived.

'Do you mind driving back cross country alone?' He was mildly worried about it. She had a good car and was an independent woman, but she was still a woman on her own.

'I'll be fine.'

'You can always have the car shipped from Nashville and fly home,' he suggested, but she shook her head. She liked the challenge, and it would be a good time to just think peacefully while she drove. 'I'll drive your car for you tomorrow, or we can ride the bus if you prefer.'

'I think it would be fun to drive,' she said as they left the lunch table in his suite. They chatted for a while, and then she went back to her own room. She wanted to buy a few things for the trip to Nashville. She was running out of clothes. She had only brought enough for the weekend at the Biltmore, and even if she only stayed a few days in Nashville, with the drive back, she needed clothes now for ten days. She was about to leave her room to go shopping when Chase called her and offered to go with her.

'Won't your fans drive you crazy?'

'We'll see how it goes.' But he liked the idea of shopping with her, and he wanted to give her an idea of what she might need. And from her perspective, suddenly she had a pal to do things with, and he made everything more fun.

They started out on foot and went to one of the huge malls she had already discovered. He was wearing dark glasses and a baseball cap, and they got through two stores before anyone recognized him.

And he made their shopping expedition an adventure. Stephanie burst out laughing at the first thing he chose for her. It was a red-sequined stretch jumpsuit that he said would look great on her figure, and it took her a minute to realize he was kidding. She picked out jeans, a pair of white silk slacks, and a white cotton jacket, while he concentrated on a low-cut silk blouse and a black leather miniskirt that made her laugh.

'Are you kidding? I'll get arrested.'

'Not in Nashville, Stevie. Why not? It would look great on you.' She tried to imagine what Bill would say if she had shown up in an outfit like that. They compromised on a short denim skirt, and one sexy black top and a short white denim skirt she could wear with her high-heeled sandals. It was still younger looking and more revealing than most things she would have bought if she'd gone shopping on her own, but it was new for her to have the male point of view while she shopped, and she liked it. It was nice knowing what he wanted to see her in and thought looked good on her. Bill hadn't gone shopping with her since they were first married, and even then he considered it a painful chore that he was happy to give up after the first year. Her entire wardrobe was one that suited a respectably married woman, and was not meant to make her look sexy or even attractive. Everything she owned was practical, conservative, and fairly plain. Chase reminded her that she looked fifteen years younger than she was and had a great figure, and should take advantage of it. It was strange hearing him say it, and when she got home she tried on everything they'd bought. It all looked good on her, but she hardly recognized the woman in the mirror, in the short white skirt and a youthful pale pink top. She wondered what her daughters would say if they saw her.

She called Jean and told her what she was doing. She felt uncomfortable not having someone know where she was, and where she was going.

'Has he put the make on you yet?'

'No, and I don't want him to,' Stephanie said firmly. She didn't have the same fantasies as Jean. She was enjoying their friendship and didn't want to spoil it with anything more.

'Why not?' Jean asked her, and Stephanie thought about it.

'I still feel married. Maybe I always will.' She sounded sad for a minute as she said it.

'I hope not. Bill didn't when he had that affair,' she reminded her. Jean never minced words.

'That was different.'

'Yes, it was. You wouldn't be cheating if you went out with this guy. You're a free woman, Steph.'

'It's only been four months, not even that.'

'Well, keep your options open. He sounds like a nice guy.'

'He is. But it would spoil everything if we got involved. We're just having a good time, and I don't live in Nashville. And his life is completely different from mine. I'm just going to Nashville for a few days. I'll visit Michael in Atlanta, and then I'm coming home.'

'Are you trying to convince me or yourself?'

'Both,' Stephanie said, and laughed.

'Let me know where you are. And have fun.'

They talked for a few minutes and hung up, and Stephanie went backstage again that night. It felt like a familiar scene now. After three days the band was starting to treat her like one of them, and Sandy loved talking to her. Stephanie had shown her photographs of her children, and Sandy had worn the mouse shoes that day. Delilah had shown Stephanie photographs of her children too.

Their performance that night was electrifying, and the audience loved them, and knowing it was their last night got everyone even more worked up. Chase had Sandy sing a solo, and she was great. She told Stephanie afterward that she had worn the mouse shoes for good luck, although she usually wore stilettos on stage.

They went back to the diner for dinner, and Chase had an enormous steak. He was starving as usual when he finished work, and told her all about Nashville while he ate.

'You're going to love it,' he said with a look of excitement in his eyes, and Stephanie couldn't wait. It was a trip she would never have taken without him, but a place she had always wanted to visit, after reading about the music scene there. But she'd never had a reason to go.

The band went back to pack up their equipment after dinner. There was a truck that would be following the bus, and Chase had told her they would be leaving at nine the next morning. She promised to be ready on time.

She had trouble sleeping that night, she was thinking about the trip. And just as she was falling asleep, she had a text from Charlotte just checking in. Stephanie answered her immediately, and didn't say where she was or where she was going. She still had to invent a credible story for all of them, about a college friend she had decided to visit, but she didn't broach the subject yet. And Charlotte hadn't asked how she was, and assumed she was at home. She had just written to tell her mother what she was doing. She said she was going to Venice for the weekend. And Stephanie was relieved to know she'd be home in a few weeks, toward the end of June. After answering her text, Stephanie lay awake for another hour, wondering what Bill would think of what she was doing, and if he would approve. And she couldn't help wondering too what he would have been doing if she was the one who had died. But he would have had his work as a lawyer to keep him grounded. She didn't have anything except the kids, and her occasional work at the shelter, which just wasn't enough.

Stephanie was ready when Chase called her from the lobby the next morning. She'd been up since seven, her bags were packed, and she'd had coffee and scrambled eggs.

'Ready for your big adventure?' Chase teased her. It was hard to believe that they had met only three days before and had become friends. He was opening the doors to a whole new world, one that she was really starting to enjoy.

'I'm ready,' she said, and called the bell captain after she hung up. When she got downstairs, the boys in the band were just boarding the bus with Delilah and Sandy, who waved at Stephanie. She was wearing the mouse shoes again.

'You're going to wear them out,' Chase called after her, and she made a face at him and disappeared into the bus. The truck had already left with their equipment and headed to Nashville, and Chase slipped behind the wheel of Stephanie's car. She got into the passenger seat, and they took off, following the bus. The day was hot, and they had a long way to travel. Stephanie wore shorts, a T-shirt, and sandals, and Chase was wearing his torn jeans and a tank top, which showed off all his tattoos.

He turned on the radio as they drove down the strip toward the highway, and sang along to the music in his strong clear voice. She smiled at what she was listening to, her very own concert. It was still hard to believe. And as they set off on the open road, with the bus behind them by then, Stephanie started to sing with him, in a cautious voice at first. He pretended not to notice, so as not to make her self-conscious, and waited through several songs before he said anything.

'You've got a damn fine voice,' he said, keeping his eyes on the road.

'Not really. I just like singing.' He smiled at her then.

'You've got perfect pitch. And not one false note. I should hire you to sing with the girls.'

'Yeah, right.'

He flipped through the stations then, until he came to some country music, and sang along with that, and she joined him on the ones she knew. She got braver as he got louder, and they were having a good time.

'Have you ever thought of writing lyrics?' he asked her, and she shook her head.

'I don't think I could.'

'You said you like to write. You should try it sometime. It's fun. I'll show you how it works. All you need are some couplets and a refrain. You just tell a story with words, about who screwed over whom, who broke whose heart, and how long they've been crying ever since. You know, just like real life.' She laughed.

'You make it sound so simple.'

'It is. Just listen to the songs.' She knew he wrote his own music and lyrics, and most of his songs were touching, told a story, and were very good. And the melodies were easy to sing. 'I'll bet you could do it if you tried. We can try it when we get to Nashville. Hell, I'll turn you into a country singer yet.'

'Oh God, that's a frightening thought. You'd be out of business in a week.'

'Maybe not,' he said, smiling at her again. She was easy to be with, and they were quiet for long periods, as Nevada slid by them. He was happy to be going home. He told her about the house he had remodeled a few years before, with a professional sound studio in it, where he recorded, and about his dogs. It sounded like a good life, and he didn't seem to mind being alone.

'After Tamra, I needed some time off,' he explained to her when they talked about it as he drove. 'It just got too intense, but that's how she is. She set fire to all my clothes once, when she thought I'd cheated on her.' He smiled at the memory now, but he hadn't then.

'And had you?' Stephanie asked with interest. There were lots of temptations in his world, and he was a good-looking man.

'Not that time,' he said laughing. 'I used to be pretty wild when I was younger. I gave that up after my first few years with her. It wasn't worth the headache. Before her, I was kind of a bad guy. I was thirty-two when we got together, and I settled down after I turned thirty-five. She never believed me, though. She always thought I was cheating on her. She's a hotheaded woman. She cheated on me, though. She left me a few times, but she always came back. I was the one who wanted out in the end. I wanted a peaceful life, and I couldn't do that with her.'

'Why did you take her back?' Stephanie was curious about him, and he was very open with her.

'She was a beautiful woman and hard to resist. I finally figured out that wasn't enough. I needed someone I could talk to. Tamra was too self-centered to listen. She never cared about anyone but herself. We sang great together, though. I thought I'd take a hit when we stopped recording together, but actually my albums have done better since she's been gone. I always believed the fans liked her. Turns out I have better sales on my own.' The bus passed them a couple of times once they were on the open road, and some of the boys in the band hung out the windows and hooted and waved. He knew they would be having lunch on the bus by then, but Stephanie had brought them sandwiches from the hotel so they wouldn't have to stop. He ate his with one hand while he drove, and she offered to take a turn so he could rest, but he said he was fine.

And she ate her sandwich as he continued driving. He put the radio back on then, and as she looked out the window and listened to the music, she fell asleep. He glanced over at her and smiled, and when she woke up two hours later, they were just passing Gallup. He said he wanted to keep driving until dark and get as far as they could that day. There was a motel in Elk City, Oklahoma, where they usually stopped. It wasn't fancy, but it was clean, and he said there was a great truck stop nearby, with a diner where they liked to eat.

'I'll help you plan your route back to California when you leave Nashville. You need to stay in decent hotels. You can't stay in the kind of dives we do when we're on the road. I could write a guidebook to the worst motels in the world,' he said with a grin, but she appreciated his concern for her. 'As long as you stick to the main highways, and stay in good hotels and motels, you'll be fine on the way home,' he reassured her. By then they were getting to Albuquerque, New Mexico. She felt as though she were getting a geography lesson as they drove. She would have liked to see Albuquerque, but they didn't have time. Chase had told her, before they left, that they would be driving on average fourteen hours a day for both days. It would have been easier and more relaxing on the bus, where they could stretch out on the couches, eat in the kitchen, use the bathroom, and walk around. But Stephanie liked being in the car with him, and talking as they drove. On the bus they would have had to be sociable with the others. This way she had Chase to herself.

When they stopped for dinner that night in Amarillo, Texas, they met up with the others on the bus. Sandy sat down next to Stephanie as soon as they walked in. She had been dying to talk to her all day. Everyone was looking a little raggedy by then. They had been watching movies on the bus on the large screen in the living room, and Sandy had slept in Chase's room. She was the only one he allowed to use his room. It was off limits to everyone else. And he put an arm around her after dinner, as they walked out of the restaurant. Stephanie liked watching him with her. He was so fatherly, and affectionate and kind, and stern when he thought he had to be. He told her to go to bed and sleep when they got back on the bus. They would be laying voice tracks of her when they got back to Nashville, and he didn't want her getting overtired.

He talked to the bus driver for a few minutes, estimating how much longer until they stopped for the night. While Chase was talking to him, Alyson called Stephanie on her cell. It was the first time she had heard from her all week, which was just as well.

'Oh my God, I'm so sorry, Steph. It's been a nightmare. The kids have been sick. They came down with chicken pox the night we got home. They're covered with them, and I know the baby is going to get them as soon as these guys get over them. I haven't left the house since we got back. How are you?'

'I'm fine,' Stephanie said cheerfully. It had been a great week, but she didn't want to explain it to her.

'I don't know when I'm going to get out of here,' Alyson said, sounding exhausted.

'I'm going to Atlanta to see Michael. And an old friend of mine from college.' Alyson was happy to hear it. She knew that Stephanie had hardly left the house since Bill died.

'That'll be good for you,' she said kindly. 'I don't think I'll be able to get out till next week. And if Henry comes down with it, then I'll be stuck all over again.' Henry was her two-year-old.

'I'll come and see you when I get back,' Stephanie said.

'That would be great. Give my love to Michael. When are you leaving?'

'Soon,' Stephanie said vaguely, as Chase walked toward her, and she saw the bus pull out. 'I'll call you,' she said, and hung up quickly. She didn't want Alyson to hear Chase talking if he said something to her, but he was cautious. He didn't know if it was one of her kids or someone else.

'Everything okay?' he asked as they got back in the car. They had a few more hours to drive before they stopped for the night in Elk City.

'It's fine. That was one of my two best women friends. Alyson. Her kids have chicken pox. She has young kids. Her husband is a doctor.' She had mentioned them to him before, and as she said it, her life sounded so staid and bourgeois compared to his. But now everything seemed to be changing. She didn't feel like a boring housewife anymore, on the road to Nashville with Chase and his band. She looked over at him as he started the car, and he looked tired. 'Do you want me to drive for a while?' she offered, and he shook his head and turned the car back onto the road.

'I'm fine,' he said easily. 'I like driving. It reminds me of all the years I drove the van, when we were on the road on tour in the early days.'

'I like driving too. And I'm wide awake, if you want to switch off.'

'You can ride the bus anytime you want,' he suggested, and she smiled.

'I'd rather ride with you. It's nice talking to you.' He looked pleased when she said it. 'And being alone,' she added shyly.

'I like it too,' he said gently. 'I keep wondering about the hand of fate that made us run into each other on that hiking trail.' And now it felt as though they had known each other forever. She had admitted things to him, particularly about her marriage, that she had said to no one else. And he had been equally candid with her, even about cheating on Tamra. 'Destiny is a strange thing,' he added. 'Sometimes I think people are brought into our lives to teach us lessons.'

'I believe that too,' she said softly, but she couldn't imagine what she was teaching him. He was teaching her to be more spontaneous and seize the moment, which was what had convinced her to go to Nashville, but she had decided to go to Las Vegas on her own.

'You've led a more stable life than I have. And you spent more time with your kids. I was too busy building my career and going on tour when my boy was little. He pretty much grew up without me. I was all over the place then, but he doesn't hold it against me. He comes up from Memphis pretty regularly to see me. And he loves the Grand Ole Opry. He has a great voice too, but you can't get him near this business. He's happy in construction.'

'Is he married?' She had never thought to ask him, and there was something about driving at night that led to confidences, revelations, and confessions. But he knew most of hers already.

'No.' Chase laughed at the question about his son. 'He's still a bad boy, like I was at his age. He's always got a string of girls running behind him. But they can't catch him. He's too smart for that, and he doesn't want to settle down.'

'He should talk to my son Michael. I'm scared to death that girl is going to convince him to get married. He's such a decent guy, and so steady and reliable, any girl would want him. And I think she has her eye on marriage.'

'He sounds like you,' Chase said gently, glancing at her in the light from the dashboard. She had let her hair down, and her face looked soft in the dim light. 'Steady and reliable. Someone you can count on to always be there for you. I've never had a woman like that in my life. I've always been drawn to the wild ones, and the bad girls. They always seemed more exciting. It took me a lot of years to figure out that they're just trouble and not much else. They're never there when you need them, and cheating with someone else.'

'That makes me sound so boring. Steady and reliable. Like a solid car, or an old workhorse.'

'They're the best kind. And the ones you want to come home to, not the ones you want to run away from.'

'Maybe that's why Bill had an affair. Because he knew I'd always be there. He was looking for excitement. She wasn't a bad girl, though, just bored with her marriage. I guess Bill was too.'

'It doesn't have to be that way, boring with a good woman,' he said wisely. 'I'd rather have a fast car now, and slow women. A fast one will always burn you. At least the ones I knew always did, every time.'

'I don't know what the right answers are anymore,' she said with a small sigh in the darkness. 'The marriages that last aren't the ones I want. My friend Jean is married to a man who cheats on her constantly, and she hasn't loved him in years. She stays married to him because he has a lot of money, and she'd rather have everything she can buy than a man who loves her. And my other friend Alyson, the one who just called, is madly in love with her husband. But she has so many illusions about him that I always feel like they're an accident waiting to happen. Like me and Bill. I never thought he'd cheat on me, and then he did. And nothing was ever the same again. We never got back to the way we felt before. So what's the answer to that one?'

'Maybe you should have left him if you weren't in love with him anymore. In spite of the kids. That's not enough reason to stay married.'

'I thought it was. I don't know. Maybe I was wrong.' She looked pensive as she said it.

'What did your kids think? Did you ask them?'

'They were too young. And we never told them what happened. I didn't want them to hate their father.'

'You're a noble woman, Stevie. And they weren't that young. From what you've told me, the two oldest ones were sixteen and eighteen, seven years ago when it happened. And your little one was thirteen. That's plenty old enough to know the difference between right and wrong. Hell, I had a kid myself when I was your son's age at the time. And he was seven when I was the age your son is now. That forces you to grow up. Young people stay kids a lot longer today. Those were different times, in a different world. Kids in the south used to marry a lot younger, especially poor ones. No one I knew went to college. You graduated from high school, got married, and had a baby nine months later. Or you got pregnant and got married. That's why I keep an eye on Sandy. I don't want her doing either one, getting pregnant or married. She has a big future ahead of her, if she sticks with it. I want to get her an album when she's ready, in another couple of years. She's not ready for it yet, but she will be. That's the best gift I can give her father. He was a hell of a fine musician. He died of a brain tumor. He was gone six weeks after they diagnosed him. That taught me something too, about life, and how fast it can change.'

'She's lucky to have you,' Stephanie said quietly. 'You're a good man too,' she said and meant it. 'You're steady and reliable.'

'Reliable,' he grinned at her, 'but not always so steady. At least I didn't used to be. Now I'm just old and tired.' But he sure didn't look it. He still seemed young and sexy. Jean wasn't wrong about that. Stephanie realized too how shocked Alyson would be to see her with him, not to mention her children. They were a slightly incongruous pair. She was a Pacific Heights housewife, and he was a star on the country music scene, and everything that went with it, including his good looks. But there was a lot more to him than that.

'I don't think "old and tired" is the way I'd describe you.' She laughed in the darkness at his self-deprecating description.

'Well, you don't look like anyone's boring wife, I can tell you. Your husband was a fool to be after greener pastures, with all due respect. And if you'd bought that black leather miniskirt I picked out for you, I'd be beating guys away with a stick, to keep them off you,' he said with a guffaw, and she laughed.

'Yeah, and they'd be cops trying to arrest me for indecent exposure. The white one I bought is short enough.'

'Nah, we'll get you into some decent clothes in Nashville,' he teased her. But he liked the way she dressed – she managed to be clean cut, respectable, and sexy all at the same time. He knew she was the kind of woman you married, not just slept with. Her husband just hadn't known what a prize he had. But he didn't want to press the point and say it to her. Chase had been proud every time he left the hotel with her, and she had no idea how beautiful she was. He admired her innocence and honesty. He found everything about her refreshing. He was tired of the jaded women he met constantly, and the lunatics and women who wanted to go out with him just because he was Chase Taylor, or for what he could buy them. He

Danielle Steel

could have had a dozen women like that every day. But he had never been with anyone like Stephanie. He knew it the minute he met her.

'You know what I think the answer is, Stevie?' He thought about it for a long moment. 'I think you have to wait for the right person to come along, even if it doesn't happen till you're ninety-eight years old. It's just not worth messing with the wrong ones. They break your heart or screw up your life every time. I guess that's why I haven't bothered for the last couple of years. I've been around that track too often. I don't need to go around it again. You always wind up in the same place, right back where you started. I can't be bothered.'

'I still feel married to Bill,' she said softly, in the confessional atmosphere of the dark car as they drove along the highway.

'You probably will for a while,' he answered, not looking at her. 'It just shows you're a good woman, and you were a good wife. You don't have anything to reproach yourself for on that score. And I'm sure he knew it too.'

'Maybe,' she said thoughtfully, but she wasn't sure. 'We didn't even say goodbye to each other that morning. All we talked about was the weather. And his last word to me was "thanks" as he walked away.'

'That's a lesson for you right there. When you fall in love again, you'll talk about the things that are important.'

'Yeah, I guess so.' But she couldn't imagine falling in love again. Like Chase, she didn't want to get her heart broken. And Bill had injured hers severely. She had never really recovered. She realized that now. She had just been on autopilot for the last seven years of their marriage, and maybe even before, and so had Bill.

They rode along in silence for a while, and then he started singing in his soft, deep voice, and she sang along with him a capella. They sang a few songs, and he turned to her. 'We sound pretty good together. We'll have to record that. After you write me some songs.'

'I'm not going to write you any songs. They'd be awful.'

'Try it. You might like it.' He was teasing her, but he had a feeling she might be good at it.

He talked to her about Nashville again then. He was happy she was going with them. And it was eleven o'clock when they finally drove into Elk City. He headed down the main street to the simple, but comfortable hotel where they had stayed before. The others were piling out of the bus, when Chase pulled up beside them. They needed six rooms for all of them, and he had had Charlie call ahead. The desk clerk was waiting for them and had all their keys ready. They always spent the night there on their way to or from Vegas.

The boys in the band slept in pairs, and Sandy and Delilah shared a room. And he had reserved two rooms for him and Stevie. They happened to be next door to each other, and he walked her to her room to make sure they had given her the best one. She was carrying a tote bag with what she needed, and had left her suitcase in the trunk of the car. His was on the bus, and he was carrying a backpack with his toilet kit, clean underwear, and a clean T-shirt. He was satisfied with the room they'd given her and turned to look at her from the doorway.

'Sleep tight, Miss Stevie. Call me if you need anything. I'll be awake for a while.' The band had gone to eat at Friday's at the hotel, but Chase said he wasn't hungry. And all Stevie wanted was a bath. She felt grimy after riding in the car all day. And they had another long day ahead tomorrow. They had agreed to ride the bus and have one of the boys drive her car.

'Thanks for the nice room, Chase.' He had insisted on paying for it with the others.

'Of course. I tried to get a rollaway to put you in with Sandy and Delilah, but they didn't have one,' he said with a twinkle in his eye, and she laughed.

'That would have been fine. I've had worse.'

'Not on my watch.' He smiled at her then and left, and she gently closed the door. And a little while later he could hear her bath running, and he tried not to think about her getting in it. Those kinds of thoughts always got him in trouble, and she wasn't the kind of woman you could take lightly. And he didn't want to. He didn't want to do anything to spoil the trust they were building. He could tell that she felt safe with him, and he wanted to keep it that way. She brought out the best in him, and had ever since he met her. This wasn't Tamra or the women like her. She was a lady, and a woman he respected. He walked into his bathroom then and turned on the shower and washed off the dirt of the day. He put on clean shorts and lay on his bed then, still thinking about her. He kept thinking back to the day he had met her, sitting on the bench, looking out at the Grand Canyon, and then walking along the trail with her. And seeing her from the stage, and his excitement knowing she was there. He was beginning to feel as though she had been in his life forever, and he hoped she would be. He had no idea what they would be to each other, maybe just friends, but he knew that something important had happened that day on the trail. Whatever this was, Chase could feel the hand of destiny in it. He felt like a boy again when he thought about her. Just a country boy, and as he thought it, a song started dancing through his mind. He could already hear the music, and the words that came into his head as he fell asleep were 'the country boy and the lady' . . . the music sounded great, and all he needed now were the rest of the words.

Chapter 10

It was easier riding the bus, the next day, than it had been driving her car for so many hours, and two of the men from the band took turns driving it as they went through Oklahoma, and then into Arkansas, which Chase said gave him nightmares just thinking about it. He had hated his childhood there. He said he had felt stifled in the tiny town he grew up in, there was no opportunity to grow and be something more, and most people got stuck there forever. And he admitted that even as a kid, he had had big dreams.

They sat on the bus and talked to the others, and Sandy monopolized Stevie every chance she got, showing her gossip in fan magazines and dresses she thought were terrific. She wanted to know Stevie's opinions about everything, and Chase smiled as he watched them, and finally rescued Stephanie and invited her to watch a movie in his bedroom. They had to sit on his bed, propped up against big pillows, and he let her pick the movie. He had one of the guys make them popcorn in the microwave, and he and Stephanie sat engrossed by the movie, and he loved her choice. The others were eating microwave pizza when they finished, and he and Stevie helped themselves to a slice, and looked out the windows as they sat at the dining table. The bus was a wonder of practicality, luxury, and comfort, with a sound system better than most homes had.

It was early evening when they reached the Mississippi River, and Stephanie was amazed by how wide it was, and how much activity there was on it. They crossed over at Memphis, and had another three and a half hours to get to Nashville. But everyone on the bus was coming alive by then and was excited to get home. Chase sat next to Stephanie and told her again about the sights he wanted to show her in Nashville. He had to work for a few hours the next day, but he planned to pick her up by noon and show her around the city. She already knew about the full-scale replica of the Parthenon and could hardly wait to see it, and he wanted to show her Andrew Jackson's home, which he said was a tribute to one of the great love stories of the south. The president had designed the gardens himself for his wife, Rachel.

Everyone was animated in the last hours on the bus, and Delilah couldn't wait to see her boys. Chase had already made a reservation for Stevie at the best hotel in town, the Hermitage, which this time she insisted she would pay for, and he had agreed to let her. The hotel was in downtown Nashville, and Chase had told her it housed one of the best steakhouses in the city. He ate there often.

It was ten o'clock by the time they drove up to the hotel entrance, after a twelve-hour drive, but they were home. Chase had the bus stop at the hotel first, and the boys who had been driving her car dropped it off, so she would have it with her. And he watched the bellman unload her suitcase and then walked her into the elegant lobby. He stayed with her while she checked in, and went upstairs with her to make sure she liked her room, and she assured him she loved it. The hotel had all the graciousness and elegance of the south that she had expected. Then he looked regretful as he left her.

'I'm sorry to run out on you. I need to get these guys home so they can work tomorrow. They've got to start laying down the music tracks in the studio for our album. I'll call you in the morning.'

'I'm fine,' she said, and then gently put a hand on his arm. 'Chase, thank you for everything.' He could see that she meant it, and was touched. She was such a gentle woman. He had been making notes all day for the song he'd thought of the night before, 'The Country Boy and the Lady,' but he hadn't told her about it.

'We haven't even started,' he said, and then kissed her cheek. 'Wait till I show you the city tomorrow.'

'I can't wait. I'll take a look around in the morning.'

'I'll call you,' he promised, and then hurried down the hall with a wave, as the bellman and elevator man looked at him in awe. They were used to seeing stars around the hotel, but Chase Taylor was about as big as it got in Nashville. And just seeing their reaction to him, Stephanie realized again just what a huge star he was. She had already gotten used to being with him, and he was so natural and relaxed that sometimes she forgot about it.

She settled into her room then, unpacked her suitcase, and ran a bath, and she was suddenly glad that she'd been brave enough to come, and called Jean in California.

'So how is it?' Jean asked with an expectant tone. 'Is he there?'

'No, he had to get the band home. Jeannie, it's fantastic here. I love it. It's so . . . so southern.' They both laughed at what she said, and Stephanie told her about the two days on the road, the places they'd gone through, her day on the bus, and how beautiful the hotel was.

'Shit. We'll never get you back to San Francisco.'

'Yes, you will. I live there. But this is so much fun.'

'I'm happy for you,' Jean said, feeling emotional about it. Her friend had had such a hard time in the last few months that she was genuinely grateful that something good had happened to her. And meeting Chase Taylor sounded like a good thing to her. He had already turned Stephanie's life around in a short time. And even if nothing came of it, it had been a great experience. Her voice sounded different. And she seemed more hopeful about life, and excited about what she was doing. She had finally stopped mourning, and had begun living again.

They talked for a while, and then Stephanie got into the tub. And she was just getting out of it and had wrapped herself in a towel when Chase called her. He was home after he dropped everyone off. And the first thing he did when he walked in was call her.

'I know this sounds ridiculous,' he said, sounding embarrassed, 'but I already miss you. You're nice to be with, Stevie.'

'So are you.' They had talked nonstop for two days, when they weren't singing, laughing, or watching a movie. The trip from Vegas to Nashville had been great with Chase. 'I could definitely get used to your bus as my favorite mode of travel.'

'Maybe I should send it back to California with you. They could tow your car,' he said seriously.

'If you do that, I might never send it back. I think I'd better drive home. Besides, how would I explain it to my son?' She laughed at the thought.

'Is everything okay at the hotel? Did you order something to eat?'

'I was thinking about it,' she admitted, but she was almost too tired to eat. The bath had made her sleepy.

'The food is great there. They have one of the best chefs

in the city. We'll have dinner at the steakhouse one night.'
There was so much he wanted to show her, she'd have to
stay a month. And he had to fit his work in somehow.
'Get a good night's sleep. We're going to be busy tomorrow.
And I have to be in the studio tomorrow night. Will you
come?'

'Of course, if you'll have me.'

'The boys say you're our mascot. And Sandy loves
you.'

'Is that polite for groupie?'

'You can be that too.' But he was always respectful of
her. He treated her like a porcelain doll, and he was very
southern in his manners and how he addressed women.
She liked it. For a poor boy from Arkansas, he had learned
quickly a long time ago, and behaved like a gentleman
despite the long hair and tattoos. He was more polite than
any man she knew in San Francisco.

He sounded sorry to hang up, and she ordered
chamomile tea, which arrived on a silver tray, with a plate
of delicate butter cookies. She loved the hotel he had
picked for her. And after she finished her tea, she texted
all her children, sent them her love, and said she hoped
that they were fine. Then she called Alyson to see how her
kids were doing. She sounded frantic, Stephanie could
hear them crying in the background, and Alyson got off
in under two minutes. But Stephanie felt like she'd done
her duty. She got into the big, comfortable bed, turned on

the TV, watched a movie, and fell asleep halfway through it.

And the next thing she knew, the sun was streaming into the room, and when she got up, she peeked out her windows at the view of Legislative Plaza, in front of the Tennessee state capitol building. She ordered breakfast and got dressed and walked around downtown near the hotel. She was back long before noon, when Chase had promised to pick her up. He arrived a few minutes late and looked harried. He said he had been getting things organized at his house all morning.

'We've only been gone a week, but everything goes wrong when I'm away. My sprinkler system broke and created a lake in my backyard. One of my dogs got loose and probably got my neighbor's dog pregnant, for the second time. My housekeeper is threatening to quit, and the gardener broke his arm and didn't come. The guys were late coming to the studio this morning, and Sandy thinks she's catching a cold, and we need her to lay voice tracks for the new album.'

'Are you sure you want to go sightseeing today? We don't have to. I feel guilty tying up your time,' Stephanie said apologetically.

'We don't have to. I *want* to!' he told her with his dazzling smile. He had driven over in the vintage Corvette he loved, and they left the hotel five minutes later. They went to the Parthenon in Centennial Park first, so she could see it in broad daylight, and he promised to bring her back at night, when it was even more impressive. He told her it had been built for the Tennessee Centennial Exposition in 1897. He was an encyclopedia of local historical facts, and she was fascinated by all of it.

Then he took her to The Hermitage, Andrew Jackson's estate, to visit the house and the grounds. They even saw the log cabin Jackson and his wife had lived in from 1804 to 1820, the mansion they had lived in from 1820 onward, and the historic gardens he had designed for his wife. There was something so touching about it, as the docent who conducted the tour brought the presidential couple to life, with personal details that made them seem more human. And she explained that they had had a hundred and fifty slaves working on the property at the time to care for the plantation and the farm. Farming had been Jackson's passion. Stephanie found it fascinating, and Chase admitted that he hadn't visited the historic home in a long time, and enjoyed seeing it as well.

And after that they went to a little catfish place on Music Valley Drive for a late lunch. Then he drove her past the dozens of storefronts that doubled as music venues. It was here that one sensed that Nashville was all about music. Every store they saw had some kind of live music being offered. He explained to her that they were in the West End of the city, and the street they were on was called Music Row. And then he pointed out the renovated homes and old warehouses that housed the big-label music companies now. He said there were countless recording studios there as well, although he now preferred his own. But this was where all the action was in the music world that made its home in Nashville. Two blocks away he took her to Elliston Place, where he said all the nightclubs were, and she noticed a number of cafés with live music. He said some of the best music in town was played on that block, and he had played there himself when he was young. And on the way back to the hotel, they passed Vanderbilt University. It was late afternoon when they got back to the hotel, and they stopped at the Oak Bar for a drink. Her head was spinning from everything they had seen in a short time. And she said her favorite had been the tour of The Hermitage, Andrew Jackson's home. And she was touched hearing about how much he had loved his wife. There was something both poignant and inspiring about it.

'It's kind of cool that two hundred years later, we're hearing about how much he loved her. I don't think they would say that about anyone I know.' She was smiling as the waiter poured them each a glass of champagne. Chase toasted her to celebrate her arrival in Nashville.

'Well, they're not going to say that about anyone I went out with, two hundred years from now,' he said as he took a sip of the champagne. He had enjoyed showing her the sights all afternoon. And he was going to take her to Brentwood, the suburb where he lived, that night. There wasn't much to see there except stately houses – it was where many of the wealthier residents of Nashville had their homes. He had lived in Franklin before that, a small historic town, but he liked his much bigger new home in Brentwood. And he had a small cottage on the estate for Sandy, which gave them both a little space from each other. He had provided a wonderful home for her.

'What a terrific city,' Stephanie said, looking relaxed and happy. 'It's so alive.'

'San Francisco is beautiful too.' He had been there many times, and played concerts at the Oakland Coliseum, and Shoreline Amphitheatre in Mountain View, and the HP Pavilion in the city. And he had played the Fillmore when they were still booking him into smaller venues. He had always loved that one for its 1960s aura and history. But now they could only book him into larger ones when he went on tour, because the crowds at his concerts were so huge.

He hated to leave her after the champagne, but he said he had to get back and check on the band, and see how things were going in the studio.

'They're like kids. They start slacking off if I'm not around.' He had arranged for his assistant to pick her up and drive her to Brentwood at seven o'clock. It was only twenty minutes out of the city, and he would drive her back himself in the Corvette. She had had a great time with him all afternoon, although everyone recognized him, but they would have anyway, no matter what he drove. 'I have the day off tomorrow. And there are some other things I want you to see. I have a surprise.' He was trying to organize her introduction to Nashville, while keeping a hand in his work. And she knew they were playing a concert in six days. It had been sold out for months.

He left her in the lobby, and she heard the Corvette roar off two minutes later, as she went upstairs. She had had a fabulous day so far, thanks to Chase.

She changed into jeans and comfortable clothes for their time in the studio that night. And he said there would be plenty of food for everyone to eat. She couldn't wait to see his house. She knew how much he loved it, and how important his home was to him. He talked about it a lot, and what a job it had been to renovate it. It was an old Colonial mansion on extensive grounds. It was part of an old plantation that had been divided into lots years before, and he had the main house and gardens closest to the house. The old slave quarters had been torn down when the property had been split up.

She hardly had enough time to check her e-mails and change her clothes before it was time to pick her up. One of his assistants was waiting outside the hotel in a 1940s panel truck. It was cherry red, and she was enjoying seeing all the things he had told her about that she knew he enjoyed. He had shown her a picture of the truck on his phone. He had rebuilt the engine himself. Wanda, his assistant, was a young girl about Michael's age from Savannah, who had worked for him for three years, and it was obvious how much she admired him and liked him, as she raved about what a terrific person he was all the way to Brentwood. He was obviously good to work for, since the band said that about him too. Wanda chatted easily with Stephanie all the way to the house.

And when they got to Brentwood, she was amazed by the size of his home. It was an enormous, imposing, stately mansion that looked like something out of *Gone with the Wind*. And there were equally large homes and even a few larger ones in the area around him. But his was one of the most beautiful ones there.

'Wow!' Stephanie said, breathless for a moment, as she looked at Wanda. Nothing had prepared her for this.

'It's nice, isn't it?' Wanda said, with a vast understatement about his home.

'It certainly is,' Stephanie said, as she followed her inside, after they left the truck parked out front. It looked incongruous sitting there but somehow seemed perfect with his image. The fabulous house, and the vintage panel truck he had restored. And the moment they stepped inside, she was impressed with how quietly elegant it was. He had beautiful antiques interspersed with more recent

171

pieces, and it all seemed to work. The colors were sub-dued, and there was something peaceful and welcoming about it. The inside of the house wasn't showy, but it was exquisitely done. And he had some very fine paintings that she liked too. He had obviously put a lot of time and effort into doing his home. Despite his humble beginnings, he had refined taste and the money to indulge it. The house was like him, impressive and discreet.

Wanda led her into an enormous state-of-the-art kitchen, all done in beige and black granite, and from there you could see the beautifully kept gardens behind the house. There was a huge round table in the middle of the kitchen where more than a dozen people could sit comfortably for easy dinners. And they walked through the kitchen into the elaborate high-tech world he had set up behind it, which was the studio where they recorded. He had built it as an addition onto the house. And Stephanie could see Sandy's cottage at the back of the garden, which looked like a little gingerbread house that was perfect for her. Everything about the house and what was in it was great, and infinitely more than she had expected. But she was beginning to know that it was typical of him. Nothing had been done to show off, it had all been designed to live in, comfortably and well, with beautiful things around him, where the people he cared about would be comfortable and feel at ease. It was both casual and impressive all at once. She found him in the studio, talking to the band, while two sound technicians were playing with the mix, and Chase was explaining what he wanted changed. He sounded patient, but looked intent, and totally focused on what he was doing. He didn't even notice for a minute that Stephanie had arrived. Wanda said goodbye and discreetly disappeared. She worked in Chase's office but had nothing to do with his music. And then suddenly he saw Stevie and broke into a grin.

'You're here.' He looked pleased, and she nodded, still slightly overwhelmed by the house and everything she'd seen on the way in.

'This is quite a place,' she said admiringly. It made her realize again just how important a star he was. He made it so easy to forget. He was so normal and human scale, in his dealings with people and in the way he looked, that it was hard to associate his appearance and demeanor with his stature in the world. But even Jean had reminded her that Chase Taylor was a huge celebrity. And the house was in keeping with that, no matter how discreet it was, or how simply and tastefully he had decorated it. The art alone was worth a fortune, as were the antiques. 'I love your house,' she said simply, and he looked thrilled.

'I was hoping you would like it,' he said, as an oversize golden retriever came to lick his hand and check her out. 'That's Frank. George is asleep upstairs.' She knew that George was an English bulldog he had brought back from

Europe after one of his tours. They were his beloved friends. Frank was wagging his tail frantically with a ball in his mouth to get their attention, and she reached out for it. 'Don't even start,' Chase warned her. 'He'll never leave you alone after that. He's obsessed. He follows me around all day with his ball. And he sings. He howls whenever we play. He can't stay in the studio when we do, or all we'll hear on the tracks is him.' Everyone laughed when he said it, because they all knew it was true. And Stephanie patted Frank's head. She hadn't had a dog since Charlotte left for college. Their Lab had died three years before, and Bill didn't want her to replace him. He said it was too much work and made no sense with the kids gone. But she missed having a dog, particularly now, and she'd been thinking of getting another one. Seeing Frank made it seem like an even better idea. His devotion to Chase was complete.

'When can I meet George?' she inquired, and Chase promised to take her upstairs when they finished work. He shooed Frank out of the room then, and closed the soundproof door of the studio, and pulled up the stool he had gotten for her. It was comfortable and very high, and he placed it so she could see everything going on in the room and watch them work. And it was close enough so he could see her too. He handed her a set of earphones so she could hear the music on the tracks, and listen to the mix. It was an impressive high-tech studio, and she could tell that the equipment had cost a fortune, but this was where they recorded his albums. It was the heart and soul of his life, and his work.

They started a few minutes later, and she made not a sound for the many hours that they worked. They worked for four hours without taking a break, and then at a sign from Chase, they all stopped what they were doing.

'Let's eat,' he said to everyone there. He was satisfied with what they'd done so far, and was finally willing to take a break, although they had several hours left to do. He turned to Stephanie then for the first time, and he looked at her intently. He was very serious about his work. 'What did you think?' he asked her, although she knew nothing about his business. But she could tell how skilled and meticulous he was. He paid attention to every detail, and made them go over the same pieces again and again until they all got it right. And he was just as demanding of himself, and a relentless taskmaster with Sandy to teach her her craft. She had performed beautifully on what they'd recorded.

'It sounded fabulous to me,' she said honestly.

'We have a lot more to do,' he explained. 'We won't finish it tonight.' He walked into the kitchen and she followed him, and a lavish spread had appeared on the granite counters, of southern fried chicken, barbecued ribs, salads and pasta, sashimi, and cold lobster. It was an incredible meal, and they were all ravenous as they dug in, even Sandy. They had worked hard. And Stephanie heaped food onto her plate along with them. She hadn't realized how hungry she was too until now. And the food looked too good to resist. She helped herself to lobster and sashimi and some ribs.

They talked about what they'd been recording, during dinner, and Chase outlined what he wanted to finish that night. He didn't fool around while he was working, although he chatted with Stephanie while they ate, and made small talk with the others. They all helped themselves to thick slabs of chocolate cake and cheesecake, and an hour after they'd started eating, they went back to the studio and got to work.

It was three in the morning when they finished. Stephanie was surprised to see that they looked exhilarated instead of exhausted. It was obvious that they loved what they were doing, and equally so that they admired and respected Chase. Charlie said that he was a genius. He had an infallible sense for his music.

The members of the band left quickly and promised to be back the next morning. Chase told them he wouldn't join them until the afternoon, and he looked at Stephanie mysteriously as he said it.

'We're going somewhere tomorrow,' he told them, and no one seemed to mind. They had enough to work on, on their own, until he got back. He had given them all assignments and told Sandy to rest her voice. She had worked hard that night, and he didn't want it to show in what they recorded the next day.

And then finally they were alone in the kitchen where he said he spent most of his time.

'Do you want to come upstairs for a minute?' he asked her with a mischievous expression. She had an instant's hesitation, then quickly agreed. She was sure he was only going to show her the house and would never cross any boundaries with her, without her permission. He had always been respectful of her so far, and never took advantage of her or treated her as more than a friend, which was all she was prepared to be for now, in spite of Jean's fantasies about them. She didn't share her friend's point of view, of sleeping with him for the hell of it, because he was handsome and who he was. She wanted more than that if she came to care about him. Stephanie had never been promiscuous even before she married Bill, or when she was in college. Bill was the only man she had ever slept with, and she wasn't ready to move on. She still felt as though Bill was her husband, even though he was gone, and she had said as much to Chase.

He led her straight to his bedroom, down a long hall, with important paintings hanging all along the walls. And his bedroom was an enormous, simply decorated room overlooking the garden. She could hear George before she saw him. He was snoring louder than any man, lying on Chase's bed, with his head on the pillow, his eyes closed, and his tongue hanging out of his mouth. It was the portrait of bliss. He looked at both of them then, opening one eye with acute annoyance, picked up his head briefly, glanced at her, dropped his head back on the pillow with his eyes closed, and snored even louder, as though to admonish them for waking him at all.

'That's George,' Chase said with a fatherly tone. George's face was one only a mother could love, and Stephanie couldn't help laughing.

'He's gorgeous.' Chase could see that she meant it, and was delighted by her response.

'He's got really bad manners. And he's a rotten host. He hates it when I have people over. Frank loves it. George never comes downstairs when anyone's here. I took him to a hotel with me once, and the people in the rooms on either side complained all night because he snored so loud. The hotel never let me bring him back. He sounds like a 747 taking off.' But Chase was crazy about him, and she could see it. 'I wanted you to meet him.'

'If this is some kind of test, he doesn't look impressed.'

'No, he doesn't. That's standard behavior for him. If he didn't like you, he'd growl. He's fine. He's just snoring. I have to wake him in the morning, or he'd never get up. He's the laziest dog alive. Frank walks him around the garden on a leash, and George hates it. He'd rather stay in bed. And he eats enough for two men. I worry that he'll get fat.' He already was, but Stephanie didn't say it. They watched the sleeping dog for a few minutes, and then Chase put an arm around her shoulders and walked her out of the room and toward the stairs. 'Come on, I'll take you home.' He looked happy to have introduced her to his dog.

'You must be exhausted. I can take a cab.' She felt guilty making his night any longer than it had already been, after their intense work session.

'I'm fine. I'm used to this. And you're not taking a cab anywhere,' he said sternly. He walked into the garage and opened the door to the Corvette for her to get in.

And on the way back to the hotel, he kept another promise. He drove her past the Parthenon in Centennial Park, so she could see it all lit up at night. It was even more beautiful than in the daytime, as he had said. And a few minutes later, they were back at her hotel. He got out to open the car door for her and looked down at her for a minute.

'I loved having you there tonight. Thanks for coming out to the house.' He made it sound like she'd done him a favor, instead of the reverse.

'I loved it too. I wouldn't have missed it.' She knew it was such an important part of his life, as was his music. 'And I'm glad I got to meet Frank and George. Particularly George, even if he wasn't impressed.'

'I'll discuss it with him in the morning. He really has to behave better when someone I really care about comes to visit. He hasn't had any experience with that,' he said with a gentle glance into her eyes, as the doorman turned away discreetly. She didn't know what to answer. She was too touched to think of anything to say.

'Thank you,' she whispered, as he put a finger under her chin, and tilted her face up to his. She thought he was going to kiss her, and she wanted him to, but she was scared.

'I meant what I said. I'm not going to do anything you don't want me to do, Stevie. This is just the beginning. And we have all the time in the world.' She nodded, and her eyes filled with tears at how kind he was. He kissed her on the cheek then and walked her inside. He left her at the elevator, and she hugged him and thanked him again. She wasn't sure what she was thanking him for, dinner, the visit, letting her be in the studio, seeing his home, or the extraordinary human being he was. And as she walked into her room in a daze over everything she had seen and experienced that night, she realized it was everything, the remarkable combination of who he was. When she got into bed in her nightgown a few minutes later, she fell asleep in five minutes with an enormous feeling of peace and well-being. She had never been as comfortable with anyone in her life.

Chapter 11

The morning after their late-night studio session, Chase called Stephanie at ten a.m. about the 'surprise' he had mentioned the night before. He didn't explain what it was but told her to be ready to leave at eleven, and he wouldn't give her even a hint of what was in store. She couldn't even guess and had no idea what to expect.

'What should I wear?' She sounded perplexed.

'Oh . . . let's see . . . how about a ballgown? I'd love to see you in a sexy evening dress.' And then he chuckled. 'Just kidding. Wear whatever you want, shorts, jeans, something comfortable.'

'Running shoes? Hiking boots?'

'Anything goes. Barefoot if you like.' In the end, she put on white denim shorts and a pink T-shirt, and wore her sandals, and she was in the lobby right on time. He pulled up in the Corvette, and as soon as she noticed the stir it was causing, she ran outside. There was already a crowd gathering around the car, when people realized it was Chase Taylor. She slipped between the fans, opened the door, and hopped into the car, and Chase waved at the onlookers as they sped off.

'Sorry. I came out as fast as I could, before one of the fans got into the car instead of me.'

He laughed. He was used to it. But she wasn't yet, and people were even more aware of him here than they had been in Las Vegas. He was a huge star here and exactly why people came to Nashville, to see country music celebrities like him, and he was one of the biggest. It still amazed her that she was riding around Nashville in the Corvette with a big country music star. To her, now he was just Chase.

He drove onto the highway, heading in the direction of the airport, and pointed out Opryland to her a little while later, where everything had started, and she wondered where they were going as they drove by it. He took a turn right before the airport and pulled up in front of a hangar, where a small private jet was waiting. It was a Falcon, and the pilot, copilot, and stewardess were waiting outside expectantly, and smiled when they drove up, and Chase stopped the car and turned off the engine as Stephanie looked at him.

'We're flying somewhere?' She was surprised.

'Yes, we are. It's a long drive but a short flight from here, and it's something you have to see. An important piece of Tennessee folklore and history, but not exactly the Grand Canyon.' The look in his eyes said he was teasing her as they boarded the plane. Even more than on his bus, she was in awe of the sheer luxury of the plane, and the fact that he had chartered it just for her. It was above and beyond anything she could have imagined, or would expect anyone to do for her. She didn't have the remotest idea where they were going.

It was noon when they took off, having avoided all the chaos of the airport and security. They just drove up, parked, and boarded the plane. The stewardess offered her coffee, tea, soft drinks, or champagne, and Stephanie had just finished a cup of coffee with croissants while chatting with Chase, when the pilot radioed to the tower in Memphis that they were coming in for a landing. They were assigned a runway after circling for five minutes. Stephanie looked out the window and still couldn't guess why they had come here as they made a smooth landing, and taxied up to a private hangar similar to the one they had departed from in Nashville. An SUV with a driver was waiting for them.

'Come on, Chase, where are we going?' She was dying to know, as they got into the car and the driver took off.

'You'll see,' Chase said mysteriously, thoroughly enjoying the secret. Stephanie had absolutely no way of guessing what he had in mind.

It was a short drive from the airport, and only when

they turned down Elvis Presley Boulevard did Stephanie begin to suspect. They stopped in front of a large home with tall white columns that she had already noticed were typical of many fine homes in the south. Two white lions sat on brick pedestals out front, and the sign that said 'Graceland' finally told her where she was. He had brought her to the famed home of Elvis Presley in Memphis, for the tour that was a must. She turned to Chase with a broad grin the moment she read the sign.

'You are so funny to do this. I never even thought of it!' She was delighted and intrigued to be there.

'You have to see it. I'd have driven you, but it's a three-and-a-half-hour drive, and we just didn't have time. So I thought we'd come by plane.' She knew he had spent a fortune to get her there, and had been incredibly generous and thoughtful to think of it.

They took an audio tour of the downstairs, which included commentary by his daughter Lisa Marie, and sound clips of Elvis himself.

The upstairs was closed to the public, and Chase told her that he had heard they kept it private in deference to the family, although no one lived there anymore, and they didn't want fans gawking at the bathroom on the second floor where Elvis had died. So they were confined to the ground floor, where they saw Elvis's living room, music room, parents' bedroom, dining room, and kitchen, and

184

on a floor below it, his TV/media room, pool room, and the famed Jungle Room.

The dominant color, particularly in his parents' bedroom, was white, with a deep purple velvet bedspread, and his mother's closet had been sealed with glass to show off some of her clothes. Elvis's bedroom, on the closed second floor, was not on the tour. But in his TV room, they saw the three televisions he used to watch at the same time. His bar and billiards room were on display. The staircase to the upper floor was white with mirrors, and there were stained-glass panels of brightly colored peacocks. Parts of the house were gaudy, as Stephanie would have expected, and she was reminded on the tour that he had bought the house at twenty-two years of age.

After the main house, they visited the museum and trophy building, with his vast collection of gold and platinum records, his wedding tuxedo, and Priscilla's wedding dress. They quickly saw his father's office, and Elvis's shooting range and racquetball building, which had become home to some of his most extraordinary costumes, sequined and gold jumpsuits, and a stunning array of the outfits he was remembered for having performed in. It was an amazing collection of his clothes.

They saw thirty-three of his vehicles, including his famed pink Cadillac, a 1975 Ferrari, a 1956 Cadillac Eldorado convertible, a red MG, several Stutz Blackhawks, Harley-Davidson motorcycles, and more. And they finished the tour in the Meditation Garden where Elvis was buried, near his parents and grandmother, and from there, Chase and Stephanie walked back onto the street. It had been fascinating and a piece of folklore that Stephanie wouldn't have wanted to miss. It was an odd experience going there, and some of it was a tribute to bad taste, but it was the symbol of an era, and a personal view of a man who had made huge contributions to American popular culture and had been revered by generations. She was thrilled that they had come, and grateful to Chase for bringing her, and taking the time from his busy life to do so.

'I loved it,' she said quietly to Chase as they walked back to the car. As always when visiting someone's home, once they were gone, one felt slightly in awe of moving in what had once been their footsteps and glimpsing their private lives, and yet Elvis and the family had wanted people to be there, keeping his memory alive. 'Thank you for bringing me,' she said as they drove back to the airport. And half an hour later they were back on the plane and in the air heading toward Nashville, where she got another glimpse of the Mississippi River. They ate sandwiches on the plane and were back at Chase's home in Brentwood by four-thirty. Chase had to do some more work in his office, so she lay next to the pool, and she thought about what they'd seen that day and since she arrived. Her favorite so far had been Andrew Jackson's home, The Hermitage, but she agreed with Chase that Graceland was a must. And it had been an ideal way to see it. Chase was doing so much to make her comfortable and happy, show her his city, and do everything possible to make her feel welcome and at home. Chase was a remarkable man.

He joined her at the pool at six o'clock, just before the band arrived. They had a quick dinner in the kitchen, and by seven they were back at work in the studio, changing arrangements and recording Sandy's voice, and then Chase's, as he sang two new songs. He still wasn't happy with the mix, and they made several corrections that night. He was a perfectionist about every detail, and Stephanie had new respect and insight into what it took to record an album. They finished that night at two o'clock in the morning, and he drove her back to the hotel again. He looked tired, after another long day, partially because of her, since he had spent most of the day taking her to Graceland. She thanked him for it again when she got out of the car, and told him he didn't have to get out.

'I've got a lot of paperwork to do tomorrow, and some writing on that last song. I'm not happy with the lyrics. But you're welcome to spend the day at the house with me. You can lie by the pool while I work.'

'I don't want to intrude,' she said politely, hesitant to bother him while he worked.

'You're not. I love having you around.' He smiled the

smile that women swooned over. 'Bring your bathing suit. We'll take it easy. I'll cook you dinner tomorrow night. I gave the boys the night off.' It sounded very appealing, and she agreed. 'Just come on over whenever you wake up. Call Wanda, she'll pick you up.' Stephanie had her own car, but Chase wanted her driven. She promised to call his assistant, and went back to her hotel room after an amazing day. Everything about Nashville was fantastic so far, especially Chase.

She took him at his word and called Wanda the next day, who showed up in the vintage red Chevrolet truck at noon and drove her out to the house, offered her something to drink, and then disappeared discreetly. Stephanie changed into her bathing suit in a changing room and lay on a chaise longue next to the pool with some magazines and a book. Chase wandered out of the house at three o'clock. He looked relaxed in bare feet, a white T-shirt, and torn jeans, and sat down on the chair next to hers. She had been dozing in the sun after a swim. It was a hot day, and the iced tea that Wanda had given her was still sitting next to her.

'Hi.' She smiled at him lazily. He had some sheet music in his arms, and a stack of printed e-mails and notes. 'How's your work going?'

'Okay. I'm still stuck on those damn lyrics, but I got a lot done today. Sometimes you just have to sit there and do it.' But it was a nice way to work, at home, in a house as beautiful as his. Stephanie felt peaceful being there, and had enjoyed the silence all afternoon. He lay down in the chair next to her then and began scribbling some notes, and then turned to her with a look of frustration, and handed her the piece of paper he'd been writing on. 'What would you add to that? I need two more lines for the refrain. I'm no writer, I'm a musician. I hate having to do both.'

She closed her eyes and thought about it for a long moment, then took the pencil from him and scribbled something, and handed it back to him.

'I'm no writer either. How does that sound?' She looked hesitant. He read it, nodded, and looked at her with a broad grin.

'You're better than you think. That's good. Very good. It works.' He sang it a capella with the rest of the refrain, and it sounded good to her too. 'You got the beat just right. It's all about the beat – you can't have an extra syllable hanging out there. And I like the words. You're hired,' he said, as he set the paper down, pulled off his T-shirt, took off his jeans with a swimsuit under them, and dove into the pool. He had a long lean athletic body, and he surfaced at the other end after swimming the length of the pool, and then swam back to her. 'I like it when you're here, Stevie. This is nice. I don't feel like I have to entertain you, but I like knowing you're around somewhere. You're easy to be with. And you write good lyrics.' He grinned at her.

'Thank you. I like being here too.' They sat side by side at the pool, each of them reading after that until the end of the afternoon. Wanda called out to him from the house when she left for the day, and it was pleasant knowing that he didn't have to work in the studio that night and could do things at his own pace and relax.

They sat at the pool until almost seven o'clock, and then he asked her if she was hungry. He had promised to cook dinner for her, and they went to look at what was in the fridge. He had a daily housekeeper who took care of the house and shopped for groceries for him, but he didn't like having staff there at night, unless he was working and needed help serving food.

They decided on steaks and a big salad, and he had just started heating the grill when they saw Bobby Joe walk through the garden to the little gingerbread house at the other end, where Sandy lived. She had a separate entrance, but Bobby Joe knew the code and often came through the main gate.

'That damn kid. I keep telling him to go the other way and he never does.' They saw him with Sandy a few minutes later, and she waved. Stephanie went outside to call across the garden to her, and she could see that Bobby Joe was scowling and looking unhappy about something, but Sandy looked happy, blew Stevie a kiss, waved goodbye, and then went behind her house to get her car.

'Bobby Joe's not looking too happy,' Stephanie commented while he cooked their steaks.

'He never does. I keep telling Sandy, he's jealous of her. She's going to go a long, long way and be a big star, and he knows it, and he's not. He's good enough, but he doesn't have what it takes. He'll always try to make her feel bad for that. It'll never work. He'll just keep grinding at her, and bitching and sulking, and punishing her, until she gets tired of it. She'll figure it out. He's not a bad kid, just kind of mediocre and a jerk. She can do better than that. She needs someone who's proud of her and makes her feel good about herself. That's what we all need,' he said, smiling at Stephanie as she finished tossing the salad, and he put their steaks on two plates.

'It sounds easy, but that's harder to find than you think.' Bill had often been critical of her too, and she didn't like it. And she hated the kind of snide cutting comments that Fred and Jean made to and about each other. It was so easy to take cheap shots.

'Yeah, it is,' he agreed, as they sat down at the big round table in his kitchen. He had put out placemats and linen napkins, which he admitted he only bothered to do when he had guests. 'I never had that problem with Tamra. She wasn't one for subtle comments and put-downs. She just hit me on the side of the head, or took a swing at me. She was more direct.' He laughed as he said it, and Stephanie could just imagine what she'd been like. A wild country girl with a hot temper and loose fists. It seemed like a poor match with his gentle, patient ways, but that was probably why it had worked for as long as it did. 'She went after me with a frying pan once. She was very down market.' He chuckled. 'I've never hit a woman in my life, and she took full advantage of it.' Stephanie was sure she did, and then looked worried.

'Do you think Bobby Joe hits Sandy?' He had seemed pretty angry a few minutes before, and once on the bus, when he wanted to go to the casino and she didn't and had to work.

'No, I don't,' Chase said, and appeared relaxed. 'I'd kill him if he did, and put him in prison after that. He just hurts her with what he says. He's always pissed off. She'll get tired of it eventually. We all do.' The steaks were delicious, and she told him so, and he was pleased. 'I like to cook. I don't get much time for it, but I can do anything I want in this kitchen. It's got some pretty fancy stuff. Most of the time I just make ribs or steak. I'm a southern boy.' He grinned at her. 'I make pretty good grits too, but you have to be southern to like them. You can't feed a Yankee girl on grits,' he teased her, and she laughed.

'I should try them while I'm here.'

'You won't like 'em. Most Yankees don't. They're a southern thing.' She forgot how southern he was at times, but she liked that about him, good manners and respect for women, and a certain old-fashioned courtliness despite the long hair and tattoos, which she was getting to like too. They went with his look, and it worked on him. He was so good looking, he could get away with it, and even not shaving for several days, which made him even sexier.

He offered her an Eskimo bar for dessert, and they sat talking in his kitchen about the work he had to do that week, and the concert they were playing that weekend.

'I'm going to see Michael in Atlanta tomorrow,' she told Chase. 'I called him this morning, and he's free tomorrow night. Unfortunately, I have to invite Amanda too. They're a package deal.'

'Why don't you invite him to the concert this weekend? I'd love to meet him and his southern belle.'

'She's a piece of work,' Stephanie said, looking unhappy. Amanda had been involved with Michael for three years, and was beginning to look like she might be there to stay. He had met her when he first moved to Atlanta, and hadn't dated anyone else since. She was the same age as he was. Stephanie and Louise thought she was manipulative, always trying to work Michael toward her goal of marriage, although she was always sickeningly polite, and seemed insincere to them.

'Maybe he'll meet someone else.' Chase was optimistic.

'I don't think so,' she said, worried. 'He's a very loyal

guy. He never looks at other girls. He's been with her since he was twenty-two, too young to settle down. She's got a prize and she knows it. She's not going to let him go,' Stephanie said.

'You settled down when you were very young,' Chase pointed out to her, and he was right.

'Yeah, but I'm a girl, and his father was twenty-six.' That was only a year older than Michael was now, which scared her even more.

'Well, ask him to the concert. I want to meet your boy. Hopefully, you'll meet mine too, one day.' He had thought of dropping in to see him at work the day before when they went to Memphis, but they didn't have time since he had to get back to work himself.

'I hope I will,' Stephanie said kindly, and promised to ask Michael to come to the concert when she saw him the next day.

'How long will you be in Atlanta?' he asked, seeming worried.

'Just one night. He's too busy to have me hang around. The Braves keep him running all over the place. He never gets home to San Francisco anymore, except for Thanksgiving and Christmas.'

'That's the way it works when they grow up,' Chase said philosophically. 'I'm going to miss you,' he added. 'What am I going to do when you go back to California?' She wasn't sure what she was going to do either. She was having such a good time with him. But they had done pretty well so far. They had managed to turn a single VIP comp concert ticket into a nine-day adventure, and she hadn't left for San Francisco yet, and wasn't sure when she would. She was thinking about stopping to see Louise in New York on the way back, as long as she was this far east. She hadn't made up her mind yet, or talked to Louise about it, who might be too busy for a visit anyway. Louise worked hard at her job too.

'I've been thinking the same thing, about when I go back,' she admitted, with a wistful look.

'Then don't leave, Stevie,' he said as he put an arm around her, and then circled her with the other arm and held her close. She didn't pull away or resist. She felt safe and comfortable in his arms and had gotten used to him day by day.

'I have to,' but she couldn't remember why, as she said it.

'No, you don't,' he argued softly, his face very close to hers. 'You can do anything you want . . . like stay here.'

'And what would I do here?' she asked in a whisper. She had no life here, except in relation to him, although she loved being there and everything they did.

'You could write lyrics for me,' he answered, 'or we'll figure out something.' And before she could answer him again, he kissed her gently on the lips, and she felt as though her head were spinning. His lips were as gentle as butterfly wings, and yet his kiss was strong and deep, and she was breathless when he gently pulled away and looked down at her, with the most loving look in his eyes she'd ever seen. 'I'm crazy about you, Stevie,' he said softly. 'I don't want you to leave. I will miss you every day until you get there, as soon as you leave. This has never happened to me before.'

'Me neither,' she said, and he kissed her again, and this time it was filled with more passion on both sides, not just tenderness. He was hungry for her but didn't want to scare her. He knew how new this was to her. But she didn't feel frightened in his arms.

'I don't want you to go,' he said again.

'We'll have to figure this out,' she said vaguely, but she didn't see how. She had a life and house and friends and history in San Francisco, and a home that her children expected to come home to for holidays and family events. And he had a life and career in Nashville that was a major enterprise and industry and couldn't be ignored. They weren't kids with a movable life, and they lived across the country, in entirely different worlds. She reminded herself too that they hardly knew each other, and she couldn't throw her whole life out the window after ten days, but he wasn't asking her to. He was telling her how much he cared about her and wished she could stay, which was enough for now. It didn't scare her, but she didn't see how they could resolve it.

They kissed again as they left the kitchen, and they watched a movie together, lying on his king-size bed, with Frank and George on either side of them. George snored so loudly while he was sleeping, they had to turn up the volume on the movie so they could hear it, and they both laughed. She even loved his dogs. Most of his girlfriends had hated his dogs, and said they should be yard dogs, and Tamra had been allergic to them, so he really did have to keep them outside until she left. But Stephanie loved the fact that he had dogs.

He didn't try to make love to her that night. He just lay next to her with an arm around her, holding her close, and they kissed from time to time. It was sweet and innocent. They were in no rush, although she could feel how powerful his body was, and sense his passion when he kissed her, but he never pushed her farther than she wanted to go, nor lost control of himself. He was a wise and gentle man, which made her feel completely safe.

'There's no room for me in your bed anyway,' she teased him, pointing at the dogs, when they talked about not rushing into making love. It was a big commitment that neither of them wanted to make lightly, until they were sure of what they felt. It was still very new, and they both agreed it was smarter to wait awhile. 'The boys take up the whole bed,' she said, as Frank stretched his long legs in his sleep, pushing her closer to Chase, and George snored even louder.

'I think we can work something out. I'll talk to the boys about it,' Chase assured her. 'Maybe we can negotiate time-shares on the bed.' They both laughed, and after the movie, they lay there and kissed for a while. He was dying to feel her body naked on his, and the wait to discover it was tantalizing, but they agreed it would only make things better once they decided they were ready. 'I hope our kids are as sensible as we are, before starting relationships,' Chase said, laughing.

'I doubt it,' Stephanie commented. 'I don't think that happens till you're our age.'

'It's never happened to me before,' he admitted. He had been impulsive about his sexual and amorous entanglements in the past, which had always gotten him into trouble. This time they were both being smart.

And with regret they got off his bed and went downstairs. He drove her back to the hotel, and they lingered in his car, kissing, before she got out. He had told her where to stay in Atlanta, which was a better hotel than the one she usually stayed at. And she promised to call him when she got there. It was a four-hour drive from Nashville, and she was planning to walk around, do some shopping, maybe go to a museum, and meet up with her son after work, with Amanda, for dinner. And she was going to return to Nashville the next day.

'We'll go out to dinner when you come back. There are some great restaurants here.' He was dedicating all his spare time to her – he wanted to spend as much time as he could with her before she left Nashville. 'Have fun in Atlanta,' he said, as he kissed her for a last time and looked into her eyes. 'Should I tell you again how much I'm going to miss you?' She smiled at him. It was nice to hear.

'I'll call you tomorrow,' she said, then ran into the hotel, waved from the door, and hurried upstairs to her room. She still had to pack for her overnight stay in Atlanta. She was leaving the rest of her things at her room at the Hermitage Hotel, which seemed simpler for one night.

Chase called her on her cell phone just as she was about to go to sleep. She answered it and could hear a roaring engine before she heard his voice, then realized it was George snoring, when Chase said hello and she started laughing. 'Do you have any idea what it sounds like with George lying next to you?' Chase laughed too, told her to sleep tight, and they hung up. She fell asleep thinking about him and how nice it had been lying in his arms. She hadn't been kissed like that in a long time.

Chapter 12

Stephanie woke up at seven a.m. to drive to Atlanta. She left the hotel at seven-thirty for the four-hour-plus drive, and checked into the Ritz-Carlton on Peachtree Street that Chase had recommended. It was as lovely as he had said, and her room had a perfect view of the Atlanta skyline. She spent the afternoon walking around Atlanta, went to the High Museum, and waited to see Michael when he finished work. They met in the lobby of her hotel at six o'clock.

Amanda was with him, and she was as perfectly groomed as he was. He had to wear a suit and tie at the Braves. She worked for an ad agency as a junior copywriter and had a good job. She had gone to Duke and was a bright girl, but there was something sharp and cunning about her that Stephanie had never liked. She was very ambitious and very demanding of Michael. They each had their own apartments in the Atlantic Station area, but they had spent virtually every night together at Michael's for the past two years. He made noises occasionally about renting an apartment together, but much to his mother's relief, they still hadn't. She was still hoping that Michael would break up with her eventually, and keeping their own apartments was simpler. Amanda had always had an agenda.

She'd been pressuring Michael for a while to get a better-paying job so they could buy an apartment or a house together, but Michael was in love with his job with the Braves. And in the three years since he graduated from college, he had done well. Stephanie was satisfied with his progress and thought he was nicer to Amanda than she deserved. Her mother was in real estate, very successfully, and her father worked for a bank. And she had an older brother and sister who were successful in business, and both were married. In their family, money was key.

'Where would you two like to have dinner?' Stephanie asked them, and Amanda immediately suggested Bacchanalia, an expensive restaurant where they'd been before. She knew that Michael preferred more casual dinners, but he deferred to her. It was the kind of aggressive greediness, typical of Amanda, that always annoyed Stephanie, and concerned her for the future.

They were already having dinner when Michael asked his mother what she was doing in that part of the world.

He'd been startled when she'd called him and offered to come to Atlanta the next day.

'I'm a little bit at loose ends right now,' she said honestly with a sigh, and they both knew why. 'I got an invitation from a friend from college who lives in Nashville. I haven't seen her in years, and I thought it might be nice to come and see her. And it gives me a chance to see you too.' The drive cross country to see a long-lost friend was so unlike her that Michael didn't know what to say. He could always count on his mother to be in the same place. She never ventured far from home, and never on her own. Even when his father was alive, they had taken only modest trips to Tahoe, Santa Barbara, Los Angeles, Palm Springs, or New York to see his sisters, and they went to Europe once every few years. He couldn't even imagine her driving to Nashville, Tennessee, and even less so alone. She looked well though, and said she'd been having a good time.

'We went to Graceland yesterday,' she volunteered, which surprised him even more.

'Graceland? Since when are you interested in Elvis?' He had died when she was twelve, and she'd never listened to his music that he could remember. Her taste ran to other things, like ballads, Motown, or the occasional rap song they had played when they were young that she had liked.

'My friend suggested it, and I thought it would be interesting to see his home. It really is a phenomenon to see how someone like that lived. And Nashville is so alive with all the country music. Which reminds me. By a total fluke, I met Chase Taylor through my old friend. He's playing a concert this Saturday, and he invited you both to come, with VIP tickets, backstage passes, the whole shebang. I think you'd enjoy it. I'll go with you if you want.'

'How much longer will you be in Nashville, Mom?'

'Just a few more days. I'll stay till the concert if you decide to come. I want to see Louise in New York next week, and then I'll drive home.'

'By yourself?' He looked shocked when she nodded. 'You've become quite a wanderer since Dad died.' He sounded genuinely surprised and a little worried about her. She didn't tell him about Las Vegas, or the Grand Canyon where she had met Chase.

'I don't have much to do at home, except my volunteer work at the shelter, which is a little haphazard,' she said honestly. 'You guys are gone . . . and Daddy . . . there's nothing I have to do there now. Everyone I know is married and busy with their lives. I really want to get a job.' He felt suddenly sorry for her, and she could see it in his eyes.

'I'm sorry, Mom,' he said quietly, and he looked so much like her, it was startling. He was tall and thin and athletic, with the same blond hair and blue eyes. He was the male version of her. People always commented on it, and even she could see it now, as he gazed across the table at her with pity. He had suddenly gotten a glimpse of how lonely his mother was, enough to drive across the country to visit her son and daughter and a college friend. He didn't like to think of her traveling alone like that. It pushed the invitation to the concert right out of his head.

'I'm having a good time,' she said, and seemed to mean it, and she didn't mention how much she dreaded going home. 'What about the concert this weekend? It's on Saturday. He seems like a nice guy, and he's a big star.' She was grateful that Michael hadn't asked her the name of her college friend, she knew she would have had to come up with one fast.

'He sure is. And you're a country music fan?' It was a whole new side of her he'd never seen before.

'Not really,' she said honestly. He knew her better than that. She couldn't lie to him about everything, and she never had. She hated doing it, but she had no other choice. There was no way he would understand the chance encounter at the Grand Canyon or what Chase was beginning to mean to her. And it was too soon after his father's death to introduce a new man into his life, or even into hers. 'But that's what Nashville is all about,' she added. 'Why don't you both come?'

Amanda seemed as though she liked the idea, particularly of the backstage passes, and the weekend with

Michael's mother, where she would score brownie points with her. Michael wasn't as sure, although he'd be happy to see his mother again.

'Can I let you know tomorrow, Mom? The team's away this weekend, but I think we had some plans.'

'Sure, sweetheart. He was very nice about getting us tickets. I can let him know tomorrow.' She tried to sound casual about it.

'I'd like to meet your college friend too,' he said warmly, trying to let her know that he cared about what she was doing and what was happening in her life.

Stephanie knew that if he came, she'd have to come up with an excuse for why her mythical friend wasn't there. Maybe she could say that she was sick, she thought to herself – if Michael came, which didn't sound like a sure thing. But she would have loved to introduce him to Chase. She was proud of her son. She smiled across the table at him, then glanced at Amanda. She was a pretty girl, with hair and eyes as dark as he was fair. There was just something so determined about her, as though she had Michael in her control, which made his mother nervous. Amanda seemed older than her years and ready to settle down. And Michael just seemed to be going along. He was innocent and young. Amanda was more mature for her age.

They had a nice dinner together, and then the two young people went home to his place, and Stephanie went back to her hotel. She was leaving the next morning to go back to Nashville, since he said he was busy all that day and evening. And Michael spoke to Amanda about his mother on the way home.

'I'm worried about her. She tries to act like she's happy, but I know she's sad.' He knew her well. 'She's lost without my dad.'

'Don't be silly,' Amanda dismissed his fears. 'She's never looked better. She's a beautiful woman. She'll have a new man in her life in no time. I'll bet she gets married again.' It was not what Michael wanted to hear.

'You don't know my mom. She really loved my dad, and was devoted to him. I'm sure she'll never marry again, or even have another man.'

'At forty-eight?' Amanda laughed at him. 'Dream on. She's pretty, she's got money, there will be a man in her life within a year.' Michael looked straight ahead as he drove home and didn't say a word. 'And look how independent she is. She drove all the way across the country alone.'

'She had to be desperate to do that,' he said through nearly clenched teeth. Amanda wasn't listening to him and had missed the point of his concern. 'She doesn't even like to go to Tahoe alone.'

'Maybe she turned over a new leaf when your dad died. I think it's great. And look at all the people she's meeting. What about the concert on Saturday night?'

'I'm not that crazy about country music. Are you?'

'Who cares? VIP tickets and backstage passes to meet Chase Taylor is pretty sweet.'

'Yeah, I guess.' He didn't look excited about it.

'I'd like to go,' she said firmly. 'Besides, it would be nice to see your mom again. Why don't we go?'

'I'll call her tomorrow,' he said, looking unhappy.

And in her hotel room, Stephanie was talking to Chase. 'How was it?' he asked her.

'Nice with Michael, except for Miss Control. I always feel that she has him by the throat and runs his life.'

'Did you invite him to the show?'

'He said he'd let me know tomorrow. I got the feeling that she wants to go.'

'Good. Then I'll get to meet them both. I want to check out this girl myself. I'll let you know what I think.'

'I hope they come.' She liked the idea of seeing her son again and had taken a reservation for them at the Hermitage Hotel just in case. 'I'll be back in Nashville tomorrow by lunchtime,' she said, and he sounded pleased.

'I'll pick you up in the afternoon, and we can come back to the house. I have rehearsal tomorrow night for the show.'

'That sounds like a plan. See you tomorrow,' she said warmly, but when she hung up, she was thinking about her son. No matter how polite and pleasant Amanda was to her, she just never liked her. And she always, like Michael, did whatever Amanda wanted. She ran the show.

Michael called her as soon as she got back to the hotel in Nashville, and he surprised her. They had decided to come for the concert. He told her honestly that Amanda wanted to meet Chase.

'He's a nice guy. You'll like him too. And his music is really good.' She didn't tell him that she had helped him with a few lyrics to one of his songs, or that she had watched them record an album, or that she'd driven to Nashville with him. There was a lot Michael didn't know, and didn't need to for now.

He said they'd be in Nashville on Saturday afternoon before the show, and she promised to meet him at the hotel. Chase would be busy at the Bridgestone Arena, where the Country Music Association Awards were held every year, but this was an independent concert set up by a famous promoter of country music. It was a venue that Chase liked, and he was looking forward to it.

She was pleased she would see Michael again before she left for San Francisco. When Chase picked her up that afternoon, she told him and he was happy for her. He was excited to see her, and gave her a kiss as soon as they drove away from the hotel. He had a lot to tell her about their preparations for the concert the next day, and Chase looked annoyed when they got to his house and he saw a dozen tourists outside, holding a map. They were easy to get at the visitors' center and the Ernest Tubb Record Shop, which sold maps to the homes of the stars. Chase took one look, then drove past the house and behind the property, to the entrance to Sandy's house. Her car wasn't there, and he could see she was out as they drove through the back gate and parked the Corvette in the garage. It would have been easier living in a gated community, or behind tall walls, but he loved his house. It was worth putting up with the occasional tourists gawking outside, or tour buses that drove by. They couldn't see anything from the street, and they kept the shades closed on the front of the house. And all the windows had been replaced with bulletproof glass before he moved in. Stephanie thought it was sad that he had to worry about things like that. But it was a reality for him and the price of being a major star.

They chatted in the kitchen while he checked his e-mails at his desk, and answered a few. Wanda came in and out and said hello to Stevie. She had become a fixture overnight, and Wanda liked her and could tell that Chase was very taken with her. And finally the band arrived, and they started rehearsal in the studio and played until midnight, stopping only for a quick dinner. He'd written a new song for Sandy and was introducing two for himself. They all agreed that the show was strong and fresh, and Stephanie liked their new songs. During a break he whispered to her that one of them was about her. It was called 'The Country Boy and the Lady' and he was going to try it out for the first time in public on Saturday night. She loved it when she heard the words. He told her he'd written it since their return to Nashville, entirely inspired by her. The melody was as beautiful as the lyrics.

After rehearsal, they made out in his car like two teenagers when he took her back to the hotel. Things were heating up between them, like a slow blaze taking hold.

The next day she waited at the Hermitage Hotel for Michael and Amanda to arrive. When they did, Amanda looked genuinely excited about the concert, and Michael was happy to see his mother. They wandered around some of the music shops that afternoon, enjoying the live music, and Michael asked about her friend, whom he was looking forward to meeting. Stephanie turned to him with a disappointed look, exhibiting acting skills she never knew she had.

'Shit luck. She came down with the flu last night, and she's sick as a dog. I'm so disappointed. I wanted you to meet her, although she tells some pretty awful stories about me in college that you don't need to hear.' He smiled. 'She called Chase Taylor, and he's giving us the tickets and passes anyway. Everybody seems to know people involved in music here. So we're all set for tonight.'

'That's too bad she's sick,' Michael said, thoroughly convinced. It never dawned on him that his mother would lie. Or be involved with a country music star. Both concepts would have seemed preposterous to him, and Stephanie felt a little guilty for not telling him the truth, and hoped that nothing she or Chase said that night would give them away. She had told him the story she would tell Michael, and they had picked a fictional name for her college friend. Laura Perkins. It sounded perfectly credible to them, and it did to Michael too.

They had dinner at the hotel's excellent Capitol Grille that night, and at eight o'clock they left for the Bridgestone Arena, where Stephanie knew Chase had been rehearsing and setting up for the past eight hours. He always oversaw the preparations himself, and never trusted the event producers or venue managers to do it right. He had sent a car and driver for them, which Michael thought his mother had arranged, and as soon as they showed their tickets, they were escorted to the first row, dead center, where Chase would be only a few feet away from them. Amanda was so excited, she was practically squealing and called a friend from work on her cell to tell them where they were, and that they'd be meeting Chase backstage.

'I never knew you liked him this much,' Michael said, looking surprised.

'Are you kidding? He's gorgeous,' she said, with her heavy southern drawl. She always made a point of saying that southern men were better looking than Yankees, 'except for Michael, of course.' But the added compliment never sounded totally sincere. She chatted with Stephanie then, while Michael checked the baseball scores on his BlackBerry. The Braves were in Philadelphia that night, and he was happy he didn't have to go. He went to a lot of their out-of-town games. Amanda loved going with him, especially when they stayed at fancy hotels, paid for by the team, who treated their employees very well. And she liked their room at the Hermitage Hotel too. His mother was always very generous with them. Amanda just expected it, but Stephanie did it for her son.

The arena was packed, and the concert was due to start at eight-thirty, but it didn't begin till nine. Stephanie wondered what was happening and hoped nothing was wrong, but she couldn't go backstage to ask. Sandy had been feeling squeamish that day, and she hoped she wasn't sick. The last time she had spoken to Chase was before dinner, and he had said that everything was fine. He had sounded busy, and they had gotten off quickly. And as she started to worry, the house lights went down, and the opening band started playing. Bobby Joe and his group played a short set and left the stage. And then the big band came on, and the music exploded through the sound system, and a moment later Chase was on the stage, as dynamic as ever, grabbing the audience's attention, and his fans screamed his name as he started to sing one of his new songs. He saved the one about Stephanie almost till the end, and the audience fell in love with him all over again.

She could see that Amanda was mesmerized, and Michael was enjoying it too. The concert had been fabulous, and the crowd applauded and screamed and begged for encores when it was over, and he played three. And then he took his final bow and left the stage as the spotlight followed him off. It had been a fantastic performance, and Amanda was jumping up and down and clapping her hands, as an usher appeared next to them and asked them to come backstage. Chase had looked straight at her several times during the performance with a look that was filled with his feelings for her, but the people around them just thought it was part of his act, and she was a lucky fan. But she knew exactly what it meant, just as she did when he sang the song he'd written for her. She just hoped Michael didn't figure it out too, but there was no reason why he would.

They followed the usher up onto the stage, into the backstage area, past all the sound technicians, and into a trailer they had set up for Chase behind the arena. It was almost as luxurious as his bus. Amanda was wide-eyed as they walked up the steps into it. Stephanie introduced them both to Chase.

'Thanks so much for coming to the performance,' Chase said to Michael, who looked amazed.

'Thank you for the tickets.' They talked about baseball for a few minutes, and Chase said he was a Braves fan. Chase couldn't have been more welcoming to both young people, and he gave nothing away when he spoke to Stephanie. He played it to perfection when he told her how sorry he was that Laura couldn't come and he hoped she wasn't too sick. Stephanie assured him it was just the flu, just as Sandy bounded into the trailer with a look of fury and walked right up to Chase, oblivious to Michael and Amanda, and even to Stephanie for once, as Michael stared at her. She was wearing the sequined cowboy shirt and skin-tight jeans she'd worn on stage, and her straight blond hair was hanging down her back to her waist.

'Bobby Joe is such an asshole!' she said to her guardian, and even surprised him. 'He said I sang flat for the first half of the show, and I was completely off by an octave for the new song.' Chase tried to keep a straight face. It was just more of Bobby Joe's antics to make her feel bad about herself. She still hadn't figured it out.

'You were great!' he reassured her. 'Believe me, if you'd sung flat or been off by an octave, I'd have given you shit myself. He's just jealous, and we cut his set short tonight because of the new songs. He's just pissed.' And then he reminded her of her manners. 'Sandy, we have guests. This is Stephanie's son Michael from Atlanta, and his girlfriend Amanda.' He looked serious and circumspect as he said it and gave her a look to telegraph to her not to say too much. She got it immediately. She was a very bright girl.

'Oh, hi,' she said, looking embarrassed. 'Sorry for the complaints. My boyfriend thinks my singing sucks,' she said, looking up at Michael, thinking she had never seen anyone as handsome in her life, except maybe Chase.

'You were fantastic,' Michael reassured her, as their eyes met and held. Stephanie felt as though she could see sparks coming from them, and she smiled. Amanda was too busy fawning over Chase to notice. She had her back turned to Michael and never saw the exchange. But Chase did, and so did Stephanie. Something had happened between the two young people without words.

'I need to rehearse that song some more,' Sandy said vaguely, but she looked as though she had no idea what she was saying, and Michael didn't seem to care. 'You live in Atlanta?'

'Yes, I do. I work for the Braves.'

'I love baseball,' she said suddenly sounding very southern, even more so than Amanda, who was charming Chase, and he kept her busy so Michael and Sandy could talk. He was on Stephanie's team.

'You'll have to come for a home game sometime,' Michael said vaguely to Sandy, his eyes never leaving hers, oblivious to Amanda.

'I'd like that,' Sandy said, completely forgetting about Amanda, and that she had a boyfriend herself. It was as though Michael and Sandy were alone in the room. And then more people crowded into the trailer, Chase got busy, Sandy was pulled away to talk to someone, and Stephanie led Michael and Amanda out of the trailer. She noticed that her son seemed dazed. Amanda was talking to him a mile a minute about how incredible Chase was and how charming, and he didn't hear a word. He glanced at his mother with a blank look, as though he were under a spell and a bomb had hit him the minute Sandy walked in. She was seven years younger than he was, just eighteen, but he didn't care. She was the most beautiful, enchanting girl he had ever seen.

They had a nightcap at the hotel at the Oak Bar, and Michael literally didn't say a word.

'Are you okay, sweetheart?' his mother asked him, and he nodded.

'Yeah, I'm fine. We lost tonight in Philly.'

'Oh, I'm sorry.' But they both knew he wasn't thinking about the Braves. She wondered if he would say anything to her about Sandy, but he couldn't. And he had no idea how well his mother knew her. Amanda was still rhapsodizing about Chase.

The young couple went to their room shortly afterward, and Amanda thanked her profusely for the tickets. Michael just said he was really tired and disappeared into the room.

Stephanie went to her room, lay down on the bed, and

turned on the TV. It was two hours later when Chase called her after he left the arena, while the band was still packing up their equipment, and he was on his way home. He had been there for fourteen hours and he was tired, but it had been a very successful show.

'It was terrific,' she told him, as she turned down the TV. And she was happy that her son had suspected nothing between them. Chase had played it very straight, out of deference to her.

'Yeah, it was pretty good,' he said, as he drove the Corvette with the top down. It was a beautiful June night under a full moon. 'I think we had some magic here tonight.'

'I loved our song,' she said, still very moved that he had written it for her and sung it while looking at her that night.

'Me too. But that's not what I meant. I meant in the trailer afterward. Your son looked like he was about to faint when Sandy walked in. I heard birds chirping, harps playing, violins. The two of them looked mesmerized by each other. I tried to keep Little Miss Busybody occupied so she didn't notice.' Stephanie laughed at what he said.

'I thought maybe you were falling for her,' Stephanie teased him.

'Not likely. And I know exactly what you mean about her. I know the type. She's pushy, but in a very hidden way. Even hardly knowing her, I got the feeling that she's

217

after money. It's all she talks about, who has what. But I think something happened there tonight, with Sandy. I hope he does something about it.'

'I doubt he will. He's totally faithful to Amanda. It's a terrible thing to say, but I'm not even sure he loves her.'

'Yeah, but something happened tonight,' Chase insisted, trusting his instincts, and Stephanie hoped he was right. 'It was like watching a movie. He fell for her like a ton of bricks, and so did she. Sandy was telling him how much she loves baseball. Hell, she doesn't know a ball from a bat.' Stephanie was still laughing, and she wondered if Chase was right and something might come of it. It seemed unlikely to her, but stranger things had happened. She had met Chase. 'Can you slip him her number somehow?'

'I don't know how. What would be the excuse?' Stephanie asked him.

'Tell him to invite her to a game,' Chase said simply.

'Are you promoting a romance between your ward and my son?' she teased him.

'Yes, I am,' he said unashamedly. 'And I'll be doing you a big favor if it works,' he reminded her.

'Isn't that the truth. I'd owe you big time for that one!'

'I'll remind you of that one day.'

They talked about the concert again then, and he was pleased. He told her he'd call her the next day, when he woke up.

She was planning to see Amanda and Michael for brunch at the hotel before they headed back to Atlanta.

The next morning at the hotel restaurant, Stephanie thought that Michael still looked distracted, and he was unusually quiet, while Amanda chattered endlessly about the charms of Chase, how handsome he was, and how great the concert had been. She thanked Stephanie profusely for inviting them, and then went upstairs to pack her bag and brush her teeth before they left, while Michael spent the last few minutes with his mother.

'Mom,' he said, sounding serious for a minute, and she was suddenly worried that he would ask her again how she knew Chase, but he had given nothing away the night before, and neither had she. 'You wouldn't have his daughter's number, would you?' He didn't see why she would, but he had to ask, just in case. He looked desperate and almost sick, which touched her heart.

'Do you know what's funny? As a matter of fact I do. She was with Chase when my friend Laura introduced me to them, and she gave me her number. She's not his daughter, by the way. He's her guardian. Her parents died, and her father left her to Chase when she was fifteen. She told me all about it when she gave me her number.'

'How old is she?' He still looked concerned. He was afraid she might be sixteen or seventeen. She looked young.

'Eighteen.'

'She's legal at least,' he said with a grin, and his mother didn't say a word. She was ecstatic that he was even remotely interested in her. Maybe Chase was right, and she had seen the magic happen in the trailer the night before herself. Stephanie looked up Sandy's number on her cell phone and texted it to him. And as soon as she did, Amanda appeared back at the table, carrying her overnight bag and ready to leave.

Stephanie walked them out to Michael's car and hugged him and thanked him for coming.

'I'm glad I did,' he said, looking her in the eye, and she nodded and then hugged him again. She couldn't say anything about his calling Sandy in front of Amanda, but she hoped he would. And she knew she couldn't pry after this. He was a man. It was up to him. But her fingers were crossed that the magic had been real. She wanted that for him even more than she wanted Chase. Michael had his whole life ahead of him, and she wanted it to be good, not spent with a woman who didn't really love him and saw him as a good catch. Amanda had convinced Stephanie of it in the past three years.

She waved as they drove away, then went back to her room at the hotel. Chase called her a little while later, and she drove out to Brentwood to spend the day with him by the pool. He broached a painful subject with her that afternoon.

'When are you leaving, Stevie?' He knew it would be

soon. She had agreed to wait until after his concert, and she had wanted to see her son, but there were no more reasons left to delay. She had called Louise while she was waiting to hear from him, and she said that the only day she had time to see her mother was Thursday, which meant that Stephanie had to leave Nashville on Tuesday, to get from Nashville to New York in two days. It would give her another day together with Chase, but after that she had to face reality and leave. She was as sad about it as he was, and all Chase wanted was to figure out a reason for her to return. Soon. Or he'd go to California to see her if he had to. He couldn't imagine his life without her now.

'I'm leaving Tuesday,' she told him sadly, 'so I can get to New York Wednesday night. Louise has some time on Thursday, and Friday I'll head back to California.'

'Are you sure you don't want me to send you back on the bus and tow the car?' He was even more worried about her now that he knew her better. But she insisted she'd be fine.

'I'm a big girl.' She smiled at him. 'I've never done it before, but I kind of want to. I have a lot to think about on the way back.' Him, her life, and where to go from here.

'You could come back here,' he said hopefully, but he knew she wouldn't. At least not for a while. He wanted to give her space and time to assess her life and make some plans, but he wasn't going to stay away from her for long. He couldn't. She meant too much to him now, and she was under his skin, and woven into his heart.

'I'll come back to Nashville,' she said, and meant it. 'I just don't know when.'

'I can come out to see you.'

'I'd like that,' she said quietly. It would make him seem like part of her real life, not just a fantasy of some kind or a dream. The truth was pretty hard to believe. She had taken a wrong turn and gone to Las Vegas, met a country music superstar at the Grand Canyon, and been following him ever since, back to Vegas, across the country, and to Nashville, where she had never been happier in her life. But now she had to go home and figure out who she was without Bill. She had to put Bill to rest, before she could open her arms to Chase. She knew she was falling in love with him, but she didn't know what it meant, or how it would work, or if it even could.

She had been living her life in service to her husband and children for so long that without them now she felt as though she had no identity. And she wanted to come to Chase as a whole person, and not just become his shadow too. She felt like she had no shadow of her own, and the things that had validated her existence and identity were no longer true. She was no longer anyone's wife, which had been her principal role for twenty-six years. She had no children to take care of at home. She had no career. No one needed her anymore. She lived in an empty house in San Francisco, and she felt like a fifth wheel with her friends. But she couldn't just run away and hide in his very full life in Nashville. She had to find out who she was first, and her own identity, now that she was a free woman, not just attach herself to his. He understood that but it frightened him when she explained it to him over dinner that night, when they cooked together again, and chatted in his kitchen for a long time.

'I'll be waiting for you,' he said calmly, trying to sound more confident than he felt. What if she decided that she liked her old life best, with her old friends, and without him, in her familiar city and home? He wanted to share his world with her. But she was a woman with dignity, who wanted to establish some purpose in her life, and not be totally dependent on him to meet her needs. He loved her for it. He loved her for everything she was. He just hoped that she would find her way through the maze and come back to him. It was all he wanted now.

Chapter 13

Stephanie and Chase spent a quiet day together on Monday. She knew he had a lot to do, but he said he wanted to be with her. They took the dogs for a long walk in Centennial Park, as long as George would allow since he hated to walk and kept sitting down and glaring at them. They kept the conversation light and tried not to worry about the future. Neither of them knew what would happen. All they knew was how great the last two weeks had been. That was already something, and it felt like a huge blessing and stroke of luck to both of them. A few minutes more or less on the trail at the Grand Canyon, and they would never have met. She could have decided to drive straight back to San Francisco and not returned to Vegas, or never gone to the Grand Canyon at all, or not come to Nashville. Instead they had seized every opportunity they'd been given and made the best of it, and the result had been perfect. Neither of them would have traded the time they had shared for anything else in the world. Now they just had to figure out how to keep it going, with his very busy life, and hers three thousand miles away. And her life wasn't busy. Far from it. She seriously questioned how much she had to bring to the relationship. She had to find herself and get back her self-confidence before she could be with him. She had to sort it all out when she got home. And Chase truly hoped she would decide they should be together.

They lingered in each other's arms that night, and she was sorely tempted to make love with him. But she didn't want to confuse the issues further. She knew that once she did, her commitment to him would preclude all clear, rational thinking. She wanted to stay as lucid as she could while she thought about everything, and he didn't want to interfere with that, although he was dying to make love with her and had to force himself not to pressure her. He wanted to make love to her more than he had ever wanted to with any woman. She stayed with him until four a.m., and they alternately kissed and dozed in each other's arms. She had to force herself to get up, and he drove her home at four-thirty.

'I think we need to make love, just so we get some sleep,' he teased her. And they sat and kissed again in the car, and then she left him. She was leaving the next morning, and she had no idea when she'd see him again. They just had to trust that the right things would happen, as they had till then. These had been the happiest two weeks of her life, and his. She was the woman he had been looking for, and hadn't known it. And he was the man she wished she'd married. But if so, their lives would have been very different, and maybe it wouldn't have lasted when they were young. They both felt ready now to take on a serious commitment, but they knew they couldn't decide that after two weeks.

She finally extricated herself from his arms and walked into the lobby of the hotel. And he had a heavy heart as he drove back to Brentwood. He lay on his bed with his clothes on and thought about her. And she lay in bed at the hotel and watched the sun come up. She hardly got any sleep. And he was sleeping soundly between his two dogs when she drove out of Nashville, and saw the Parthenon for the last time. It was still early, and the city looked magical in the early morning light under a pastel sky. She headed for the highway that would take her to Knoxville and then on to Roanoke that night, and Chase had promised to call her along the way.

She got the first call from him at noon, after she left Nashville that morning. 'How's it going?' he asked in his now familiar drawl on speakerphone in her car. It was a hot June day. She had the air conditioning on in the car, but she could tell it was hot outside too. She had just passed Fall Branch, Tennessee, after four hours on the road.

'It's okay. I miss you,' she said, sounding as sad as he did, but it was nice having someone to miss, and the memories of the past two weeks to take with her. It felt like a dream now. But it was also real.

He told her what he was going to do that day. He had meetings with his record label, and he had to audition new drummers. Charlie had had an offer to play with a band in Vegas, and was leaving after five years, which was a big deal, and she knew that Chase was upset about it. He had to get off the phone after a few minutes and promised to call her later. He called her after the meeting at three, and then much later, when she had just checked into the Hotel Roanoke that he had recommended. She called Louise to tell her that she was halfway there, and Louise was at a dinner party so they didn't really talk. And when Chase called her to say goodnight, Stephanie was already half asleep, so they didn't stay on long. Their lives were already taking divergent paths, and they were on different rhythms. He had just come home from band auditions, and they still hadn't found a drummer to replace Charlie, whom he liked and felt at ease with.

Stephanie left Roanoke at seven the next morning, while Chase was still asleep, and she had no reception on her cell when he called her as she went past the Blue Ridge Mountains. She drove steadily and didn't stop for lunch. She drove into a truck stop late that afternoon and bought a sandwich and kept driving. She finally reached the George Washington Bridge and crossed the Hudson River into New York at six-thirty. She called Chase to tell him, and he was in a meeting and couldn't talk. She missed him fiercely, but she was looking forward to seeing Louise the following day. She was at a big Sotheby's art auction that night and couldn't see her. And as she drove toward the Carlyle Hotel where she always stayed, Sandy called her. They had had a tearful goodbye on Monday, and Sandy told her that Bobby Joe was still being a jerk to her.

'He keeps telling me I have no voice, and that Chase only uses me in the band because he feels sorry for me.'

'That's ridiculous,' Stephanie said, angry at him. Bobby Joe was such a cocky little bastard. 'Chase has an important career. He's not going to screw up the band with charity cases. Bobby Joe is jealous, Sandy, that's all it is.' She didn't dare ask her if Michael had called her. She hoped he would. They chatted for a few minutes, and Stephanie got off the phone as she got into the heavy traffic on the West Side Highway, then drove across town through Central Park to the Carlyle Hotel on Madison Avenue. It was an elegant hotel, and they knew her from her frequent visits to Louise and Charlotte. She'd had an e-mail from Charlotte the day before – she'd gone to Paris with friends and was having a ball traveling in Europe. She was due home at the end of the month, and she didn't sound like she was looking forward to it. Summer in San Francisco was not going to measure up to living in Rome for the last year. And she was going back to NYU in August for her senior year.

Stephanie checked into the hotel, ran a bath, and ordered room service, and she was lounging on her bed when Chase called her. He was happy to hear her voice, and relieved that she had gotten to New York okay. He had interviewed more drummers and found one who might work, but he wasn't sure yet. He wanted to play with him a few times, and he'd gotten another booking in Vegas. He was rehearsing with the band that night. He said he missed her, but she didn't see how he had time to. And her life at home was so staid compared to his. She had talked to Jean about it while she drove through New Jersey.

'Stop looking for problems,' Jean had told her. 'It sounds like you met a great guy, and now you're trying to find reasons why it won't work.'

'They might not be hard to find,' Stephanie said, sounding worried. 'Our lives are so different. His is going a hundred miles an hour. Mine is dead in the water. I'll get lost if I'm with him. I don't even know who I am yet. I need some kind of activity of my own so I can bring something to the table too.'

'You'll find something to do. And he didn't fall for you

Danielle Steel

for the career you don't have. He fell for *you*. Don't forget that.'

'What's to fall for? I'm boring.'

'No, you're not. You're a smart, interesting woman. And he loves you. Or at least it sounds like it.'

'He says he does, but what does he know?' Stephanie said, feeling sorry for herself, and Jean laughed.

'Just stop it. And I can't believe you didn't sleep with him. I would have.'

'I need to think about it, and figure out what I'm doing before I jump into the deep end.'

'You're much too sensible, and much too noble. Live a little. You only live once, Steph. We don't get another go-around. All we get is this one.'

'I'm trying not to screw up my life, and his.' She sounded earnest about it.

'You won't. What does he say?'

'That he loves me.'

'Take it and run,' Jean advised her. 'Or give me his number.' They both laughed and hung up a minute later. Stephanie still hadn't told Alyson what she'd been doing, other than visiting Michael in Atlanta. And the baby had gotten the chicken pox after the others, so she was still busy. It was hard to believe that they'd all been in Santa Barbara together only weeks before. Her whole life had changed in the meantime.

She went to bed early that night, after talking to Chase.

They talked several times a day. And she went to the Metropolitan Museum the next day, and then went for a walk in Central Park all the way down to the Plaza Hotel, and then back up Madison Avenue to the Carlyle. She was meeting Louise at seven.

When Stephanie got to Louise's apartment on Eighty-ninth Street, Louise had just gotten home from work, and she looked stressed. There was another art auction the next day, and she had a lot to do to help get it ready, and they'd found a mistake in the catalogue she was afraid she'd get blamed for. She was a pretty girl with dark hair and blue eyes and looked like her father. Michael and Charlotte looked like Stephanie, but Louise was the image of Bill's mother.

Louise finally started to calm down by the time they got to the restaurant, a small French bistro near her apartment that she had suggested, and Louise said as soon as they ordered how weird it was that her mother was driving around like a lost soul, visiting them. She had said as much to Michael a few days before, and he had said he thought their mother was lonely.

'I visited a friend from college,' Stephanie said staunchly, sticking to her story. 'I had nothing else to do, and I wanted to see Michael and you.'

'And now you're driving back to California? Mom, that's crazy. People do that in college, not at your age.' Stephanie always felt she had to defend herself to her older daughter. Louise had turned criticizing her into a full-time job since high school. And at twenty-three, she was still at it. 'I take it the monster is still with Michael. Did she come to Nashville?' Stephanie didn't tell her about Sandy, or she'd have something to say about that too.

'Yes, she came with him. She loved the concert.'

'And that's another thing. When did you become a fan of country music?' Louise was always suspicious of her mother, and now she had good reason to be and didn't know it.

'My friend Laura from college lives there, and she introduced me to Chase Taylor. He gave us comp tickets to the concert.'

'Why?'

'I guess rock stars and country music stars do that. We all enjoyed it.'

'It sounds insane to me. Why don't you go to Europe and visit Charlotte?'

'Because she has better things to do than hang around with me. She's busy with her friends from school before she comes back to San Francisco. The last thing she'd want is me showing up.' And Louise didn't look too pleased about it either. Whenever Stephanie visited New York, Louise acted as though she was intruding on her. She had always been happy to see her father. And she began extolling his virtues again before the end of dinner.

The father who had always been there for her, for all of them, who had taught her everything she knew, who was the most patient, giving, loving, finest man on earth – who in truth had spent as little time as possible with them and had never been there. It was Stephanie who had done everything for them, which Louise no longer remembered.

'Life is never going to be the same without Daddy,' she said mournfully, as tears rolled down her cheeks, and Stephanie felt sorry for her.

'I know it won't, sweetheart. But Daddy wouldn't want you crying about him all the time. And you'll feel better about it in a while.' It had only been four months, although Michael was doing better than his sisters. He was sad to have lost his dad but was less devastated by it. Louise had always idolized him and was his favorite child.

'What about you? Are you feeling better?' she asked her mother in an accusing tone, wiping away her tears with her napkin.

'Sometimes I feel better. I miss him all the time, but I'm trying to get my life back on track. We can't sit here and just mourn him forever. That doesn't mean we don't care. But we have to have a good life without him.' Stephanie was gentle but definite about it.

'It's not the same, Mom. Who's going to take care of us now?' She was echoing Stephanie's own panic until she'd realized she'd been relying on herself anyway, when Bill was alive.

'I'm still here. And Daddy provided for all of you.' She wanted to tell her daughter that she had to move on, but even in her head the words didn't sound right.

'It's not about money. I could call him anytime I had a problem.' Stephanie wanted to shout 'No, you couldn't.' He had never been there to listen, to them or to her. He always sounded irritated when she called him at the office. And once the kids left for college, he never called them. How had Louise forgotten? He had been a solid husband and father but not an attentive one. She was the one who always listened to their problems, but Louise refused to give her credit now. According to her, all the credit went to her father. She just couldn't accept what he hadn't done for them, and since his death, she had created a fantasy father and negated everything her mother had ever done.

But Stephanie didn't want to call her on it. She wasn't going to get in an argument with her daughter about who was the best parent. In Louise's current state of mind, it would have been a losing battle.

'Are you going out with anyone?' her mother asked her, trying to change the subject, which would at least put them on level ground, without her distorted memories of her father.

'No,' Louise said bluntly. She was a pretty girl, but

inclined to be too serious and work too hard. 'I haven't met anyone interesting in months. And I'm in no mood to go to parties since Daddy died.'

'You have to go out,' Stephanie told her gently. 'You can't just work all the time.'

'Why not? Daddy did. You don't understand, Mom. You've never had a job.' Louise dismissed her as a lowly housewife.

'I had a job when I was your age. I stopped working when I was pregnant with Michael, and Daddy wanted me to stay home after he was born, and then I had you and Charlotte.' As usual, she was defending herself and getting nowhere. 'I want to get a job now,' she threw into the conversation.

'Doing what?' Louise looked as if she thought it was a ridiculous idea.

'I haven't figured that out yet.' Stephanie was embarrassed to admit it.

'Why don't you just do volunteer work for the Junior League or something?' She thought it was all her mother was good for, lunching with socialites to plan fashion shows for charity. Stephanie was sure they did good work, but she needed more in her life than that, especially now that she no longer had a husband or kids at home. She wanted to do something meaningful. Her work at the shelter was a start.

'I'd like to do something more important. I like the

work I'm doing now at the adolescent homeless shelter,' she explained to Louise, 'but I'd kind of like to get a paying job.'

'You don't need one.' The conversation faltered then, and after dinner Stephanie walked her back to her apartment.

'Do you want to have lunch tomorrow?' Stephanie asked her, and Louise shook her head. She looked as though she were eating herself up with grief over her father. It took a lot of energy to keep the fantasy going, and in order to validate it, she had to reject her mother. Stephanie understood it, but she didn't like it, and it was tough being on the receiving end of her daughter's anger. Instead of being angry at her father for dying, as Stephanie had been herself, Louise was furious at her mother for her father's slights.

'I can't,' she said to her mother's invitation. 'I have to work on the auction. It's tomorrow night.'

'That's fine. Then I'll leave in the morning.' She had nothing else to do in New York, and had only come to see Louise, which as usual hadn't been pleasant. She hoped that one day it would get better.

'Thanks for coming, Mom,' she finally said as they stood in the doorway of her building. Although not a fancy address, it was modern and clean, and safe for her, with a doorman, which was a comfort to her mother. 'I'm sorry I'm still so down about Dad. I just don't know how to get out of it.'

'Maybe you should talk to someone. I am. And it's been helping.'

'He'll still be just as dead if I go to a shrink,' Louise said, and as she said it, she burst into tears and melted into her mother's arms. It was the first sign of closeness Stephanie had felt from her all evening. She held Louise in her arms, and let her cry, and wished there were something she could do to help her, but only time was going to ease the pain she was in. It made Stephanie sad for her. She had been much too young to lose her father, they all were. Louise had taken it the hardest of all of her children, since she had been the closest to him.

'Think about it,' Stephanie said gently, about talking to a therapist.

'I don't have time. I'm too busy. You have nothing else to do. I'm working.' She could never resist taking a swing at her mother.

'You can make time, at lunchtime or after work. I think it would help you.' Louise shrugged and dried her tears again and hugged her mother.

'I'm okay. I just miss him.'

'So do I.' It was true, but Stephanie still had a lot of unresolved issues about him, and now they never would be. She wanted to deal with that before she made any big decisions about Chase. She didn't want to go to him with a lot of heavy baggage. She needed to empty those bags first, and arrive with a clean slate, and she knew she wasn't there yet. Like Louise, she needed more time to heal the pain, although for different reasons.

'Take care of yourself, I love you,' Stephanie said, and hugged her again, and then with a depressed look, Louise waved and walked into her building. It hadn't been an easy evening, but it never was with Louise. She never gave her mother a fair shake, particularly since Bill died.

Stephanie walked back to the hotel in the balmy evening and told Chase about it later. He was sympathetic. He said that in his opinion girls were harder than boys, although he hadn't had too rough a time with Sandy, and she wasn't his child, which made a difference.

'And I'm probably a lot tougher than you are.' He already knew Stephanie was a gentle person, maybe too much so with her daughter who, to him, sounded like she needed a swift kick in the butt to get her going and stop blaming her mother. He wasn't sympathetic to her cause. Everyone had hard knocks in life, which he felt were no excuse to take it out on someone else.

'I think girls have issues with their mothers,' Stephanie said rationally. Louise certainly did. 'I am so tired of hearing how fabulous Bill was to them, when in fact he did so little.'

'It sounds like they need a dose of reality about their father,' Chase commented.

'It's too late for that now. You can't malign the dead, even if it's true.'

'So he goes down in history as a saint forever?'

'It looks that way,' Stephanie said, sounding discouraged. And even though she was difficult to be with, she felt sorry for her daughter and helpless to take away her pain over losing her father.

'So when do you leave New York?' he asked, changing the subject.

'First thing tomorrow morning.' He had helped her plan her route. And he was still sorry she wasn't willing to take the bus and tow the car.

'Call me if you have any problem,' he said firmly.

'Can you change a tire long distance?' she teased him.

'No, and don't you do it either. Call a towing service if you have car trouble or a flat tire.'

'I promise.' She was looking forward to the trip, although she hated that it was taking her farther away from him, but the sooner she sorted out her life, the sooner they could be together.

He promised to call her the next day while she was driving, and she knew he would. He had been totally reliable so far, and always kept his word, even when he was busy. He made time for her, and she felt like a priority to him, and she loved it.

She went to bed that night thinking about Louise and

wishing that there were some way to help her. But all
Louise wanted was her father, which was the one thing
her mother couldn't give her. It was a totally no-win
situation, and Stephanie was trying to accept it. It was up
to Louise to figure it out now, particularly since she
didn't want her mother's help. She had to do it on her
own.

Chapter 14

When Michael and Amanda got back from Nashville, things had been a little rocky between them for a few days. Michael had been withdrawn and distracted. And Amanda was stressed over a new ad campaign she'd been assigned to.

And every day at lunch, Michael stared at the number his mother had texted to him at brunch on Sunday. But he couldn't think of an excuse to call Sandy. And he felt wrong even thinking about it. He had been faithful to Amanda for three years and had only cheated on her once at the beginning, and he didn't want to do anything behind her back now. But finally, on Wednesday, after a tense time with Amanda the night before, he called Sandy.

She had been rehearsing a new song with the band, and they had just taken a break. Bobby Joe had come by and told her he didn't like it. And Sandy didn't like the new drummer Chase was trying out.

'Hello?' She was exasperated when she heard her phone, and she didn't recognize the number.

'Hi,' he said, feeling thirteen years old again. It had been three years since he'd called a woman other than Amanda, and he felt rusty at it, although he'd gone out with a lot of girls in college. 'It's Michael Adams. I met you at the concert last weekend, with my mother . . . Stephanie . . .' He tried to jog her memory, as though he needed to. She knew exactly who he was the moment she heard his voice.

'Hi, Michael.' She seemed happy to hear him. Her voice was soft and breathless. He loved the way she sounded on the phone. 'How are you?'

'I'm fine. I was wondering how you were. That was a great concert. You were terrific.'

'Thanks. I was trying out a new song Chase wrote for me. I still need to work on it.' She was thinking of Bobby Joe's harsh criticism of the way she sang it. 'What have you been up to?'

'Working. I work for the Atlanta Braves.' She remembered.

'That must be cool, for a guy,' she said, and giggled. 'I don't know too much about baseball,' she admitted this time. 'I work all the time. Chase is a pretty demanding teacher, but he's the best there is. He thinks I have talent, so he's tough on me. And he works really hard himself.'

'I think so too,' Michael said, about her having talent. He was thrilled to be talking to her. She could have said anything – he just liked hearing her voice, young, breezy, and sexy. 'You sing like an angel.'

'That's what my dad used to say. Not everybody thinks so.' She was referring to Bobby Joe. 'I love to sing, though. It's great doing something you really love. Do you like what you do?' she asked him.

'I love it. I want to manage a team one day. I need a lot more experience to do it, and I'll probably go to grad school. Would you like to come down for a game some-time?' As he said it, he was wondering how he would pull it off with Amanda. She didn't come to all his games, but she was around all weekend. And what would he do with Sandy once she got there?

'I'd really like that.' She sounded as though she meant it, although she wondered how that would sit with his girlfriend, and then the band started signaling to her that they were going back to rehearsal. 'That sounds terrific. I have to go back to work now. We're at rehearsal. Call me again sometime.'

'I'd like that very much,' he said, feeling awkward, but happy that he'd called her. He could just imagine her at rehearsal, with her long blond hair and big blue eyes, singing her heart out.

He thought about her all afternoon, and when he got home that night, Amanda was in an even worse mood.

She told him why at dinner, which consisted of the takeout he'd brought home. Amanda didn't cook. Sometimes he did. Or they ate out. Amanda loved going to nice restaurants.

'I have to go to Houston for client meetings all weekend. I hate this new client. They just rejected our whole presentation, and they want to brainstorm with us.'

'I have a home game this weekend anyway. I have to be here.'

'I hate Houston,' she said, looking glum.

'When do you leave?'

'Friday morning. They're sending a plane for us, and I won't be home till Sunday night.' He nodded, but all he could think of that night, as he lay in bed next to Amanda, was Sandy. It was a rotten thing to do to Amanda, but a force greater than he was was pushing him to do it. He called Sandy back the next day and tried to sound casual about it. He invited her to the game on Saturday and suggested she come down on Friday night. He said he'd book a hotel for her. Fortunately they didn't have a performance that weekend.

And she was thinking about Bobby Joe before she answered. This would serve him right. She was tired of his criticizing her all the time. He'd been mean to her for months and was getting worse lately. And going to Atlanta for the weekend didn't mean she was going to do something wrong. Besides, Michael had a girlfriend too. Maybe they could just be friends.

'I'll come,' she said, sounding breathless. 'I don't like to drive alone. I think I'll fly. Chase's secretary can book it for me.' All she had to do was find an excuse to give Bobby Joe, but lately he wasn't spending much time with her on weekends. It was going to be a little dicey to get away for a whole weekend, though.

She asked Wanda that day to make the reservation for her, and Wanda mentioned it to Chase after she booked the ticket. Sandy hadn't said it was a secret, so she assumed she could.

'Atlanta?' Chase looked blank when his assistant told him. 'What's she doing in Atlanta?'

'I don't know. She didn't tell me.' But he had a sudden suspicion. He asked Sandy about it that night when he saw her, and Bobby Joe wasn't around.

'You're going to Atlanta?' He looked her straight in the eye, and she nodded. 'To visit anyone I know?' He still expected her to let him know what she was doing, although allegedly she was a woman, not a child. But he kept a close eye on her.

'Maybe.' Her voice was very small as she said it.

'Michael Adams?' She nodded again. 'Does Bobby Joe know?'

'I didn't tell him. I'm not going to do anything, Chase. Just go to a baseball game and hang out with him. He's nice.' Chase wanted to add 'so is his mother,' but he didn't. This was about Sandy and Michael, not about them. Chase was all in favor of it – he just didn't want her to get hurt. And Michael had a girlfriend. And she had Bobby Joe, although Chase didn't like him.

'Be careful. It sounds complicated. For both of you.' And then he said something she hadn't expected. 'Sometimes you just have to seize the moment, and figure it out afterward. Carpe diem. It sounds like that's what you're doing. And sometimes that's a good thing. Just take care of yourself.' He grinned then. 'And if you get pregnant, I'll kill you.' He always said that. 'And Bobby Joe won't be too pleased about it either.'

'I'm staying at a hotel. And I'm not going to do anything crazy. I don't even know him.'

'At your age and his, you can get to know someone mighty quick.' He smiled ruefully at her.

'Yeah, like you and Stevie,' she teased him right back, and he grinned. He was a good sport and never minded her teasing him, which was one of the many things Sandy loved about him. He didn't act all uptight like a father, but he still expected her to behave.

'You mind your business, girl,' he said about Stevie. 'And say hi to Michael for me. What are you going to tell Bobby Joe?'

'I don't know yet. I hate lying to him.'

'Tell him I'm sending you as a scout, and you have

to go.' She nodded, grateful for the excuse. 'And have some fun. You deserve it. Something tells me he's a good boy, and he looked nuts about you when he met you.'

'I like him too,' she admitted.

'Well, play it cool. You don't want to be his "other woman".'

'I won't be,' she said with a look of self-assurance, and with that she threw her arms around him and thanked him. She called Michael back after that and told him everything was all set for Friday. She was arriving in time for dinner.

He was beaming when he hung up the phone. It had all worked perfectly. Amanda was going to Houston. Sandy was coming to Atlanta. And whatever happened happened. He felt ready to do something new and different. Amanda didn't own him yet.

When Sandy arrived on Friday, Michael was waiting for her at the airport. Amanda had left on the private jet that morning. And he looked nervous. Sandy had only brought carry-on with her, and he carried it for her, one small rolling bag, and a garment bag with a dress in it in case they went someplace fancy. Other than that, she had brought shorts and jeans.

He took her to the hotel he had booked for her, the Hyatt Place in the heart of Atlanta, and he had paid for it when he booked it. It seemed like the proper thing to do. And that night he took her out to dinner. He could tell she was nervous too. She talked a lot, and looked at him with wide eyes. But by the time they got to dessert, they had both started to relax, and Michael looked mesmerized by her. She was the most beautiful girl he'd ever seen. She was small, but perfectly proportioned, and she was mature for her years. She said she had grown up a lot since her dad died, and she'd been working in the music business since she was fourteen. She wanted to go to college, but she hadn't had time. Chase kept her really busy.

They talked about him for a little while, and Sandy told Michael what a great guy Chase was, and how he had taken care of her for the last three years, and even built her a house of her own in his garden.

They walked back to the hotel from the restaurant where they had dinner, and she seemed very relaxed with him. She said she was looking forward to the baseball game the next day. It was a day game, and they were playing at noon. And after the game, he wanted to show her around the city and take her out to dinner at the Top Floor, which he said was a beautiful place. And after that, he thought they might go dancing. He realized that he was courting her and acting like he didn't have a girl-friend, and he wasn't sure what to do about it. He was thoroughly enjoying being with her. She was such a sweet person and so much fun to be with. And she was interesting to talk to, and totally impressed by him because he was so much older.

'Do you like to dance?' he asked, looking hopeful.

'I love it.' She smiled shyly at him.

He said goodnight to her in the lobby like a perfect gentleman, and didn't try to kiss her. He just wanted to get to know her, and from everything he had heard that night, he thought she was a wonderful person. And there was a childlike naïveté about her that he loved. She was innocent and wise at the same time, kind of like his mother. She reminded him of her in some ways, and he could see why his mom liked her.

They had a wonderful time at the game the next day, and ate hot dogs and pretzels. He bought her an ice cream, which she dribbled down her chin, and he teased her about it. They were like two peas in a pod, and agreed about a lot of things. The Braves won, which made everyone happy, and afterward they took a long walk and talked. There was something he wanted to make clear to her before they went any further. Amanda. She had texted him twice that day to tell him how much she hated their client, and never asked how he was or what he was doing, which was a relief. He didn't want to lie to her, although he knew he was committing a 'sin of omission' by not telling her Sandy was there. And she wasn't in Atlanta by accident. He had invited her to come. He knew he'd have to take responsibility for it at some point. And he wanted to with Sandy now. He liked her too much to lie to her.

'There's something I have to tell you, Sandy,' he said, as they sat down on a bench in Centennial Olympic Park. She looked instantly worried. He hated to say it, but he knew he had to. 'I've had a girlfriend for three years. She came to the concert in Nashville with me. She doesn't live with me, but she stays with me a lot of the time. It's been pretty serious for three years. But I've been realizing that we're at different stages in our lives and want different things. She wants to move in together, buy an apartment or a house, and get married eventually. I'm not ready to make that kind of commitment to anyone. And to be honest, I don't think she's the woman for me. I haven't told her that yet, though, which makes things awkward for us. I had no right to ask you here this weekend. I thought maybe we could just be friends. But talking to you, and seeing you, I realize I want more than that. I'd like to go out with you. But I need to clear things up with Amanda first. She has no idea that I've realized recently that she's not the right girl for me. Anyway, I wanted you to know that my situation is a little bit complicated right now. And after three years with her, I owe it to her to do it right and be honest with her. I just don't know when. I want to find the right time to say it to her. And then I'll be free' – he looked nervously at Sandy – 'if you even want to go out with me.'

She was listening to him and watching him intently as he spoke to her, and his confession induced her to do the same.

Sandy looked momentarily embarrassed. 'I lied to my boyfriend too. I've been going out with him for a while. But I told Chase I was coming here. He approved. No one likes the guy I'm going out with. He's in our opening band, and he's a jerk. He was nice at first, and now he picks on me all the time. He's pretty mean. Chase says he's jealous of me. But whatever it is, he says a lot of nasty things and puts me down, which really hurts. I've been thinking of breaking up with him. And I really liked you when I met you, so I came. I thought maybe we could be friends too. And I really like your mom, she's so sweet.' She didn't say a word to him about his mother and Chase. Chase hadn't told her not to, but she thought it best to be discreet. She didn't know how much Michael knew, and people were touchy about their moms, especially going out with guys. So she kept her revelations about her and Bobby Joe.

'I'm kind of in the same boat,' Michael admitted. 'You knocked my socks off when I met you, Sandy. And I didn't know what to do. I asked my mom for your number, and when Amanda told me she was going to Houston, I invited you for the weekend. If anything happens between us, I don't know what I'm going to do. And I need to talk to Amanda anyway. Something about that just isn't right for me.' And it was very different being with Sandy. She was younger than Amanda, and her expectations of him were entirely different from Amanda's, who wanted so much more. Sandy was easier for him, more lighthearted and more fun.

'Yeah, like me and Bobby Joe.' They looked at each other and grinned. 'Maybe we should relax and have fun. We don't have to decide anything right now. Chase told me about something called "Carpe diem", enjoy the day. Why don't we just have fun together and see what happens?' she said sensibly. It sounded right to both of them. He took her hand then, and they continued walking back to her hotel. They both felt better after their conversation. They had been honest with each other, although they hadn't been with the people they were dating, and felt awkward about it. He took her to her hotel then, and he went home. And when he picked her up for dinner, she blew him away again. She was wearing a short, tight, sexy red dress with her long blond hair, great figure, and high heels. She looked even better than she did on stage. She was spectacular.

'Holy shit, Sandy! You look incredible!' She smiled when he said it. It was a vast improvement over Bobby Joe's constant criticism and put-downs. They talked incessantly at dinner, and they danced afterward until three a.m. When he took her back to the hotel, Sandy said she'd never had so much fun in her life, and he felt the same way. He kissed her chastely on the cheek, and promised to call her in the morning for breakfast the next day before they left for the airport. He never took her to his apartment, or went to her room at the hotel, and she didn't ask. They had a totally wholesome, nonstressful weekend, talking and laughing, and teasing each other. It had exceeded their expectations, which created a whole new problem for them. They were both in committed relationships that weren't working, and they had to deal with them now, if they wanted to date each other. They were honorable people and didn't want to lie.

When he said goodbye to her at the airport, he looked down at her with a gentle smile.

'Thank you for coming to Atlanta, Sandy.' It had been brave of her.

'Thank you for being so nice to me.' She was wearing a pink cotton dress and flat shoes. She looked like Alice in Wonderland with her long blond hair.

'You're easy to be nice to.'

'Will you come to Nashville sometime?' she asked, as they waited for her plane. An announcement said it was starting to board, and she was sad to leave. They didn't know when they would see each other again or what would happen now.

'I will. I'll call you tonight.' And then he remembered that Amanda would be home, probably at his apartment, and it reminded him of the difficult situation he was in. He had just spent a fantastic weekend with Sandy, he liked her even more than he had hoped, and now he had to deal with Amanda if he wanted to pursue this as more than just a friend.

'Thank you for everything,' she said as she stood on tiptoe to kiss his cheek, and before he could stop himself, he had put his arms around her and kissed her on the lips. It was a long sensual kiss, and she looked startled when they stopped. 'I thought we weren't going to do that,' she said softly.

'Yeah, so did I. Look, I'll come to Nashville in a couple of weeks. We've got some away games. I can come to Nashville then.' But for a minute, she felt like she was dating a married man, and she didn't like how it made her feel. He could see it in her eyes. For now at least, he was in a relationship with someone else.

'Maybe you shouldn't come to Nashville until we both work things out,' she said, and he nodded, and realized that she was right. She was young, but no fool, and she didn't want to get hurt. He didn't blame her – neither did he.

She had to go through security then, and she waved as she went through. He watched until he couldn't see the blond hair and pink dress anymore, and then he went back to his apartment and thought about her for the rest of the afternoon. He didn't know what to do about Amanda, or when. And Sandy was thinking of him as she flew home.

Chapter 15

Michael and Sandy weren't the only ones to make confessions over the weekend. Chase didn't want to compromise the openness and honesty that he and Stephanie shared. She started her drive west the same day Sandy flew to Atlanta, and Chase called Stephanie on her cell phone in the car. She answered on speaker, and she was excited about the trip.

'How's it going?' Chase asked her. She had the radio on and a bag full of snacks and bottled water on the seat next to her.

'It's fine so far.' She smiled.

'I just want to tell you something that's probably none of my business, but I want to keep the communication clean between us. I think that's important so we know we can trust each other.'

'It sounds serious,' she said, listening to what he said as she dealt with the traffic leaving New York.

'It probably isn't, but it could be in time, depending how things work out,' he said, sounding relaxed, and he cut to the chase. 'I discovered the other day that Sandy is going to Atlanta for the weekend.'

'She is?' Stephanie sounded surprised. 'You should tell her to call . . .' she started to say, and then stopped, and understood. 'Is she going to see Michael?' She hadn't expected that, and neither had he.

'Yes, she is,' he said simply.

'What did he do with Amanda?'

'I think she's away for the weekend.'

'Wow, I don't think Michael has ever done that before. He's usually such a straight shooter. He must be crazy about Sandy, to take a risk like that. I hope nobody tells Amanda,' Stephanie said. They both knew that she didn't like her, so she couldn't pretend to be sad about it. 'Well, that certainly is an interesting turn of events. I wonder what he's going to do about it.'

'She's in the same boat with Bobby Joe. And he'll have a fit if he finds out,' Chase said.

'They're younger, and it's not as serious as Michael's situation with Amanda. I guess they'll just have to work it out,' Stephanie replied.

'Yes, they will. And all we can do is watch from the sidelines, and see how it shakes out.' She was as intrigued as he was now. 'I just wanted to be sure you knew, so you won't feel I'm holding out on you, or hiding something.'

But she didn't think that anyway, and she was grateful he had told her. It only enhanced their trust of each other.

'Thanks for telling me,' she said gratefully, and he was relieved. They both wondered how it was going to turn out. It was another one of the mysteries of life.

On her trip home, Stephanie covered seven hundred miles across four states on the first day. She drove for eleven hours, stopped for gas twice, and bought sandwiches at truck stops and didn't stop for meals. She wanted to get off to a good start. And Chase called her all along the way. He wanted to know how she was, and warned her to pull over if she got tired, and take a nap. She could hardly move she was so stiff when she got out of the car at a clean-looking motel just off the highway in South Bend, Indiana. As he had asked her to do, she called and told Chase where she was. None of her children had said that. Michael didn't think about it, and Louise was busy with the auction, texted her thanks for dinner that morning, and didn't think of her mother again all day.

'Put the chain on the door,' Chase told her, but she already had. He didn't like the idea of her staying in motels along the way, but it had been easier than looking for a decent hotel, which would probably have been worse. And she felt safe. She had noticed that there were two old ladies in the room next door, and a family with their kids in sleeping bags on the floor in the same room as their parents. She had no sense of danger when she got into bed, and Chase was satisfied. He worried about her, and had called her many times that day, even when he was busy, to check on her and give her a quick kiss. She was very touched. Bill had never been as attentive as that, even in the beginning, and in recent years not at all. He assumed she could take care of herself, and everyone else, and he wasn't wrong. But she loved the way Chase treated her, as though she were precious to him, and important in his life. She hadn't felt that from a man in years.

She fell asleep almost instantly after they hung up. And she awoke just after dawn the next morning. She showered and got back on the road and stopped at a McDonald's for breakfast. She drove through Illinois and Iowa that day and stopped at one point to walk around at a truck stop and stretch her legs. She didn't try to get as far as she had the day before and only drove for nine hours and stopped at a motel in Omaha, Nebraska, that night. The days were beginning to blur, and the only contact she had with the world was with Chase. She loved it when he called. And it gave her a thrill when she heard him on the radio when she put a country music station on. She sang along with him and could hear Sandy in the background. She missed her too, and wondered how she was.

She pushed harder again on the third day, and had a scary incident that night, when she drove on for a while after taking a nap. She stopped at a diner instead of a

truck stop, and when she left, three men followed her outside. She could sense them behind her, but wasn't paying
attention, until one of them grabbed her arm and yanked
her toward him. He literally lifted her feet off the ground
while the other two laughed, and there was no one else
outside to help her. All three of them were young and
looked tough and were driving eighteen-wheelers.

'Come on, baby, come see my cab,' the one who had
pulled her said to her, and for an instant she was terrified,
then realized that she was the only one she could depend
on, and if she didn't defend herself, she was about to be
raped, or worse, by all three as they formed a circle around
her with an evil look in their eyes.

There were plenty of people in the diner, mostly other
truckers, but no one outside. She hesitated for a long
moment as she looked her main attacker in the eye, and
then took a powerful swing at his nose. Blood gushed
from it instantly as he screamed and clutched it with both
hands, and she was sure she had broken it, just as one of
the two others grabbed her long hair and pulled hard as
he dragged her toward him, and with ingenuity and guts
she didn't know she had, she elbowed him hard in the
throat at the level of his Adam's apple, and he made a
gurgling choking sound and let her go. She had frightened
them by then, and the remaining uninjured one shouted
at her, as he helped his friend with the broken nose. 'What
are you, a fucking cop?' She had used two maneuvers that

she had learned at a self-defense class in college and had long since forgotten, but they came back to her at the right time. All three men jumped into their trucks and started the engines, and a moment later they drove off as two other men came out of the diner, and saw her sitting on the pavement shaking from head to foot, while she wondered if she'd have to do it again. But they were older men with big paunches, and one stooped down to help her. She felt like she was going to throw up and realized she was covered with blood from the guy with the broken nose. It was all over her jeans and white T-shirt and even on her shoes. He had bled a lot.

'Did you fall?' the man asked her. 'Do you need a doctor?' All she could do was shake her head, feeling dizzy. She couldn't talk for a minute.

'I'm okay,' she managed to croak out, looking deathly pale. 'Those guys came after me and grabbed me.' She indicated the three big trucks lumbering back onto the highway, and the two truckers shook their heads.

'You shouldn't be driving alone at night.' She nodded agreement and went back into the diner with their help to get a glass of water, and one of the waitresses helped her clean up in the bathroom while she told her what had happened.

'You could have been raped,' she said solemnly, and Stephanie had been certain she would have been, and they were powerfully built guys. She had taken them by surprise, and herself. She thanked the waitress, and one of the others brought her a glass of ginger ale and some cookies, and she felt better, although her hands were still shaking. She asked where the nearest motel was, and they told her to drive another forty miles to a Best Western that was in a decent area. She didn't know if she could do it, but she got back in her car a few minutes later, and started to calm down as she drove. Chase called her then, and she wasn't going to tell him, but he could hear something wrong in her voice and was frightened.

'Did you have an accident?'

'Almost,' she said cryptically, her voice still shaking.

'I told you to pull over if you got tired. What happened? And what are you doing driving at this hour?' He sounded worried sick. He wanted to be there with her, and he felt helpless.

'I thought I'd get some extra miles in tonight. I took a nap in the car this afternoon. And I stopped at a diner to get something to eat a little while ago. Three guys followed me out, and one of them grabbed me.' She told him that one had yanked her arm and lifted her off the ground, and the other had pulled her hair and wanted her to come to his cab. Then she told him what she'd done. There was shocked silence at the other end.

'You did *that*? I'd better watch myself around you.' He couldn't believe that she'd had the guts to defend herself and break one man's nose and hit the other in the throat, which was exactly what she'd been taught to do. Chase was horrified at what could have happened to her if she hadn't. She could have been kidnapped or killed and dumped by the side of the road somewhere. Then he turned serious. 'Okay, the fun is over. I want you to put your GPS on and head for the nearest airport. Ditch the car. You can send someone back for it later. I want you to fly home.'

'Honest, Chase, I'm fine.' And she meant it. She had almost stopped shaking, and she was exhilarated by what she had done. She had actually taken care of herself and proven she could, with no man at hand to help her. Nothing like it had ever happened to her before.

'You may be fine, but I'm not. I'm going to be worried sick until you get home. I want you on the next plane.' It sounded appealing even to her, but she didn't want to quit now. It was kind of an endurance contest driving from New York to the West Coast, and now she wanted to finish what she'd started.

'I'm almost halfway home now. It's stupid to fly.' But it was also amazing to think that what she could have done in six hours by plane would take her six days by car, with danger, and endless hours of driving every day.

'I'm scared to death of what could happen to you. I have been since you left Nashville. Please, Stevie, be a good girl. Get on a plane tomorrow, and find a decent place to stay tonight, not some shit motel along the road.'

'They told me about a Best Western in Rawlins. I'm only a few miles from it now.' She could already see the sign for it in the distance, and she took the turnoff while talking to him. It was nicer than any place she'd stayed so far. And she could see the manager in his office. She told Chase she was going to check in, and he told her he'd call her in five minutes.

She got a clean, comfortable room, and Chase called her, as promised. He sounded completely unglued by what had happened, and as she lay on the bed and they talked, he marveled again at her courage and clear-headedness, faced with the three truckers.

'I should never have let you do this. I should have sent you with the bus.'

'I wanted to do it. I wanted to see if I could. I've always wanted to drive cross country.'

'But not alone.' She was in Wyoming by then, and it brought back memories for him of his road tours, driving through the night after a show to get to the next venue. But there were always at least half a dozen others in the van with him. It was why he had bought the bus as soon as he could afford it. Even he, as a man, had never driven cross country on his own by car. He was badly rattled about her incident, and they talked for a long time that night until she was nearly asleep. And he told her to call him the minute she woke up, or if she wanted to talk during the night.

The sun was streaming through the thin curtains when she woke up nine hours later. She felt stiff and exhausted from driving, and she had a bruise on her arm where the truck driver had grabbed her. It hadn't been a bad dream. It was real. She called Chase and woke him up, but he was happy to hear her voice.

'I want you to call me every hour, and I swear if you don't, I'm calling the state police, in every state you're crossing.'

'I'll be fine,' she promised, but she was shaken too by what had happened the night before, and she swore to him she'd be more careful about where she stopped. And she wouldn't walk out of any more diners alone. She had learned her lesson.

She didn't drive as far that day, she was still tired from the day before, and she stopped at a very respectable place for breakfast and ordered scrambled eggs, toast, and coffee. She bought sandwiches so she wouldn't have to stop for lunch. And by nightfall she was in Utah and went to a Denny's. She had talked to Chase all along the way. He was talking her home day by day, hour by hour, and keeping even closer tabs on her now. Originally, he hadn't been too concerned about the trip, but as he got closer to her, he worried more.

By the fifth day, she had made it through Utah, and to Nevada by evening. And the sixth day she pressed on after nightfall, so she'd get home that night. She pulled into her driveway at midnight, and just sat there for a minute. It felt as though she had left for the weekend in Santa Barbara months before. Her house looked quiet and dark. She got out of her car, dragged her bag up the front steps, and let herself into the house. She turned off the alarm and turned on the lights, and Chase called her just as she did. It was two in the morning for him.

'What are you doing awake? I was going to text you. I didn't want to wake you up.'

'I'm just happy to know you're home. And I don't care what you want to prove, please don't ever do anything like that again.' But she had a huge sense of accomplishment as she looked around her house. She knew now that she could take care of herself, whatever happened. She had learned important information about herself, and now felt less vulnerable than she had before. And her voice sounded strong to Chase as they talked.

'How does your house look?' He meant tidy or not, not how fancy, and she understood.

'It's okay, empty, lonely. You're not here,' she said softly, sounding like a woman who couldn't have broken anyone's nose in a hundred years. 'It's not as nice as your house,' she said, remembering his. 'It feels like a relic of the past, from another life.' Her children had grown up in the house, and her marriage to Bill had waxed and waned, and she had lived here when he died. Now all those memories were intertwined, and she felt overwhelmed by them as she walked around. 'Time for another trip,' she said jokingly, and he groaned.

'That's not funny, unless you want to charter a plane. Get some sleep now. We'll talk tomorrow.' She knew they would. He had literally talked her across the country, watching over her like a guardian angel, and he had delivered her safely home. She dragged her large bag upstairs to her bedroom, bumping it on each step, but she got it there and set it down. And as she glanced around her bedroom and thought of the three men outside the diner, she realized she would never be afraid again.

Chapter 16

Stephanie could hardly wait to see her friends. She called Jean and Alyson the morning after she got back from her trip. Jean had been waiting to hear from her and knew she was driving cross country. Alyson had only just come up for air after the kids were sick and had no idea where Stephanie had been. She had lost track the week before. And it seemed impossible to believe, for all of them, that Stephanie had been gone for three weeks. Even more so for her, in those few weeks, her whole life had changed. And now she was back where she had started, having met new people, done new things, stepped into Chase's world in Nashville, seen two of her children, and driven across the country by herself. She felt like a different person, and yet everything at home was the same.

The three women agreed to meet for lunch on Union Street the next day. And somehow Stephanie expected them to look different, because she felt so different inside.

There was no way to tell them how much she had seen and experienced, or even why she had gone to Las Vegas instead of coming home, had followed Chase to Nashville to explore his world, and then wanted the challenge of driving three thousand miles alone. Their lives were so safe and predictable, she knew they'd never understand the feelings she had, of being alone and vulnerable since Bill died. She had needed desperately to find out if she could take care of herself now, and the night she was almost raped by three men, she had. It gave her self-confidence and a feeling of independence and security that she'd never had before.

She strode into the restaurant and saw her two women friends sitting at a table, talking quietly, waiting for her. Alyson was wearing jeans and a sweatshirt, her hair was a mess, and she had circles under her eyes after weeks of too little sleep taking care of her sick children. And Jean had had a manicure and a facial, and had her hair done and blown out that morning. She looked terrific in a white cashmere Chanel tracksuit. And Stephanie was wearing one of the pink T-shirts she'd bought in Las Vegas, with a pair of ragtag jeans. She looked young and healthy, with her hair in a ponytail, and her big blue eyes the color of a summer sky. There was a sparkle in them that Jean hadn't seen in years. They smiled the moment they saw her, and Stephanie kissed them both on the cheek before she sat down.

'Hello, ladies,' she said with a broad smile. Just seeing them made her feel better about coming home.

'Welcome home,' Jean said, delighted to see her friend. She instantly noticed the change in Stephanie.

'I'm sorry I look such a mess,' Alyson apologized. 'I was about to get ready when the dog got sick, and I had to drop her off at the vet.' Her life was one of children, dogs, a house to run, kids' lives and after-school activities to organize, and a husband who wanted her full attention every night. There was never any time left over for her. Stephanie had lived that same life for twenty-six years. She had thought she still missed it, but when she looked at Alyson, she realized that there were advantages to her new life. 'Wow, you look great. I can't believe you drove home from New York. Why?' Alyson asked her. They all knew what they were going to order. They had the same salad every time, with iced tea for Stephanie and Alyson. And Jean always ordered a glass of white wine.

'I just thought it would be exciting to drive home. I decided to go to Nashville to see my old friend Laura Perkins from college.' She had almost become real to Stephanie by now, she had mentioned her so many times. 'And I wanted to see Michael in Atlanta. I decided to go to New York to see Louise at the last minute, and by then, I was there, I had my car. It seemed stupid to ship it back, and I've always wanted to do it, so I drove. It took six days, and it was great.' She didn't mention the incident outside the diner. She knew it would have terrified them for her. And she was fine, although it had scared her too, and Chase. She had been very lucky and instinctively used her wits. Chase had said afterward admiringly that she 'had balls.' 'What about you two? What have you been up to?' Stephanie asked them.

'I'm on the benefit committee for the Diabetes Ball in September. I just got put on the ballet board. And I'm spending Fred's money as fast as I can. I bought a new sable coat last week,' Jean said with a grin. 'I can wear it when we go to New York in the fall.'

'I've been nursing sick kids,' Alyson said, looking apologetic. She had nothing to contribute to the conversation compared to the other two, but they loved her anyway. She was a good person, a great wife and mother, and their friend. She didn't have to prove anything to them. 'And Brad just got a distinguished service and life-time achievement award from the Orthopedic Surgeons' Board,' she said proudly, and Stephanie had to resist saying 'What about *you*?' It was always about him or the kids, just as her life had been until now. Now it was finally her turn. They were almost the same age, but Stephanie had finally graduated. With young kids, for Alyson, time for herself was years away. Stephanie had never felt as free or as comfortable with herself as she did now.

'Okay, so tell all,' Jean said as their salads came. 'Who did you meet? Any cute men in Nashville or New York?'

She knew about Chase but didn't want to let on to Alyson that she did.

'Jean!' Alyson said with a shocked look. 'Bill's only been gone for four months and one week, I'm sure Stephanie doesn't want to think about dating for at least a year, if then.' As she said it, Stephanie thought about her long, hungry kisses with Chase. But she hadn't expected that either, so she couldn't blame Alyson for thinking it was out of the question. Stephanie still considered what had happened with him an aberration. She had never even thought about 'dating' until then. And she still told herself they weren't 'dating,' they were friends. With a hint of future romance. But she couldn't deny, even to herself, how close they were and how much she liked him.

'Don't be ridiculous,' Jean said, taking a sip of her wine. 'You don't expect her to sit around alone for the rest of her life? Look at her, she looks thirty years old. Some hot guy is going to sweep her up in a New York minute. And they damn well should.' She didn't say anything, but she had noticed that Alyson needed to get her nails done, and she had three inches of dark roots. Unlike Stephanie, she wasn't a natural blond. But she never had time to take care of herself and lately didn't seem to care. The only time she dressed in something other than jeans and sweat-suits was when they went away on their couples weekends. The rest of the time she said she didn't have time, and the kids got food, markers, or paint on what she wore anyway.

'Are you thinking about dating?' Alyson asked Stephanie with a look of amazement after what Jean had just said.

'No . . . not really . . . I don't think so. I don't know,' she said, looking embarrassed. 'Maybe one day. I'm not ready yet. Bill's clothes are still in the closet, his flip-flops are next to the bed, his glasses are in every drawer in the kitchen.' But more than that, he was still in her head. But now so was Chase. But she didn't want to say that to Alyson. 'I guess I'll have to eventually. It's hard to figure out. I still feel married, and if I slept with someone else, I'd feel like I was cheating on him.' That much was true, and she had said it to Chase. He understood.

'That never stopped him when he was alive,' Jean said wryly and finished the glass of wine. She was always more outspoken when she drank, and Alyson looked uncomfortable. She never said anything to remind Stephanie of that terrible time. And Alyson was sure he had never done it again. They had been back together for years. And Stephanie had never shared with her how dead their marriage had felt after that. She hadn't even admitted it to herself until now. 'That's how guys are,' Jean added, and Alyson looked pained. 'It never seems to bother them to cheat on us. But if we do it, it's the end of the world. What makes them think they're any different from us?

We like cute guys too. We're just too scared to do anything about it. They're not. They never care about the consequences if they want to get laid.' Alyson hated Jean's theories about men, and changed the subject.

'So when is Charlotte coming home?' Alyson asked Stephanie.

'Next week. She hasn't told me what day. She's been all over Europe with her friends. She's going to be bored stiff here. It'll do her good to take it easy for two months before she goes back to school in New York. I really miss having her in the house.' And she knew it might be the last summer, since she would be graduating in a year and working after that, maybe in another city, like Michael and Louise. 'It was great seeing Michael, although Amanda is still firmly entrenched. I'm scared she's going to get him in the end.'

'I hope not,' Jean said firmly. 'He's such a sweet boy.'

'She wants to buy a house with him. I hope they won't. Then he'll really be stuck with her, married or not.' But knowing that he had invited Sandy to Atlanta, Stephanie wondered if things in his life had changed. He hadn't said a word to her. And all she knew was from Chase.

'I'm sure that's what she has in mind,' Jean said, suspicious. 'Let's hope she doesn't get pregnant first.'

'Don't even say it,' Stephanie said, rolling her eyes with a look of dread.

Jean picked up the check, although Stephanie offered to – the three of them always took turns paying – but Jean was happy to do it today. And Stephanie's cell phone rang while Jean was paying. It was Chase.

'Hi,' she said discreetly, lowering her voice. 'I'm having lunch with friends. Can I call you back in a few minutes? We're just leaving.'

'Of course.' He had gotten used to checking in on her all the time, while she was driving, but now she was home, so things had changed. 'Sorry, Stevie.'

'No worries. I'll call you when I get home.' Her house was only a few blocks away, and she saw that Alyson was watching her with interest when she hung up.

'Who was that? Your whole face changed when you answered.' Jean had seen it too, and was smiling. She could easily guess who it was.

'It was Laura,' Stephanie said quickly, not knowing what else to say, but Jean knew the truth, and Alyson didn't. Stephanie just didn't feel ready to tell her about a man. She didn't think Alyson would understand. Jean did, and was more open-minded about it, and even enthusiastic. She had been encouraging Stephanie to get involved with Chase since the first day. But Stephanie sensed that Alyson would be shocked, and maybe even disapprove out of loyalty to Bill.

'Since when is Laura so important that you drove across the country to see her? I never heard you mention her before. And you didn't tell us in Santa Barbara that you were going there,' Alyson challenged her.

'I decided at the last minute, when she called to invite me,' Stephanie said, trying to sound vague, and wondering if it was true that she looked different when Chase called. She was always happy to hear his voice. 'We were friends in college, and we recently reconnected. She just lost her husband too. So we're both at loose ends.' The story was getting more convoluted, and the lies were taking on a life of their own. Her fictional friend had even begun to seem real to her, and was really just a disguise for Chase, to her kids and now to her friends. 'Laura' was her excuse for spending two weeks getting to know Chase and discovering his world. But what she had just said to Alyson sounded plausible to her, and she seemed to relax about it.

'Well, I'm glad you have her to be with,' Alyson said kindly. 'I feel so guilty sometimes that I'm so busy with the kids. I always want to spend time with you, and then something happens and I can't.' She looked genuinely sorry, and Stephanie knew that Alyson cared about her, and was just overwhelmed by her life. 'Why don't you have Laura come out to visit you here, if she's alone now too?' She hated to think of how lonely Stephanie must be in the empty house without Bill.

'She probably will,' Stephanie said easily. 'We had a nice visit while I was there. We even went to Graceland.'

'It's good for you to have someone to do things with,'

Alyson said sympathetically. And then all three women hugged each other as they left the restaurant and promised to get together soon.

'Say hi to Laura for me,' Jean whispered to Stephanie as she kissed her goodbye, knowing full well it was the code name for Chase.

'I will,' Stephanie promised, and went back to her car, happy to have seen her friends. She was home five minutes later and called Chase. She was out of breath from running up the stairs.

'Sorry. I couldn't talk in front of them.'

'I didn't mean to bother you. I just missed you. And we're going to work in the studio in a few minutes. I wish you were here.'

'So do I,' she said honestly. 'I have nothing to do here. I'm almost sorry I came back.' She was planning to go to the shelter to work, but they just didn't need her enough. They had plenty of volunteers. And she had to get ready for Charlotte to come home in a few days. And while she was driving home, she had decided to put Bill's clothes away. She wanted to do it before her daughter got home. It would be upsetting for her to see her mother empty his closets.

'You can come back anytime,' he reminded her, and she smiled, thinking about it.

'I'd like that a lot.' And she hoped he'd come to San Francisco one day, although they had no plans.

'I'll call you when we finish,' he said. She could hear the others shouting out to him, and knew he had to go. And a minute later they had said goodbye, and he was off the phone. She sat thinking about him for a long time, with her cell phone still in her hand, remembering the good times they'd had in Nashville, and lying in his arms on his bed. She was startled when the phone rang as she held it. It was Charlotte, back in Rome, after her trip to Paris.

'Ready to come home, sweetheart?' her mother asked her, and there was a brief silence at the other end. For a minute, Stephanie thought the line had gone dead.

'Actually . . . that's why I called you, Mom. Everyone's going to the South of France next week, and I got invited to Corsica, and St. Tropez. Could I, do you think . . . would it be okay if I stay another month? I promise I'll come home at the end of July, and spend August with you.' Stephanie was disappointed to hear it, but she didn't have any fabulous plans to offer Charlotte, the weather was always bad in San Francisco in the summer, cold, foggy, and windy, and she knew that Charlotte would have nothing to do when she got home. And it was hard to compete with Corsica and St. Tropez.

'I guess so,' Stephanie said quietly. It made her sorry she had come home from Nashville. With none of the kids home in July, she could have stayed there with Chase. But her children never planned ahead, and even when they did, they changed plans at the last minute, as Charlotte wanted to do now. 'Okay.' She agreed to what Charlotte was asking, and reminded her that she had to give up her room in the apartment she had been assigned the following week. They were student apartments provided by the university. She had five roommates, and Charlotte had to vacate her room.

'I'm going to leave for St. Tropez before then. Thank you, Mom!' She sounded ecstatic that she didn't have to come home. After they hung up, Stephanie lay down on her bed, wondering what to do next. She wanted to empty Bill's closets, but she wasn't ready to do it on her first day back. She had the whole month of July to do it now. She lay there and closed her eyes, thinking of Chase, wishing she were with him in Nashville. The house seemed emptier than ever now that she knew Charlotte wasn't coming home.

Chapter 17

After Sandy's visit, Michael felt like everything had changed. When Amanda came home from Houston, exhausted after the weekend, she found Michael remote and strange. He wanted to talk to her, but thought he should give her a chance to catch her breath.

She didn't say anything about how quiet he was for the first few days, and thought he was busy at work or in a bad mood. He was trying to plan what to say, as nicely as he could.

'What's up?' she finally asked him on Friday night, when they went out to dinner, and were going to meet up with friends. 'Bad week at work?'

'No, just busy.' He didn't meet her eyes.

'You've been acting weird all week. Are you feeling okay?'

'Yeah, I'm fine.' But he had verbalized things to Sandy that he had never admitted to himself, that he couldn't see himself spending the rest of his life with Amanda, marrying her, or having kids. They were just too different, and her career ambitions no longer seemed to mesh with his. It sounded corny, but he wanted a wife or woman more like his mother. Amanda thought of everything in terms of the investment, of time, energy, or money, rather than the people involved. She wasn't a nurturing person. She was a money-making machine in a dress. And she kept talking about what they could do with their two combined incomes, rather than how much she loved him. Listening to her now turned Michael off. And he hated to admit it to her, but he was done. All that remained was to tell her. The hardest part.

She had been talking to him about the house she wanted to buy with him all night during dinner, and she could see that he had tuned out. He and Sandy had been texting each other all week, and he had called her when she got home, right before Amanda got back. He felt awkward calling Sandy now, until he worked things out with Amanda, but texting seemed okay. The subtle shadings of modern technology. And sending her an e-mail would definitely be too much. He didn't want to make promises or issue invitations until he was free. And Amanda still wanted to buy a house with him, and expected to marry him one day. They weren't engaged, but in her mind, they might as well have been. All the same expectations were there. Amanda was too ambitious, demanding, and grown up. Sandy seemed like an irresistible little elf. He kept thinking of her in the pink cotton dress and ballet flats when she left. She looked like a beautiful little girl, but at the same time she was a woman, and he was overwhelmed with desire for her. It was all he could think of every night when he went to bed with Amanda, and the haunting visions of Sandy just wouldn't go away. He was afraid that Amanda would guess before he had a chance to clean things up. She had noticed something off about him, but had no idea what.

'So what do you think, Mike? Should we go house hunting this weekend?' Amanda was like a dog with a bone. 'I looked online, and there are three open houses in Buckhead at really reasonable prices. I think we should take a look.' Buckhead was a beautiful, very substantial part of town. But not where Michael wanted to live. It was where older people who made a lot of money bought homes.

'I don't feel ready to buy a house,' he managed to blurt out, and she gave him a startled look.

'You don't?' She had just given him the perfect opening for what he wanted to say, but he was scared. And knew he had to say it anyway. In fairness to them all.

'That's such a big commitment,' he said, about a house in Buckhead. 'What if I lose my job, or you do? How would we handle the mortgage?' Even without Sandy, he was worried about it.

'My dad says he would help us.' And then she narrowed her eyes and looked at him. 'Are you having second thoughts about us?' That had never even occurred to her before, but she sensed it now. He always seemed so steady and on track, and now he was sidling around, like a nervous horse. She'd been talking to him about a house for six months, and had never picked up any skittishness before.

'Look, we're both twenty-five years old. What's the rush? I like my apartment. You live in a nice place. Why do we have to buy a house?'

'It's a great investment. My dad says we're just wasting money with rent. He said he'll help us with the down payment, and you have the insurance money from your dad, which is just sitting there. Why not put it into a house?' She had it all figured out, and assumed a lot. Michael had thought of buying a house with the insurance money too, but more modestly, and on his own. And he knew his mother didn't like the idea of his buying real estate with Amanda. She had asked him what would happen if their relationship didn't work out. If they owned a house together, it would be complicated and more like a divorce.

'I think we're both too young.' He sounded hesitant as he said it, thinking of Sandy and the weekend before. He had no idea what to do about her yet, and the prospect of looking at houses with Amanda only made his anxiety worse.

Danielle Steel

'I'm not too young to buy a house,' Amanda said with determination. 'And you're not either. You're just scared,' she said, hoping to embarrass him into it, but he surprised her and agreed.

'Yes, I am. You make a lot more money than I do. What if I can't hold up my end?' Given the houses she wanted to look at, and the area, it was going to be a stretch for him, a big one. She wanted a serious house, and her daddy said she could have it. But more than that, she wanted Mike to go with it. Michael felt like her father was buying him as well as the house. It made him feel claustrophobic.

'Let's just see if there's anything we want,' she said firmly.

'I don't know if I can afford it,' he said, feeling as though he were shouting into cotton. She didn't want to hear him, and after he paid for their dinner, they left the restaurant and went to meet up with friends at Strip.

Amanda noticed that he never said another word for the rest of the night, and drank a little too much. He wasn't falling off his bar stool, but he was vague and distracted. But she was confident she would ultimately convince him about the house. And if she couldn't, her father would for sure. She could hardly wait to look that weekend.

Michael texted Sandy from the bar that night, while no one was watching. Amanda was busy talking to their friends. He wrote to Sandy that he was thinking about her. She had been answering promptly all week when he texted her, and sent back funny little quips that made him smile, or sent smiley faces. But this time, when he needed to hear from her, she didn't answer. It made him feel lonelier than ever, standing right next to Amanda. And all he knew was that he didn't want to be railroaded into a house he didn't want to buy, or forced to stay with a woman he had only recently discovered wasn't for him. And the one who was, was barely more than a child, just eighteen, and had a boyfriend too.

Sandy was rehearsing with the band that night. Chase had written some new songs that he wanted to try out. She was only singing backup with Delilah, but she was distracted and couldn't get it right. It was unusual for her, but this time she couldn't remember the words. And Bobby Joe was sitting on the sidelines and smirking at her. Without a word, he managed to convey just how stupid and inept she was by rolling his eyes.

Chase came over and said something to her during a break. 'Is Bobby Joe distracting you?' He had seen him grinning derisively at her, and Sandy looked away, after she made the same mistake four times.

'No,' she said, embarrassed and apologetic. 'I don't know why I can't get it right.' The words were simple to remember. 'Just dumb, I guess,' she said under her breath, as Chase spun around and grabbed her by the shoulders.

'What did you just say?' he asked, looking intently at her. 'If that little asshole makes you feel like that about yourself, get rid of him, Sandy. He's never going anywhere, except a bar on West End Avenue, or some shoestore with live music. You're going to be a star one day, and not because of me. You've got everything it takes, he doesn't. He should be playing a washboard somewhere. So don't let me hear you saying how dumb you are, Sandy Johnson, or I'm going to kick your ass.' She smiled when he said it.

'Sorry, Chase.' He nodded with a serious expression, and then glanced at her. She seemed troubled.

'Does this have anything to do with last weekend in Atlanta?' He lowered his voice to ask her. She hesitated and then nodded. He was like a father to her, and she always told him the truth, even more than she had to her own dad.

'Maybe.'

'Is Michael giving you a hard time?' She shook her head instantly, with a wistful look in her eyes.

'No, he's real nice to me. It's just . . . well, you know . . . he's practically engaged to that woman. She wants him to buy a house with her. It's almost like they're married. He says he doesn't want to stay with her, but he hasn't done anything about it yet.'

'She wants a lot of things,' Chase said knowingly. 'But

"almost" doesn't put a ring on your finger or win horse races. I told you to be careful. But that doesn't mean you won't get him. I saw the way he looked at you after the concert. That boy is crazy about you. If he says he'll get out of his relationship, he will.' Chase sounded convinced. 'Have you heard from him since last weekend?' Her eyes lit up when he asked.

'Yeah, about five times an hour.' She laughed, and Chase grinned at her.

'I'd say that's a nice start. You didn't sleep with him, did you?' She shook her head emphatically. She wouldn't have done that while still involved with Bobby Joe. She was a girl with principles, and Michael respected her for it. Chase was pleased with her answer. 'Good. Keep it that way. It'll drive him crazy,' he said, smiling broadly. Not having slept with Stephanie was doing that to him. All he wanted was to put his arms around her and make love to her. He was obsessed with her. Sandy laughed at what Chase told her, and a few minutes later they started rehearsal again, and this time she got it right.

They broke for the night around midnight. Bobby Joe had waited for her, and he'd been drinking beer all through rehearsal. He was fairly well lubricated when they walked from Chase's house back to her cottage in the garden, and he sprawled out on the couch.

'You sure muffed that the first hundred times tonight,' Bobby Joe said, gloating at her. He loved it when she

287

screwed up. It always made him feel better, and he never missed a chance to point it out. She remembered what Chase had said about him earlier in the evening. That he was going nowhere fast. He was a good-looking boy with a mediocre talent in music that wouldn't take him far.

'I needed to get the melody right, and learn the words. It came out good the last time.' She seemed pleased, and Chase had loved it.

'You're lucky he lets you sing backup. He only does that because of who you are. You'd never get a job anywhere if you had to do it on your own.'

'What makes you say that?' Sandy asked him, as she stood very still and watched him. He had just gotten up to help himself to a beer in her fridge.

'Everybody knows it. You're cute, babe, but not long on talent.'

'Why would you say something like that to me?' She was outraged, especially after Chase's pep talk that night. 'Just to make me feel bad and hurt my feelings?'

'No, because it's true. The truth always hurts.' He shrugged as he said it, went and got the beer, and put the bottle to his lips. And then he glanced at her with a wicked grin. 'Come on, baby, let's go to bed. I'm tired from listening to you sing all night. Let's have some action.' He was treating her like a cheap slut, and suddenly added to everything else he had said, it was just too much. She hadn't been looking for a showdown with him, but she had no other choice.

'You actually think I'm going to sleep with you after you say things like that?'

'What's the matter? Can't stand the truth, that Chase only lets you sing for him because he feels sorry for you and promised your daddy?' Bobby Joe was always mean as a snake when he was drunk.

'I may be a shit singer,' she said with her chin trembling, and her eyes blazing, 'but I'm not some cheap trick you picked up in a bar. You can't insult me, and expect to wind up in my bed. Get your ass out of my house, Bobby Joe.' And she meant it. He wasn't impressed.

'Why? You think you're too fancy for me, because Chase has money and you live here? Get real, baby, you're no better than I am, no matter where you live. You don't impress me. You're just a hillbilly from the gutter, like me.'

'No, I'm not. And it's not where I'll wind up one day, like you. I work my ass off, while you sit on yours drinking. You're not going anywhere, Bobby Joe, but straight down-hill. I'm going to be someone one day, on my own, not because of Chase. And you're going to be nothing. And you can't treat me like shit and say mean things to me anymore, because you're jealous. You're nothing but a pile of shit with a mean mouth. Now get out of my house.'

'Come on, baby, let's go to bed.' He stood up unsteadily

and tried to paw her, and she gave him a shove. He fell back on the couch and sat there, laughing at her while she shook with rage.

'You've got three choices,' she said through clenched teeth. 'I call Chase or the police, or you get your ass out of here under your own steam. Your choice. You're a mean little shit, and I'm finished. I don't need someone to treat me like this. I'd rather be alone.'

'You can't make me leave,' he said cockily, and she looked him right in the eye with a deadly calm.

'Watch me. You've been badmouthing me since you started going out with me. I'm done. Get out.' She said it clearly, as she picked up her phone and pressed 9-1-1 for the police. As she did, he lunged at her, grabbed the phone, and disconnected the call.

'Don't be stupid.' He was angry by then. This wasn't a fun game anymore. 'Let's go to bed. You can blow me.' She could see that he was really drunk. He was unpleasant when he was sober, but a lot more so whenever he drank. And he had gone over the line.

'It's over. Go home. And don't come back here. You can talk to Chase about if he still wants you to open for him.' Bobby Joe looked panicked at that. She had gotten him the job.

'Come on, Sandy,' he pleaded with her. 'You know I love you.'

'No, you don't. You treat me like shit, because you're

jealous. Go find someone else to treat mean. We're finished.' He got up off the couch then and hesitated. He made a sloppy pass at her, trying to get amorous and pull her toward her bedroom, and she pushed him away. 'I don't need garbage like you in my life.'

'Go fuck yourself, Sandy!' he shouted at her as he walked to the door and yanked it open. 'I don't need you either.' He slammed the door behind him, and Sandy walked to her room and lay down on the bed. She knew she had done the right thing, and she wouldn't miss him. He had been awful to her, and Chase was right. She didn't deserve it. No one had a right to treat anyone like that, drunk or sober. He'd been doing it for a long time, and she'd let him. He'd never laid a hand on her, but had beaten her up with his words, and tore her down every chance he got, to make himself feel better. She wouldn't miss him.

She lay there for a long time, thinking about what he'd said, and she never looked at her phone again that night. She fell asleep on her bed, with her clothes on. And she never saw the text from Michael. And she forgot about her phone the next day when she went to see Chase.

She told Chase about Bobby Joe the next morning, when she saw him sitting at the pool. He was reading the Sunday paper.

'I broke up with Bobby Joe last night,' she said, sitting

down on a chair next to him. She seemed okay, but a little tired. She'd been up late, and she'd barely slept after he left.

'Are you all right with it?' he asked with a look of concern, and she nodded.

'Yeah, I am. He's been treating me like dirt forever. I kept thinking it would get better, but it didn't. He was nice in the beginning, when he wanted a job, opening for you.' She shrugged, and Chase smiled.

'I guess I need to start auditions for a new opening band. I was tired of him anyway. He plays the same old stuff every time. I'll have Charlie let him know.' Charlie was not only the drummer, but he also hired the opening acts, with Chase's approval. He was leaving, but still dealing with the other band members until he left. 'Bobby Joe's a nasty piece of work. I'm glad you're done with him. Time to move on.' He didn't say a word about Michael, and neither did Sandy. And it didn't make any difference anyway, she reminded herself as she dove into the pool a few minutes later. She was free now. But he wasn't. At least Bobby Joe was gone. She was glad. He was a jerk. And she knew she had hung on to him longer than she should. She'd been afraid to let him go.

Amanda and Michael visited three houses on the same street in Buckhead that Saturday. Two of them were enormous, with extensive wings and grounds, and the last one had five bedrooms. All of them were serious family homes, and just looking at them with her made Michael nervous and confirmed everything he thought.

'So when are you two getting married, or are you already?' the realtor running the open house at the last home asked them with an Alabama drawl.

Amanda smiled at the question, and Michael felt sick as he wondered what she would answer. He didn't say a word, which was often his way of dealing with questions he didn't like. And he didn't like that one. He had told her he wasn't ready.

'We're just looking,' Amanda said blandly, and smiled conspiratorially at Michael. She was being coy, and as they drove away, she was excited. 'Oh my God, do you believe how gorgeous that house is?' She acted like she was ready to move in, with or without him, or if she had to drag him there by the hair.

'Are you insane?' he finally exploded. 'Did you see the price? Do you know what I make? And I'm not putting all my dad's insurance into that house, or asking my mom to help. We'd need four kids to fill that house.'

'It's a great investment,' she said calmly. Her mantra.

'So is Buckingham Palace. I can't afford it. You should marry Prince Harry. And we don't need a house like that, or any house. We're not getting married.'

'Not now. But one day. Right?' She gazed at him directly as she asked the question, and suddenly he thought

293

of what he had said to Sandy only a week before. That he couldn't see himself married to her, or having children with her. Now or later. He had just never said it to her, and he'd only been sure about it for the past few months, when she'd started pressuring him about a house. At first he thought he wasn't ready. But now he knew she was the wrong girl, which was very different. He had never been sure of that before. Now he was. He pulled the car over and put it in park, and looked at her long and hard. And he spoke clearly and firmly when he finally did.

'No, Amanda. Not one day. Never. I can't. We'd be miserable together. We don't want the same things in life.'

'Of course we do. You're just scared to buy a house. Everyone is when they buy their first house.'

'I don't want to marry you,' he said simply. 'Ever. It's not right. You need someone more like you. I'm never going to be that person. You need a guy like your father.' He was all about money, ambition, and power. Michael wasn't. He was more like his mother, oblivious to superficial values.

Amanda sat staring at him for a long moment, and set her lips in a thin line. 'Take me home.' He started to drive her back to her place, which she rarely went to, and then he felt like a monster when he saw she was crying. He pulled over again, and put his arms around her.

'I shouldn't have pushed you about the house. We can wait, Mike. I just wanted to get us started. I'm in no rush.'

She didn't want to lose him. He was a great catch, she had made her mind up about him three years before, and still felt the same way. She was convinced he had a great future ahead of him and would do well, especially with her behind him.

'Yes, you are in a rush,' he said honestly. 'And that's okay for you, but it isn't for me. I just realized recently that I don't want to marry you. I don't think it's right for either of us. I wanted to tell you, but I didn't know how.'

'We don't have to get married for a long time,' she negotiated with him, and he shook his head.

'No,' he said firmly. 'You need someone else. And so do I.' She looked panicked then as she heard what he said.

'Is there someone else?' He could be honest with her, and he was glad he had gone no further with Sandy the week before, and had been truthful with her about Amanda.

'No, there isn't.' He didn't add the words 'not yet.' She didn't need to hear them. And it was beside the point. All that mattered was that he knew he didn't want a life with her. He wasn't even sure he loved her. And he wasn't sure if Amanda even cared. She wanted a lifestyle, and an investment, more than the man who went with it. His mother had been right all along.

He drove her home then and stopped outside her building on Cheshire Bridge Road. She got out slowly and looked at him through the window. 'Why don't we think

about this, Mike? You panicked. Let's give it some time.'
He already had. Three years. Long enough to know what
he didn't want, and with whom. He shook his head as he
looked at her, not knowing what else to say.

'I'll drop your stuff off this week' was all he could think
of. Amanda looked shocked as he drove away. She let herself into her building then, ran upstairs to her apartment,
and threw herself onto the bed. But she had to call her
father and tell him what had happened.

'I always knew he was the wrong guy,' her father said
calmly. 'No guts. No ambition.' It was a harsh thing to say
about Mike. He worked hard, had a good job, and was a
nice boy. 'Good riddance,' her father said roughly, and
Amanda felt sad as she hung up. She loved him, and
thought he loved her too. She always believed they
wanted the same things, but they didn't. And maybe her
father was right, and Michael. They both said she needed
a man like her father. And when she thought about it, she
knew they were right. She wanted a guy who wanted one
of those big houses in Buckhead, and would kill himself
to get it for her. A man who wanted to stretch and grab
the brass ring and win the prize. Amanda wanted all the
prizes, but not necessarily the guy. It wasn't about love for
her. It was about power. And that wasn't Michael.

Sandy never saw the message Mike had sent her from the
bar until late Saturday, when she fished her phone out

from between the couch cushions where Bobby Joe had thrown it the night before. She answered it just saying that she was thinking about him too, and hoped he'd had fun the night before. But he didn't answer. When he saw her text, he was sitting in his apartment, thinking about Amanda and what had happened that day. He felt empty and alone every time he thought of Amanda. He wasn't sure how or why it had unraveled so quickly, but a three-year relationship had ended. It was something to think about, and he needed time to mourn it. He didn't want to just reach out to Sandy, or tell her what had happened, as though he could end one relationship and start another five minutes later. *Hi . . . I'm free now . . . let's go play.* He owed Amanda more respect than that, so he didn't respond to Sandy.

He packed Amanda's things in boxes – the clothes she'd left at his house, her books, her tennis and gym clothes, a sculpture they'd bought together. Three years of memorabilia that were at his place and not hers. It took him an hour to gather it all up, and another hour to pack it. Three years in two boxes. And he called his mother that night and told her. He sounded sad.

'I'm sorry, baby,' she said to her son, and she meant it. Stephanie had never liked her, but he had, and that was enough. She was sorry for the disappointment and his aching heart. He sounded very unhappy and a little shocked.

Danielle Steel

'I don't know what happened. All of a sudden, I just had to tell her. I only figured it out a few weeks ago. She's been pushing me to buy a house. I just didn't want to do that, but she kept pushing. I nearly broke out in hives when we looked at that house.' Stephanie smiled at what he said.

'One day you'll find the right person.'

Amanda called Michael that night and sounded as shell-shocked as he was. But she didn't argue with him, or beg to get back together. In her heart of hearts, she knew he was right. She reminded him to put her skillets in with her other things. She had paid for them and wanted them back. And the new microwave she had just bought for his apartment. In the end, it came down to that. Frying pans and a microwave and a box of old stuff. She reduced it all to the merely practical. He wondered if she'd even miss him. He felt empty when he hung up. Three years of his life had just gone down the garbage disposal, and he'd flipped the switch. And he knew he should have done it long before.

He went for a run that night to try and clear his head. It helped a little. And he thought about Sandy when he got back. He wanted to call her, but he knew it was too soon. He needed time to put Amanda behind him and wipe the slate clean. And when he went to bed, he dreamed of Sandy. They were buying a big house, and Amanda was the real estate agent, and she kept pushing. In the dream,

298

he shouted at her, and then he and Sandy ran away, laughing, with Amanda shouting after them. The dream seemed clear to him when he woke up. Amanda was the saleswoman, trying to sell him a house he didn't want. And Sandy was the girl of his dreams.

Chapter 18

In the end, Michael waited a week, and then decided to call Sandy. She had sent him a couple of texts, which he hadn't answered, and he felt guilty about it. It was a few days before the Fourth of July weekend. He had dropped off Amanda's things and hadn't heard from her. She had moved on, without sentiment or regrets. He was disappointed, but he wasn't devastated or heartbroken, which told him he'd done the right thing. He'd been thinking about Sandy a lot. She hadn't told him what had happened with Bobby Joe in her texts. And since she didn't hear from Michael in response, she assumed he was still with his girlfriend. She sounded surprised to hear from him, and was downtown shopping with a friend. But she was as easygoing as ever.

'Sorry I haven't answered. I've been a little tied up here,' he said, feeling awkward at first.

'That's fine. I've been busy too.' She had been sad not

to hear from him, but she respected him for not chasing her at the same time, when she knew he had a girlfriend. They'd kissed at the airport, and he had told her he needed to make some decisions. She assumed he had decided to stay with Amanda. 'How are you?'

'Fine.' The Braves had been on a winning streak, which everyone in Atlanta was excited about, hoping to get to the playoffs and World Series.

'We're playing a big concert on the Fourth of July. Five big bands. Chase is the lead act, so we've been rehearsing day and night.'

'Sounds intense,' Michael said, thinking of the concert he'd been to when he'd first seen her. 'How's the rest of your life?'

'The same. Well, almost. I broke up with Bobby Joe.' That was a major piece of news to him. 'He acted like a real asshole. All the time, actually. But he got drunk one night while we were rehearsing, and he was such a jerk, it finally did it for me. Chase just hired a new opening act for the band. That'll really fry his sorry ass,' she said, laughing, and Michael was smiling.

'Yeah, I think so.' He hesitated for an instant and then decided to tell her. 'I broke up with Amanda. No new opening band, though.' Sandy laughed.

'What happened?'

'Pretty much what we talked about. I knew I didn't want to marry her, and she backed me into a corner about buying a house with her, and I had to tell her. It's better this way.'

'Why didn't you tell me you two broke up?' Sandy sounded surprised.

'I thought I should wait a little while, out of respect for both of you. But I missed you too much, so I called you today.' He was smiling as he said it. They were both quiet for a minute. It changed things between them, and made things seem more serious than they had been when she went to Atlanta. They were both free now, and she was thinking about it and what it meant. So was he.

She decided to be brave first. 'Do you want to come to the Fourth of July concert here?' Her heart was pounding as she asked him and waited for his answer. 'You can stay at Chase's. He has a guest room.' She didn't want him to think that she was inviting him straight into her bed. She wasn't. She had taken Chase's advice to heart.

He was thinking about it, but his answer came quickly. He didn't want her to change her mind.

'I'd love it. Are you sure Chase wouldn't mind?'

'No, he'll be fine.' She sounded happy and excited, and so did he. He was going to come down two days before and spend the weekend with them. She told him that Nashville went all out for the Fourth with barbecues, picnics, and a parade, and their concert. There was another one the day before at Opryland. 'Come ready to party,' she told him, and he laughed. She was excited when she hung up, but tried to be calm about it, and she told Chase about it the day before Michael arrived.

'Can I use your guest room this weekend?' she asked casually when she saw him at rehearsal, and he looked surprised.

'Sure. Who's coming? Anyone I know?' He couldn't imagine who she wanted there. Once in a while she had a girlfriend come to visit who'd moved away, but they always stayed in the cottage with her. Why not this one?

'Michael Adams.' She tried to sound nonchalant about it, and his eyes grew wide.

'Michael Adams, as in Stevie's son?' She nodded, and smiled. 'Is he bringing his girlfriend?' he teased her, and she shook her head.

'They broke up.' He smiled at that with a wicked look.

'My, my . . . isn't that interesting . . . and you and Bobby Joe broke up too . . . happy to have him,' he said, and winked at her, and they both went back to work with the band.

He told Stephanie that night.

'I'm having a guest this weekend,' he said benignly when he talked to her after rehearsal. He was tired, but excited about the concert on the Fourth. There was nothing he liked better than playing. He always said he was born to sing and play his guitar.

'Anyone special?' Stephanie asked, wondering if it was

some big country music star. He knew them all, and there were a number of them playing at the concert on the Fourth.

'I think so. I think you will too. A young man by the name of Michael Adams. He's coming from Atlanta.' It took a moment to sink in, and then she screamed.

'My Michael? How did that happen?' She had spoken to Michael two days before, and he'd said nothing about it. She was suddenly glad she hadn't decided to go to Nashville too. It would have been harder to explain to Michael about 'Laura' a second time.

'Sandy invited him,' Chase filled her in. 'He's staying in my guest room, all very proper.' She knew Michael and Amanda had broken up because he had called her about it, but she hadn't heard from him since. And he hadn't mentioned Sandy. But she was pleased.

'Well, I'll be damned.' Stephanie sat on her bed and grinned. 'That is very good news indeed. I wonder if he'll tell me.' She suspected he would eventually, but not just yet.

'Well, act surprised if he does. I don't want him to think I'm spying on him.'

'You have to tell me all about it,' Stephanie said, sounding excited.

'Of course. I just wish you were coming too.' He was wistful as he said it.

'So do I,' she said, remembering his kisses. She was

planning on going to a barbecue at Brad and Alyson's in Ross over the Fourth. Chase had invited her to Nashville, but she wasn't ready to go back. She still felt she had to make some decisions about her life first.

'Well, let's see what happens now, with these two. Life is funny, isn't it?' She thought about it as he said it. It certainly was. 'It's all about fate and destiny, and opening the right door at the right time, and having the guts to walk through it. It's amazing how everything changes in the blink of an eye.' One minute he was all tied up with Amanda, on a straight path toward a marriage Stephanie had thought would make him miserable. And now he was headed in a totally other direction, with a country music singer who sang like an angel. It was like Stephanie taking the road to Las Vegas instead of San Francisco, and then going to Nashville with him. All you had to do was be brave enough to do it. She had been, and now her son was too. She was thrilled.

Chapter 19

The Fourth of July party at Brad and Alyson's house in Ross was the epitome of everything Stephanie had been afraid her life would be like as a widow in San Francisco, with all the people they had known, in the familiar world where she now felt like a misfit. And everything people said that night just made her feel worse. They all told her how 'sorry' they were for 'her loss,' like a mantra they had to say the moment they saw her. Then they asked how she was 'doing,' as though she were in treatment for a terminal disease, which it was in a way. Widowhood was the end of life as she knew it, but it was inconceivable to them that there was any form of life beyond it. Their pity for her radiated from their eyes like gentle daggers that pierced her heart. She had never missed Bill more than that night, and she didn't even know why. He would have hated the evening, complained about going, made her leave early, and told her how stupid Fourth of July parties were and that they shouldn't have gone. She always wanted to stay at parties longer than he did, and he always made her leave early because he had a meeting the next day, or an early golf date on a holiday or Sunday.

The party was held in Brad and Alyson's beautifully manicured garden at their house in Ross. All of their neighbors were there, most of whom Stephanie knew, and even those she didn't were sorry for her when mutual friends told them about Bill's death on the ski slopes nearly five months before. She felt as though she should have worn a black veil or widow's weeds to the party, but she didn't need to. They treated her that way anyway. She was 'Poor Stephanie' in their eyes, and nothing was going to change that. And while feeling sorry for her, the wives were slightly suspicious of her, as though she were dangerous now, and the husbands were much too friendly and a little too cozy, which proved their wives right. There was no way to be herself or a normal person in their midst. Alyson was nervous throughout, worried that the caterer wasn't doing things right, and she went inside several times to check on the kids. Brad was too jovial and acted like he'd had a lot to drink. The waiters were passing trays of margaritas, and no matter how many Stephanie had, she felt painfully sober throughout the evening, even if slightly sick.

And Brad had kept an arm around her for a little too

long as he asked how she was doing, and he said they didn't see enough of her now. He asked what she'd been up to but didn't listen to what she told him, and she had the feeling that if she'd read the Yellow Pages to him as an answer, he would have smiled and listened in the same sympathetic way. He told her she looked great, but she didn't feel it. Jean and Fred were there too. Jean was flirting with several men after too many margaritas, and Fred fell asleep in a chair before the buffet dinner. Stephanie felt disconnected from everyone there although she had known them for twenty years.

They talked about nothing, and just talked at each other while they ate and drank all night, asked about one another's kids but didn't listen. The fourteenth time someone asked her, after telling her how sorry they were about her loss again, she wanted to tell them that Michael was in jail, Louise was turning tricks in New York, and Charlotte had gotten knocked up in Europe. She didn't, but they wouldn't have heard her anyway. It was the most depressing evening she'd spent in years, and Alyson asked her solicitously if she'd had a good time, somehow conveying the message that she knew she couldn't possibly since she'd come alone, and no longer had a husband.

Stephanie quietly called a cab to take her home, since she'd arrived in one so she could have a drink or two. The others had driven themselves, and would be driving home drunk all over Marin, as they always did. She wanted to scream on the ride home, and she watched the fireworks from the cab on the Golden Gate Bridge. They were pretty, but the evening had been morbidly depressing. And she couldn't even call Chase to tell him about it, since he was on stage in Nashville at that moment. She was happy to know that her son was there and wished she were too. She had slipped away and only said goodbye to Alyson. She just couldn't face all the others to say goodbye in her new role of 'Poor Stephanie.' It was the first party she'd gone to since Bill died, and it had been unbearable for her.

She paid the cab and went inside to the dark house and silence that were familiar now. There was no one to talk to about the party, and she didn't want to anyway. She put on jeans and an old sweater, and she didn't want to go to bed, so she finally tackled the project she had dreaded most, knowing she couldn't get more depressed than she already was. She started emptying Bill's closet, and laid his jackets and trousers one by one on their bed. She and Michael had already discussed it, and he was much taller than his father, and thinner, there was nothing he could wear or wanted to keep. And his feet were three sizes larger than his father's. So she was going to give it all away.

She had put boxes aside in the garage for the project, and she brought them all upstairs. It was nearly four o'clock in the morning when she finished, and all of Bill's suits, slacks, sports coats, shirts, ties, shoes, underwear, and everything he'd ever worn, including his tuxedo, was neatly folded in boxes, and taped closed. She didn't even feel the tears running down her cheeks. And all of his drawers and closets in his dressing room were empty. There was no sign of him at all except in the photographs of him around the house in silver frames. He was a ghost now. He was gone.

She fell asleep on the bed with her clothes on, too tired to change, and she walked around the house the next morning, as though seeing it for the first time. She moved some chairs around, and a table. She pushed her desk to the other side of the room, and she was surprised by how much better things looked when she was finished. She even rehung some paintings in the living room and dining room, and took down one Bill had loved and she didn't. They'd bought it in London, of a hunt with the hounds tearing a fox apart. She was going to put it in a storeroom they had downstairs, she didn't want to see it anymore. She took out some silver bowls she'd put away, and a small statue she loved that Bill had hated, and the house started to look more feminine as she moved things, and put things away. She was desperate suddenly to make it her own, and no longer theirs.

And that afternoon she moved some of her clothes into his closet. She felt like a traitor doing it, as though she were burying him again. But she didn't want to live in a shrine. It was her house now, for as long as she chose to live there, and she had a feeling he would have done the same thing.

She carried all the boxes down to the garage to give them away, and Jean called as she was coming back up the stairs. She'd been busy all day. And she hadn't heard from Chase yet, which was unusual for him, but she was glad she hadn't. She needed to do this alone. She was relieved that it was Jean.

'Great party, wasn't it?' Jean said happily, and Stephanie hesitated for a long moment, not sure what to say, and decided to tell her the truth.

'I hated it. I felt like a freak all night. 'Poor Stephanie . . . I'm so sorry for your loss . . . what have you been doing? . . . oh poor you . . . and how are the children doing?' It's like I have no identity anymore except as whatever is left of Bill. I felt like I was on furlough from a mental institution. And why was Alyson so nervous all night? She looked like she needed a Xanax or a Valium or something.'

'You know how Brad is. He wants everything perfect, so she gets nervous. But I thought she did a great job. I'm sorry you had a tough time, Steph. It was the first time you went out. It'll be better next time.' Not unless she got new friends, Stephanie thought to herself. The prospect of going through that again made her want to scream. She'd felt like a whole person in Nashville, where no one knew her, but the night before had been her worst nightmare come true. She felt buried alive with Bill.

'I emptied all his closets last night when I got home. I just couldn't take it anymore. I was suffocating. I feel like I've lost my identity. It's like they think I'm nobody without him. And I think so too. No job, no career, no kids anymore, no Bill. There's nothing left of me. That's all I ever was, the service department for all of them with no identity of my own. I need to do something with my life, but I just don't know what. There's no me.'

'Yes, there is,' Jean said soothingly. She could hear how upset she was, and she understood. 'You were a great wife, and you're still a great mother. You didn't have time to be you when they were all here. You were taking care of them. The same thing would happen to Alyson if Brad died. Good wives don't make themselves known, they're too busy nurturing other people, unless you're a bitch like me.' Stephanie laughed at what she said, but Jean had a definite personality, was true to herself, and took care of her own needs. Stephanie knew she hadn't. She had always been quiet and discreet and done what Bill wanted and what worked for him. It never occurred to anyone, least of all him, what she needed or what worked for her.

'Maybe I was too scared to speak up,' she said to Jean. And she thought Alyson was too. She was so terrified to lose Brad, or piss him off, that she had stopped being anyone except the person he wanted her to be, not who she had been. 'What's wrong with us, acting like that? And then they die, or leave us, and there's no us left, just the shell of what we once were. That's not who I want to be anymore,' Stephanie said firmly, 'I want to be me. I just don't know who that is yet.'

'You'll figure it out,' Jean said calmly. 'I'm proud of you, Steph. You've grown up since Bill died.' And her drive across the country had been a rite of passage of some kind, as much as the trip to Nashville with Chase. She had been brave enough to enter and explore new worlds, which she could never have done with Bill. And Stephanie had the strange feeling that if Bill had returned from the dead at that moment, she wouldn't have wanted to be married to him anymore, even if she was lonely now. She was beginning to like who she was becoming too much to ever give it up. She was never going to let anyone do that to her again.

They talked for a while, and Chase called her late that afternoon. He apologized for not calling sooner, but they had left the concert and gone out to all the bars with live music, so he could show Michael, and they had done the same again that day. Chase said they'd had a ball. It was what Nashville was all about, and they were going to the Grand Ole Opry that night, which Michael wanted to see too.

'Don't let him wear you out,' Stephanie said apologetically.

'He won't. This is what I love. And he knows a lot about country music. I was surprised.'

'He loved it when he was a kid. How are he and Sandy doing?' She was dying to hear about that. She was so excited about his being there with her, and breaking up with Amanda. She was so relieved for him.

'They're getting along like a house afire. He's so sweet to her, it's really cute to watch. She's never known anyone like him, except me.' He laughed. 'The boys she meets around here are a little rough around the edges, especially on the music scene. Or they're sucking up to me. Michael is a man, and he acts like one. He's very protective of her.' Chase loved what he had seen, and it was easy to see how attracted they were to each other. They were always kissing and holding hands when they thought no one was watching. 'I think we have a real romance on our hands here.' He was happy to see it. Her son was a lovely person, Chase trusted Sandy with him completely, and they had been very well behaved the night before. Michael had said goodnight to her in the garden, and had breakfast with Chase in his kitchen that day.

He couldn't stay on with Stephanie for long because they were going to the concert at the Grand Ole Opry, but she was thrilled with the report, and it boosted her spirits as she continued to change things around the house. And she ate dinner alone in the kitchen at ten o'clock, and sent Alyson an e-mail, thanking her for the party. She wondered what Chase and the others were doing at that moment, and wished she was there.

Michael told Chase that the Grand Ole Opry was everything he had expected and more, although he had enjoyed Chase's concert even more the night before and loved watching Sandy perform. Just as it was for his mother, it was a whole new world for him. He met Randy Travis, Tim McGraw, Carrie Underwood, and Alan Jackson when he went out with Chase and Sandy afterward, and Chase's son Derek had come for the night from Memphis and was staying with friends, and Michael enjoyed meeting him too. He was a smart guy, and good to talk to. And it was obvious how much he and Chase liked each other and enjoyed each other's company.

But the highlight of the weekend for Michael was Sandy. He was absolutely dazzled by her, and was mesmerized by her solo at Chase's concert. She had a powerful voice that soared on the high notes like a gospel singer. Chase had taught her how to maximize the range of her voice. The crowd had gone wild when she finished, and so did he. And when she wasn't working, they laughed and talked and had a great time together. It was so different from everything he'd experienced with Amanda, who was so much more intense than he wanted to be. Sandy was like a summer breeze, gentle on his cheek. And when he kissed her, it drove them both to the edge of passion, but they managed to stay within sane boundaries for the entire weekend, although with some difficulty. His body ached for her every time he touched her, and hers did the same. But Chase was impressed by how reasonable they were and how well they behaved. Michael was a responsible young man, and Chase wasn't sure he could have done the same at his age.

'I was a lot wilder than he was,' Chase told his mother. 'You've got a good boy, Stevie.' She was proud of him too, and slightly concerned for Sandy. She was only eighteen, and Michael was seven years older. She had a long way to go, and a big career ahead of her, before she could settle down, no matter how in love they were, and Chase agreed.

'It would be a shame if she gave up her career now to get married and have babies. It's the only thing I'm afraid of for her. She shouldn't give up the chance she has now to make it big.'

'Michael won't expect her to,' she reassured him, 'and he's not ready to settle down either.' That had been one of the problems with Amanda. That and the fact that she was the wrong girl for him.

'He might be before she is, and it's threatening for a guy to have a woman you love exposed to so many things, opportunities, and good-looking guys. It's heady stuff. But she's got a good head on her shoulders.'

'So does he,' Stephanie said, although all of this was new to him.

When Michael went back to Atlanta on Monday night, he told Sandy before he left that he loved her, and she said it to him too. It had hit them with the speed of lightning, and gone off like rockets. He promised to come back in two weeks for the weekend, when the team had an away game. He couldn't come before that, but Sandy looked like she was floating on air when she went back to her cottage after he left.

She worked harder than ever for the next two weeks. She wanted to prove to Chase that she wasn't going to let romance distract her or destroy her career. If anything, it would fuel it, and he was impressed, and he said as much to Michael when he returned.

'You're good for her. That's the way it should be,' Chase said quietly. They were drinking a glass of wine by the pool, while Sandy was getting dressed to go out to dinner at the 1808 Grille. 'A bad love life can really screw up your career, if you're in a creative field. You can wind up too upset to work, although I always write more songs when I'm sad. But a good relationship can inspire you and give you strength.' And for the moment, Sandy was soaring. Chase hoped it would stay that way.

Sandy came out of the cottage a few minutes later, and they left for dinner. Chase sat at the pool for a long time after that, thinking about Stevie and how much he missed her.

And two days later he had a surprise for her. His agent had called him that morning. Stephanie had just gotten up when he called her, and was shuffling around her kitchen reorganizing the pots and pans and dishes.

'What are you doing this weekend?' he asked her.

'Cleaning out my garage. Why? I want to get rid of all the old tools that are broken and don't work.' It had become a sacred mission now to weed through everything in her house.

'Want help?' She didn't know what he meant. She thought he was offering to hire someone for her, which would have been just like him.

'No, I'm okay. I'm just taking my time. But thanks for the offer.' She was becoming more and more independent, and he could hear it. He didn't mind, and he admired her for it.

'That's too bad,' he said, pretending to sound disappointed. 'I thought I'd come out and give you a hand.' There was dead silence at her end as she absorbed it.

'Are you serious?'

'Yes, I am. I have meetings with a record label in L.A. next week. I thought I'd come to San Francisco first for the weekend, and we could go down to L.A. together.'

'Oh my God.' She was beaming as she said it. It was all she wanted. She hadn't seen him in weeks. 'When?'

'How soon do you want me?'

'Now.' She was laughing and sounded excited. Her hands were shaking.

'I'll come tomorrow. That gives us four days together in your fair city before we go to L.A.' It was Wednesday, and he would be there on Thursday. 'How long can you stay in L.A., or can I stay in San Francisco if we go back?'

'Charlotte's coming home in two weeks. I'm free till then.' And the homeless shelter was so flexible that she could make up the time.

'I'll stay till then,' he said, sounding as happy as she did.

It felt like the best news she'd had in years. She could hardly wait to see him, and told Dr. Zeller about it that afternoon. Stephanie had already seen her several times since she got back from her road trip cross country. And the therapist always gave her something to think about.

This time she asked her why she had never left Bill, after the affair, or even before that.

'It doesn't sound like you had a very satisfying life together. He was always busy, never at home. Even when he had free time, he spent it playing golf with clients or friends, and not with you. He wasn't there for his children, and you had to cover for him and be mother and father to them a lot of the time. So what exactly did he give you? It doesn't sound like sex was a big issue. So what kept you there?'

'Dedication. Duty. Responsibility. The kids. I wanted to be a good wife. I didn't want to deprive them of their father if I left. That was after the affair.'

'Twenty-six years of dedication and duty. Wow, Stephanie. I'm impressed. Did you love him?'

'Yes.' But she knew she hadn't stayed because of love. Dr. Zeller made it clear that she didn't believe her and wasn't really as impressed as she said.

'Any other reason you can think of?'

'What about you?' Stephanie asked. 'Why do you think I stayed?' She seemed to doubt Stephanie's word and had made that clear.

'What about fear?'

'Fear of Bill? Like he'd beat me up if I left?' That sounded ridiculous to her. Bill had never laid a hand on her nor threatened to. He wasn't a violent man. If anything, he was disengaged and disconnected from her.

'Fear of being alone,' Dr. Zeller said quietly, and Stephanie felt as if she'd been hit by a two-by-four in the solar plexus. She couldn't breathe. 'Fear of never finding anyone else. Of venturing out into the world. Your life with Bill was safe. You knew what you were dealing with. Fear of the unknown, a lack of confidence in yourself.' The therapist was well aware that Stephanie had already changed, or she would have never gone to Las Vegas, the Grand Canyon, and Nashville and driven cross country. She would never have dared to do anything like it six months before, before Bill's death. Now she had lost her excuse not to, and was facing her fears at last. She sat in her chair for a long time with tears in her eyes and nodded as she looked at the therapist.

'I think you're right,' she said softly.

Dr. Zeller nodded back with a smile. 'So do I. You're doing great, Stephanie,' she praised her. Stephanie was open to gaining insight into herself, and doing something about it. 'Have fun with your country music star. He sounds like quite a guy.' She was aware that Stephanie hadn't slept with him. They had talked about it when she got back. Stephanie didn't feel ready, and the therapist knew it was up to Stephanie if she wanted to or not. It was her decision. And if she didn't, someone else would come along. Of that Dr. Zeller was sure. She was a beautiful woman, with a fine mind, a good heart, and a lot more guts than she knew or gave herself credit for. And she was starting to open all the old doors and look at all the secrets buried there.

They had come far again that day. She was pensive as she walked out of the office and drove home. Stephanie realized now that she hadn't stayed with Bill for all the noble reasons she claimed, but because she was afraid to leave him. She knew it was true. She was making important discoveries for her future life. If she chose to have one. The other option was to bury herself alive, but she wasn't going to do that. She had already made too much progress to turn back.

Chapter 20

Stephanie felt like a kid as she waited at the San Francisco airport for Chase the next day. He had taken a commercial flight, which he rarely did, but had chartered a jet to take them to L.A. And she wanted to jump up and down, she was so excited to see him. The minute she saw him walk off the plane with his long steady stride, their eyes met, and with no thought for who might see them, he pulled her into his arms and kissed her hard. He knew he had missed her, but he only realized just how much when he was holding her again.

'I'm so happy to see you,' she said, melting into his embrace. She just wanted to stand there while he held her, but they walked slowly through the terminal and down to the baggage claim area so he could pick up his bag. He couldn't take his eyes off her, and he kept an arm around her shoulders as they walked. And she was surprised to realize that there was no awkwardness between them.

They had talked so much and so often since she'd been home that it was as though they had never left each other.

He had already told her that he had taken a suite at the Ritz-Carlton. He didn't want to make her uncomfortable, staying in the house she had shared with Bill, even if he slept in a guest room and they never touched each other. It was wiser this way, he said, and she agreed. In spite of the changes she had made, she still felt Bill's presence in the house, and there was so much history there. She was glad Chase had thought of taking a suite at a hotel. It was no different from her being at the Hermitage Hotel when she was in Nashville, they could still be together all the time. And they would be together at the Beverly Hills Hotel in L.A. He had booked a two-bedroom bungalow, and a cabana at the pool. But he was still looking forward to seeing her San Francisco house, and discovering her world, just as she had seen his.

She had thought about introducing Chase to Jean while he was in town, but she decided not to. She didn't want to crowd him, or burden him with friends who would make a fuss over him. She wanted him to herself. And they needed time alone. He had been busy in Nashville when she was there, although he had made time for her. And he would be in L.A. as well. Their four days in San Francisco were going to be pure relaxation and pleasure. And it was a beautiful day when he arrived, without the usual heavy summer fog. She had told him to bring a coat and some sweaters, since it was always chilly in the summer, and he had. And she had promised to take him to the Napa Valley, and anywhere else he wanted to go. All Chase wanted was to be with her.

'Are you hungry? Tired? What do you want to do?' She turned to him as they got in her car. 'Do you want to go to the hotel and relax, or get something to eat?' He just sat there smiling at her before he answered, drinking her in with his eyes. He was wearing a dark blue V-neck sweater, faded jeans, and cowboy boots. And as Jean would have said, he looked sexy as hell. Stephanie smiled as she watched him.

'How about we drop my bag off at the hotel and figure it out? Is there a beach we can walk on? I want to see the Golden Gate Bridge like a tourist. But all I really want to see is you. That's what I came for. The bridge is second best. You're first.' He had seen the Golden Gate Bridge before, but now he wanted to see it all again with her. She started the car, and he didn't offer to drive since he didn't know his way around. And it was only a twenty-minute drive to the city, past the old Candlestick Park, where the 49ers played. They saw the skyline of the city, the financial district, and the Bay Bridge as they drove into town. And they took a turnoff to downtown, so she could take him to the hotel.

She left her car with the doorman, and followed him

into the lobby to check in. The manager on duty escorted them to the club floor and his suite. It was one of the best in the house. And they had champagne, fruit, cookies, chocolate-dipped strawberries, and a cheese board set up in his room. He was an important VIP, and they were excited to have him there – but not nearly as excited as Stephanie was to see him. And he mentioned to her that Michael was coming back to Nashville again for the weekend. He went every week now, unless the team had a home game.

'They're so cute to watch,' Chase said about Michael and Sandy. Stephanie couldn't wait to see them together.

Stephanie offered to drive him around the city to show him the sights, and then go for a walk to the Golden Gate Bridge, and he ordered coffee for both of them from room service before they went out. They sat down in the living room of the suite to wait for it, and as they were talking, he leaned over and kissed her again. It was like a whisper on her lips. The waiter interrupted them with the coffee, and as soon as he left, Chase pulled her into his arms again. All he wanted was to feel her body next to his. He had his arms around her, and she was pressed against him. They were both breathless when they came up for air.

'I've missed you so much,' he said, nestling against her hair, and she looked up at him with all the tenderness she felt. Everything about him felt familiar to her now. It was as though they had always been together, and without a word they walked into the bedroom and lay on the bed, smiling at each other.

'I love you, Chase,' she said softly, and as she said it, he kissed her again and gently peeled her clothes off, and they got into bed together.

'I love you, Stevie,' he said as he began making love to her. It was the most natural thing in the world, and what they had both been waiting for. And when it was over, they lay in each other's arms. 'You're a beautiful woman,' he said to her softly, running a hand down her body still pressed against his. 'What are you thinking?' he asked her, worried that it had been too soon and she'd have regrets.

'That I'm the luckiest woman in the world. And if I hadn't gone to the Grand Canyon, I would never have met you that day.' They both felt as though they were meant to be together, and had come from opposite sides of the world to find each other.

'That was my lucky day for sure,' he said, and slowly pulled away from her. He walked into the bathroom with his long, lean, athletic body, and ran a bath for both of them. They slipped into it a few minutes later, and lay there at each end of the tub, and smiled at each other.

'Thank you for coming out here,' she said, as he pulled one of her feet out of the water and kissed it, as she giggled.

'I was going crazy without you in Nashville. Even if I

didn't have the meeting in L.A., I couldn't have held out for much longer. My life is nothing without you now.' And then with a serious expression, he asked her the question she had been asking herself for weeks. 'How are we going to work this out? I don't want to be away from you, Stevie. Do you think you could come to Nashville and spend some time with me? We can figure out a way to spend time here too.' But at least she had no children to keep her here anymore. She was free. But she still felt anchored in San Francisco, for reasons she hadn't been able to figure out since she got back. She wasn't working, she was only attached to Alyson and Jean, and yet she felt as though leaving would be running away somehow. But she had so little to keep her here, except a house and the holidays she spent here with her kids. All she had here now was history, and the man she had fallen in love with lived three thousand miles away. 'Why don't you come for a while after your daughter goes back to school?' he suggested. He knew Charlotte was planning to spend a month with her before she went back to NYU, and he didn't want to interfere with that. But he wanted her back with him as soon as she could.

'We'll figure it out,' she said softly, and she was determined to try, but she didn't want to give up everything familiar to her either. Her whole life had revolved around Bill and her children for twenty-six years – now she didn't want it to revolve around someone else. There had to be a place for her in his world too, where she felt useful and productive and had something real to do. 'What would I do in Nashville if I spent time there?' she asked him honestly while they got dressed. He had taken a clean white shirt out of his suitcase, and put it on with his jeans. Stephanie had no other choice than the clothes she'd picked him up in. He knew she'd asked him a serious question, and he tried not to be distracted by her body as he answered her. All he wanted to do was hold her and look at her and make love to her again.

'What do you want to do? You can do anything you want. You can handle PR for me if you like. I always need help with that.' She was a smart woman, and he thought she'd be good at it. She'd already given him several good ideas about how to handle his publicity and dealing with the press. He was unhappy about the PR firm they used, and had been thinking of switching to one in New York or Atlanta. And Stephanie could oversee that. She was toying with the idea, and there were things about it that appealed to her, but she didn't know what it would be like to work for him, or if it would interfere with what they had. Working for him would make things different. 'You can do volunteer work like what you do here. Or something in the music business. I could get you some interviews.' He was anxious to help her with anything he could, particularly if it convinced her to spend more time with him.

'I'm not sure what kind of job I could do if I'm not there full time.' But she'd have the same problem finding a job in San Francisco, if she was going to be running to Nashville all the time. The one thing she didn't want was to give up her identity and be some kind of satellite to him. She had done that for too many years. Bill hadn't asked her to, it had just worked out that way, married and with children. And Chase was a far more powerful entity than Bill had ever been. All Bill had ever wanted her to do was be a wife and mother to their kids. That wouldn't be an issue with Chase. 'Do you want more kids?' she asked him, looking worried, and he burst out laughing.

'Hell, no. I did that when I was a kid myself. I want time with you! Not changing diapers, or chasing teenagers around when I'm in my sixties.' They had been careful, and she didn't want any slips either. She still had to worry, for a few years anyway. And she didn't want a baby at her age. She smiled to herself thinking how furious her kids would be if that happened.

'I agree with you. Let's try not to make any mistakes,' she said gently, and he added, 'Let's leave the baby-making to our kids.'

'Not just yet though, please.' She thought her kids were all still too young to have children responsibly. They were still children themselves in many ways. 'I'm not ready for that.' And she looked so young that even though she was old enough, he couldn't imagine her as a grandmother. He was far more concerned that their passion would lead to a pregnancy for her, and it could.

'Maybe you should go on the Pill,' he said, looking worried. 'What did you used to do?'

'What we did today,' she said discreetly. 'We didn't need birth control very often. I guess our marriage was in pretty bad shape.' She could already tell that wasn't going to be the case with them, and she wondered if he was right about her going on the Pill. 'I'll talk to my doctor about it,' she said, as he put his wallet in his jeans, and pulled his cowboy boots on. They were ready to go, and he stood there for a minute, looking at her, admiring her beauty, and desperately in love with her. And she was just as much in love with him. She felt bonded to him now that they had made love. It was why she hadn't wanted to do it until they both felt ready. It was too important to her to take it lightly, or have a casual affair with him. Their relationship already felt serious to both of them. They still didn't know how they would work out the geography or the demands of his career, but they were committed to try, and making love had sealed their union.

'Well, I guess we just turned this into our honeymoon,' he said with his sexy southern drawl as they left the suite, and she grinned. It felt that way to her too.

She drove him down to the marina, where all the sailboats were, and they drove past it and parked the car next to

Krissy Field. They walked onto the narrow beach and watched the windsurfers coming in, and the fog bank roll in through the Golden Gate. It was chilly, and they had both brought sweaters with them and put them on. Chase held her hand as they walked, and she kept smiling up at him as if to make sure he was real.

'Have you ever been to Alcatraz?' he asked her as they looked at it across the Bay.

'Once with Michael, for a report he had to do for school in fourth grade. I've never been back since.' But it looked cold and bleak.

They walked all the way to the Golden Gate Bridge at Fort Point, and then wandered slowly back to where they'd left the car, and she offered to take him to the house. They drove there, and she showed him around, but it felt like someone else's house to her now. And in spite of all the changes she had made and the things she'd moved around, it still felt too much like Bill. She made them something to eat, and they shared a sandwich in the kitchen, and he told her to pack a bag. He wanted her to stay with him at the hotel, and she agreed. They went back to the Ritz at five o'clock and had high tea in the lobby and laughed about it. She felt like a tourist in her own city. Chase had asked the concierge to make them a reservation at Gary Danko, but they wound up in bed instead, and decided not to go out. They lay there, talking, and they watched a movie and ordered room service, which they ate in the living room of the suite, wearing the plush terrycloth robes that were provided by the hotel. It all felt lazy and luxurious and exactly what they wanted to be doing. They were happy they hadn't gone out. And then they went back to bed and made love again. It was even better as they learned each other's bodies, and they wound up back in the giant bathtub at one o'clock in the morning, laughing about silly things, and talking about their childhoods, and she told him funny stories about her kids that made him laugh. She had a way of making him happy and just feel good about life, and he did the same for her. He felt like he'd known her all his life, and they were becoming best friends as well as lovers. It was everything she had ever wanted and never had. It was so different from what she had had with Bill, which was more serious and less playful, because that was the way he was. She felt like a different person with Chase, yet still herself.

It was after two a.m. when they finally fell asleep, and when she woke up in the morning, he was in the living room, reading the paper, and he smiled when she walked into the room and sat down next to him with her terry-cloth robe open. She felt totally at ease with him, as he did with her. He had his underwear on and nothing else. It was a comfortable domestic scene they were both enjoying to the fullest. He put down the paper and kissed her and asked her what she wanted to do that day.

'I thought we could go to Napa and have lunch up there. There are some terrific restaurants, and some very pretty wineries.' It sounded like fun to him too, and this time he drove, and she gave him directions as they sped along. She put the radio on, and one of his songs was playing, and he sang along in a strong, sexy, clear voice. She knew the song now and sang along with him, and he grinned at her at the end of the song.

'You have a mighty fine voice, Miss Stevie.' He had told her that before, but she was still shy about singing around him. 'If you ever want a job with the band, just say the word.' He was teasing her, but he really was impressed by her voice. For an untrained voice, she had power and range. It was a perfect voice for country music, and she loved learning his songs. She paid special attention to the words now, knowing he had written them all.

They visited the Mondavi Winery, and had lunch at Bouchon, and then drove north to Calistoga, and drove past countless wineries on the way, and they stopped for a drink at the Auberge du Soleil on the way back. They sat on the terrace and enjoyed the view of the valley, and then they drove back to the city and had room service again. She loved the time they spent in bed together, cuddling and making love. She was soaking up his affection and love. She realized now that she had been starving emotionally for a long, long time. She had just never thought about it before. It wouldn't have changed anything if she had. She and Bill had been disconnected for too many years when he died. And as she thought about it, she realized that she didn't feel as married as she had before. The bonds that had linked her to Bill were slowly disappearing, and were being replaced by what she felt for Chase, which was pure and clean and very powerful. She had no doubts about what they were doing or how she felt about him. She was very much in love, and she knew that he was too. It was a perfect balance and an even exchange, which was something she had never had in her marriage. She had always given more. But Chase gave just as much to her as she gave him.

On Saturday, they drove to Stinson Beach in Marin County, just past the Golden Gate, and walked the full length of the spectacular white sandy beach, which stretched for miles. They had dinner at a local restaurant, and drove the winding road home along the cliffs, and looked at the lights of the city sparkling in the distance. There was no fog that night, which she said was rare in July. And the view from the bridge, on the way back, was glorious with the city all lit up. They went back to the hotel, and on Sunday they stopped at her house to pack for L.A. They were flying down that night on the plane he had chartered. And when they checked out of the hotel, she felt as though they had formed a new and deeper bond to each other. The past four days had changed everything again. Now she felt like they belonged together, as though nothing had existed before or would come later. Their relationship had been born in those four days, and she could see that Chase felt the same way. He was careful and gentle with her, and found a thousand different ways to protect her and demonstrate his love. And she was excited about going to L.A. with him, and staying in a bungalow at the Beverly Hills Hotel, where the stars hung out, or met at the Polo Lounge for lunch or dinner. Sometimes she forgot that Chase was a big star too. He was something else now to her, the man she loved, part of her private life, and not a public person. But the moment they checked in to the hotel, three people in the lobby asked for his autograph, which brought it home to her again.

'Sometimes I forget who you are,' she said with a grin, as the manager on duty took them to the bungalow. It was one of their best ones, with two extra bedrooms they didn't need, but Chase liked to have space to move around. And this time he carried her over the threshold, to remind her that this was still part of their unofficial honeymoon. The hotel sent them a bottle of Cristal after that, not sure if they were newlyweds or not, but they did it for good measure.

They'd had champagne on the flight down on the chartered jet too. With him, she was getting used to luxuries he took in stride but constantly provided for her. The jet itself had been fabulous and an extravagantly comfortable way to travel.

'You're going to ruin me for real life,' she said as she got into the Ferrari he had rented, and they left for dinner at Mr. Chow, which was one of his favorite restaurants in L.A., but as soon as they got out of the car, they were faced with a wall of the paparazzi who flocked there to catch a glimpse of the stars who came to dine. They snapped their picture going into the restaurant. Chase strode right past them with an arm around her and escorted her into the restaurant. He paid no attention to the photographers other than a discreet wave as they walked by. It startled Stephanie for a moment, but she felt him strong and protective beside her.

'Are we going to be all over the tabloids now?' she asked, looking worried. She hadn't thought of it before. People noticed him in Nashville, and asked for autographs, but the press had paid no attention to them. Here it was different, and there was a feeding frenzy of press photographers when they walked out.

'We might be,' he said, in answer to her question. 'Do you mind?'

'Of course not, I'm proud to be with you. But I might have to say something to my kids if that happens. You don't look like Laura Perkins.' He laughed as she mentioned her mythical college friend, but in L.A. they could have been together for a number of reasons, none of which Stephanie could think of now, but she'd have to think on her feet and improvise if her kids challenged her about it.

She still thought it was too soon to tell them she was dating, not to mention the fact that she had fallen madly in love. She knew they would be upset about it, out of loyalty to their father.

They went to bed early that night because his meeting at the record label was at nine the next morning. He was meeting his entertainment lawyer there, and his dramatic agent, to discuss possible promotions to go with a new album. And this time he didn't invite her to join him. This was in the big leagues and not a little meeting she could go to. It was a very big deal, involving a lot of money. He promised to meet her back at the Polo Lounge for lunch. And in the end, she went to the cabana he'd rented for them, and lay by the pool all morning. She was thoroughly enjoying the hotel and being in L.A. with Chase.

He came to find her at the cabana when he got back, and he looked gorgeous as she watched him thread his way through the chairs around the pool.

'How was it?' she asked, as he sat down at the foot of her chair, and leaned over to kiss her.

'Pretty damn good,' he said, pleased with the meeting. And as he said it, two women glanced over at him and whispered something to each other. He was recognized everywhere, and Stephanie felt important just being with him. It was exciting, and still a new experience for her. And a minute later, one of them came over and asked for his autograph and told him which of his hits were her favorite songs. He heard it all the time, and she was impressed by how gracious he was to fans, who always came over at the wrong time, or intruded during a meal. He was unfailingly polite and obliging to them. After the fan thanked him for his autograph, she was smiling from ear to ear as she walked away and gave a thumbs-up to her friend.

They went shopping at Maxfield's after lunch, and Chase bought some new clothes, black leather pants that were cut like jeans, and a black leather jacket that looked great on him and that he said he'd wear on stage. Everyone knew him there, and they made a fuss over Stephanie too. When she admired a Balenciaga bag she thought was too expensive, he surprised her and handed it to her when they got in the car, along with a cashmere scarf she'd loved, the same color as her eyes.

'Chase! What are you doing?' She was embarrassed by his generosity, but touched by it too. No one had ever spoiled her that way before. What he'd given her just from a random afternoon of shopping was more thoughtful than any Christmas gift Bill had ever given her. Chase was an entirely different breed. He amazed her constantly with his kindness, generosity, courtly manners, and good taste.

'I'm just loving you, that's all,' he said as he kissed her. And the two paparazzi who had been following them as they wandered in and out of shops on Melrose snapped their picture. It was almost sure to become news or wind up on YouTube. Stephanie was becoming mildly concerned. There was going to be no way to conceal their relationship if they were all over the press, but she knew it went with the territory with Chase, and she had to get used to it, and accept the risk of it happening at some point.

Later she told Jean about it when she called her that afternoon, when they went back to the pool.

'What am I going to tell the kids, if they catch us?' she said.

'I take it you're no longer a virgin,' Jean said drily.

'That's beside the point,' Stephanie said discreetly. She was not going to discuss her sex life with her friend, no matter how close they were. 'I just don't want the kids to make an issue of it.'

'You know they will. And he's a big star, Steph, it's bound to come out, and probably soon if you're all over L.A. together.'

'I can't hide in our room.' And she didn't want to. She was having too much fun with him.

'The kids will get used to it,' Jean said calmly. 'They can't expect you to be alone forever.'

'I think they do.' And they didn't expect her to date a country music star. Even Michael didn't suspect, and he was dating Sandy, but Chase had told her not to say anything to him. And their relationship hadn't been as engaged when Stephanie was in Nashville, so Sandy didn't know their current status either, but she knew enough to upset Michael if she told him. So she promised Chase she wouldn't.

The matter was taken out of their hands two days later when YouTube ran a clip of them kissing as they left an antiques shop, and there was a photograph of them on the cover of a tabloid, going into the hotel. Chase was wearing a tank top with all his tattoos showing, and Stephanie was wearing shorts and sandals, and they had their arms around each other's waists. Louise called her mother as she and Chase were getting up, and they had just ordered breakfast and were sitting on the patio of their room. Louise was livid.

'What the hell is that about, Mom?' she said for openers.

'Is what about? What are you so angry about?' Stephanie was still half asleep and hadn't seen the video or the tabloid. They were on the front page.

'You're having an affair with a rock star? Do you have a tattoo yet? What kind of hypocrite are you?'

'I'm not a hypocrite. And I don't know what you're talking about.'

'Have your boyfriend show you what's on YouTube. I'm assuming you're dating him, and it wasn't a one-night stand. I'm not sure which would be worse in this case.'

Danielle Steel

She was almost in tears. 'How can you do that to Dad?'

'I'm not doing anything to Dad,' Stephanie said, trying to sound as calm as she could in the circumstances. 'And yes, I am dating Chase Taylor. I was going to tell you about it, but I thought it was too soon. It just happened. I didn't expect it either.'

'It didn't "happen," Mom. You weren't kidnapped by aliens or taken hostage. You did it. That's a decision. How can you be so disrespectful to Dad?'

'I have never been disrespectful to your father. He's not here, Louise. I am. And Chase is a wonderful man. I think you'll like him a lot.'

'I'm never going to meet him!' Louise shouted at her over the phone, sounding hysterical. 'And I can't believe you're whoring around five months after Dad died. What's wrong with you?'

'Don't speak to me like that!' Stephanie shouted back, and her voice was shaking. She couldn't believe what Louise was saying to her, even if she was upset. Being called a whore by her daughter didn't sit well with her, to say the least.

'And you were in Nashville with him, I guess. You lied to us, Mom. I'll never trust you again.' She was sobbing by then, and Stephanie was crying too.

'I didn't lie to you. Nothing had happened. This only started recently.'

'Well, if you have any respect for Dad, and any decency, you'll stop it immediately.' She was still crying as her mother closed her eyes and listened.

'I'm not going to stop it. I have a right to a life, Louise. Your father is dead, I'm not. And I'm not doing anything I need to apologize for, and certainly not to you after the way you're speaking to me. Get a grip on yourself.'

'You're making an ass of yourself, and embarrassing us. I just talked to Charlotte, and she doesn't even want to come home now. For God's sake, Mom, you're on You-Tube! You didn't even know what that was last year.' But she did now, in spades. It was just unfortunate that Louise had seen it, and they'd been on the front page of *The Globe* too. Chase was listening and could guess what had happened, as he gently reached out and touched her hand to let her know he was there and how sorry he was. They hadn't been as careful as they should, and he knew better, but he was so happy with her, and they'd been enjoying each other and L.A., and had gotten relaxed and not careful enough about the press.

Louise shouted at her for a few more minutes, and then hung up, still hysterical. And Stephanie looked at him unhappily as their breakfast arrived and the waiter set it up.

'I'm sorry, baby. Do you want to go back to San Francisco today?' he asked her.

'No, I don't. I love being here with you. She thinks I'm being disrespectful to her father. But they want to bury me with him. She's always tough on me. She'll have to get over it this time.' But it didn't sound like she would any-time soon.

The next call was from Alyson, who had heard about it from someone and was desperately worried about her friend.

'Is that really you?' she asked in a shocked tone. She had called Jean too, who didn't seem surprised or upset, and told Alyson to calm down, but she called Stephanie anyway. She was sure that the photo had to be a fake of some kind, but Stephanie told her it wasn't.

'It's me,' she said in an exasperated tone. She didn't need Alyson bugging her about it too. 'I'm sorry I didn't say anything about it, but we're trying to keep it quiet.'

'Well, the whole world knows now,' Alyson said with obvious disapproval. 'What do the kids say about it?'

'Louise just called me a whore when she called me. I haven't spoken to the others.'

'Do you even know this guy? Don't you think you should stop seeing him?' She made her disapproval clear.

'He's a wonderful man, and I love him,' Stephanie said simply. 'The kids will have to get used to it.'

'Are you serious about him?' Alyson sounded even more shocked at that. Clearly, Stephanie had lost her mind.

'Yes, I am serious about him,' Stephanie confirmed, as Chase looked over at her with a slow smile. He was sorry about all the trouble she was having, because of him. 'Alyson, I'll call you soon,' Stephanie said, and cut her off before she could say any more, but it was obvious that Alyson was shocked and concerned for her friend. Her perspective was so narrow and her world so small that she couldn't even conceive of what Stephanie was doing. Alyson led a sheltered life dictated by her husband and was naïve. Jean had been supportive about Chase from the beginning.

'Are you okay?' Chase asked her, looking worried. 'It sounds pretty bad. Who was that? Your other daughter?'

'No, my friend Alyson. This is so far out of her realm, she thinks I'm crazy. My friend Jean is your biggest fan, though.' She didn't want him to think that everyone in her life hated him. This was not a warm welcome for him.

The next call was from Michael two minutes later. He wasn't shouting insults like his sister, but he sounded worried.

'Are you okay, Mom?' he asked her, which was more than Louise had done before hurling slanderous accusations at her.

'I'm fine, sweetheart. I guess you've heard about me and Chase.' At least Michael knew him and liked him. Stephanie was grateful for that.

'Yes.' Louise had called to warn him, and he had looked online to see for himself. 'It's actually not that bad,' he tried to reassure her. 'Louise is just upset because of Dad.'

'I know, and I'm sorry you had to hear about it this way. I just wasn't ready to tell you yet. I didn't realize it would wind up all over YouTube.'

'He's a big star, Mom. You can't hide for long.'

'So I gather. So what do you think? At least you know him.'

'I'm kind of upset about Dad,' he said honestly, in his clear, concise way, but he didn't sound angry. 'But I'm happy for you. He's a good guy. Are you two serious about each other?'

'I think so.'

'Because if you're just fooling around and having fun, it's not worth it. But if you're serious, you have my approval, if you care.'

'Of course I care. I love you. Do you mean what you just said?' She was touched by how compassionate and understanding he was being.

'Yes, I mean it. And I know that you and Dad were never really happy after he came back. If Chase makes you happy, then I'm glad.'

'He does. Thank you, sweetheart. Maybe you can calm your sister down about it.'

'You know Louise. She'll get over it. She just needs to

go nuts for a while, and beat everybody up. I think she got Charlotte all excited about it.'

'I'll call her.'

'Tell Chase he has my endorsement,' Michael said quietly. 'Let me know if there's anything I can do.' He really was a great kid, and made up for the other two, even Louise's vitriolic reaction. She told Chase about the call and called Charlotte a minute later. She was almost as hysterical as Louise, but not as rude. She was younger, and still more respectful of her mother. She didn't take the liberties Louise took.

'I'm not coming home if he'll be there,' she threatened.

'He won't be. And you *are* coming home when you said. No more extensions.'

'This is so mean to Dad. How could you, Mom?'

'I'm not married to him anymore, Charlotte. He's gone. And Chase is a terrific man.'

'You're cheating on Dad, Mom,' Charlotte said miserably. 'He would never have done that to you.' Stephanie caught her breath when she heard, and was tempted to tell her the truth, that he had cheated on her when he was alive, but she would never do that. It would be too hurtful to the kids, and there was no point exposing him now, just to absolve herself.

'We don't know what Dad would have done in these circumstances. He might have had a girlfriend by now, but we'll never know.'

'But you do, and it's just not fair to him, or to us. I'm embarrassed you're my mom. And you can make me come home, but you can't make me meet him, ever. Keep him away from me,' she said, sounding almost as vicious as her sister. Stephanie could already see now that it was going to be tough when she returned, probably with arguments day and night.

The calls from her family stopped after that, and she and Chase discussed it over breakfast.

'Is there anything I can do? Do you want me to call them and tell them how much I love you? Maybe it would help.'

'I don't think so. They're defending the memory of their father. And now I've become the whore of the village. The only thing that will fix this is time, and seeing for themselves that you're a great guy. That won't happen overnight,' she said wisely.

They went to the Getty Museum that day, but she was distracted, and all she could think of were her kids, and how they had reacted to her getting on with her life. She wanted them all to calm down, but that wasn't in the cards for now. They were flying around the ceiling, throwing rocks at her and Chase, and mostly at her.

She had a heavy heart all day, but they decided to stay in L.A., as planned, for the rest of the week. Stephanie was not going to give in to them. A new era had dawned.

Bill's reign in her life had ended and would not continue from the grave. She was no longer afraid, of him, or her kids, or anyone.

Chapter 21

The time Chase and Stephanie shared in L.A. was idyllic. They went to restaurants and shopped, spent a day at Venice Beach, and had dinner in Santa Monica at Giorgio Baldi. They went to a few parties Chase had been invited to by other country music stars, and they spent quiet time together at the hotel. It was perfect. And they stayed away from the press as much as they could, although *People* magazine ran an item on them, and they were on Page Six of the *New York Post,* which made Louise even madder. She sent her mother furious e-mails all week, and Stephanie stayed calm in the eye of the storm and so did Chase. There was nothing else they could do. She wasn't going to give him up because Louise was unhappy. She'd have to adjust. Stephanie hadn't heard from Charlotte again, and decided to let sleeping dogs lie until she got home. There would be plenty of time to discuss it with her then.

They flew back to San Francisco on the same chartered

jet, checked back into the Ritz-Carlton, and had five more days together there. Chase rented a house for them at Stinson Beach, where they hid out and saw no one. They spent long lazy days, walking on the beach, or making love and watching movies in bed.

Stephanie talked to Alyson again, and she was as unreasonable as Stephanie's daughters had been, so she avoided Alyson after that, and put her on the back burner too.

And through it all, their relationship got stronger, and Stephanie was glad they had two weeks together to discuss their plans and how to deal with her kids, although Michael had continued to be supportive. It helped that he and Chase had met.

Everything blew up again when, in one of their futile conversations about their mother, Michael admitted to Louise that he was dating Chase's ward. She went crazy all over again.

'For God's sake, Mike, have you lost your mind too? What is it with you? What about Amanda?'

'We broke up.' Louise didn't like her either, but at least she was respectable, in Louise's opinion, not some country music singer who she assumed was out of a trailer park.

'So now you're dating an eighteen-year-old Okie? Please tell me this isn't happening to us. I feel like aliens took over our family when Dad died. You and Mom have gone nuts. What's happening to you? This is straight out of a soap opera. Well, don't bring her to meet me.'

'I wasn't planning to,' he said in an icy tone. 'I know better, with that razor mouth of yours. She doesn't deserve that, and neither does Mom. Chase Taylor is a great guy, and I like him. And he's wonderful to Mom, more than Dad ever was. That's what we should care about, not all the rest. All the stuff in the press is bullshit.'

'Don't talk about Dad like that. He was great to our mother,' Louise said in a fury.

'No, he wasn't,' Michael reminded her. 'And they almost divorced when you were a senior in high school. You know that as well as I do, so don't tell me how great he was to Mom. He was never home. He didn't want to be, and Mom ended up picking up all the slack for him, whether you want to admit it now or not.' She didn't.

'I'm sure whatever it was that they fought over wasn't such a big deal, since Mom went back to him,' Louise said hotly.

'She did that for us.' Michael kept the pressure on her, for the truth.

'Because she loved him,' Louise corrected him.

'I'm sure she did love him, but he was never there for her, or for us.' He was being brutally honest with Louise, but it resolved nothing. She continued to praise their father, and crucify their mother. She didn't want to hear anything Mike had to say in her defense.

The battle raged on for the whole time Chase was in

San Francisco, and eventually Stephanie stopped answering her older daughter's calls and texts. There was nothing else she could do to protect herself, and Chase. They just had to weather the storm.

On Chase's last day in San Francisco, they took a walk in the park, bought take-out sashimi afterward, and took it back to the hotel. They had spent a lot of time in bed all week. There was no question in either of their minds about the seriousness of the relationship. They just had to find a way to make it work, in both cities, and in spite of two of her kids. But she wasn't going to let Louise or Charlotte spoil it for her. She wanted to protect the relationship with Chase.

Stephanie was lying in Chase's arms, after they made love on their last night together, and talking quietly about when they would see each other again. She had promised to come to Nashville as soon as Charlotte went back to school, in a month. It seemed like an intolerable amount of time to both of them. And Stephanie knew she'd probably have to put up with Charlotte's assaults about Chase while she was there. Stephanie was hoping to calm her down. She was usually easier than Louise.

'You can't even imagine how much I'm going to miss you,' he said mournfully, as he rolled over on his side and looked at her. She kissed him then and snuggled close to him in bed. She loved feeling his warmth beside her at night, and she couldn't imagine living without him every day either. They were deeply in love.

Stephanie took Chase to the airport when he left. She walked him into the terminal and said goodbye to him right before security. She was wearing dark glasses and a hat, which felt ridiculous to her. By the time Chase left, she was convinced that she was the luckiest woman on earth, and he said the same about himself. It was a match made in heaven, with the daughters from hell. He promised to call her as soon as he arrived in Nashville, and as always, he did. He was at home by then, and miserable as he looked around his kitchen. The woman he loved was nowhere to be seen. She was living three thousand miles away, and he had to get through the next month without her.

The day after Chase left, Charlotte flew home from Paris. She arrived from the airport angry, and stayed that way. She hardly said hello to her mother, when Stephanie picked her up and drove her home. From the moment she came through the door, she complained about being forced to come home, and was painful to be with. She wanted to be in Paris or Rome, or anywhere in Europe with her friends, not at home. And her mother's relationship with a country music star was all the provocation she needed to be angry at her all the time, and attack her whenever she could, encouraged by her older sister.

It was the middle of the afternoon, but midnight for

Charlotte, flying in from Paris. But she was young and had slept on the plane, so she had plenty of energy to attack her mother. Stephanie had made her something to eat, and they were sitting at the kitchen table, when Charlotte gave her an angry look. She had been barely civil until then, even if she had hugged her mother when they met.

'So where is he?' she asked as she finished her sandwich and favorite potato chips, which Stephanie had gotten for her, and pushed her plate away. The look she gave her mother was instantly confrontational. The gloves were off.

'If you're referring to Chase,' Stephanie said calmly, 'he's in Nashville.'

'When did he leave? I assume he was here till I came home.' It was none of her business, but her mother nodded.

'He left yesterday. He has an album to record.' He was doing duets with another famous country music singer. And Stephanie acted as though her involvement with him was normal.

'Don't you feel a little ridiculous being a groupie at your age, Mom?' There was a derisive tone in her voice Stephanie didn't like. Whenever Louise called, hers was one of pure rage. Charlotte was subtler and younger, and didn't have the guts to be as rude, but she was bad enough.

355

'I'm not a groupie. We're dating.' It was honest. She was hiding nothing from her.

'You're sleeping with him,' Charlotte accused her, with the self-righteousness of youth. Stephanie didn't comment. 'And in my father's bed, I suppose.' Stephanie was instantly angry at her comment, but didn't show it.

'It's none of your business, Charlotte, but we stayed at a hotel.' It was a small town, and she would have found out anyway. Someone always knew someone who saw something who . . . she preferred to tell her herself.

It would have been infinitely worse if they had stayed at Stephanie's home, no matter which bedroom they slept in. She was glad they hadn't, and he had been wise enough to stay at a hotel. It was better for her too, not just her children. 'That's disgusting. Aren't you afraid of what people will think of you? My father's been dead for about five minutes.'

'Dad died six months ago, Char. And you can't predict what will happen in life, or who will come along. I wasn't going to date at all until I met him. And my dating Chase doesn't mean I didn't love your father. I loved him a lot when he was alive. But he's gone now, which is sad for all of us. And now this happened. And six months is respectable. Some people don't wait that long.'

'Decent people wait a year,' Charlotte informed her.

'*Some* people wait a year, some don't. I waited five months. And you wouldn't feel any better about this if we'd waited another six months. Why exactly are you so angry, Charlotte?'

'You're being disrespectful of our father,' Charlotte said with fury. 'And look who he is and what he looks like. He's a hillbilly, Mom!' Chase was a lot of things, but not that. He was a very sophisticated, intelligent, successful, incredible-looking man. Just different from their father, with his long hair, tattoos, and torn jeans.

'He's just different from Daddy, Charlotte. And he's a very cool guy. You'll like him.'

'No, I won't,' she said with a stubborn look. 'And I hear Michael is dating his illegitimate daughter or something. What did you do? Double-date?'

'He came up from Atlanta with Amanda for a concert Chase invited them to. And Sandy is his ward. Her parents died. She's two years younger than you are, and an amazing girl. And you never liked Amanda, so don't act all holier than thou about her,' Stephanie warned her. Charlotte hadn't spoken to Michael, she had heard it all from Louise.

'I think you and your sister are being incredibly disrespectful of me, and a man you don't even know. I understand how sad you are about losing your father, and so am I. But I have a right to live too, and this is what I'm doing, whether you and Louise like it or not. And your father would probably be doing the same thing – dating someone.' *After all, he did it while he was alive,* she thought to herself but didn't say to her daughter. 'You wouldn't like that either.'

'I doubt that, and he wouldn't be dating some rock star with tattoos.'

'You never know.' Stephanie smiled at her. 'Love takes you by surprise sometimes.' But Charlotte looked even more upset by what she said.

'Are you telling me you love him?' She made it sound like her mother had admitted to a crime, and Stephanie faced her calmly and looked her in the eye.

'Yes, I am.' She never lowered her gaze, as Charlotte got up from the table, left the kitchen, and stomped upstairs to her room. Stephanie kept busy with some projects at her desk, paying bills, and she was startled when Charlotte burst into the room.

'What the hell did you do to the living room? I just went to look for something, and I saw it. It looks awful.' It didn't look awful. It looked different. Things had changed. A lot had changed, including her mother, which was the biggest and most threatening change of all. And the biggest change was that Stephanie was happy, which came as a shock to her kids since Chase was part of it.

'I moved some things around,' Stephanie said quietly. 'I'm sorry you don't like it.' She didn't offer to move it back, and wasn't going to. Charlotte stormed out of the room again then, and Stephanie heard crashing noises a few minutes later and ran down the stairs to see what had happened. Charlotte had tried to move the furniture in the living room, had knocked over a small table, and a large vase had crashed to the floor and broken. She was on her knees sobbing in a pool of water with the flowers all around her.

'OhmyGod, what happened?' Stephanie asked as she ran to help her, and cut her foot on a piece of broken glass. Charlotte couldn't stop sobbing, and just knelt there with a desperate look.

'I can't remember how it was,' she kept saying over and over. She had tried to move everything back, and couldn't get it the way it was before, because she'd never really noticed. She just knew it was different now. 'You changed *everything*!' she screamed at her mother hysterically, as Stephanie bent down next to her and tried to put her arms around her, and Charlotte pulled away. 'Don't touch me! I hate you!' She sounded five years old as she said it, and there were tears in Stephanie's eyes. This was all so hard. Charlotte ran out of the room then and left the mess. She didn't see that her mother's foot was bleeding – she was too distraught to be aware of anything but herself. Stephanie heard the door of Charlotte's room slam, and cleaned up the mess herself. She felt suddenly guilty for the things she had moved around. But she had needed to do it for herself. Her children weren't at home anymore. She lived there every day.

She threw away the pieces of the broken vase, put the

flowers in another one, cleaned up the water, put the furniture back in order, and bandaged her bleeding foot. The cut wasn't deep, it was just superficial. Charlotte didn't come out of her room for several hours. It had been a tough first day home so far.

Stephanie talked to Chase quietly from her room later that night and then called Jean. She couldn't call Alyson anymore, she was too upset that Stephanie was involved with Chase, so she would be no help about the kids, or support for Stephanie. Alyson had told Jean she thought it was shocking, since Bill had only been gone for five months. And what was she doing with a man like that? She needed to go out with someone like Bill or Brad or Fred, one of them, not some rock star.

'Why not?' Jean asked her bluntly. 'You think Brad is so great, well, good for you. Fred sure isn't. And Steph was unhappy with Bill for the last ten years. She looked like her soul was dead. Now she's alive. Is that really what you want for her now? To be miserable again. Because I sure as hell don't. The best thing that could happen to her was to meet a real guy who loves her, and she has. That's good enough for me. And I don't give a damn what he looks like, where he comes from, or how many tattoos he has. And if you love her as a friend and want her to be happy, that should be good enough for you too, *and* her kids. At least they have an excuse to bitch for a while, Bill was their father. As her friends, we have no excuse to beat her up. How can you be so narrow-minded, just because he works in the music industry and has long hair and tattoos? Who cares? I'd go for him in a hot minute, and maybe you would too if you weren't married to Saint Brad.'

Alyson had been deeply offended by what Jean said and hadn't spoken to her or Stephanie since, in about a week. Stephanie was letting her cool off and mellow out a bit, but Alyson really didn't understand the broader world, or men who weren't traditional or professionals and looked like Brad. She thought the whole world should be like them. And Brad and Alyson were fiercely loyal to Bill. Brad had told Alyson that he didn't approve of what Stephanie was doing either. He thought it was disrespectful to the memory of Bill for her to be dating so soon, and he thought her dating Chase was in terrible taste. His narrow-minded views dictated Alyson's, since she parroted everything he thought and said. She was the 'perfect' wife, as Stephanie had been. But Steph couldn't do it anymore, and didn't want to. She had far more respect for Jean, who always said what she thought, whether Fred or other people liked it or not. Stephanie's friendship with Alyson had just taken a heavy hit. But Jean was still there, rooting for her, an outspoken voice of reason, well aware of the compromises and courage it took to get through life.

Stephanie told her about the incident of the broken vase in the living room, and how sad she was about it when she saw how distraught Charlotte was. 'Maybe I should have waited a while to start moving things around, but it was so depressing. It looked like Bill was going to come home any minute. It felt like *Groundhog Day*. Nothing changed, except he never showed up.'

'You can't live in a tomb, Steph. You did the right thing. And the simple fact is you live here and the kids don't. They want to breeze through here when they feel like it, pick up clean laundry and some cash, and find everything the same, particularly you, chained to the wall in your bedroom, waiting for them, even if they only show up for Christmas and Thanksgiving. Well, guess what, life doesn't work that way. Particularly for you, with Bill gone. You have every reason to change things and move on and get a life for yourself. You didn't have one with Bill. You had his life and theirs, and yours as their slave. Now you're free. Use it. My girls aren't much better about changing anything around here. The drapes in their old bedrooms were in shreds, so I replaced them last year. The girls had a fit when they came home for Christmas. And they're twenty-eight and twenty-nine years old, for chrissake, and who cares what color the drapes are? They hadn't been home in two years, since I go to Chicago to see them. But when they saw the drapes, they demanded I put the old ones back *immediately*!' Stephanie felt better as she listened. She always did with Jean. She was so reasonable and practical, and took shit from no one.

'So did you change the drapes back?'

362

'Of course not. I'd thrown them away. But even if I hadn't, I wouldn't. You have to move forward in life. You can't sit in the same place, unless you want to, that's a choice too. But you can't sit there because someone else says you have to, because your moving forward makes them uncomfortable. This is good for your kids, Steph. It tells them that no matter how much you loved someone, you have to move on. They do too. They can't expect you to sit there and be buried alive with him. That would be really scary. And I'd be worried about you. They're going to have to suck it up sooner or later.'

'Well, the girls sure aren't ready to do that. It nearly broke my heart when I saw Charlotte sobbing in the living room, trying to move everything back. She was crying because she couldn't remember how it used to be.'

'That's my point. And pretty soon the new way will seem normal. And so will Chase if they ever give him a chance. So when am I going to meet him?' She understood perfectly that she hadn't so far. They needed time alone together.

'The next time he's out here, I promise. He wants me to come to Nashville when Charlotte goes back to school.' She sounded worried about it.

'And?' Jean could hear the hesitation in her friend's voice. Stephanie was honest about it.

'Here, we're kind of suspended between two worlds. We have nothing to do except be with each other, and we had a great time in L.A. But in Nashville he has a life, an empire to run, albums to record, rehearsals, concerts, a thousand things to do every day. He takes me with him, but I fit into *his* life, it's not *our* life. I did that with Bill, and I don't want to do it again. I'm scared to lose me. I become no one except some kind of appendage in other people's lives.'

'You're going to have that with any busy guy with a big career. Maybe Bill was particularly self-centered that everything had to be his way and about him, and Chase sounds like he makes a real effort to include you, for now at least. But he has a career, a big world, a huge, successful business. If I still cared and wanted a real life with Fred, I'd have to follow him around. Let's face it, he wouldn't be coming to Botox shots and the hairdresser with me. Sometimes you just have to accept that one person has a bigger life, and you have to go with it. Bill never paid attention to you, so you got lost in the shuffle. I don't get the feeling Chase would do that, from everything you've said.'

'Maybe not.' Stephanie was pensive. She was thinking a lot about it, and what she had to contribute to their life, and Jean had a point about his career and her having to adapt to him. 'He said I could handle PR for him if I come to Nashville.'

'So?'

'That's just a made-up job, like helping him write lyrics. He's doing fine without me.'

'Then get a real job in Nashville. But wherever you are, if you're with a big successful guy, you're going to have to accommodate his career. It won't work otherwise. The same would be true if you had a busier career than his. The secret is to find someone who is reasonable about it, not like Bill, who never paid attention to you or cared what you thought as long as you did what he wanted, or Brad, who expects Alyson to be some kind of drone. I think *reasonable* is the operative word here. Fred was pretty good about it, until he started screwing every bimbo in town. He'd be a decent husband if he could keep his pants on. Maybe that's why I stick around. I actually used to like him. It's not just about the money.' Stephanie always suspected that was true, although there was so much bitterness and distance between them now that they really didn't have a marriage, and neither of them made any effort to bridge the gap. Their roles had been set in stone for years. He chased women, and she spent money. But they were both good people. Stephanie was sad for them that things had turned out as they had. And Jean had made the valid point that she would have to adapt to any man's career, since she didn't have one of her own. Her career had been Bill and their kids. She just didn't want to trade it in now and have her career be Chase. She had to have an identity of her own. She was getting there, but the cake wasn't baked yet. She was still in the oven. And it was a shaky time for her to be making big life changes. She didn't want to do anything prematurely. They had waited to sleep together and that had felt right. Now she needed time to adjust to the rest. But Chase wasn't pushing. He just missed her. And she missed him.

After Charlotte's outburst in the living room on the first day, she looked up all her friends and was hardly home after that. She was out all day, went to her friends' homes almost every night. She went to Tahoe for a weekend, went camping for two days in Yosemite, and Stephanie almost never saw her. She flew through the house, and they never had a meal together. Stephanie finally caught five minutes with her in the kitchen when she was waiting to be picked up to go to a concert at the Oakland Coliseum.

'Do you want to get a manicure together tomorrow?' Stephanie asked her pleasantly. Charlotte had been home for a week, and Stephanie wanted to spend at least a little time with her.

'I can't. I'm going to Sonoma. Heather's parents have a new house there.'

'What about the next day?'

'I don't have time, Mom.' She had kept a wall up between them. Officially, it was about Chase, but partially it was her age, and she was still mourning her father. And she blamed her mother for everything on the planet, mostly because she was alive and Bill wasn't. 'I want to see my friends while everybody's still home. This is our last summer. Next year after we graduate, everyone will be working, and nobody will come home, and I probably won't either.' Stephanie wanted to say 'What about me?' but she didn't. Charlotte was driving the point home that she wanted to spend her time with her friends, not with her mother.

Two days later she was looking for something in a drawer when Charlotte walked into her bedroom.

'Do you know where my tennis racket went?' Charlotte asked her, looking annoyed. She had discovered that her mother had moved the contents of the closets around too, and she didn't like it, even though it seemed to work better. And she'd noticed that some of her father's things were gone, like the old sports equipment he no longer used, and a set of barbells that had been rusting in the garage for years.

'I moved all our sports stuff to the basement closets,' Stephanie said over her shoulder as Charlotte wandered toward her father's dressing room with a sad look. Stephanie didn't say a word as she watched her, and Charlotte opened a door and saw that the closet was empty. One by one she pulled them all open, and saw her mother's winter coats in one, some evening gowns in another. But her father's clothes were gone. She turned to her mother with a look of horror.

'What did you do?' she asked in a choked voice. 'Where

Danielle Steel

are Daddy's clothes?' She acted as though her mother had committed a sacrilege, and Stephanie's face was as pale as her daughter's when she answered.

'I gave them away, Char. I had to. I couldn't live with them staring at me in the face every day. I have to live here.' Her daughter said not a word, she turned on her heel and strode out of the room, and a moment later Stephanie heard the front door slam, and the car Charlotte was using drive away. It didn't matter what Stephanie did anymore, she was always wrong. Any sign of life or change or even healing on Stephanie's part was treated as a crime. There was no question in her mind now. They wanted to bury her with him. And as long as she refused to lie in the grave with him, they would hate her.

She talked to Dr. Zeller about it the next time she saw her, and they agreed that to some degree it was normal. Still, her children appeared to be carrying it to an extreme degree, and Chase was such an easy target for their anger at their mother.

'Whatever I do is wrong,' Stephanie said unhappily with tears running down her cheeks. 'It's not like I've forgotten their father. I haven't. I loved him. But he's gone, and the truth is for at least the last ten years, we had a lousy marriage.'

'Then why do you feel so guilty about moving on?' her therapist challenged her, and Stephanie thought about it.

'Maybe because they're so angry at me.'

'Or because you think you don't deserve a better life?' Stephanie thought about it for a long time, and then nodded, and blew her nose.

'He never cared about what I thought, or what I wanted. He never asked me. Nothing I said ever made a difference. And now the kids treat me the same way. They don't care that I love Chase and he loves me and he's a great guy. I'm just supposed to sit here and pretend I'm still married to their father. Well, I don't want to be. I did it. It's over. But they won't let it be.'

'Some of that is normal behavior on their part. Most young people really don't care how their parents feel. Parents are a vehicle to meet their needs. And some of their anger over their father's death is normal too. But he set a bad example in how he treated you, and you're trying to change that. It's also normal that they don't like that. Change is hard. But you can't let it stop you from leading your life. You have a right to a new relationship, and if it's the one you want, you have a right to move forward. They'll adjust in time, despite the stridency of their accusations now. You have to seize opportunities as they come along. You can't let them stop you.' Stephanie nodded, and then told her about her concerns about Chase's life in Nashville.

'He has a huge career. I don't know how I'd fit in. Or if I'd lose my identity the way I did with Bill. Chase is larger than life.'

'You can't lose your identity unless you give it up. No one can take it from you,' she reminded her. 'And I don't think you'd do that again. Bill and Chase also sound like very different people. Bill was much more autocratic with you, and sounds pretty inconsiderate and indifferent. Chase is always trying to find ways to include you.' What she said was true, and as always, gave Stephanie food for thought when she left her office.

But in spite of what the shrink had said, Stephanie had another big fight with Charlotte that night, because Stephanie wanted to sell Bill's car. No one used it, or ever would. Seeing it every day depressed her, but having it in the garage reassured Charlotte. It was part of the fantasy that her father was still there and would come back to drive it.

'I won't sell it now,' Stephanie finally agreed after a two-hour battle that led back to the closets and Chase and even the rusty weights she'd gotten rid of. 'But we have to sooner or later. It's just going to sit there.' And she didn't think keeping it was healthy for her, or the kids. He wasn't coming back, for the car or anything else. They had to face it. But they weren't ready, and she was. She was willing to defer selling the car for a while, but not forever. It was a minor victory for Charlotte. They were all fighting to crawl back into the womb of life with their father. And Stephanie wanted to cut the cord. Their needs were different and a constant cause of conflict now.

Charlotte agreed to have dinner with her mother a few days before she left. Stephanie tried to pick a place she'd like. Charlotte wanted the days after that to spend with her friends. And by the time Stephanie drove her to the airport on the day she left, Stephanie felt as though they'd hardly seen each other. It had been a tough summer, full of change and arguments between them. Louise was barely speaking to her, and still angry whenever Stephanie called her. She preferred to send her texts.

Charlotte had opted to stay in the dorms again at NYU, although she had debated about getting an apartment with friends. But her best friends were still in the dorms, so she decided to stay there too. It was exciting to be going back for senior year, and Stephanie was happy for her, and sad that they had spent so little time together, but she knew it couldn't be any different. Charlotte wouldn't let it.

Stephanie hugged her before she went through security, and Charlotte turned back once to wave and smiled at her mother. And much to Stephanie's amazement, she shouted 'Love you, Mom!' They were the only kind words Stephanie had heard from her all month. She wondered if what they were going through was just a process, and their way of mourning Bill. Maybe they had to be angry at their mother to get through it. For just an instant, Charlotte looked like the little girl she had been, and then she was gone, and Stephanie drove back to the city. And it was peaceful and calm when she got back to the house. No doors were slamming, no one was shouting or angry at her. No one was staring at her accusingly and telling her what a monster she was, what bad taste she had, or how terrible she looked in a dress or a pair of shorts. It was blissfully peaceful, which made her sad. She had never been happy to see any of her children leave before, and this time she was. The house just wasn't big enough for them both.

Chase called her an hour later. 'Is she gone?'

'I came back an hour ago, and I hate to say it, it's a relief.' Thinking about it, she was dreading Thanksgiving and Christmas, when she and Louise would both be home, constantly angry and accusing her of something. 'Who ever said having kids was easy?' she said with a rueful smile, as she sat down in her kitchen, enjoying the peace and silence. It was no longer lonely, it was a vast improvement over the tension of the past month.

'How soon can you get your gorgeous ass down here?' He couldn't wait to see her, and the following weekend was Labor Day weekend. He was playing a concert in Memphis and wanted her to come with him. 'And I want you to stay as long as you can this time. You don't have to rush back.' And she realized it was lucky she hadn't found a job yet, or she couldn't have gone at all. Maybe Jean was right, and the less busy person had to accommodate the busier one. It made sense. 'Can you come tomorrow?' She smiled at how anxious he was to see her. She couldn't wait to see him too, but she was tired and discouraged after her month with Charlotte and her constant accusations and attacks. It had been incredibly stressful. She felt like she'd lost both her daughters as well as Bill.

'Give me a day to get organized here. How about if I come the day after tomorrow, on Tuesday?'

'Fantastic. I'll book the ticket.' She had to fly to Atlanta on Delta and change planes, and he apologized that there was no first class, only business.

'I don't care. You can have them throw me in with the luggage. I'll be there,' she said, smiling. For the month of her daughter's abuse, it had been hard to keep the joyful feeling in their relationship, but Chase hadn't missed a beat, and he was waiting for her now, with a voice filled with excitement.

'I've missed you, Stevie. I can't wait to see you.'

'Me too,' she said, smiling. And for the first time in a month, she didn't feel guilty. She couldn't wait to hold him and kiss him and love him, and he felt that way too. And she knew that she had earned it.

She called Jean and told her she was leaving in two days. She left a message for her therapist, canceling her appointment and told her why, that she was going to Nashville. And she told the shelter she would be gone for a while and would let them know when she was back. And she didn't call Alyson, because she didn't want to listen to her accusations either, about what she felt Stephanie owed Bill and shouldn't be doing. And she went upstairs to pack. She was about to do what Chase said was his big philosophy of life. She was going to seize the moment and the day that life was offering her. Carpe diem!

Chapter 22

When Stephanie landed at the Nashville International Airport, Chase was waiting for her as soon as she left the gate area, and he swept her off her feet and spun her around so hard she was dizzy. People watching them smiled even before they realized who he was. And they stood kissing, as people walked around them.

'OhmyGod! I'm so happy to see you!' he said, with an arm around her waist as she beamed. She was just as happy to see him, and felt as though she hadn't seen him in years, instead of just a month while Charlotte was home. And even his dogs welcomed her when they got to the car. He put her two suitcases in the trunk, and stood holding her again for a long moment as they kissed. And then they got in the car to go home. She could hardly wait to be back at his house. He had ordered two huge flower arrangements for her, and there was a bottle of champagne chilling in the kitchen. He couldn't do enough for her.

He played some of the new songs he'd written when they wandered into the studio, and she loved them. And as they sipped the champagne, Sandy bounded into the kitchen and threw her arms around Stevie. It was exactly the opposite of what she was experiencing with her daughters. All the girls did was accuse and criticize her right now. Sandy was thrilled to see her, and Stephanie gave her a huge hug and kissed her on the cheek, and then looked at her in a conspiratorial, motherly way. A lot had happened since she'd last seen her.

'So how are things going with Michael?' According to him, things had never been better, and Sandy seemed that way too. She was shy and momentarily embarrassed when she answered.

'He's so good to me, not like Bobby Joe, or any of the others. He takes real good care of me, Stevie. He's so respectful, and we're so happy together.' Stephanie was happy to hear it. Sandy deserved it. She was young, but she was a woman, and she had lived a lot for her age, on the road with her father, and now with Chase, dealing with her own career, its demands and discipline, and learning the ropes of the music business. There was a lot of pressure on her, and she was a sweet person. And it was easy for Stephanie to see why Michael loved her. They were some of the same reasons why she loved Chase – they were real, decent, honest, hard-working, bright, good people. There was a real dignity and integrity to them, a kind of natural nobility that she had come to have a deep respect for, and Michael had discovered too. Stephanie was happy that Michael and Sandy had found each other and had had the wisdom and courage to grab what they'd been offered. And when she saw her son that weekend, the happiness she saw in his eyes confirmed it. He had grown into his manhood over the summer, and she loved the way he treated Sandy. It was obvious how in love they were, just like her and Chase. There was nothing but good vibes around them, not like the tension and manipulations Stephanie had always sensed with Amanda. He tried to come up every weekend, and Stephanie was thrilled to see him, as a bonus for her.

Stephanie and Chase had had a busy week in Nashville before they got on the jet he had chartered to go to Memphis, just as he had when they went to Graceland. The others were going on the bus, but Chase wanted to get there more quickly. He had a dozen deals hanging fire at the moment, and he wanted some time alone with Stevie. He talked to her about what he was doing, and asked for her advice. Although she'd never had reason to use it professionally, he found she had a good head for business and a commonsense, pragmatic way of analyzing things, and she was creative about coming up with alternate solutions he hadn't thought of. They complemented each other well, and she was fascinated by his career. There was no aspect of his life he didn't share with her, in sharp contrast to Bill, who had never told her what he was doing and acted as though she wouldn't understand if he talked to her about work. He always implied that the only thing she could do was take care of kids, and he had other people to talk to about his work.

There was not a single aspect of Chase's life that she didn't know about or contribute to in some way, even if just as a sounding board, and he kept telling her she had a gift for lyrics, which she thought was just his way of being nice to her. They talked about everything he was doing, which made her head spin, and he made love to her as no one ever had before. Their love for each other was growing day by day, and she felt totally at ease with his band and in his world, and he loved to tease her about it.

'All you need now, baby, is a tattoo with my name across your chest, with a heart, and my initials on your ass. Now that would be something!' He loved what a lady she was, and how smart she was, and told her constantly how beautiful she was. Stephanie felt as though she had died and gone to heaven, and she found that she really loved Nashville. She drove herself around in the vintage Chevrolet truck he lent her, and sometimes she took the dogs with her. She was becoming a familiar sight around Nashville. He surprised her with a black sequined jumpsuit that was vintage Chanel, he had found it on eBay, and it fit her perfectly when he gave it to her.

'Now you look like a country music star's lady' – He

narrowed his eyes, looking at her spectacular body in the jumpsuit that fit her like a second skin – 'and maybe a little like Elvis.' She laughed, and she actually wore it in Memphis, and wound up on YouTube, and Louise sent her a nasty text about it, and Stephanie didn't care. She was happy.

The concert in Memphis at the FedExForum was a huge success, and she stood backstage with Michael while they watched Sandy and Chase perform.

'That's quite a look, Mom,' Michael teased her about the jumpsuit, but he had to admit, she looked incredible in it, and not like the mother he remembered in denim skirts and flip-flops from his childhood. It was a whole new image. She felt like a new person, having kept the best parts of the old one, but she was free to be herself now and felt like she was growing every day. And she liked sharing it now with Michael. She had never expected him to be with Sandy, but she suited him to perfection. And when they had minor arguments because Sandy was stressed or tired, or nervous before a performance or after long nights in rehearsal with no sleep, or he was tired after working all week in Atlanta, the arguments always ended with one of them teasing the other out of it, joking about it, or with a kiss. Stephanie loved watching them together.

'It's quite a life, isn't it, Mike?' Stephanie said as they stood backstage together. 'They're both so talented. It's hard to imagine being able to do that. I always wished I could be a singer. I wish I had a voice like Sandy,' she said enviously, but with admiration for Sandy's talent.

'You could always take lessons and have some fun with it. You have a nice voice, Mom. I remember when you were in that choir in Marin.'

'I'd feel silly doing it around Chase.' Michael understood that – he felt daunted by Sandy sometimes too. Her singing voice was so huge, it filled the room sometimes. Despite her talent, Sandy looked up to Michael too. They had achieved a good balance of mutual admiration and respect.

The crowd went crazy at the concert in Memphis, Derek had been backstage with a new girlfriend, and they went back to Nashville late that night, with everyone asleep on the bus. And Michael went back to Atlanta on Sunday. The following week, Stephanie and Chase went to one of the playoff games with the Braves, and they took Sandy with them on a private plane. Sandy stayed in Atlanta for a few days with Michael, and Stephanie and Chase came back on the plane after the game. Chase was a big sports fan, and went to the World Series and the Super Bowl every year, and before they left, he had promised to take Michael with him.

'Thank you for being so nice to my son,' she said as they flew back to Nashville. It was the end of September by then, and she'd been there for a month, and it was beginning to feel like she always had been. She had no plans to go home, and no reason to, and he made her so comfortable in his Nashville life. He was in the process of planning a tour in the spring to cover a dozen major cities. He hadn't toured for a while, and his manager thought he should. And there was a promoter offering him a fortune to do it, although he had told Stephanie that tours like that were grueling, but it was part of his business.

He told her about the business meetings he had coming up that week, as they flew home from Atlanta. It was a long list, and he said he hoped she'd come with him. He teased her sometimes that she had become his new partner. She went everywhere with him.

'I don't want you to get tired of having me around, or feel you have to take me to all your meetings,' she said when they talked about it.

'I never get tired of having you here, Stevie.' She kissed him when he said it, and she never got tired of him either, but by the time she'd been there for six weeks, she realized that everything they did was about his work and his career, his recordings, his rehearsals, his photo shoots, his plans, his concert tour, his interviews. She didn't mind it being all about him, and he included her in all his major decisions, but she felt she was losing her own self again. She was his shadow and nothing more. She had nothing to contribute other than her presence and her love, and no life of her own. Nothing to confirm to herself who she was.

She tried to express it to him, but he didn't hear her. He just kept telling her how important she was to him, and no woman in his life had ever meant as much to him, as they went from one meeting to the other. She was with him at everything he did, but he had the talent and the career, and she felt as if she were along for the ride. All she added to his life, as far as she was concerned, was the fact that she loved him. It didn't feel like enough in exchange. She needed something more to do than helping him pick what shirt he wore to a photo shoot, or what outfit he wore on stage at a concert, or select what photograph worked best on the cover of a CD. She loved it, but it seemed like too little for her to do. And by mid-October she was starting to look distracted and unhappy.

'What's wrong, baby?' He had been sensing for weeks that something was bothering her, although she never complained to him. She felt like she was losing her identity again. She had been the boring wife and carpool mom of a lawyer for twenty-six years, and now she was the girl-friend of a big music star, wearing sequins. What had really changed? She tried to make his life better in count-less ways, but always felt it wasn't enough.

'Maybe I need to go home for a while, and try to figure out who I am,' she said to Jean in one of their early morning conversations. She had been struggling with it since Bill's death eight months before, and she still didn't have the answers. She was wondering if she ever would.

She had taken the wrong fork in the road years before when she gave up having a career when she married Bill, and now it was too late at her age. She had no special talent. There was no business she wanted to start. She had no job experience, so she had nothing to sell in the job market. All she could do was what she was doing for Chase, follow him around and look adoring. It didn't feel like enough to her, even if he was happy. She explained it all to him again, and he looked worried.

'Do you feel like I don't respect you?' That was the last thing he wanted, because he did, a lot, but she was quick to shake her head.

'God, no! I just feel like a bimbo, and I am losing myself in your life.'

'You give me the strength and inspiration to do what I do, which is an incredible gift to me. I'd be nothing without you, Stevie. Or I'd be the half man I was before.'

'That's not true, and you know it.'

'Yes, it is,' he said emphatically. He had already written half a dozen songs to her and said they were his best songs. 'You need to feel loved if you're a creative person, to keep the juices flowing. I know you love me. That's a first for me. I was limping along until you got here.' It made her feel important to him, and she knew she was, but she still felt she was shortchanging him and herself. She needed to offer more and bring more to the table than styling his photo shoots, loving him, and inspiring his songs. She wanted to be more than just his muse.

'You deserve better than that, Chase.' He didn't like the look in her eyes when she said it.

'What are you saying?' His blood ran cold as he asked the question. He was afraid of the answer. What if she left him? He was as insecure as the next guy, despite his good looks and his stardom. And people were unpredictable. You could never predict human nature.

'I don't know. I've been thinking I should go home for a while, and figure out who I am and how to contribute to your life in a meaningful way, without losing myself. Maybe I'll never figure it out. Maybe I'm just meant to be someone standing on the sidelines, cheering. Maybe all I am is a natural fan, and no one in my own right. But I want to be more than that, Chase. I owe it to you and to myself. I need to find my place in the world and in your world. I need some time.' This was all so new to her.

'You want to go home?' He looked heartbroken as she nodded sadly. She knew she had to. She was losing herself again in his identity, and couldn't find her own.

'For how long? A couple of weeks or forever?' He looked frightened as he asked.

'I don't know,' she said honestly. She didn't want to promise something she couldn't deliver. And she felt like she had a lot of soul-searching to do. She had been a wife and mother for more than half a lifetime. And now she had become a kind of professional girlfriend to a rock star. But who was she in all that? And what did she have to give? She needed to find the answer.

'Shit, Stevie, I'm going to be lost without you. You can't leave me now.' But he knew she could, and it sounded like she was going to.

'I have to, or you're just going to wind up with some dumb bimbo on your hands who helps you pick your shirts out, or listens to your concert tour plans. You deserve a whole person. And I want to be that person. I just have to figure out how to get there.'

'Maybe you already are there. Sometimes we make life more complicated than it needs to be. Sometimes we already are the person we want to become, and we don't know it.'

'Then I have to find that out,' she said firmly, but she hated to leave him as much as he hated to see her go. She had never been as happy, but she also knew that something was missing in herself. She didn't know what piece, but there was a hole in the puzzle and she wanted to find the pieces to fill it. Otherwise she would feel incomplete and empty forever. And she wanted to be a whole person for herself, and for him. Chase was already satisfied and happy with what he had – he wasn't asking for more. But she was setting the bar high for herself and didn't want to let herself or him down.

'When are you thinking about going?' he asked her sadly, afraid of the answer. It was mid-October.

'I don't know. A couple of weeks maybe. Before Thanksgiving. The kids are coming home for the holiday anyway, so I have to go home by then.' She would have liked to invite him to come to San Francisco, but with Charlotte and Louise's hostile attitudes, she didn't want to expose him to that, so she couldn't invite him, although she knew that Michael had invited Sandy, which she thought was brave of him.

For the next two weeks, Stephanie could sense a kind of lingering sadness between them. Chase was unhappy that she was going back to San Francisco, and she didn't like it either. She was much happier in Nashville with him, but she thought it was important for the long haul, so they didn't run into trouble later, as she and Bill had. Jean pointed out in their regular conversations that he was a different person and thought she was crazy to leave him.

'What if you lose him?'

'Then it wasn't meant to be,' Stephanie said quietly. She believed in what she was doing and that she needed to leave for a while. His life was so all-consuming that she had to get away to get some perspective about him, herself, and their life.

'Stephanie, why are you doing this?' Jean challenged her. 'Are you being self-destructive?' Anything was possible – maybe she thought she didn't deserve him.

'I don't think so. I just don't want to be Alyson or me the way I used to be, just a robot serving my master.' It was a hell of a thing to say about their friend, but Jean didn't disagree with her, although she thought Stephanie was being a little harsh.

'You were a hell of a good wife and mother – let's not get carried away here. But you never thought about yourself, and neither did anyone else. Bill certainly didn't. But Chase loves you, Steph. It's not going to turn out like your marriage to Bill.'

'Maybe the problem here is me, not them,' she said honestly. 'I do it to myself. I do everything for everyone to make their lives easier and better and then I don't know who I am, and they don't care. I'm the full-service wife and mom, and now I'm the full-service girlfriend. Maybe that's okay, but I need to decide that, not just do it.' Listening to her, Jean hated that Stephanie was putting a good relationship at risk, with a man who genuinely loved her, after being unhappy with Bill for all those years.

'Don't doubt yourself so much, Steph,' she said gently. 'The man loves you. He's not a fool. Maybe you should just trust his judgment and enjoy it.'

'Maybe I'll come to that conclusion too. But I'm not there yet.'

'Don't lose him. Be careful,' Jean said to her. 'Guys like him come along once in a lifetime.' Stephanie knew it was

true, but she felt like she had to earn him, and she hadn't.
Not yet. And maybe never, she admitted to herself.

And Chase tried to talk her out of going before she left.
'You're just going to sit in that depressing empty house,
trying to figure out what? You don't need a fancy career to
impress me, Steph. I don't care about that. I'm not
asking you to only be in my life and give up who you are.
I love you as a person. Hell, come back to Nashville and
go to medical school if you want. Do whatever you want.
But please, please know that I love you and need you just
the way you are. You don't need to be more or less or
different.' She could see in his eyes that it was true, and
when they made love the night before she left, it was
bittersweet and they both cried.

'Maybe I'm scared to be dependent on you,' she
admitted as they lay in each other's arms and talked afterward. 'What if you die, or leave me? Then what would I
do? I'd be no one again and have lost my whole identity,
if my identity is you.'

'So you're leaving me instead? Isn't that a little crazy?'

'Maybe I am a little crazy,' she said with a sad smile.
But she wasn't, and he knew it. She was looking for something, and striving to be better, and above all to be herself.
He respected that about her, but he didn't need it for himself. He loved her just as she was. He thought she was
terrific and a lot more whole than she gave herself
credit for. 'Just give me some time to make some sense

of all this,' she whispered as they drifted off to sleep.

'You can have all the time you want. Just come back to me, Stevie . . . that's all I want . . . come back . . . soon . . .' he said as he reached for her, and they both fell asleep.

Leaving her at the Nashville airport the next day was agony for them both. She had been there for two months, and his life in Nashville was part of her now, just as he was. She felt as though she were ripping out a piece of her heart when he kissed her and they said goodbye, and she could see that he was crying when he walked out of the airport. And tears were streaming down her cheeks when she went through security. She felt crazy and stupid now for what she was doing, but in calmer moments it seemed right. She needed to be away from him to find herself.

And as the plane took off on the runway, she watched Nashville shrink below her, and thought of him with Frank and George, and Sandy. She felt like she was leaving home, and had no idea when she'd be back again, if ever.

Chapter 23

Stephanie was as miserable in San Francisco as Chase had predicted she would be. The weather was terrible – it rained for two weeks straight when she got back. The house was depressing and felt dead around her, in spite of the changes she had made. And there were still subtle signs of Bill everywhere. She couldn't exorcise him from the house, or her head. She spent hours walking on the beach, trying to understand what had gone wrong with their marriage. Was she at fault? Was he? Had they simply outgrown each other? She was staring out to sea in the fog one day, thinking about it, when a funny little dog walked up to her and sat down on the sand, staring at her. He had fluff on his head and a bushy tail, a long spotted hairless body that looked like polka dots, and a pointed face. He looked like a joke someone had assembled out of random parts. He was small, and appeared to be part miniature dachshund and part Chihuahua, with a dash of Yorkie, and sat looking at her as though he expected her to do something.

'Don't look at me,' she said finally. 'I can't figure my own life out.' He cocked his head to one side, wagged his tail, and barked at her. His body was dark and spotted with no fur. She wondered if it was a skin problem from poor diet. His ears, the pouf on his head, and the one on his tail were blond and looked like a bad bleach job. 'Has anyone ever told you how ridiculous you look?' she said to him, and he barked at her again and then followed her when she resumed her walk down the beach. She noticed that he had no collar and tags. He appeared to be a stray, but she didn't want to take him home in case he was lost and someone came back for him. And he gave her a heart-breaking stare as she got in her car. He was still sitting there, whining softly as she drove away, feeling guilty for leaving him at the beach.

She told Chase about him that night when he called her. They still spoke every day, and she hated how sad he sounded. She'd been home for two weeks and hadn't found any miraculous answers to her questions about her life.

'Maybe you should rescue him,' Chase suggested. 'He sounds too small to just abandon out there at the beach, and a car could hit him.'

'I felt terrible when I left him, but I was afraid someone would come back for him and then they wouldn't find him. Maybe I'll look for him tomorrow.' She had been going for long walks every day, but she only got more and more depressed, and she felt lost now and missed Chase terribly. She was even avoiding Jean now, who kept telling her she was insane to have left Chase in Nashville, and that he loved her. She loved him too, but she wanted to be more to him than she currently had to offer.

Chase told her before he hung up that she could take the dog to the SPCA or keep him and put signs up that she had him, with her phone number, so someone could reach her. And then he told her again how much he loved her. And no matter what she did now, or said to herself, she felt unworthy. Bill had criticized her for years, and now her daughters did at every opportunity, and she was feeling worse about herself instead of better. Maybe they were right.

She went back to the beach again the next day, to follow Chase's suggestion about the stray, and she had brought some signs with her and a staple gun to put them up on lampposts. She walked for an hour in the rain and didn't find him, and she hoped nothing had happened to him, and felt guiltier than ever. Now she had abandoned a dog too, not just the man she loved in Nashville. 'You are seriously messed up,' she said to herself as she walked back to her car in the parking lot. It was the only one there, other than an old wreck with no tires or windows, and as she opened her car door to leave, she saw a flash of movement behind her, as the same stray dog leaped out of the rusted old car and stood barking at her. His fur was plastered to his head in the rain, and she had never seen a dog look so pathetic, or so ugly. He was no beauty, but he was lively. And his blond matted hair that looked like a toupee made her laugh at him, and stoop to pet him.

'Well, hi, there. I've been looking for you.' He'd cleverly used the abandoned car for shelter. 'You are a mess.' She could almost hear him saying she didn't look so great herself, and she stood there in the rain trying to decide what to do, and left her car door open. With one glance at her, he jumped into the car, sat on the front passenger seat, and barked at her, as though to tell her to get in and let's go home. She took the posters she'd made out of the car then, walked to three lampposts in the parking lot and attached them with the staple gun, and went back to where the dog was waiting on the front seat of her car. 'Okay, you win,' she said to him, and with that he lay down on the front seat and went to sleep as she smiled at him.

She stopped at the supermarket on the way home, and bought some dog food, and a collar and leash in the pet section, and she called the SPCA from her car phone, and described him. They said they had no missing dogs listed with that description but the man she talked to listened carefully when she described him as a miniature Appaloosa, dachshund, Chihuahua, maybe Yorkie mix.

'I'm not so sure of that,' the man at the SPCA said after she'd described him. 'He sounds more like a rare pedigree breed, they're called Hairless Chinese Crested. Their bodies are hairless and kind of brindle and spotted, with ears, head, and tail with what looks like a wig with a bad blond dye job. And they do look a little like a Chihuahua, only slightly bigger, right?'

'Exactly.'

'They're rare and expensive. Someone will call us,' he assured her. And in the meantime, she made a bed for him in the kitchen, he slept a lot, and he was happy to see her whenever she walked into the kitchen. She told Chase about him, and he said the dog sounded ridiculous.

'I thought he's a mutt,' she told Chase the first night. 'But he isn't, he's some rare breed called Hairless Chinese Crested. He's the silliest thing I've ever seen, and he's really sweet.' She sent him a photo of the dog, with her cell phone, and Chase called her back laughing.

'Are you kidding? That's not a dog, he looks like he's wearing a wig. We should get him a job in Vegas.' They both laughed about it. But by the end of a week no one had claimed him. She'd even left a notice with Pets Unlimited, which had an adoption center, but no one called. She sat looking at him in the kitchen a week after she'd found him and shook her head. She had debated about giving him to the SPCA to find a home for, but he was so cute and funny, she didn't want to give him up.

'Looks like it's you and me, kid. But you've got to stop wearing that bad toupee. You just look silly.' He barked at her as though he thought so too, and his middle section looked naked and even more absurd with the spots. 'I think you need a good haircut and a sweater.' She took him to a pet shop that morning and bought him a red sweater and red collar and leash, and the pet shop owner recognized the breed immediately and told her how rare they were.

'I've always wanted one, but they're too expensive and look kind of delicate to me.' He wasn't though, and had survived his homeless life on the beach, and when she took him to a vet, they told her he was about a year old, very healthy, and slightly small for the breed. They gave him his shots in case he'd never had them, and asked Stephanie his name. She stared at the dog blankly.

'I don't know. He didn't tell me.' The dog barked and looked more like a normal Chihuahua in the red sweater, and she couldn't think of any Chinese names. 'Pedro. Pedro Gonzales,' she said with a straight face as though she'd just remembered, and they wrote it down and opened a file for him under Pedro Gonzales Adams. She had a dog. She called Chase as soon as they left the vet, and she sounded elated.

'I'm keeping him. No one called for him. His name is Pedro.'

'I wish you sounded that excited about keeping me. I

can't wait to meet him,' Chase said with a loving tone.

'The vet says he's about a year old, very healthy, and a little small. And he is that Hairless Chinese Crested breed. He really looks weird.' He had seen that from the picture from her cell phone.

'My vet says I'm forty-eight, and very healthy too, and, listen, if you're into blond wigs like that, I'll wear one.' But he was happy she had company. She had been sounding so down and lonely, and he felt that way too. Sometimes he was frustrated by her search for herself, which was keeping them apart, but he tried to be patient about it, so as not to upset her further, and slow things down. He hoped she'd come to some positive conclusions for them soon. She had been doing volunteer work for the homeless shelter again when they needed her, and her kids were coming home for Thanksgiving in a few days. But she still had no answers and she was no closer to coming back to Nashville than she had been before she left. Chase was going to Memphis for Thanksgiving with his son, and Michael had invited Sandy to San Francisco for Thanksgiving, and she was coming. Her girls were in an uproar over it, but Stephanie supported Michael's decision to bring her.

'Mom, it's our first Thanksgiving without Dad. He can't bring her.' Charlotte had objected, and Louise was incensed.

'Yes, he can. It will be good for all of us to have someone

new here.' She didn't want them crying all day. It was going to be hard enough as it was. And she saved Pedro as a surprise.

Charlotte and Louise flew home from New York together and arrived on Wednesday afternoon, and Michael and Sandy landed two hours later. By Wednesday evening, Stephanie had her whole family at the house, and was facing the weekend with trepidation. The girls knew she had left Nashville three weeks before, and they were hoping that her romance with Chase was on the rocks, but no one asked. And she didn't know the answer to that herself. She and Chase still spoke to each other, sometimes several times a day, and were in love, but Stephanie couldn't figure out how to be part of his life without feeling she had given up her life and everything she was. And she felt that there was no way to do it by half measures. She was either in or out, as far as she was concerned, and for now she didn't know which. And Chase was so miserable he was writing songs about her every night. He said it was one of those extreme times when the only outlet for his sadness was in the creative process, which made her feel even more guilty. She was still in some kind of downward spiral, and the only thing that cheered her up was Pedro, and the calls from Chase.

The girls were the first to arrive, and Charlotte went out to the kitchen to get a drink, and Pedro was standing in the middle of the room in his red sweater, staring at her, and she screamed as her mother and sister walked into the kitchen.

'Oh my God, what is that?' Charlotte said, laughing at him. 'He looks like a rat in a wig.'

'Don't listen to her,' Stephanie instructed him. 'His name is Pedro, and he happens to be a very fancy breed called a Hairless Chinese Crested.'

'Where did you get him?' Louise asked with interest, and even she looked amused. He was so funny looking, even in his fancy red sweater. And his name seemed to suit him.

'We met on the beach.' She picked him up as she said it, and he licked her face. He was affectionate and very well behaved, and rarely left her side. She couldn't imagine how his previous owners had lost him. And she had sent away for his dog license and ordered ID tags. She'd even had a chip put in his shoulder with her name, address, and phone number on it in case he got lost again. She had fallen in love with the funny-looking dog, and both girls liked him.

Charlotte and Louise were more pleasant to her than they'd been in a while, and Louise was the first to ask her, with a hopeful look, 'So is it over with your rock star?'

'No, it isn't. We're trying to work things out, or I am.'

'It must be a pretty uncivilized life in that business. He looks a little rough around the edges on YouTube.' Stephanie didn't like the remark.

'He's not,' Stephanie said quietly, 'other than long hair and tattoos. He's a gentleman, and a lovely person. I'm the problem, he's not.' She hadn't liked the tone of what her daughter had said. Louise was all too willing to think and say bad things about him, and about her mother too. And even Sandy, whom she'd never met.

'I hope you're going to be nice to Sandy,' she said to both of them, but she considered it unlikely, and she thought Michael was courageous to bring her, but he wanted to be with her for Thanksgiving. And Stephanie could only imagine what it would have been like if she had tried to include Chase. They would have been extremely rude, and she didn't want him subjected to their abuse. He was a good man, and she loved him, and he deserved a lot better than that.

The girls went to their rooms, and Stephanie came downstairs the moment she heard Michael and Sandy arrive, and Stephanie gave her a big hug. Sandy looked thrilled to see her. And as they were hugging, Pedro came out of the kitchen to check them out. Michael burst out laughing as soon as he saw him.

'What on earth is that?'

'His name is Pedro, and he lives here,' she said with a broad grin, as Sandy hugged her again, and Michael picked the dog up.

'I've never seen a sillier dog in my life. Or is he some kind of hamster?' She told him about the breed, and they both laughed as Michael set him down and Pedro began dancing around in circles and barking. He looked like a wind-up dog on the sidewalk, the kind street vendors try to sell to children. It seemed to be some kind of trick he had been taught, and Stephanie had never seen him do it.

'How's Chase?' she asked Sandy softly as they walked upstairs to Michael's room with her bags, and her face grew serious immediately.

'He's very sad, and he looks awful. All he does is stay up all night and write songs about you.' What she said and her expression when she said it nearly tore Stephanie's heart out.

'I really miss him,' she said to Sandy as they walked into Michael's room and she set her bags down. Sandy was wearing jeans, a white V-neck sweater, and a leather jacket with her blond hair loose down her back. She seemed like any other girl her age, and she was wearing very little makeup. She only wore heavy makeup and sexy clothes when she was on stage. A moment later Charlotte walked into her brother's room, and the two girls looked each other over. Stephanie couldn't help thinking they were like two dogs circling each other. Charlotte was curious and cool, and Sandy seemed nervous and held Michael's hand. Stephanie was letting them share the room. There was no point pretending they weren't sleeping with each other. She would have done the same for the girls, although Bill would never have allowed it for any of them. Things had changed. They were Stephanie's rules now, and Michael had thanked her for it, and added that he would never have brought Sandy home if his father were alive. Stephanie had always been more practical and more relaxed, and Bill more puritanical for their children.

And Louise walked in a moment later, glared down her nose at Sandy, shook her hand, and left the room. It was what Michael and his mother had expected of her.

They all had dinner in the kitchen that night, and afterward they all went out to meet up with friends who were home for Thanksgiving. Sandy hung back for a few minutes before they left and thanked Stephanie for letting her come, said they had a beautiful house, and told her how much she missed her in Nashville.

'I miss you too,' Stephanie said sadly. And a few minutes later they all went out separately to meet up with their own friends. She heard them come in after midnight, but didn't get up to see them, but the next morning they all had breakfast together.

Charlotte and Sandy helped her set the Thanksgiving table, and Louise went to her room without saying a word to Sandy, and Michael appeared to make sure that Charlotte wasn't being rude to her. But much to Stephanie's surprise, the two girls got along really well and discovered that they liked the same music. And Sandy got excited when she saw they had a piano. She went over and played a few chords, and then sat down for a minute, and sang a few lines of a song, as Charlotte came over and watched her.

'Do you sing?' Sandy asked her.

'A little.' Charlotte looked suddenly shy.

Sandy asked her about a song they both liked, and she started to play it, and they sang it together. They had a good time and sang together for a while, and Michael joined in, and Stephanie even joined them for a few minutes. It was fun and Sandy looked happy, and then they went to finish setting the table, and at six o'clock they sat down to Thanksgiving together. Stephanie had called Chase in Memphis, and told him how much she loved him, and how happy she was to have Sandy with them. He sounded tired and lonely, just as Sandy had described, but as always he was gracious to her. He never complained about the torture she was putting him through, or put her down for her need to find herself. He was hoping that if he let her do what she needed to do, she'd come back to him, but it didn't look promising at the moment.

Stephanie said grace before they started the meal, and said a blessing for Bill, and the girls' eyes filled with tears, and then they all started eating. The conversation was lively, particularly between Charlotte and Sandy, who seemed to like each other, and Louise was more restrained and said very little to anyone, especially her mother. And Michael hovered over Sandy, trying to make sure that everyone was nice to her, she felt comfortable, and Louise didn't attack her. He was relieved that his youngest sister liked her. And when they needed a neutral topic of conversation, they talked about Pedro, who was sound asleep, lying on his back and snoring softly. They all agreed that he was the weirdest dog they had ever seen, but very sweet. And Stephanie loved him.

And much to Stephanie's relief, they managed to stay off the subject of Chase until almost the end of dinner. And as she sliced the apple, mince, and pumpkin pies and put scoops of whipped cream on them, Louise couldn't control herself any longer and turned to Sandy.

'What do you and Chase usually have for Thanksgiving, Sandy? Grits? Or spare ribs?' She couldn't seem to help herself, and Stephanie looked horrified. Michael glared at her as though he wanted to kill her.

'No, we have turkey,' Sandy said pleasantly. 'We even eat it with a knife and fork.' She was unfailingly polite, but Louise had gotten the message to back off.

'That was unnecessary and just plain rude,' Stephanie said to Louise as they cleared the table and set the plates down in the kitchen. 'Why would you be rude to our guest?'

'Why would Michael bring her here the year Daddy died? You might as well just have invited Chase here.'

Danielle Steel

'Rest assured, if we stay together, next year I will,' Stephanie said sternly, and Louise looked as though she were about to scream as Michael walked into the kitchen.

'If you ever say something like that to her again, I swear, Louise, I'll hit you.'

'Don't threaten me. You shouldn't have brought her.'

'Why? Because you can't control your mouth? You may get away with being a bitch to Mom, but don't try to pull that shit with me, or Sandy.'

'Oh, poor little thing, does she need you to defend her?' Louise asked, sounding just plain nasty. Stephanie hated to see that side of her take over her personality as it had for the past year. She sounded bitter and angry. But as she said it, they heard a clear strong voice behind her.

'No, I don't need Michael to defend me,' Sandy said in a drawl that was pure Nashville. 'I can kick your ass all by myself, Louise, but I figured it would be rude to your mom if I did. So why don't we just make an effort to be polite for her sake?' Sandy turned and stared Louise right in the eye. Louise was taller and stronger, but Sandy looked as though she meant it, and Charlotte burst out laughing, as Michael smiled.

'Don't mind my sister,' Charlotte said easily. 'She's rude to us all the time. It's kind of her trademark.' And as she said it, everyone in the kitchen relaxed, and Louise stormed out of the room and went upstairs.

'I'm sorry, Sandy,' Stephanie apologized to her, and put an arm around her and gave her a hug.

'I'm sorry I said I'd kick her ass,' Sandy said, appearing genuinely contrite. 'I just figured that if I didn't say it, she'd be baiting me all weekend, and I knew no one would like it, and it would upset Michael.'

'I'd like to see you kick her ass,' Charlotte said with a grin. 'She always kicked mine when we were little.'

'I think she's just really sad about your daddy, and she doesn't know how else to express it,' Sandy said wisely. 'And I guess she's upset about your mom and Chase.'

'I kind of have been too,' Charlotte admitted. 'We don't want her to go out with anyone yet.'

'You'd like him,' Sandy said simply. 'He's a really great guy. And he loves Michael . . . and your mama. He wrote a song about her, and it's number one.' Charlotte started to look upset and then relaxed. She didn't admit it, but she liked Sandy, and she was willing to concede that maybe Chase was a good guy. They went to play the piano together after that, and sang duets. Charlotte had a pretty voice, and combined with Sandy's powerful one, they sounded terrific. Stephanie smiled as she listened to them while she cleaned up the kitchen and Michael helped her.

'Well, I think you won over Charlotte.' She smiled at him. But Louise was another story. She lived in an armed camp of her own making, and she was about to lose

Charlotte's support about Sandy, and maybe one day about Chase too, although they weren't there yet.

Louise went out with her friends later that night without saying goodbye to anyone. Charlotte decided to stay in, and invited some of her friends over, and they sat at the piano playing and singing for hours, and all of them loved Sandy. And Stephanie and Pedro went to her room. She was listening to the music and missing Chase, when Jean called her at nearly midnight.

'Holy shit,' she said with fervor when Stephanie picked up.

'What's wrong?' She thought something might have happened to Fred.

'Alyson found out tonight that Brad had an affair with their last au pair, the one who quit so mysteriously and just disappeared. It's over now, but he had a baby with her, the same age as Henry' – their youngest. 'She showed up on their doorstep tonight, with the kid, and accused him of lying to her and screwing her out of the support he'd been paying her for two years until a few months ago. Poor Alyson is in a state of total hysteria. The woman told her, standing in their dining room in the middle of Thanksgiving, with Alyson's parents there, that he's having an affair with the new au pair too. Apparently, she kept her key and let herself into the house while they were eating. I don't know what's going to happen. But Alyson wants to kill him. It looks like Saint Brad isn't as perfect as she thought after all. I always knew he was full of shit. And now she knows it.'

'OhmyGod! Now what?' Stephanie was shocked.

'She says she's going to divorce him, and she probably will. I don't know how he's going to bullshit his way out of this one. Not with a two-year-old as evidence.'

'Oh, poor Alyson, and she thought their life was so perfect, and she's so in love with him.'

'I think she got cured of that in a hurry tonight. She made him leave the house in the middle of Thanksgiving. He refused, and she started to call the police, so he left.'

'And what happened to the au pair with the baby?'

'She left with him. I think he just wanted to get her out of there. Alyson said the kid looks just like him, so he can't deny it, and he didn't try to. The au pair said they had DNA tests to prove it. And Alyson is going to fire the au pair she has now, since the other girl claims he's sleeping with her too.' It was a lurid tale, but somehow Stephanie believed it. And he had been a little too friendly with her too, ever since Bill died.

'Wow!' She was speechless.

'You should call her. Her parents are here from Michigan, and she's been crying all night.'

Stephanie called her five minutes later and heard the whole story again in more detail. Alyson couldn't stop sobbing hysterically and said she never wanted to see him again, which seemed unlikely. They had three children together. But she said she was filing for divorce on Monday, and the way she said it, Stephanie thought she would.

'I'm so sorry, Alyson,' she said sincerely, and felt terrible for her. It was an awful story, particularly knowing that her ex au pair had been pregnant and having a baby at the same time as she was.

'I'm sorry too,' Alyson cried into the phone. 'I've been mean to you about Chase, but I was worried about you, and I thought it was shocking that you were going out so soon after Bill died, and with someone so different. Brad kept telling me it was a terrible thing to do . . . and look what he did . . . he's such a prick. How could he do that? I hate him.' Her words came out in a rush, and Stephanie felt desperately sorry for her. She had fallen from the heights of innocence and trust to the depths of betrayal in an instant. 'I'm sure you know what you're doing,' Alyson said about Chase. 'I just love you, Steph, and I don't want anything bad to happen to you. And now look what happened to me.' She cried for a while longer, and then they got off the phone, and Stephanie lay on her bed thinking about her. It was hard to imagine the rotten things people did to each other, and she remembered when she had found out about Bill's affair and how hurt she had been. She realized now that she should have divorced him, and she thought that Alyson should too. Their relationship would be irreparably damaged forever. There was no way to repair that kind of hurt and betrayal.

* * *

Stephanie was still thinking about it when she ran into Louise alone in the kitchen the next morning. She didn't say anything to her. They had all said enough the night before. Louise looked depressed as she drank her coffee, and then glanced mournfully at her mother.

'I'm sorry I was rude to Sandy last night. I don't know what's wrong with me. I'm just mad at everyone all the time. I'm mad at you for being with Chase, if you still are. I wish you were still with Daddy. I'm mad at Daddy for being dead. And at Michael for being with Sandy.' And then she grinned. 'And maybe I'm just mad that Charlotte was ever born. She was such a pain in the ass when she was little, and sometimes she still is.'

'It's big of you to admit it.' Stephanie leaned over and kissed her cheek. 'I was mad at Daddy for a while for dying too. But it didn't help. I feel better now.'

'You really weren't happy with Daddy, were you?' she asked her mother, and Stephanie was careful about what she answered.

'I used to be. We were happy for a long time. And then I think we got sloppy about our relationship. He was too busy, I was busy with all of you, and we kind of got disconnected.' Louise nodded, she remembered. 'And there was a point where we probably should have gotten divorced, but we didn't. We just stuck it out, not connected anymore. I guess I was too scared to get divorced, and I really did love him. But it wasn't much of a life for either of us.'

'Why do you think that happened?'

'What I said. Sloppy, busy, lazy, careless. You have to take good care of relationships and work at them. We didn't.'

And then Louise asked her a question that took her breath away. 'Did Daddy ever cheat on you?' Stephanie hesitated for a long moment and wondered if someone had told her.

'What difference does it make? If he did, it was probably because our marriage wasn't good anymore, and that didn't help it. But I don't think people cheat in happy marriages they take good care of. Unless they're just plain stupid.' Like Brad Freeman. 'And Daddy wasn't stupid.'

'Meg Dawson told me a long time ago that Daddy had an affair.' She was Jean's older daughter, and five years older than Louise. 'I was about sixteen and I didn't want to believe her.' That was exactly when it had happened, and Meg must have heard it from her mother.

'He might have,' Stephanie said, sounding noncommittal.

'Maybe it would help if I knew the truth,' Louise said, sounding lost. 'I've blamed you for a lot of things, Mom. Maybe I was wrong. Maybe some of it was Daddy.' She had told herself a lot of fantasies about her parents' marriage and how much they had loved each other. But she had never forgotten what Meg had said and hoped it wasn't true.

'That's possible.' She smiled gently at her. 'You don't need to be mad at Daddy. He's gone now.' Louise's eyes bored through her, and finally Stephanie nodded. 'Yes, he did. But I stayed anyway. He was going to marry her and she changed her mind so he came back to me.' Stephanie hated saying it to her, but it was true. And she made no editorial comment about how selfish he had been, or how much he had hurt her. She just gave her the facts and let her make her own decisions.

'And you stayed because of us?'

'In part, and also for me. I finally realized that recently. I was scared to leave with three kids, on my own. So I stayed, and I guess I shouldn't have. I never forgave him. I just lived with it. That makes for a lousy marriage. We stayed pretty much away from each other after he came back.' Louise nodded.

'Do the others know? Michael and Char?'

'No, I never told any of you. You didn't need to know. And I hope I'm not wrong to tell you now. It doesn't matter what we did. Your father loved you very, very much.'

'He loved you too, Mom,' she said quietly, 'He told me so, a bunch of times, about a month before he died too. He said you were a really good woman, better than he deserved, and he loved you.' Tears sprang to Stephanie's eyes as she said it. 'I guess he didn't know how to show you.' Stephanie nodded. He didn't.

'Thank you for telling me,' she said, and blew her nose as Michael walked in with Sandy. Louise put an arm around her mother then and gave her a hug.

'Thank you, Mom, for telling me the truth.'

'About what?' Michael asked, happening on the scene in the kitchen, and Louise turned to Sandy.

'Sorry I was such a bitch last night. I do that sometimes. Ignore me. Everyone else does. Every family needs one,' she said, smiled at Sandy, and grinned at her brother, as he looked at her in amazement.

'Wow, what happened to you?'

'Mom put marijuana in my cornflakes. It really helps.'

'Yeah, I'll say.' Michael looked stunned at Louise's change of attitude.

They chatted easily over breakfast, and Louise and Stephanie exchanged a long look across the table. Something important had happened. Stephanie wasn't sure what yet, but something had definitely changed. And Charlotte looked happy as she bounded into the kitchen too. They all took a walk on the beach together that afternoon, and made plans to go out to dinner together. Stephanie told Chase all about it when he called her, and she assured him that Sandy looked like she was having a good time.

And that night she went to see Alyson, who was a total

mess, sobbing and crying. Brad had tried to see her that afternoon, and she wouldn't let him in the house. And Stephanie was sad for her when she went home. She drove across the bridge thinking about them, and what a fraud Brad had been. Poor Alyson, but at least she wouldn't be living a lie, or pretending to forgive him. She said she never would, and Stephanie believed her. And as she thought it, she realized where she and Bill had gone wrong. She had pretended to forgive him, and he had pretended to still love her. He didn't, despite what he'd said to Louise, and she knew it. And she hadn't loved him either. Not for the last seven years of their marriage. It had been dead for her then. And as she thought it to herself, she felt free as she drove across the bridge. She could admit it to herself now. She had stopped loving her husband seven years before he died, and maybe long before that. She felt sorry for him now. But she didn't love him.

Chapter 24

In the weeks between Thanksgiving and Christmas, after the kids left, Stephanie did a lot of thinking. She went on long walks with Pedro, who was great company and the silliest-looking dog on the planet, everyone agreed. She had found a big piece of herself after talking to Louise over Thanksgiving. It was liberating to admit to herself that she hadn't loved Bill in years. It didn't make her feel awful about herself. It was honest. She just didn't. And she had stayed with him and betrayed herself by not having the guts to leave him. Instead, she pretended to be noble.

She went to see Alyson several times, who had filed for divorce as she said she would. She would only speak to Brad through lawyers. The love story of the century had been a fraud while he slept with their au pair and had a baby with her. He certainly wasn't the first man who had done that, or the last. But Alyson's fantasies about their marriage had all been lies. She had given up her identity for a marriage that had been a sham and a man who had been a liar. Stephanie knew it would take her years to figure out why she'd done it.

Stephanie and Jean talked about it a lot and felt sorry for her. And Jean reminded her that she had never trusted Brad, nor any other man. She believed that given the opportunity, they were all cheaters. Her father had been, her brothers were. Bill had been. But in spite of that, Stephanie trusted Chase and was sure he was a good person.

He had been fiercely busy between Thanksgiving and Christmas. He had a Christmas album out and was promoting it, and had sent it to her. It was beautiful and made her cry when she listened to it. They had no plans to see each other, although they said they loved each other. But she knew she had hurt him badly when she came back to California to sort out her life. And she hadn't figured it out yet. She didn't know what she was waiting for, but she hadn't tried to find a job, and working at the homeless shelter for a few days over the holidays wasn't enough to keep her busy, not after a husband and three kids.

And she was torn between keeping old traditions and making new ones. She put up their Christmas tree with all their familiar decorations on it, while listening to Chase's Christmas album, which was the number-one hit

Danielle Steel

in the nation. She decided to give the Christmas party that she and Bill gave every year, two weeks before Christmas, and was sorry she did it. It was depressing. Half the men there, all of them married, either hit on her or implied it, and would have been more than willing to cheat on their wives, which made her feel slightly sick.

And she still spoke to Chase almost every day. But he didn't ask if or when she was coming back, and she didn't say. They avoided the subject so it wouldn't be final. She didn't know, and she had been back in San Francisco for six weeks, which felt like an eternity to both of them. And they were both afraid that it was over between them, but they were too afraid to ask, and didn't want to know.

The children were coming home for Christmas, but Michael wasn't bringing Sandy this time. She had to be in Nashville with Chase for Christmas, since they had a Christmas concert. But Michael was meeting her in Las Vegas for New Year, where she and Chase were playing a big concert on New Year's Eve. Michael had promised to be there.

The morning the kids came home, Stephanie got a package from Chase. It was a beautiful simple gold bracelet with 'Carpe diem' engraved on it. Seize the day. And on the other side, his initials and the date. She cried when she opened it and put it on. She had a present for him, but she hadn't sent it. It was a long gold chain with a medal with an angel on it, to watch over him, with her initials and the date on the back. She hadn't had the heart to mail it to him, but she did after she got the gift from him. She put the bracelet on and was wearing it when the kids came home, but no one noticed. She never took it off.

And predictably, Christmas Eve dinner was hard without their father. Everyone cried, even Stephanie when they toasted him. But they were happy to be together. And Louise seemed in better spirits than she'd been in a long time, and she spent most of the holiday with her mother, while Charlotte ran around seeing friends. She was going skiing with some of them at Tahoe, and Louise was going back to New York for New Year's Eve to celebrate with friends. Michael was going to Las Vegas to be with Sandy and Chase. Stephanie was going to spend New Year's Eve alone at home, with Pedro.

'What are you punishing yourself for?' Dr. Zeller asked her when she told her.

'I'm not punishing myself. I don't care about New Year's Eve. Besides, I don't have anyone to be with.' Jean and Fred had gone to Mexico, and Alyson was staying home.

'Yes, you do,' her therapist corrected her. 'You have Chase.'

'He didn't ask me. He's playing a concert in Vegas.'

'Why don't you go? He'd be happy to see you, from everything you tell me.'

'I'm not ready.' She looked frightened as she said it.

417

'Do you suppose you're punishing yourself for staying married to a man you didn't love? And you didn't love yourself enough to leave him? Don't you think that was punishment enough?' Stephanie said nothing as tears filled her eyes, and the last piece of the puzzle fell into place. She felt as though she were choking and couldn't breathe. It was hard to hear, but it was true. She hadn't loved him in years. And now she was paying penance. Depriving herself of a man she did love, and who loved her. It was terrifying to hear. And she was still thinking about it when she was driving home.

All of the kids left the next day, the day before New Year's Eve, and Michael asked if she wanted to go to Las Vegas with him.

'He'd love to see you, Mom. Sandy said Christmas was really rough.' She just shook her head and tried not to cry.

'I want to stay here.' She really didn't, but didn't know what else to do.

She spent the night alone in the empty house, as she had for two months since she got back, with Pedro. And when she went to bed that night, she carefully took her wedding ring off and put it in the jewelry box on her dresser. She was done. At last.

New Year's Eve dawned bright and clear. It was a perfect day, and she took Pedro for a long walk. She hadn't heard from Chase in two days, and she knew he was busy. Their New Year's concert was a big deal. Michael was staying at the Wynn with Sandy and Chase.

And that afternoon, when she got back to the house, Stephanie opened a bottle of champagne and poured herself a glass. She planned to be asleep long before midnight. Jean called her from Mexico to see how she was, and Stephanie said she was fine.

She was playing with the dog in the kitchen, as he batted the gold bracelet on her wrist. It was bright and shiny and new, and she loved it. And Chase had sent her a text to thank her when he got the angel on the chain before he left Nashville. He said he loved it too and needed an angel in his life.

The dog kept playing with the bracelet, and as she pulled her wrist away from him, she read the words again. Carpe diem. Seize the day. It was everything Chase believed about life. It was how their story had started, and why she had gone to Nashville in the first place, and how she had fallen in love with him. They had seized the opportunities they'd been given, and suddenly she knew what she had to do. She didn't have to punish herself anymore. She had a right to this. And so did he. She grabbed the dog and ran upstairs. It was four o'clock, and she could get to the airport by five-thirty, if she could get a seat on a flight. They had one on a six-thirty flight to Vegas, and she booked it online. She threw the sequined jumpsuit he'd given her into a bag, with some jeans and sweaters and shoes, underwear, a nightgown, makeup, and toiletries, and ran out of the house at five. She stopped at a pet store and bought a traveling bag for Pedro. He was wearing his red sweater, and she bought him a tiny Santa hat at the pet store, and was on the highway to the airport by five-fifteen, and at the airport at twenty to six. And she made her flight. They were due to land in Las Vegas at seven-thirty. Jean called her as soon as they did.

'You sound breathless. Where are you?' Jean sounded a little drunk.

'I'm at the airport . . . in Las Vegas . . .'

'You go, girl!' Jean said, beaming. Finally, something decent was happening in someone's life. She was so pleased, she gave Fred a kiss on the cheek when she hung up.

'What's that for?' he asked with a look of surprise.

'Because you're cute, and I love your credit cards. Happy New Year,' she said, and he laughed.

'I love you, Jean, even if you are expensive as hell.' They went downstairs for dinner then, and he told her how nice she looked. She told him she should, her dress had cost him a fortune and was Lanvin. And they had a very nice dinner together.

By then, Stephanie had checked into the Wynn and had called the concierge. It was nine o'clock.

'I need a ticket for Chase Taylor's show,' she said, sounding desperate.

'I have two seats left for tomorrow's show at eight,' he said primly.

'I need one seat tonight, the eleven o'clock show, as close to the front as possible.'

'I'm sorry, we can't – ' he started to say, and then paused. 'I have a comp seat that someone is selling for five hundred dollars.'

'That's disgusting of them,' Stephanie said disapprovingly. 'People who get comp seats should never sell them. They were a gift. But I'll take it. Put it on my bill.'

'Of course.'

An hour later, she bathed, did her makeup, brushed her hair, and put on the jumpsuit. Pedro was eating sliced turkey, and seemed to like the room, and had slept on the plane. And at the last minute she took him when she left the room. She put a sweater over her arm to hide him, and was at the theater at ten to eleven. It was the same theater where she had seen him perform for the first time, which seemed fitting, and an usher took her to a seat in the front row, and never noticed Pedro, who went to sleep on her lap. He still had his sweater and Santa hat on.

The show began fifteen minutes late. It was the opening band that had replaced Bobby Joe, and they were better than he was. She didn't see her son anywhere, and assumed he was backstage. And at twenty to twelve Chase came on, looking spectacular in black leather jeans and a black leather shirt she had bought him. He looked more beautiful than ever, and she just prayed he still wanted her. They had been apart for two months. The theater was pitch black as he started, and he opened with 'The Country Boy and the Lady,' which she recognized immediately as one of the ones he had written to her. The audience was mesmerized and went wild when he finished. The fans were more excited than usual tonight, it was New Year's Eve, they'd had a lot to drink, and Chase was more on than she'd ever seen him. He connected with his audience and was electric on stage. He warned everyone as midnight approached and timed it perfectly. He sang one of his biggest hits as midnight ticked closer, and she quietly left her seat, holding Pedro, and approached the stage. Fans had already pressed closer, and a rim of people were standing right beneath him as he sang, and then as though he sensed her, he looked down, and saw her gazing up at him in the shiny black jumpsuit, with Pedro in her hands. At first all he saw were her eyes, and he almost stopped singing, and then sang right to her. He sang his heart out, and as the song ended and the clock struck midnight, she held Pedro up so he could see him, and he burst out laughing, and then told the audience that the next song was to the woman he loved. Stephanie just stood there and watched him. It was a beautiful song she hadn't heard yet. And his eyes never left hers as he sang it to her, while she watched him with all the love she felt for him in her eyes. The audience cheered at the end of the song, as an usher touched her shoulder and whispered to her.

'Mr. Taylor would like you to come backstage now.' He had taken a sip of water and must have signaled someone, and she followed the usher to the stage entrance, and into the wings, where Michael was standing, waiting for Sandy. His eyes grew wide when he saw his mother, and then the dog, and he grinned.

'I'm glad you're here, Mom,' he whispered and put an arm around her shoulders. 'I'm not so sure about Pedro though.'

'I told him I'd spend New Year's Eve with him,' she whispered back, and they watched the rest of the show, both of them proud of the people they loved. His eyes never left Sandy, and she was listening to Chase with her eyes closed.

The applause at the end of the show was thunderous. He did four encores, and when the curtain came down, he came to find her, waiting for him, and holding the dog.

'That is the ugliest dog I have ever seen,' he said, smiling at her. He looked like a man who'd been starving, and had just seen his first meal in two months. 'I love you, Stevie. That's all. I love you.'

'I love you too. I'm sorry I've been so stupid and took so long to figure it out.'

423

'You okay now?' he asked her, checking it out. He wanted to know now. The last two months had been the worst in his life.

'I'm fine,' she said, looking straight at him. 'I'm not bringing you a damn thing except me, and the fact that I love you with all my heart, if that's good enough . . . and Pedro, of course.'

'That's all I ever wanted,' he said as he pulled her into his arms, put the dog down, and kissed her with all the force of the last lonely two months, when he had been terrified every day that he'd lost her. 'I may have to get back to you about Pedro, though. I'll have to discuss that with Frank and George.'

'Tell them we're a package deal,' she said, as he looked at the Santa hat on the ridiculous dog with the blond mop of hair and laughed.

'Jesus, I love you, woman,' he said, as they walked toward his dressing room, and he smiled when he saw the bracelet on her arm. 'You scared me to death.' Pedro was following them as though he knew this was where he belonged.

'I scared me too. But it's okay now. I found my way back. Thank God you still want me,' Stephanie said softly.

'That was never in question,' he said as he kissed her again, and Michael and Sandy were smiling at them from the distance, but Stephanie and Chase didn't see anything except each other as they kissed, and Chase held her in his powerful embrace, and then they disappeared into his dressing room with the dog.

A new year had begun. A new life. A new world for both of them. Carpe diem. Seize the day. They had.

Undercover

Danielle Steel

Marshall Everett and Ariana Gregory are about to collide, and life will never be the same again.

Marshall is an ex-undercover agent who has just survived the toughest assignment of his career amidst the jungles of Colombia, and is happy to put living in danger behind him. Then a routine job gone wrong shatters his world, and Marshall flees to Paris in search of peace.

Ariana knows that as the daughter of an American Ambassador, her safety is always at risk. When one close call puts her in more danger than ever, Ariana is relocated to Paris – but trouble is never far behind her.

Paired together, both Marshall and Ariana must trust each other if they are to ever find freedom from their past . . .

Prodigal Son

Danielle Steel

Twin brothers are reunited after twenty years of silence and blame when the prodigal son returns home . . .

In a matter of days, Peter McDowell loses everything he has worked so hard for – including his marriage. Stripped of everything, he has only one place he can retreat to: the home he left twenty years ago.

There, he comes face to face with his brother for the first time in years. At first, Peter dreads seeing Michael again – but to his surprise their reunion is tender and real. Only later, as Peter mulls over his late mother's journals, does he begin to question what lies beneath Michael's perfect surface.

In a race for time, Peter throws caution to the wind to find the truth. What he discovers will change their lives, the lives of their children and an entire town for ever.

Precious Gifts

Danielle Steel

One act of love will change one family's destiny.

As a devoted mother, Veronique Parker has dedicated herself to her three daughters, before and since her divorce.

Her world is turned upside down when her former husband dies suddenly, leaving her and their daughters astonishing inheritances: a painting of mysterious provenance, a château in the south of France, the freedom to pursue their dreams, and a shocking revelation from the past.

The precious gifts he left will lead them on a journey certain to change Veronique and her daughters' destinies in the most surprising of ways . . .

Pegasus

Danielle Steel

One life-changing war. A love story that would echo across the decades . . .

On the cusp of the Second World War in Europe, Nicolas and Alex are two widowed men raising their children alone. They lead contented, peaceful lives, until a long-buried secret about Nicolas's ancestry threatens his family's safety . . .

To survive, they must flee to America. The only treasures Nicolas and his sons can take are eight purebred horses, two of them dazzling Lipizzaners – gifts from Alex. These magnificent creatures are their ticket to a new life, securing Nicolas a job with the famous Ringling Brothers Circus. There, he and the white stallion, Pegasus, become the centrepiece of the show, and a graceful young high-wire walker soon steals his heart.

But as the years of war take their toll, Nicolas struggles to adapt to their new life while Alex and his daughter face escalating danger in Europe. When tragedy strikes on both sides of the ocean, what will become of each family when their happiness rests in the hands of fate?

Blue

Danielle Steel

The power of love and courage to overcome life's greatest challenges . . .

Ginny Carter was once a rising star in TV news, married, with a three-year-old son and a full and happy life – until her whole world dissolved on a freeway in a single instant. In the aftermath, she somehow pieces her life back together, but struggles to truly find meaning in her existence.

Then, on the anniversary of the fateful accident, she meets a boy who will cause her life to change forever yet again. Thirteen-year-old Blue Williams has been living on the streets, rarely attending school, and utterly alone. Ginny reaches out to him, and slowly, their friendship grows. The two form an unusual bond and become the family they each lost.

But just as he is truly beginning to trust her, she learns he has been hiding a shocking secret. Ginny wonders if she can help Blue to feel whole again, and at the same time heal herself.

Get to know
DanielleSteel
online

Visit Danielle's website to hear the latest news, read Danielle's personal notes to her readers, and sign up for her newsletter at **www.daniellesteel.com**.

You can also find out more about Danielle's two lives in Paris and San Francisco, her family and beloved dogs, and what she enjoys spending her time doing outside of writing on her blog at **www.daniellesteel.net**.

Or join over a million other fans of Danielle Steel at her Facebook page and learn more from Danielle about new releases, news and exclusive content at **www.facebook.com/DanielleSteelOfficial**.